I0539416

Unraveling

Unraveling

A Novel

NANCY BRENNAN

LINCOLN SQUARE BOOKS

Copyright © 2016 by Nancy Brennan

ACKNOWLEDGEMENTS

There is no better way to begin than by expressing appreciation to my son, Matt: You encouraged me from the moment you heard my ideas for this book. Your perceptive feedback, notations, and valued advice began with my first complete draft, through multiple versions, spanning too many years. You have been my thought partner and the tenacious nudge that kept me going to the finish line.

To my son, Mike: Since you were a youngster and to this very day, your positive attitude, high energy and spirit of adventure for pursuing outdoor challenges has never worn out. The fact that you have climbed to the peak of the Grand Tetons and explored sunken ships deep in the sea, convinced me that difficult doesn't mean insurmountable. With all your escapades in mind, I saw no reason why I couldn't sit down and write a book.

To Peter, my editorial consultant: Thank you for giving me the benefit of your literary ability and experience in helping me to get my manuscript finished, polished and published. I couldn't have accomplished this without your evaluative critique and straightforward guidance. Moreover, I will forever remember to write cause before effect—not the other way around.

To Rita and Bob, my steadfast and trusted readers: When I thought I was being overbearing sending three chapters at one time, you wanted me to keep sending you more so you could find out what happens next. I thank you so much for your enthusiasm, candid feedback, insights and suggestions.

And to all those who kept asking how my book's coming along: You know who you are. Thank you for helping to keep my vision alive despite all the intermissions.

Editing: Peter Rubie, Lincoln Square Books
Cover design: Gus Yoo

ISBN: 978–0-9909063–1-5 (ebook)
ISBN: 978–0-9981674–1-1 (Paperback)
Library of Congress Control Number: 2016961115

CONTENTS

"I wonder if I've been changed in the night. Let me think. Was I the same when I got up this morning? I almost think I can remember feeling a little different. But if I'm not the same, the next question is 'Who in the world am I?' Ah, that's the great puzzle!"

—Lewis Carroll, *Alice in Wonderland*

PROLOGUE

What's happening? she thought.

She couldn't remember the last thing she had done. *How weird is that?* But where she was now felt instinctively wrong.

What's my name? She couldn't remember. This was starting to become annoying. She was overwhelmed by a smell—gasoline, that was it!—and lightheadedness. She found herself floating face down above roads and houses, woods and fields, a car half into the tree line at an awkward angle. A steep drop off fell away on either side of the roadway with trees almost racing away from her down the hillsides. She felt languid and feeble and instantly hated the feelings.

Rubbing bleary eyes to better focus, she was startled to see below her an image of herself lying on a bed, and the sound of a repetitive monotone chirp, like some robotic bird of dawn.

Damnit! What's my name? she thought, getting irritated.

She tried to look around and see where she was, but a sudden stabbing pain in her head captured her attention and was followed by a burbling, insistent barrage of meaningless sounds and bright colors. She felt warm, afloat, and helpless. Then suddenly something was manhandling her out of her comfortable space.

"OK, lift her up on three!"

The pain and the scene faded, and she heard the repetitive little beep, then a peaceful darkness surrounded her.

She was drifting again past little points of light. The rhythm of the beep was somehow comforting as a mild pressure on her chest grew more insistent until the blackness enveloped her once more.

She was aware of a sense of euphoria. Then before her, emerging through a mist, or fog, or something that swirled around her as she walked, she saw a tall wrought iron gate and an identical fence running away on either side.

As she moved toward it, the gate swung open. Somehow that made sense. She walked into an arena awash with intense bright light. But the further she walked the more she became uneasy, and then frightened. She looked behind, but the gate had vanished in the mist. Turning forward again she saw the suggestion of a garden, of figures milling. The moment she blinked they vanished. She stopped walking.

Realizing there was nothing to be gained by simply standing there all day, she thought, *I need to know what this place is. There are answers here.*

Then she thought once more, with more than a touch of worry and annoyance, *What's my name?* and walked towards the garden.

1

THE LOCKET

Her legs ached and she was tired and thirsty. She had vague memories of walking in a garden, but now the past was faded shadows. She felt woozy and there was no sign of life or help in this barren, overcast landscape filled with dust and cracked earth and gullies. Thorny vegetation snatched at her as she climbed over rocky terrain, a veil of bugs clung to her sticky skin. There was a vague, acrid smell of drying leather.

She understood she was becoming disoriented, but had to keep moving. Somehow she knew that to stop likely meant to die out here. She felt as though she had awoken from a coma with no sense of what had been or what was to come. There was only now. She still could not remember her name or what could have happened to cause her such misery. A part of her thought fleetingly, *the amnesia of trauma*, but she wasn't quite sure what she meant by that.

The sky was a cloudless dull white, though from some hidden place an uncomfortably warm sun beat down and there was no shade to escape it. The landscape around her rolled and dipped, making any sense of place almost impossible beyond the immediacy of where she stood.

A chain necklace pinched her moist skin and she reached up and felt the heat of it on the hollow of her neck. A copper bracelet, made of dainty heart shaped links alarmingly affixed to a medical alert tag, clung snugly to her left wrist. Clues, one after another, rushed up to her, but as yet they led her nowhere. Her headache grew slowly worse, presumably caused by the heat and the glare of the unseen sun.

She trudged forward and finally reached a tree line, which threw some shade and respite. Evergreens intermingled with deciduous trees. The caustic smell of old leather faded finally, replaced by one of earth and sweetness, as though the landscape had been scrubbed clean by rain.

She collected an armful of young branches from the bases of a cluster of pine trees, and then collapsed into a makeshift bed of pine needles. She leaned back against a stone's gently curved crevice with a loud sigh of relief.

But sleep eluded her, and so she watched a clan of centipedes, obviously miffed at her intrusion, scatter in haphazard directions. She felt a growing sense of queasiness, no doubt from heat and dehydration – when *was* the last time she had eaten or drunk? She couldn't remember.

She rubbed her grimy legs, noticing fluid-filled purplish bruises and a long gouge by her shin as though at some point she had made hard contact with a sharp object. A pang of revulsion swept over her as she felt something hard protruding slightly above the surface of her skin. She couldn't imagine what it was, and put her head between her legs to stem a spontaneous gag reflex. She took slow, deep breaths to regain her composure, fighting a growing sense of urgency. With a sinking feeling she realized she needed to clean her wounds and get medical help before infection set in. But more importantly she needed to find water. Already, her tongue was beginning to stick to the roof of her mouth.

The copper bracelet, with its universal medical symbol of a snake and a staff, was her only hope of identification. She pried at the watch-like clasp with ragged nails, and it slipped to the ground. She picked it up and inspected the back of the tag. The soil-caked engraving was illegible so she spat on it, wiping it clean on the bottom of her shirt. "See Wallet Card" and a code number were all that was imprinted.

She began to cry as a new element of fear sunk in: She had no way of knowing what medical condition she might have.

Rubbing a thin denim sleeve roughly across her face to dry her tears, she wondered how she looked—terrible no doubt—and her hair! As she picked through the matted strands, she pulled out some reddish, sticky substance near the crown and examined the texture. *Berries?* While plowing through the rough brush, she had been snared by brambles laden with red berries. She recalled how tempted she was to pick some for their juice. However, the chance that this fruit could be even remotely poisonous deterred her from squeezing so much as a dab onto her tongue.

She wished that she had some wilderness survival skills. Rustling sounds nearby startled her, and she squinted in their direction. Her gaze came to rest on a pair of squirrels chasing each other around a tree trunk. Satisfied this was not a threat, she closed her eyes for a moment and tried to focus on her breathing.

She reached for the pendant around her neck, curious as to what it looked like. She found the clasp, fumbling as she unfastened it, and the necklace fell into her lap. It was a double twisted chain, delicate and seemingly made of gold. The small oval gold pendant was dented and caked in dirt. Once again, she used saliva to clean it. After shining it she gasped with pleasure. "Beautiful."

The front of the pendant had an intricate bouquet of roses etched in black and red. She gingerly turned it over in her hands, examining a fine engraving. She read, *Mom, we will always love you*, and burst into tears. She clutched it to her chest. Wiping tears from her eyes with a soiled sleeve, she looked at the pendant more closely and spotted a tiny hinge. It was a locket! But it to was caked with dirt, and no matter how much she delicately tried to pry it open, her efforts were to no avail.

Holding the necklace helped her relax. She took long, deep breaths and intermittently swatted at a cloud of brazen gnats that flitted around her head like a pestilent halo. A breeze wafted across her face. The draft felt good on her clammy skin and especially on the nape of her neck where the tendrils of her auburn hair dripped with sweat. Feeling lightheaded and thirsty, she closed her eyes and a deep sleep quickly overtook her.

She was startled awake by a sharp prick in her left arm and sat up, momentarily disoriented. To her dismay the day was already done, and twilight was gradually thickening into darkness. It wasn't long before a maddening bevy of no-see-um bugs hovered over her head. The chill of evening was slowly enveloping her, and she hugged her body for warmth. She suddenly realized she was no longer holding the necklace. In a panic, she fell to her knees groping around her woodsy bedding. "Oh thank God!" she said, as her fingers closed around the locket and brought it to her lips for a kiss. She quickly fastened it around her neck for safekeeping. A spiteful voice within whispered, *Is it really even YOUR locket? You don't remember your own name let alone whether or not you have kids.* But intuitively, she knew it was hers.

Mommy is okay and will be home with you soon, she insisted. *I promise.*

She gazed up at the night sky, and through a wide gap between the trees, a circular shimmering patch of whiteness emanated a hazy aura, strikingly stark in contrast to the bleak darkness around it. Being alone, totally clueless about who she was or where she was and with no sign of another human in sight, was freaking her out. So the prospect of making contact with someone uplifted her spirits and prompted her to head towards that direction.

It was challenging and creepy moving through the heart of a forest with nothing but transient lightening bugs and the silver moon-glow overhead to show the way. Downed branches revealed themselves as obstacles to circumvent, twigs crunched beneath her feet as she shuffled along, Pied Piper to the gnats and mosquitoes following her scent. *I would give anything to be varnished in insect spray right now.*

A low-lying, wispy, blue mist blanketed the forest floor, and she had a sense of being watched. She spotted fluorescent pairs of eyes peering at her from their protective perches on tree boughs. The sounds of small animals scurrying and scratching in the underbrush was nothing compared to the hostile groaning and growling that blended into a surround sound of roars through the trees making her neck hairs stand up.

Thirsty beyond belief and with her heart hammering in her chest, she moved deeper into the forest with no clue as to where she was heading, other than toward the mysterious shimmering white circle she could see far away.

She shuffled on course for a limbo of time before the first slanted ribbons of dawn's orange light penetrated the forest's canopy. It prompted a bustling and a twittering and chattering of birds welcoming the day. Soon the trees began to thin out, and she emerged into a grassy clearing. She paused to take in a deep breath of fresh air as she faced a panoramic expanse of blue sky. A butterfly fluttered past and landed on a rounded bush covered with yellow flowers. Soon others joined it. The sun was quickly warming the day.

She approached the point where the vegetation gave way to bald rock at the ridge of the clearing. She gasped as she suddenly found herself on the crest of a sheer craggy cliff, and looking down caused her to quickly experience vertigo. She stumbled backwards and looked more carefully around.

She had thought the circular light in the night sky was the promise of civilization, but, instead, a barren, undulating valley spread out below her, sweeping for miles to a range of cliffs on the far side. In the middle distance she saw interspersed spires of rock formations, looking for all the world like cone shaped stalagmites. And then she spotted it. If she could believe her eyes, help was at hand in the form of a lone house sitting in the valley floor. All she had to do was figure out how to get down there.

2

BEWARE OF VICIOUS DOG

The house lay due east. She didn't want to waste a moment more getting there, especially considering that her lips were cracked and sore and her throat was so dry it felt like it had shrunk to the dimension of a straw. She feared her condition would only worsen as the day went on and the sun got stronger. Hunger pangs were beginning to torment her.

She lay on a wide, bulbous ledge that jutted out past the vertical rock face, and wiggled to the edge of the cliff. Despite a panic that rose up in her, she grasped rooted stalks of tall grass for support and leaned over the rim to look down.

Below her was a ten-foot drop to a narrow strip of relatively flat rock. Beyond that was a broad slope, with a pitch of about 75 degrees, dotted with large boulders and smaller stones with clumps of scrubby bushes and other types of vegetation. After a few minutes of fighting the urge to crawl back to safety, she noticed that some parts were sharper than others, but there were definite pathways she could try and follow. Her vertigo now somewhat in check, she stood and looked around.

Nothing but rocks. So what am I supposed to do now, huh? she thought. She stood with her hands on her hips, feeling defeated.

She walked along the ridge for about thirty feet until she came upon a more negotiable spot where she could slither down to another flat ledge and see what was what from there. She sat on the edge and used both hands to grab a large clump of blue wildflowers. Twisting her body she faced backwards and dangled her legs over the precipice into empty space. Barely able to breath, she stretched until her pointed toes brushed the ledge. With the relief of a swimmer finally finding seabed underneath, she shifted her weight into the side of the cliff. Even with her feet once again on firm ground, her heart pounded and her knees felt weak. She took a few moments to compose herself in preparation for the next stage of her descent, trying very hard not to give in to her quivering muscles and a pervading pain in her back and legs.

Craning her neck, she gasped as she realized she was mere steps away from a steep incline. She took several deep breaths, drawing each in slowly and letting it out to a count of ten.

Take it slowly. Nice and easy now. Stay focused on each step, she told herself. She tried to see what was in store for her ahead if she were to traverse the slope, but the sun's glare was almost blinding, and it was difficult to assess the real height of all the shapes and formations.

Hugging the rock face at her back she inched towards her right and discovered another accessible slab about five feet below her she could hang-drop to next. Using the same technique as before she again slid over the ledge backwards. This time there were no bushes to cling to, so all she could do was claw with the tips of her fingers at the crevices in the rock until a foot touched the surface. She continued descending by zigzagging, hopping, and scampering across the rocky terrain like a mountain goat. As she approached a large area of soil she expected to find it loose and slippery, but it turned out to be hard-packed and solid, held together firmly by meandering roots.

Halfway down, she looked up, quite impressed with her accomplishment. The angle of the slope she had come down was steeper than it looked when she was perched above. She could see the giant boulders she had encountered and was horrified at the way they were looming over her, defying gravity, with seemingly nothing but small stones underneath holding them in place. All she could do was hope they were securely embedded. It was disconcerting to be in the midst of so many smaller mounds of rocks and loose shale like pieces knowing they were the products of other teetering big mamas that had crashed down and shattered. She started to panic.

The shock of a sharp pain in her head made her lose her balance. While attempting to recover traction, she stumbled off her perch and began sliding down the slope on her backside, creating a mini avalanche of small stones and loose gravel that cascaded alongside and beneath her. With her legs spread eagle and her arms waving frantically for balance she became engulfed in a cloud of dust. Blinded by the dust she tried desperately to stop her momentum by digging her heels into the surface with all her might. "Please, please, oh God, no no no no no!" she screamed. Her raspy voice echoed off the surrounding wall of rock. All she could think about was the possibility that the mini avalanche she had started might jar one of those enormous boulders loose.

As she continued to slide, she twisted her body and grabbed onto a straggly bush with both hands, praying that the roots would hold fast. They did, and with a sigh of relief, she abruptly stopped on her side. She lay in a fetal position waiting for the dust to settle, panting and coughing violently. She nestled her face in the crook of her left arm and closed her stinging eyes while she gained some composure. Once her adrenalin-spiked heart rate stabilized, she mustered some strength to lift her head. She craned her neck to look over her shoulder and found that just below her was a stretch of rocks with ruts in them, which might give her good traction. Straightening out her legs, she made sure the rocks were firm enough for a foothold before she let go of the plant.

She remained motionless, feeling a bit leery about standing up on her wobbly and sore legs. With a start, she checked for her locket and was relieved to find it was still dangling from around her neck. But her bracelet was gone. She had no sense of how far she had fallen or how much farther there was to go before getting to level ground. *But hell, if I keep sitting here, I'll dry up and cook. I'm probably burned to a crisp already.* She bit lightly on her dry tongue to stimulate whatever little saliva her body could make to relieve her parched throat. Her head felt like it was about to explode. She needed water and a doctor desperately. Feeling shaky, sore, and unsteady, she got up slowly to look ahead for the house she had spotted earlier.

There it was, below her and to the left. "Yes!" she croaked, pumping a small fist into the air. *The worst is over,* resonated in her mind several times. The rocks she had braced herself on were only about a hundred feet from the bottom of the cliff. The remainder of her descent had a bit of steepness to it and appeared to be made up of loose grit, like frozen granular snow. Compared to what she had already endured, this would be a piece of cake, she figured. She trekked along taking small steps, zigzagging back and forth, her body weary and throbbing with pain, until her feet suddenly gave out from under her.

She landed with a squeal on her butt into a heap of mushy gravel. As she stood up, the loose bedrock swallowed her feet to the ankles like quicksand. She estimated there was no more than five yards to go, and after plowing through the heavy granular surface she emitted a sigh of relief as she reached level ground. It was an odd landscape, checkered with naturally carved vertical stone monuments, which she had observed earlier and which from this perspective were at least five times her height.

She glanced up at the sun and used it as a guide to head in the right direction as best she could. A stabbing pain resurfaced in her back and legs, compounding her headache and dizziness. Her grimy legs were covered in scabby scratches and bug bites, and the penetration wound in her leg was swollen and festering. She still had no recollection of who she was or where she had come from. What she did know was that she would die soon if she didn't find water and someone to assist her.

She had been walking for but a few minutes when she was startled by a deafening roar behind her. The ground trembled and her immediate thought was that it was an earthquake. She turned to see the source of the noise and for a moment froze with fear. Careening down the mountain was one of the giant boulders that had been so precariously situated. It tumbled erratically and spewed shards of rock debris in a huge cloud of dust that spread over a wide expanse. "Run!" she commanded herself. She hobbled as fast as her adrenalin powered legs would take her, praying that the boulder would somehow miss her altogether; that it would shatter as it slammed into the rocky spires. When it did just that with explosive force, it sounded like a detonated bomb.

Thankfully, this desolate part of the terrain was flat, which enabled her to reach a safe distance from the spreading cloud of dirt and rock particles that dogged her heels. She crumbled to the ground, her heart pounding, her knees weak and trembling.

As she regained her composure, her thirst and hunger became magnified, and every joint in her body hurt. *Get up,* she told herself cruelly. *Crawl if you have to. If you don't you're dead.*

She had no idea of the passage of time, except by the lengthening shadows, and the movement of the sun above her, but she eventually came upon a rectangular sun bleached wooden sign mounted on one of the tall rock formations. Amateurishly hand printed in green paint with lowercase and capital letters in odd places was, "WeLCome to TRee cITy, pOPuLaTioN UNKNowN."

A huge floodlight that was big enough to illuminate a softball field, was positioned near the base of the sign, tilted skyward. She noticed a photo sensor attached to the frame and suspected it regulated a day/night switch. A solar panel about the size of a doormat was connected by a cable, an arms distance away. Flabbergasted, she turned and surveyed her surroundings. Not one tree was visible. Nor was there anything to even suggest the existence of a city. *This is getting more and more curious.*

Fighting her intense thirst, she continued shuffling east until the solitary house appeared close ahead, and before it, framed by the mountainous backdrop, she saw the crowns of three trees in fairly close proximity to one another. *Finally shade, however meager.* "Well now, that must be the grand entrance to Tree City," she chuckled to herself. Nevertheless, she supposed that even a meager "city" such as this could mean she would find someone to help her. Suddenly a fleeting trace of a memory surfaced: she was standing in awe at the foot of a giant sequoia tree, transfixed by the specks of sunlight passing through its towering boughs. Then it was gone.

Despite painfully weak knees, she tramp-shuffled down a slope, bending to grab the twisted stems of vines for support. As she approached the trees she saw that they were smothered with emerald green, single pointed leaves and white blossoms, the likes of which she had never seen before. She paused, barely able to hold herself up, and saw an even larger floodlight than the one by the welcome sign, turned upward, no doubt intended to illuminate all three trees. She became convinced that the light she had seen in the sky last night had to have come from one or both of these lamps.

The trees were shaped like lollipops, with clusters of white ball-like flowers with the appearance of crepe paper. If she didn't know better, she would say they were hydrangeas. However she never saw such huge specimens before. Upon examining the trees further, she became puzzled by their perfectly round shape. They had to have been pruned that way, she thought, though whoever did it would have had to use some sort of mechanical cherry picker.

She looked around for a clue as to why anyone would fuss with these trees in such a desolate place. At the bottoms of the thick trunks, in hard packed soil, were bronze plaques each embossed with the phrase "Tree City Memorial Program" and a blank inscription: "In Memory of   " but no inscribed name. This made no sense. But her priority was to get to the house, now so close she could almost touch it. *I need water. I have to find some water!.*

As she got closer to the house, she paused to take it in. She had expected to find a ranch or log cabin befitting the rustic environment, but it looked more like an English country cottage. Its two stories were built of the familiar stone indigenous to the area, held together with grayish mortar. The peaked roof was sculpted in a dark thatch that draped irregularly over the top of the exterior walls like melted cheese. The protruding stone chimney was so lopsided it looked like it might fall at any minute. An aged, red, crossbuck barn door with a curved top was in the center of a small stoop, flanked on either side by grungy bay windows.

On the second level, equally spaced apart, were three windows: casements on the left and right, and an octagonal one directly over the door. Dingy white louver shutters with broken or missing slats framed each of the windows. Dark green vines of ivy, entangled with sinuous knotted branches of a wisteria shrub, grasped at the stone surface, crisscrossing in all directions. The house had a shabby whimsicalness about it, but more than that, it struck her as being totally peculiar.

Nearby was another bleached wooden sign, this one with red lettering. Similar to the welcome sign, the words were printed in mixed lower and capital letters. She read softly to herself, "ThanK You FoR cuRBing YOUR dog." Curbing your dog? She wondered why it mattered where a dog walked around here. But more importantly, where was the water? Her parched throat was sore and ached.

Local fragmented rocks were stacked in a row about a foot high, some thirty feet from the front door, like a curb of some sort laid out parallel to the front of the house. This was another odd thing, because given the sterile environment surrounding the house there was no apparent reason to define a boundary here. Plus, that pointless curb was nothing more than a tripping hazard.

An in-ground sprinkler suddenly spewed water on what she now saw were rows of emerging seedlings about halfway up to the house. In her haste to run to the water, she caught her toe on the curb and catapulted forward, sprawling face down in the mud. Wriggling up to the sprinkler head, she began frantically slurping at it like a crazed animal.

Once she had her fill of water to the point that she was coughing and choking, she stood up and let the spray rinse some of the dried blood, muck, and sweaty stickiness off her wretched body. The coolness felt so good. Just as she finished washing her arms and legs, the water stopped flowing, and the sprinkler head sank into the ground emitting a slurping noise.

She called out to anyone who might be in the vicinity, "Hello? Anyone here?"

There was no response. Needing to rest and dry off somewhat before she knocked on the front door, she retreated to the curb and sat down.

"Well, at least it's good for something," she said to herself. After she squatted to take her seat, she noticed a row of small, red, plastic flags starting about twenty feet to the right of the house, running at right angles to the curb. A piece of wood dangling on a stake near the last flag piqued her curiosity. She shuffled over and stooped down to get a closer look. The exposed side was blank, but when she turned it over she saw the same irregular printing read, "SpoTs eLecTRonic FEncE co.—VICIOUS Dog 'n trainin." *Now that,* she thought, *is absurd.*

Folding her arms in firm resolve, she decided not to get caught up in trying to make sense of the strange scene. As far as she was concerned, there were several critical issues at hand: she had to eat, get medical help, find out where she was, who she was, and how she was going to get home. *Nothing is impossible if I put my mind to it,* she told herself.

She felt suddenly lightheaded, and plopped back on the curb just in time to vomit all the water she had gulped down. Sitting with her head between her legs enabled her dripping hair to dry off in the hot hazy sunshine that by now was directly overhead. She must have passed out, because much to her surprise the next she knew, she was lying stretched out and shaded under a beach umbrella. Her head was resting on a bunched up gunnysack, and a bottle filled with water was on the curb by her side. As she grabbed the bottle and started to drink, she discovered that her lips were sticky, and when she touched them with her finger, she found that they were thickly coated with a light green jell-like substance. "Ew!" she cried. Somewhat energized, she stood up slowly and resumed her original path towards the still closed front door, eager to meet the person who had helped her.

She remembered the sign, and looked around for the so-called vicious dog in training. Her frantic eyes spotted a metal sign she hadn't noticed before. It was maybe two feet square, behind her on the far left side of the yard, about five feet from the curb. A small solar spotlight was directed towards it. *I just* have *to see this*, she thought as she opted to backtrack a few steps in order to read it. It said "Warning" in bright red paint, and in the poorly printed black lettering underneath: "PrIVatE propertY. BeWare of ViCioUS dog." Beneath that, in smaller irregular print were the words, "HoMeowner assumes NO responsibility for MaULiNg TreSPaSSers."

She started feeling uneasy, and the sooner she did what she had to do and left, the better off she would be, she decided. She had to remain purposeful. Taking some deep breaths to gain composure and oxygenate her sore muscles, she headed back to where she had been only minutes ago. That's when she saw that the door was now partly open, and the hairs on her arms stood on end.

3

JOHN BEAM

She stared at the double Dutch style front door, its bottom portion now open. Her mind raced. *What's that all about? And why didn't anyone call out or come out to see if I was ok?* Feeling optimistic that at least she knew someone was home, she approached the house. She forgot about the recent sprinkler watering, and the moment she reached the irrigated area her front foot sunk into an oozing mush of oatmeal–like earth.

"What the...!" She yanked her foot out of the gunk, stepping back. Preferring to circumvent the soggy ground, she tested her weight on the first in a series of meandering flat stones leading up to the front stoop. Satisfied it would hold her, she boldly continued on, leaving behind a one-legged set of muddy footprints.

She took a moment to look closely at the little signs inserted into the ground next to the emerging sprouts. The names of different flowers were written on them, with numbers that she assumed were their mature height: cosmos-25 feet, sunflower-70 feet, marigold-20 feet, and many other varieties. She blinked twice, disbelievingly, because such extraordinary growth potential was more in line with science fiction than reality. "This is sheer lunacy," she muttered. "I must be out of my mind."

As she approached the door, she circumvented a thick chain strewn haphazardly on the ground. One end was secured to a metal pole and the other end was hooked to a large spiked dog collar. She began to feel queasy again, and her head started pounding. A shudder erupted in her shoulders and an adrenaline rush coursed throughout her body. She took a deep belly breath and brushed herself off as best she could. While squatting to rub off the hardened mud caked on her foot, she yelled into the house from the open bottom half of the door.

"Is anybody here? Hellooooooo!" There was no answer. "Hellooooo! Somebody! Hellooooo!"

The thought struck her: *What if that vicious dog comes bounding out and attacks me?* She struggled to pull herself up while holding on to the upper doorknob. It was very clear that given the state of her pain wracked body, no matter what, she wouldn't be going anywhere fast.

A man yelled grouchily from somewhere in the distance. "What? Go away."

"I don't mean to be a bother, sir, but I really need help," she said. "Was it you who brought me the water, the umbrella and some lip gel?"

The man continued with his long-range response. "I'm busy. How would I know if I can't see you? You'll have to wait until I'm done with my experiment. It could be ages yet. Come back tomorrow, or better yet, next week."

Considering she was at this fellow's mercy for help, she had no other option than to be patient. "Please sir, I really do need help urgently. I'm injured."

"Damn it. What's your name?" Then without waiting for an answer, "Oh, very well. Come in, and sit in the living room," adding, "and don't touch anything."

In the sweetest tone she could muster up, she said, "Thanks," and went on, "but if you don't mind, I'd really rather wait outside. Please call 911. I need a doctor. I'm injured," she emphatically repeated. "I'm lost and extremely weak. Plus, I think I have a serious medical condition, but I don't know what it is."

After a couple of minutes she heard someone shuffling to the door. She naturally expected the person to open the top half to see her. Instead, she heard muffled words coming from behind the closed upper part. Looking down and through the opening, she could see knee pads strapped to a pair of skinny legs and gray flip-flops on feet covered in dirt to the ankles.

"Who did you say you were?"

Somewhat embarrassed, she said, "I'm not really sure. I've lost my memory."

"Well that's pretty stupid, isn't it?" he said. "How do you expect me to engage in conversation with a nameless person?" He added, "I need to know your name, because I have a policy about not talking to strangers, and now that's *exactly* what I'm doing."

"Well, er... hi,... hello," she said, quite taken aback at the man's grouchiness. "Please help me. I think I need to go to the hospital, and I have to get to my children. Please. Can you give me a bite to eat and some water?" She wondered why he appeared so quickly when moments before he couldn't tear himself away from his experiment.

"Yes, I know. You already told me that moments ago, in the same order too."

Somewhat intimidated by his aggressiveness, she said, "I know it sounds crazy, but I don't know who I am." She stared at the feet on the other side of the door, but they did not budge. "I don't mean to be rude," she added, "but could you open the top door so that I don't have to talk to your legs? I'd rather talk to you face-to-face. And... you didn't say—was it *you* who gave me the water, the umbrella, and the lip gel?" She paused for a reply, but there wasn't one. "Ahhh... anyway... thank you if you did, and please... please, I desperately need another drink and something to eat or I'm going to pass out."

"It's a major problem that you don't know who you are. I told you I don't—that means do *not*—that's D-O 'space' N-O-T, talk to strangers," he replied. "Like it or lump it. It is imperative that you have a name so I can know you. Everybody has a name. If you lost your name I will help you find it later as long as I have some clues to work with. Let's brainstorm—think—what do you fill in on one of those stick on 'Hello My Name Is' labels when you go to business meetings? Do you just leave it blank? Or do you write 'unknown?' How do you sign your bank checks? What do you put on your luggage tags where it asks for first and last name? In fact, how do you own anything without a name? Not having a name is unacceptable, so I have no other recourse but to assign one to you."

She was too dumbfounded to interrupt him. Feeling woozier by the minute she leaned her shoulder against the doorframe for support. *Now what do I do? This guy is nuts.*

Without missing a beat in his steady stream of questions, the man declared, "My name is John Beam, spelled J-o-h-n. So don't you dare call me any nicknames until we get to know one another better. Otherwise, I will feed you to my giant *Dionaea muscipula*, 'Monster Mouth' which is a genetically mutated cultivar of mine. I'm in the process of getting it registered with the International Carnivorous Plants Society. Perhaps being a lay person you would be much less familiar with the genus and species than with the common name, Venus Flytrap."

Being in the position of need, she bit her tongue, doing all she could to keep from screaming in frustration and speaking angrily back to him. With no one else to immediately go to, she had no choice but to take what she could get for now. However, she decided to toughen up her response. He wasn't going to push her around like that, no matter how weak she was.

"Hey, Mr. Beam, I've been through hell today, and I don't appreciate being treated this way. I came for help, not to be badgered. Jeez! You can call me whatever you want. All I want is something to eat and drink because I'm about to faint right here on your stoop and topple over your seedlings, crushing them all." Her legs felt like rubber, and her head was starting to swim.

"Now I will open the top door," a more congenial John announced. "I heard you say you don't know who you are. So we'll have to get along with only partial introductions for the moment. In the interim, I will think of a name for you." As he spoke, he opened the top half of the door. They stood face to face without uttering a word. John stretched his neck forward and stared at her, pursing his lips all the while.

He was a blue eyed impish looking man with light red shoulder length hair and a very full matching beard that came to a point just below his chin. His skinny frame, congruent to his legs, was immersed in baggy bib overalls that ended in tattered strings just about reaching the tops of his knee pads. A familiar OshKosh B'Gosh clothing label was sewn on the bib near the adjustable shoulder straps that hiked the garment to his neckline. The long sleeves of his shirt that appeared to be made of burlap were stamped with "Idaho Potatoes" in large black letters. Greenish dust was smudged all over his cheeks and oversized horn-rimmed glasses, and sprinkled on his hair, beard, and shoulders. She didn't want to be impolite and ask about it, but obviously her expression betrayed her astonishment and curiosity. She stifled a laugh.

"What?" John asked.

"I'm wondering what all that green stuff is that's on you. And how can you see out of those glasses?"

"Oh, so it's because I'm green. Well, for your edification, it happens when I'm busy experimenting in my basement laboratory like I was when you came along. Pollen sticks to me. As to the glasses, I only need them for reading and close up work. So do you observe me doing either of those things here talking to you? Why do you ask about how I see? Are you an optimist?"

"Huh? Optimist? Given the situation I'm in now? Er ... Oh ... Do you mean optometrist? An eye doctor? Was that what ..."

John hastily changed the subject. "Here, have a homemade energy bar for all the nutritional support you need and this apple juice box. There's a little straw attached to it on the side. Here. See?" He pointed to it with a gross looking greenish finger.

She all but snatched the food out of his hand and munched voraciously on the snack. "What type of work do you do?" she asked with her mouth full. She didn't expect to get a cursory answer, but it went far beyond what she could ever have imagined or cared to know. The bar tasted so awful it made her gag. She quickly started sipping the juice, hoping John wouldn't notice.

John boasted, "I'm a botanist in the field of applied plant sciences with specialties in biotechnology and breeding. I'm very well known by most people," he added with a bit of pique. "I develop genetic modifications. I extract the best genes from plants and insert those genes into other plants so they grow with the most desirable traits. I then take the most desirable traits out of those plants and inject them into other plants, so on and so forth. By selecting and crossing plants I can create specimens that have specific desirable traits such as being fungus resistant." John took in a mouthful of air to replenish his lungs and continued.

"I'm constantly in the process of conducting experiments to formulate new strains of vegetables and other types of plant life. These plants grow enormously tall. My specialty is string beans: green, white, yellow, and brown. I'm creating a string ensemble, soon to be on the open market. Ha ha ha ha. 'String ensemble.' Do you get it?" He slapped his thighs and howled with laughter at his joke.

She humored him with a frail grin to keep the peace and struggled to suppress the urge to strangle him, although upon further thought she realized she really didn't have the strength. She felt weak, and the festering wound on her leg was itching and throbbing. She couldn't stomach looking at it now. She knelt down and lowered her head between her knees for a minute, one arm outstretched to balance herself. Regaining her balance and composure, she said, "John, that's all very interesting, but I feel very ill. Plus I have an infection in my leg and who knows where else. Can you please call the police or a doctor or get me to a hospital? I feel so faint. Can I lie down somewhere? Even on your floor would be fine."

John wasn't paying the least bit of attention to her and totally disregarded her pleas. He appeared to be preoccupied until all of a sudden, his eyes lit up. He snapped his fingers and said, "That's it. I'll call you Jane Doe. There are a lot of Jane Does around who otherwise wouldn't have an identity. Some even get the name after they are found dead with no identification on the body. I imagine that for the living ones, the name is exempt from implication in the crime of identity theft. I never heard of anyone *really* named Jane Doe and making a stink about her name being misused. But even if it were against the law, you would be safe with that name. No one could single you out for identity theft. The whole lot of Jane Does around would have to be rounded up and put into prison together. Can you imagine a chain gang that long? Nothing but a bunch of Chain Janes. How funny is that, huh?" John slapped his thighs again and laughed his head off. "But there isn't enough room in the prisons for all the Jane Does." He laughed at his new joke again. "Trust me I know. So I will call you Jane Doe. Like it or lump it."

She thanked him for her new name. As John gave his lecture like a wind up toy, never missing a beat, Jane continued to sip the drink while leaning against the house and slowly sidling downward. His behavior solidified the conclusion she had drawn earlier that he wasn't all there, so she really didn't want to hang around him for too long. She simply wanted to get the help she needed and be on her way, wherever that may be, as long as it was away from there. At this point, no longer able to sustain her weight, the world went dark and Jane crumbled into a heap in the doorway.

4

BEAM, BEANS, AND CRIMES

Jane came to lying in a wheelbarrow, drenched in sweat, inside a stifling hot and humid greenhouse. Her head was nestled on the same mound of burlap rags as before, and John was standing over her with even more green pollen on him. Except for the semblance of a grin, he could have passed for a shrub in a look-a-like contest.

Jane bolted upright and shouted, "Where am I? What happened?" She instinctively checked for her locket. It was still there. She wiped perspiration from her forehead and temples then dangled her legs over the edge and slid downward, tipping the wheelbarrow over onto its side as her feet touched the floor. A searing pain cut through her legs. They were wrapped in layers of green leaves and a mossy substance encircled with cord from her thighs to her ankles. The spot that was infected from an embedded object was thickly padded. Her lips and face were coated in that familiar gel, and her arms were oily.

"What the ...?" She scrutinizing her appendages and explored her lumpy face with her fingers.

All of a sudden it occurred to her—where's the dog? "John, where's your vicious dog? Where do you keep him? You have signs all over outside about a dog. But I haven't heard one bark or growl."

John said, "Don't worry about the dog. There isn't one."

Jane was relieved to hear there was no dog—if she could believe him. Based on what little she knew about John, no doubt his explanations for the numerous dog-related signs would be outrageous. A discussion best left for another time, she decided.

"John, what did you do to me? What's all this oily stuff?" She pointed to her legs and arms. "What's with the sticky goo on my lips and face? Huh? What happened to me that I wound up like this? I can't believe..."

"Chill out, Jane," John interrupted, sounding suddenly like some west coast surfer dude. "I suggest you lie back in the wheelbarrow, off your legs. They need to be elevated a bit longer. You'll be as good as new in no time."

Jane did as instructed, her obedience robotic.

"So you wanted to know where you are. You're in a wheelbarrow in my botanical showroom, otherwise known as a greenhouse. You've been asleep for the past five hours.

"Excuse me—what time is it?" Jane asked. "What day of the week is it? I...I don't have the slightest sense of time."

"Well, this must be your lucky day, because I just happened to hear the rooster crow six times, which is one crow for every hour, and since I'm awake I can rule out six in the morning. As far as the day of the week, well, today is the day after yesterday and before tomorrow."

My lucky day? Jane sat in disbelief, thoroughly appalled at John's insolence and outlandish remarks.

"*What* rooster? Last I knew, roosters crow in the early morning, and they don't report time. So what are you talking about?" Jane asked. "Why can't you give me a straight answer?"

John's demeanor suddenly changed. He appeared hurt. "But, it *is* a rooster, Jane. I *am* being straight with you." He was all but whining. "It's on my kitchen counter, and it ticks on a rechargeable battery."

Jane heaved a sigh, realizing her interaction with John was going to call for an inordinate amount of patience. She longed to get home to her children—they must be so upset—and she was worried about her medical situation. *What if I was on a regimen of medication for a serious health condition? What if I am severely allergic to something?* Her ruminations were making her extremely anxious. *Stop it! Think positive. You're going to be OK. John's all you've got right now, so be patient.*

John appeared to get control of himself. "As I've been trying to tell you, you blacked out in my doorway. I caught you in the nick of time or you'd have collapsed on my seedlings, probably impaling yourself on the markers. Or maybe you could have hit your head on my cast iron boot scraper. In either case I would have had a very serious problem on my hands."

"*You* would have had a very serious problem?" Jane picked up on what John said. Exasperation flooded through her. "Are you *serious*?"

The way he ignored her, she might as well have been invisible. "Again, as I was saying," he continued, "since you were pretty much coated in dirt, I hosed you down. And as I did that, I was shocked. You have a nasty bump on the top of your forehead, blisters on your face and lips, and scratches and welts all over you. I thought maybe you were attacked by a swarm of insects. The worst was the condition of your leg with that thing stuck in it. It was grossly swollen and smelling something awful from a horrid bacterial infection. I knew I had to do surgery right away and get it medicated or you would be dead in no time from blood poisoning. What a predicament that would be for me. I have no idea how I'd explain all this to officials once I had a body on my hands. So I decided I'd better take life saving measures and…"

Jane was incredulous over what she was hearing. "Surgery? What do you mean, *surgery*?" she screeched. "What did you do to me? You're not a surgeon, are you? Plus evidently, I have a serious medical condition. You could have killed me!"

"Oh please, what a drama queen you are! As I didn't kill you, unless I'm talking to a zombie, you're welcome. And no, I'm *not* a surgeon and have never professed to be one. I'm a botanist, a famous one I might add, but I *do* perform surgery. It's called grafting. I surgically attach a part of one plant to a part of another plant. That results in a mutation, which I then attempt to propagate. It takes a lot of skill, and I follow standard surgical procedures making sure everything is sterile. Now as I was..."

"You do what? You create mutations? Who's your mentor, Dr. Moreau?" Jane asked sarcastically.

John was clearly becoming annoyed. "If you are referring to the H.G. Wells novel, that doctor was a mad scientist. His mutations were humans blended with animals. I work with plants not animals or humans."

"Jeez—never mind. I don't need to be lectured. I'm sorry. It's obvious you did something extraordinary to help me," Jane said contritely. "So go on—what did you do? What's all this stuff you put on me?"

"Well, like I said, I'm a famous botanist. But what I didn't say since there was no reason to do so, was that I have a successful practice in phytomedicine—er, that's botanical medicine. Simply speaking, I'm an herbalist. I know many things about natural treatments for all sorts of ailments and injuries. I can't do anything about the popper on your head or the very distinct possibility of a short circuit in your brain, but I took care of everything else. I made an antiseptic poultice from a plant called yarrow and combined it with honey. Yarrow is a miracle wound dressing and an analgesic for pain. It's been used for thousands of years. It's also used to stop bleeding which was necessary after I took out that glassy object from your leg. Before I grew a beard I used to apply the yarrow poultice when I nicked myself shaving. That was pre-eyeglasses so it happened more often than not.

"The spongy bulge in the surgical site on your leg is sphagnum moss. It too has been used for thousands of years as a wound dressing and packing. It has a sponge-like structure that absorbs double the amount of moisture than cotton can, so it's excellent for holding a significant amount of discharge from the wound before it becomes totally saturated and needs changing. I use it to wrap around the grafted parts of my plants."

"Wait," Jane cried. "You took out a piece of glass?"

John shrugged his shoulders. "I said 'glassy.' It was smooth and shiny, but why would I know if it was glass? What do you think I am, a glazier?"

"Did you save it?" Jane asked.

"For what? Forensics? Is this a crime scene or something? Be my guest if you want to dig it out of the red biohazard container full of bloody yuck," John suggested.

Jane thought it might be something she would do later out of curiosity. At the moment John's tactless proposition made her nauseous. "Nah. Never mind. So go on—what else did you do for me?" She wanted to hear more, but also realized she was hungry and thirsty. When she had first looked around she noticed John had left her something to eat on a table behind her.

He continued. "The essential oil of the herb coriander is good for muscular aches and pains so I rubbed it all over your arms and legs. I used the gel from the leaves of the aloe vera plant for the sunburn and blisters you have on your face and lips. That's that. Like it or lump it."

"I'm sorry. I don't know what to say other than thank you. You did an extraordinary thing for me. I owe you…"

John interjected, "No charge. It's free. I…"

"I didn't mean…"

"Hey, listen up," John said, changing the subject. He started walking away and spoke over his shoulder. "As a supplement to the snack bar and juice you had, I brought you some steamed veggies, hummus with roasted peppers and a quart of milk. I have left over barbequed spare ribs that I made last night, but those are only for my supper, so I didn't include them in the carte de jour. Everything's on the drip tray on the potting bench behind you. By the way, when you were snoring, I spritzed distilled water inside your mouth using my plant mister. That's why you'll notice that your tongue isn't pasted to your palette." John's voice faded away as he disappeared from view.

He came back. "Hey Jane, did you see my glasses?"

Jane shook her head. "You weren't wearing them."

"Well of course I wasn't. That's why I'm looking for them."

Jane didn't find the mixture of dairy with vegetables and dip too appealing, but she was hungry enough to scarf down anything at this point. She took a handful of peppers and stuffed them in her mouth, chasing that down with a gulp of milk. Just as she thought, the combination was awful, but she wasn't in any position to complain. She dipped the rest of the beans in the hummus and drank the entire contents of the container.

With curiosity, she turned the empty container around in her hands to read what was on it, which was nothing much. "Tree City Dairy Farm" was printed on a crookedly affixed label, and there was nothing about the milk being pasteurized or homogenized or where it was processed. Another label with the text, "Have you seen this missing child?" contained a poorly reproduced black and white photo of a young girl in braids. Oddly, there was no contact information. She figured she would ask John about that.

She was feeling much better although her stomach was experiencing some mild cramping and gurgling. She got out of the wheelbarrow and leaned on the bench to make sure she could stand up. Her legs were wobbly but not even half as painful as they were when she got here.

"Thank you John," Jane called out. No response. "John? Where are you?" Jane looked around. "John!"

There was no answer. She looked around and decided to hobble towards a sunlit greenhouse, its vertical glass sidewalls each with centrally placed double swing doors. A high gabled roof was supported by rafters. Once inside, she saw every space on the cedar central bench and two side benches was occupied with some incredibly huge specimens of varying shrubs and flowers. Although she wouldn't swear to it, the place had to be as large as a two-bay fire station. What especially captured her attention was the massive hydrangea-like shrubs with the ball shaped flowers she had come across on her way over. There were the usual blue and pink hues, but more amazing were the unusual striped and polka dot varieties.

She started meandering down one of the two gravel walkways on either side of the central bench calling, "John?!" There was no sound other than the drone of the mechanical ventilation and exhaust system fans, which had effectively dissipated the oppressive heat. Intermittently, the hiss of an automatic water spraying system shrouded the plants with a fine mist.

At one end of the greenhouse where the natural light was sparser, flats of tiny seedlings growing under low hung fluorescent lamps were situated on horizontal shelves stacked about eight feet high and along the entire wall. The top of a rolling stepladder was leaning against the highest shelf attached to a track, much like what one would find in the stacks of a library. Nearby were potting benches, surrounded by piles of bagged soil, compost, and fertilizer.

A rusty, yellow forklift with oversized tires was parked by one of the double exit doors, its raised platform with disproportionate prongs, was loaded up with three bales of peat moss. A solar panel was mounted on the flat top of its overhead canopy. Next to the forklift was a downward sloping ramp, which Jane assumed led to the underground laboratory where John practiced his biotechnology and experimented with his plants. Garden tools and terracotta clay pots of all sizes were scattered about. The air was freshly filtered and pleasantly permeated with the wholesome aroma of damp, organic soil and cedar.

Jane was fascinated by the Obvious mutations of common plants and flowers labeled marigolds, sweet peas, roses, lilies, and geraniums. There was a long row of camellias and hibiscus the size of turkey platters and dahlias that resembled Frisbees. She was in front of what appeared to be lilacs the size of ostrich wing plumes, and was so engrossed in examining them up close that she was startled by two branches unexpectedly parting and John's grinning face emerging between them. "Boo!" he shouted.

Jane jumped. "Cripes. You just scared the life out of me. Why did you do that, and why did you disappear in the first place?"

"Boo!" John repeated.

Jane rolled her eyes in exasperation. "I get it. You succeeded in what you set out to do. I got scared. Are you happy now?" She paused. "Say, can we talk? Will you call the police for me? An ambulance? Somebody? Where's your phone. I'll do it myself."

"You ask too many questions, and my time is very limited," John announced. "Anyway I don't have a phone. There are no phones in Tree City … er, correction. To be precise, if I were on a witness stand I couldn't attest to that, because it's very possible there are phones around here and there. But the fact is, they wouldn't work because there's no phone service. Our remote topography is a whole geography lesson in itself—a mix of mountains, valleys, plateaus and plains. Didn't you figure that out getting here? That's why there are no radio frequencies, er … signals er … airwaves for broadcasting. All we get up here is static."

Jane's mouth dropped open in horror. "What? You don't have a phone? Nobody has a phone around here?" She felt tears welling up in her eyes. "That's impossible. Who doesn't have a phone in this day and age?"

"You have a very short memory," John said sounding exasperated. "Maybe that's what's wrong with you. Didn't I just say five seconds ago 'I don't have a phone.'?"

"You're very rude, aren't you," Jane said. "I DO appreciate all you have done for me so far—but if you can't help me any further, I guess I'll be on my way. Perhaps you can tell me where either the nearest town or the next house is. Or mayb—just mayb—you can find it in your heart, despite your obviously very busy day, to drive me to either one of those places or better yet, the nearest police station or hospital."

John listened to her all the while looking down at a small cloud of dust forming from shuffling his feet back and forth in the gravel.

"Fine! Fine then," John shouted. "As far as what you might call a town, where our one and only rinky-dink police station is, and where there's a twenty-four hour storefront and medical emergency center, it's down the road, well below this plateau we're situated on. By car it's about an hour's drive from this house not counting some stops depending on how much water I drink. Unfortunately I don't expect to be heading that way today or tomorrow or next week—maybe not for a month. I don't know. I simply don't know. It all depends on how my beans grow. Sorry."

"What beans? What does helping me have to do with growing beans?"

Her fear surrounding the uncertainty of who she was, how she got here, and needing to contact her family consumed her thoughts. "I'm in distress, big time, with a short circuit in my brain for some unknown reason. I have no recollection of who I am, family or friends or where I last was or where I live and you're factoring in growing beans into the equation of helping me?" Her quivering voice had reached a high-pitched note. She clasped her locket sentimentally and remembered she had yet to open it.

"Oh my. Oh my. What to do? What to do?" John was flustered. He thought a moment.

"Well, I could drop you off at the Ogar house which is closest to here and be done with this chore forever. Otherwise it's a very long walk, and you're not strong enough to make that trek, but anyway, those people won't help you. You'll be sorry. That I can promise you. They're very dangerous, and as it just so happens— well, er...er...I'm on the cusp of an investigation into a very serious crime I suspect they are involved with."

Jane burst into tears. Her degree of stress had reached a crescendo.

John immediately began holding his hands on his ears. "La, la, la, la, la. I can't hear you. La, la, la, la," he rattled on, shaking his head from side to side.

Jane had all she could take watching these childish antics. She turned away and shuffled out the nearest greenhouse door. She didn't know where she would go, but she had to get away from this lunatic. Swiping her tears away with the back of her hands, she leaned up against the fender of a rusty, faded, red pick-up truck to compose herself as her eyes adjusted to the outdoor light. Compared to when she had arrived, the sun was much lower in the sky, hinting of the darkness to come. The air was desert-like, very dry and still.

Far from what she would expect in this environment, she detected a pungent smell, somewhat reminiscent of her past night in the forest. *Rot? Mold maybe? How could the outside body of the vehicle smell of rot or mold?* Stepping back to get a better view of the truck, she noticed a five sided cube made out of solar panels mounted on the rear half of the roof. She glanced towards the open cargo area, and was fascinated to see, secured with chains, several exotic shrubs about her height. Their ample root balls were tied up in burlap and rope and to her amazement, each of them bore a thriving variety of flowers and foliage, obviously the products of John's grafting experiments. What appeared to be tomato plants were tucked in between and were bursting with bright red produce the size of dinner platters. A large open gunnysack labeled "Fertilizer—Big Dog Poop," was close to the lift gate. "Pee-ew!" she exclaimed. *But John had said there wasn't a dog?*

Looking around to get her bearings, she noticed that the greenhouse was more than double the size of the house and was situated behind it and to the right. She decided her best bet was to head towards the front yard and the road. As she hobbled along, she held the wrappings on her legs to keep them intact.

She was barely past the artificial curb and onto the hard packed dirt road when she heard a chugging engine behind her and high pitched beeps. Turning her head to look over her shoulder, she was horrified to find that she was being chased by the yellow forklift she had seen in the greenhouse, still with the bales of peat moss piled up front on its lopsided platform. Its oversized tires gave it the zany look of a monster truck. John was steering with one hand and waving the other wildly to attract her attention. As one bale toppled to the ground, he swerved the vehicle recklessly around it. If it weren't for its oversized tires, the forklift would have tipped over.

"Jane! Jane! Stop. You have to stop. You need to elevate your legs for some more time or you'll get edema."

"I don't care about edema. I might have an even more serious health problem getting worse by the moment without medicine. Thank you for all of your help. I have no intention of stopping or chatting with you further," Jane shouted, huffing and puffing as she maintained her feeble pace. "Go away. Leave me alone. I need to find out what happened to me, and I want to see my children. Regardless of how old they are, I bet they're frantic wondering where I am. Assuming I have a husband, I bet he's looking for me and probably already filed a missing person's report."

"Hey there Jane. Halt," John commanded like an army general. "I'll take you to the Ogars if you don't mind being scared out of your wits."

The forklift was now sputtering by her side, and John's head was in line with hers, his long hair tossing around and getting caught in his mouth as he spoke.

"Oh, come on. Really? *That* bad? How terrible could these neighbors be? And given I have no other choice, perhaps it's better than nothing."

There was no reply. She was feeling ill and unsteady, but although each step was an effort, she kept on moving along the dusty road, thankful that it was comparatively cooler than earlier in the day. Nevertheless, the dry heat turned the gel on her arms and face into a thick dripping substance that was the consistency of Elmer's glue. As she walked, she massaged it into her skin.

"You don't want to explain? Then skip the Ogars, John. Don't do me any favors if those people are more trouble than it's worth. I certainly don't need more aggravation, that's for sure. I've had more than enough trauma already. What about getting me to the police station? Do you mind telling me what some silly beans have to do with that?"

John was doing his best to keep the rickety forklift from veering towards Jane. "Because the timing as to what happens next for you hinges on the beans. It's as simple as that."

"Oh that really explains it all," Jane said curtly. She shifted sideways to avoid being hit by the forklift.

"Okay. Okay. Shucks. I'll help you." John flashed a congenial smile and cocked his head as he attempted to control the creeping forklift. "Listen up!" he shouted over the chugging noise. "I've got a plan. Since this is a highly irregular situation I'm prepared to drop everything I had planned to do today and instead be completely inconvenienced.

"I'll drive you to the Ogars, and you can knock on their door and see what's what over there firsthand. Then you'll understand what I'm talking about, and I am quite sure you'll very quickly rule out asking them for help. Well, that's actually phase two. Phase one, which I skipped, is that on the way over I'll tell you the story about the beans and tip you off about the crime. Here's phase three: If you help me investigate it when the time is right, I promise to be your host on the long and precarious journey down road to town or at the very least to someone closer who can help. Like it or lump it."

Jane's head was spinning. Exhausted and out of breath, she stopped abruptly. The forklift continued moving a bit farther on before going into reverse, weaving uncontrollably. Jane held her ears as its back up warning alarm blared along with a male voice recording repeatedly broadcasting, "Reversing! Reversing!" Jane stood in place, hands on her hips in disbelief as it stopped and idled alongside her.

"John, you're out of your mind. *I'm* going to stick around, for God knows how long to help you investigate a crime? What crime? How many times in your life does a lost, amnesiac, distraught woman come by your place desperate to get home?" An errant tear trickled down the side of her nose.

John ignored her comments. "Cool it. Jane. I'll help you get home." Reaching out he gently wiped her face. "Wait and see. But for now, hop on and rest your legs while we go back to get my truck." He pointed ahead to the remaining bales on the pronged platform, implying that was where she should sit. "Tonight I'll make a note to look for my eraser and adjust my to-do list for tomorrow. On the first line, I'll add, 'Pick up the cargo that fell off the forklift.'"

Surprised but touched by John's unexpected sensitivity, and ignoring his mood swings, Jane found the idea of sitting anywhere rather appealing. She hoisted herself up onto the peat moss load and just as she did that, John turned the forklift around sharply. She screamed as the bale she was on slid off, taking her with it to the ground.

"There's still another one left," John said matter-of-factly. "Get on that. Hold on to the ties." Jane gingerly got up and did as she was told, not wanting to agitate him.

It seemed like forever bouncing up and down before they made it to the greenhouse and got into the old red pick-up truck Jane had been leaning on before. Peanut shells were scattered all over the floor on the passenger side, and John made no attempt to remove them. She climbed in, and as she positioned herself on the bench seat, they crunched and crackled under her shoes.

"Ich!" Jane cried as she looked around. The entire dashboard was coated in a greenish dust. To the right of the instrument panel a gaping rectangular hole with free hanging wires was testament to an earlier existence of a radio. John started up the engine, and Jane screeched in reaction to the roar of the exhaust emission.

"Doesn't this truck have a muffler?" Jane shouted.

Seemingly undisturbed, John began to chatter vociferously. "Oh that. Pay no mind to that rumble. This here vehicle has two different engines and a special exhaust set up. Believe it or not, it can run on plants and tiny saplings. It's a photosynthetic system. That's a solar panel on the hood, and that baby aids the plants and little trees in going through photosynthesis which powers up an electric motor. This truck also has a diesel engine that is fed plain vegetable oil. The two engines work together. It's taken me years to perfect."

Jane was flabbergasted. "I don't know what to say except that I'm impressed! Where are the supply of plants and trees growing?"

John snapped, "Never mind about all that. It's not relevant to the task at hand. Like it or lump it, at this very moment I'm going to begin what I said I was going to do which is tell you about the beans and a thing or two about the crime that has taken place which I suspect was committed by the Ogars. Don't interrupt me or I'll lose my train of thought. Then I might have to start all over again, and unfortunately that won't fit in with the time frame I'm allotting for this visit. So listen up. And while you're sitting there with nothing to do, start to unravel the wrappings on your legs for the surprise of your life. The dressings are ready to be air dried for optimum healing."

5

THE OGARS

"Some time ago I was a young boy," John began as he drove. Jane was busy removing the cords and the medicinal leaves on her legs. She was anxious to see what they looked like. "No *kidding*," she said, and looked up, smiling at her own pun. John glared at her. She flashed him a smile and refocused her attention on her legs.

"My father was a sickly person," shouted John over the abominable roar from the un-muffled engine exhaust. "As a result, I spent much of my time helping my mother around our rinky-dink farm. Our barn was where the greenhouse is now, and we had a plot of land next to it where we grew vegetables, strawberries, melons, and so forth. We ate what we harvested during the warmer months and preserved the excess for the non-growing seasons. Apart from some hens, one rooster and a bunch of yakking chickens, we had a cow named Milkdude who gave us lots of fresh, creamy milk to drink or to make butter from."

"Seriously? You named your cow Milkdude?" Jane asked. "That doesn't sound like a suitable name for a cow, let alone any female."

John snapped at her. "It's no different than if you had a son named Joe Doe. A doe is a female deer. So would Joe be less manly with 'Doe' as a last name?"

Jane found John's dumb analogy bothersome. There was something peculiar about his logic, plus she didn't appreciate his ongoing condescending attitude. It egged her on to sarcasm. "So if milk, butter, and eggs were your staple food items, then you all must have high cholesterol. Maybe that's why your father was sickly."

John retorted, "Well, I wouldn't say that cholesterol is a bad thing. After all, cholesterol works well for plants. It keeps them healthy and green." He glared at her as though she were an idiot. "Anyway, who made you my family nutritionist?"

"Oh pa-leeease! Keep your eyes on the road, do you mind? And just what are you talking about: *'cholesterol* works well for plants?' You're confusing that with *chlorophyll*. You know—the green pigment—the substance that absorbs sunlight to create energy for the plant to grow and give off oxygen?! It's what we all learned in elementary school. Um, does photosynthesis ring a bell, Mr. Famous Botanist?"

John stuck his tongue out at her and laughed. "So you're also the resident science expert?"

Jane sighed. "Oh forget it." She was tired from raising her voice over the noise, and was even more nervous than before. She noticed that her palms were sweating. Considering John's idiosyncrasies and the little he told her about where he was taking her, her fear was steadily mounting. Looking out the window she saw no sign of life of any kind. Afraid that she was going to trigger some other odd behavior, Jane resolved to just let John do all the talking. She wasn't in any position to be picky since she needed whatever help she could get from him. She wished she could keep the window open more for some fresh air, but the car was kicking up clouds of dust.

"Oh my!" Jane cried as she removed the last of the dressings on her legs. Faded marks signified where the many lacerations were and the welts from the insect bites had all but disappeared. The stitches where the object was removed from her leg were impeccably neat, so much so that a sewing machine couldn't have done better on cloth. The skin surrounding the wound was a healthy color and the swelling had gone down significantly. "It's a miracle. John, it's amazing how quickly they healed."

"Yeah, well that's no surprise to me." John said. "Dang it, you made me lose my train of thought." Jane jumped as he unexpectedly banged his fist on the steering wheel. Then he continued talking calmly as though he had never exhibited an outburst. "Ah yes. Anyway, it was my job to gather hay to feed Milkdude every morning and tend to the soil so that it would produce enough grass for her to graze on. Sometimes after stockpiling the hay I would forget about it and all the other tasks I had to do. I would get in the mood to just wander about long distances to take in the world around me, looking at the wildlife, the trees and all."

Jane's ears perked up. She wondered how far away wildlife and trees could be. She was tempted to ask, but instead kept silent.

"So whenever I came home without doing my chores, my mother would go into a rage about how useless I was. 'You incorrigible runt! You dolt,' she would say, and then she would send me to bed without being allowed to eat her lousy supper. Although, that was really a blessing in disguise," John added.

"All the time my father would whine, and since my mother was always complaining about what a lamebrain I was, I used to call them Moan and Groan," John snickered. "Then one day, my mother said, 'Take Milkdude into town and sell her. We are in dire need of money. The poor creature isn't producing enough milk anyway and besides, it's cheaper to go to the community food co-op for our dairy needs.'" Jane was incredulous—*a food co-op? Around here?*

"The fact that Milkdude wasn't producing enough milk was all because of me, of course. Everything bad was because of me. EVERYTHING!" John bellowed. His voice reached an octave higher as he spoke through clenched teeth while tightly gripping the steering wheel. "Can you imagine? It was my fault there was a drought, and we couldn't grow enough grass for Milkdude to eat!"

"Holy moly!" John suddenly cried. At that moment, he swerved the truck sharply to the left, slamming Jane against the passenger door in the process. "Hold onto your hat!" In an attempt to recover, he swung wildly to the right and then to the left again, repeating the movements several more times, rocking Jane violently back and forth across the seat. When he eventually succeeded in straightening out the vehicle, Jane was on the floor in a heap amidst the peanut shells.

"John! What the. ... " Jane scrambled back onto the seat gasping and hugging her chest for security. "What's wrong with you? Are you out of your mind? Why did you do that?"

Jane looked out the smudged back window and couldn't detect anything on the road that he could possibly have tried to avoid. Now more anxious than ever because of John's erratic behavior and reckless driving, she thought of a plan. As soon as the right opportunity comes along, she would say that she needed to be on her way, if he would just point her in the right direction to someplace, she would get out and walk, no matter how far it meant. But while that would be ideal, on the other hand the fact remained that she was plain scared to be out in this God forsaken place by herself.

"Oh, cool your jets," John said. "I could be wrong, but there was something fuzz—for all I know, maybe it was more than one fuzzy something—bounding across the road back there." John demonstrated with a sweep of his hand towards Jane, almost hitting her in the face. Jane stared at him dumbfounded.

"What? You saw what?"

"Yes. That's it exactly. It's in the past, so what difference does it make?"

"What do you think it or they were? A dog or a pack of dogs?"

"No," John curtly replied.

"Then what? Do wild animals roam around here?" Whatever iota of chance there was that Jane could leave John and set out walking on her own was fizzling out. Unfortunately, it seemed, she was better off in the truck despite his reckless driving. She straightened in the seat and stared out the windshield, scanning the barren countryside as they clattered on.

Offering no other explanation for what had happened, John went on with his story. "So, now I'm getting to the good stuff about the unusual seeds and just in time before we get to the Ogars' place. See the house up there?" John pointed ahead.

Jane said, "Yeah, I see it." She stared at the dusk touched horizon and spotted the silhouette of the dwelling in the distance. She was still unnerved by what John had done. "Hold on. You're trying to change the subject," she exclaimed angrily. "What do you mean by 'something fuzzy'? There's nothing around us. I haven't seen any sign of life this whole way, not even a single weed, yet all you can say is that you saw something fuzzy in the midst of this great expanse?"

"Yup. That's what I saw," John said emphatically. "Something fuzzy. Was it a dandelion puff? No. Was it a pair of slippers? No. Was it a rhinoceros? No. Was it indistinct in the low light? Yes. That's something fuzzy to me."

Jane was so exasperated with John's answers that she gave up on the topic and let him continue speaking.

"So to continue from where you interrupted me: On the way to the marketplace leading Milkdude, this man comes up to me and taps my shoulder saying, "Hey, yo! You there!" He downright scared me out of my britches, and as you know I don't talk to strangers, so I just looked at him and didn't say a thing."

"My name is Patrick Pod," he said. "But most people call me P. Pod. Get it? Heh, heh. Howya doin'? I'm a sales associate for the reputable Seedy Seed Company. I have these here seeds I'm selling, and when I reach my quota, which is right now should you buy them, I could earn myself a brand new mountain bike. More fantastically, your name would go into a drawing where you might win one for yourself. How cool is that?"

"I didn't own a bicycle," said John, "so I imagined that having a bike would be really neat. Before P. Pod could say anything else I told him, 'Well that sounds like a great plan and all except there's one little hitch. I don't have any money which is why I am on my way to the market to sell my cow.'"

"With that, the fellow started bawling. I mean, *really* bawling like a drama king. In between his histrionic sniffles, P. Pod told me this was his only chance to meet his quota for getting the bike, because I was his last prospective customer for the day."

"As quickly as he had turned it on, he abruptly stopped his crying antics. Then he sheepishly looked around to see if there was anybody in earshot, and with a sense of urgency in his voice he whispered to me, 'My friend, time is running out, and I have to move on. So because I would like to make a deal here and now, I will do you a very big favor. I'll take the cow off your hands in exchange for some highly valuable miracle seeds. They're all I have left. These here large pole bean seeds are uniquely fortified by special hormones. You'll have truckloads of string beans to harvest. I guarantee that you'll become the most famous bean producer in the world.'"

"It all sounded quite impressive, and I was hooked when he said I would become famous. So, I handed Milkdude over to P. Pod, and I headed home with my precious trade. The last things I heard him say was 'make sure you plant them in full sun, and keep them moist.'

John continued with his story. "It was already dark out when I reached home. I remember my mother stopping me at the door with her hand out as though she were some type of county toll collector. She was screaming that I was an embarrassment to her because it was after 10 p.m. and she didn't know where her child was. I can still hear that raspy voice of hers lashing out at me, 'How dare you, you little runt. Trying to make me the laughing stock of my friends, are you?' She demanded that I turn over the money from the sale of Milkdude at the market. Instead I excitedly showed her the big seeds I got in exchange for our cow and gave her the good news that these would make us very rich farmers.

To my complete surprise, my mother took one big wallop at me and called me 'dopey boy.' She said it was my fault that we were all sure to die from having nothing to eat and the tragedy would start with me because I was to go off to bed without supper and not get breakfast either."

Jane could tell that John was getting very agitated, and he began pounding on the steering wheel again. It was very disconcerting. She didn't know what to expect next from him, and that made her exceptionally nervous. Her chest began to hurt and her head started pounding. Suddenly she felt a sting in her arm. "Ouch! Not again! I was stung," she cried as she looked out the partially open window to see if something was flitting about. The back of her hand felt like it was burning and she rubbed it rapidly. *This place sure has a fair share of insects if nothing else,* she thought.

"Oh big deal. The world is filled with bees and stingrays and whatnot."

"Stingrays? What are you talking about?"

There was no answer. Jane realized that was the extent of the input and sympathy she was going to get from John. He was more intent on finishing his story as they approached the house. She was growing increasingly anxious.

"My rage was starting to get the better of me and in the midst of my father's wailing moans and my mother's groans, I turned and ran, holding my hands to my ears. I headed along this very road and walked for hours until I heard a man's deep voice yelling obscenities and a woman's bloodcurdling screams. It was coming from that house—where the Ogars live. I had stopped dead in my tracks right about where we are now and didn't move a muscle as I started to think twice about what I was doing. It was dark and I was so frightened that going back home to my hell of moans and groans was looking like a good alternative at the time. I ran home as fast as I could, and it was a while before I could no longer hear the screeches invading the night air.

"When I got to my backyard I tripped on some stupid little sign. My dad was obsessed with signs for one thing or another. As..."

Jane could barely control a hefty laugh. "So that explains it."

"What? Explains what?" John asked. "What's so funny?"

Jane sighed. "Nothing. Never mind."

"So... You have to hear the rest of the story. I'm getting to the best part. As I catapulted forward, I hit my head on the side of our well wall—we didn't have running water at the time. The next thing I knew, it was daylight, and I noticed that my packet of precious seeds had torn and the contents had spilled out under my body."

"We have arrived at our destination," Jack announced suddenly like a tour guide. He began to decrease his speed. "This is as far as we go with the truck. I'm parking by the side of their outhouse to be out of sight."

"Their outhouse?" Jane was incredulous as she spotted the structure. "That's certainly not an outhouse. It sure looks like a gatehouse to me. For a guard or something like that. What for I can't imagine, but nothing strange surprises me anymore. Can you get to the point about the seeds?"

"I have no time to tell you about that now."

"What do you mean you don't have time? You're going to stop your story now and leave me hanging about, what did you call it? 'The best part?' That wasn't the deal. Remember phase one of your grandiose plan?"

Jane was flabbergasted. John had spooked her with his creepy story, only to abruptly leave her in a cliff hanging moment. The man was impossible. She turned to push down on the door handle to get out, anxious to stretch her taut muscles and wipe off the peanut shells that were stuck to the ointment on her arms and legs. It hadn't helped being tossed to the floor and bobbing about like a cork on the ocean.

John spontaneously reached across Jane's body to grab the door handle to stop her. She let out a screech. "Hey, hey, wait. What are you doing?" John asked. "Hold up. Jumpin' Jiminy keep your voice down. You certainly wouldn't want these people to find you."

"Now that's comical. You want me to keep my voice down, but the loud roar coming from this hunk of junk would go undetected I suppose," Jane countered.

"Shut your *geggle,* will you?" John was scowling. He turned off the ignition and the truck stopped with a sputtering sigh. "This is a really dangerous mission, and we need to do this right if, and that's a big IF, the time turns out to be now."

"Look John. I'm not going another step until you tell me what all this clandestine activity is that you're sucking me into. What are we doing here that's such a priority you couldn't wait until after you took me to the town first for help? And what happened with the beans you were telling me about—the supposedly best part of the story? Your words, not mine."

"In the exact same words as I said only minutes ago, I have no time to tell you about that immediately. Like it or lump it," John snapped. "Since we reached our destination sooner than expected, I have determined that it's more important for you to know about the crime on the table for investigation than what happened to the spilt beans. There's an AMBER alert going on. A missing girl. I heard about it from my customer, Hannah, who told me someone said it's been on the radio or television—I can't remember which. She sends me a lot of news so it all gets jumbled up in my head. You see, in addition to not having phone service, I get no airwave transmission of any kind. I would like to get talk radio while I'm driving around these parts, but as you can see from that empty space in the dashboard, I had to take the old unit out. There was too much darn static when I turned it on, and it hurt my ears."

Jane shook her head over the sheer nonsense of John's rationale for removing the radio component and leaving a gaping hole. "Is that the girl whose picture I noticed on the milk container you left for me? I meant to ask you about it, because it was peculiar not having any other information with the photo. I was wondering how..."

"A picture of a person on a milk container?" Jack laughed, looking askance at Jane. "You ninny. You're truly out of your mind, you know. Why would a person's picture be on a milk container? That would have to be a dairy cow that you saw. They're the ones that make the milk. Would you put a photo of a cow on your driver's license? I never heard of such craziness. Wait—Shhhh. Hush," John ordered. "I want to be sure no one is out front." He rolled down his filmy window and stretched his neck out to see better to his left. "Coast is clear. Let's go. Remember to keep your voice down. Sound travels faster in the night."

Jane didn't budge. "I'm not going anywhere until you stick to your deal. In short, I'm not getting involved in any scheme to help you unless you explain what's going on with the Ogars and your beans." Jane's head was pounding. When she closed her eyes, it was as though rhythmic lights flashed past, giving her a sense that she was in some sort of vehicle looking through a window as it passed street lights or headlights at speed. She could hear the moaning ring of something, a siren perhaps, that John clearly could not. It made her slightly nauseous. "Look, John. I think maybe I'm suffering from a concussion of some sort. I feel sick and can hear ringing and see flashing lights when I shut my eyes. I've got a terrible pain in my head again, and I'm pretty sure I need medical help badly. I can't be wasting all this time. I have to get myself fixed up right. Please let's go to the police."

"Yes, yes, I said I'll take you, but not right now, because in case you haven't noticed we're doing *this* activity," John replied.

"I don't understand," Jane said forlornly. "Why can't you get it? I bet my family is looking for me. I have children who need me. Speaking of which, you may have noticed that I'm wearing a locket but I can't get it open. I was hoping it has photos or something inside that can help me. Can you try and open it for me?"

John looked up and towards the left as though pondering a profound question. "Well, that's quite a predicament, isn't it? Still, look on the bright side—when we met you didn't have a name and now you do."

"Terrific," Jane said snidely.

"It's kind of dark for me to fiddle with your necklace now, and anyway if the locket is stuck, I'll need to use my chisel to pry it open when we get back."

Jane laughed. "A chisel? Why not a crowbar? Ha Ha. Funny. Yeah, it will have to wait for better light and the right tools. I certainly don't want to have it damaged."

"So we've resolved that problem then," John said seriously.

"For now, I guess. You mentioned Hannah as being a customer of yours and someone who might be helpful to me. Do you know her well?"

"Hannah? Of course! She's my long time plant customer and friend. She's far from here but closest to the road that leads downward to town. She runs a safe house for people in trouble—or something like that anyway. Every so often she sends one of her boarders to me to pick up some vegetable sprouts and drop off cooked meals. Come to think of it, one of them told me that there was a recent report on television about somebody else missing—or maybe it was a dog. I don't remember."

Jane's mouth dropped. "What did you say? When? What else did you find out? That could be about me! Jeez! Why didn't you say anything?"

"Because I have enough to think about regarding my investigations," John said. "People are talking about the Amber Alert for the missing girl, and that's the news I decided to focus on. Thinking about the possibility of there being another missing person is too much to bear. Dang it, I can't throw anything else into the mix."

"John, please, you have to take me to Hannah," Jane said, dismayed that he would be so oblivious to making the connection. "That's where we should go now. Not here at your neighbor's house. To Hannah. To get more information from her—from anybody."

"Fine. I'll take you to see Hannah, instead," John said. "But it has to be in the daytime, and anyway, tonight we're on a mission. Like it or lump it." John opened his window and checked outside again. "Still all clear."

"Daytime, when? Tomorrow?" Jane asked. "Let's go tomorrow."

"First things first. You insisted on knowing more about the Ogars—so listen up. I'll speak quickly and only explain once."

Jane was barely controlling her excitement, but she decided it was to her advantage to placate John. The sooner she helped him do whatever it was he wanted to do here, the sooner she could find her way home.

"Alright. I'm all ears," she said softly.

John nodded and continued speaking. "I learned a lot about the Ogars during the years following that first experience I had hearing all the ruckus coming from this vicinity. I spent time spying on them in addition to all the many other things I've had to do every day. The gossip is that Mr. Ogar is a pedophile in addition to being a wife beater. He's as mean as they come, and he's married to a shrew of a woman—a monster he likely created himself. On top of that, they have a very vicious dog. I heard it myself loudly barking and growling very deep growl like rolling thunder."

"Ha. Ha. As vicious as the one you supposedly have?" Jane asked.

"It's not funny. I already told you I don't have a dog. It's all a ruse. Truthfully, I put all those messages up because I've been petrified of these people. I'm projecting an image to the general public. I figured that if ever the Ogars passed by my house they would think twice about bothering me or coming on my property if they were convinced I had a very vicious dog too. And what's it to you anyway?"

John was clearly fidgety. He looked out the window again and whispered, "Coast is clear. Let's go." He pushed down onto the door handle.

"Wait a minute," Jane demanded. "That's it? All you have to say? What about the rest of the story?"

John was already out of the truck and turned around. "Shhh. I told you to keep your voice down! Stick with me as we head to the backyard. Stay low."

"Augh!" Understanding that it was futile to get John to finish his story and not wanting to be left alone in the truck, Jane got out. She watched him as he comically tiptoed past the front of the gatehouse, his upper body bent forward surreptitiously like a thief. He stopped and faced her as she approached.

"Get a load of that!" Jack said. Similar to the ringmaster in a circus, he swept his arm outward with a flare as an invitation for Jane to look at the spectacle.

There before them in the moonlight was a tall gray stone house with Palladian windows centered over the front double entry door. It had a steeply sloped roof with pronounced dormers, two chimneys spewing sparks and smoke, and tacky looking pilasters resembling flat columns. The whole house was overdone and bloated with pretentiousness, including the front yard and driveway, which were entirely paved in elaborate cobblestone designs. However, Jane thought that the absence of foundation plantings or any greenery at all gave it a glum appearance.

"What the ..!" Jane exclaimed, remembering to speak softly. "Jeez! How did this get here? It looks like a friggin' castle! All it's missing are the moat and drawbridge."

"Humpf." John ignored her comment and whispered, "Believe it or not, that used to be a log cabin out of a box which was so crude that it looked like it was made with cardboard paper towel rolls. Then I heard that the Ogars came into some highly suspicious money and turned it into a mansion. The style hardly fits in with the local architecture, wouldn't you say?"

"Local architecture? What do you mean? There isn't a house around for miles." *This building is so absurdly over the top. I bet the gatehouse was part of the builder's package deal.*

"Exactly my point. That's why it doesn't fit in," Jack retorted. "It kind of stands out like a sore head."

"Sore *what*?" Jane said.

"What? What?" John said.

"Thumb. You mean sore thumb."

"So, tell me Jane, now that we're here, do you want to go knocking on that big door to tell them your predicament and see if they can give you a ride to town? I'm sure you'll be thrilled to meet them."

"No. Forget it. Let's get on with this big plan of yours. The sooner the better," Jane said.

They resumed walking, and Jane pondered her difficult situation. Despite John's obvious brilliance with plants, his childlike qualities were beyond reasoning with. Whatever scheme he had cooked up was making her jittery. However, she was resigned to having no choice but to go along with it.

Her legs felt so rubbery that they gave out just as they reached the back of the house. She stumbled, and John grabbed her arm just in time to break her fall. He stood still holding her tightly like a vise.

"Holy moley!" John exclaimed softly, his voice quivering. "Look at that! It's enormous. Now that's what I'm talking about!"

6

THE BEANSTALK

"What's enormous?" Jane asked, squinting intensely. Her eyes followed the line of John's finger but she could barely make out a thing. If it weren't for the bright illumination of the moon, she would hardly be able to see her toes.

From what she could see, unlike the front of the house, the rear was nondescript, lacking any decorative molding or appointments. The double hung windows were three up and three down, looking very plain without grids. Apparently these people were intent on keeping up appearances but limiting their exuberance to the front of the house, even though from what she could fathom there was no one around to impress. An odd, flickering, mellow light formed an eerie backdrop to the upstairs windows and gave her goose bumps.

"What is it exactly that I'm supposed to be looking at?" Jane asked. "What's with that flickering light on the second floor? Let's get out of here. This is very creepy."

John ignored her. "Jumpin' Jiminy! Are you visually impaired too? Look under the right side window. See the vine? It's huge! It's truly your lucky day, because it's only been two weeks since I planted it!" John was obviously very excited, and could hardly control his enthusiasm.

"You planted a vine on somebody else's property?" Jane asked.

"You are surely scatterbrained! The beans. Remember? The B-E-A-N-S? You know, the beans I got from P. Pod. I planted the beans over there, and they grew into that giant vine."

"Oh. Sure. Right. The bean story you never finished telling me about."

"So, this is where you come in," John said, ignoring her sarcasm. "I want you to stand at the base of the vine and catch me if I fall. Two stories is kind of high and unforgiving to a slip of the foot."

"You want me to do what?" Jane was incredulous, remembering at the last moment to keep her voice low. "Are you crazy? You're not thinking of climbing that thing, are you?"

"Why are you freaking out?" John whispered harshly.

"Because I'm not having any part of this if you're going to break in and commit a burglary. No way, no how. All I want is to get the heck out of here and to your friend Hannah which is where you said you would take me." Jane's head was pounding and a familiar feeling of nausea swept over her. A knifelike pain sliced into the top of her skull, and she felt about to faint.

"Shut your geggle," John whispered. "We're wasting precious time. I told you I would drive you there, but you seem to have a problem remembering the orchestrated plan that I will now review. It was a conditional offer if you recall, and dependent on how my beans grow. That was first and foremost. Now it just so happens that this is your lucky day, because the extraordinary vine is there in all its glory. So the next step is for you to help me with my investigation."

"*We're* wasting precious time? Well, I have a conditional offer too," Jane snapped. "I'm not going any further to help you with your scheme until you do some explaining." She stood rigidly with her arms folded, staring intently at John and trying to ignore the somehow disturbing upstairs lights of the building in front of them.

"Humpf. Well, in a nutshell, I'm conducting criminal investigative work regarding that missing girl who could very well be held here by the Ogars against her will. I want to snoop around and see if there are any clues to her whereabouts in the house. Maybe they have her in their basement, or as you might befittingly call it, their *dungeon*. If I get caught and go to jail for breaking and entering, I'll make sure I go by myself, because I have no desire to be locked up with you in the likes of a skinny vertical crate that's our one-celled jailhouse."

Jane's patience was waning and her apprehension mounting, especially considering the possibility that the Ogars' ferocious dog might be let out any moment, and they could both be torn to shreds. Nevertheless, she continued to stand her ground.

"Can't you please get to the point?"

"Well, if I find her I'll take her home and compare her to the photo," John responded. "About the vine: it's just like what happened many years ago." He had leaned in closer to Jane, speaking softly into her ear. "Listen up. I'll make a long story short and do it in less than sixty seconds. Like it or lump it."

With a touch of drama, John took a deep breath in and began to speak rapidly, all the time looking at his illuminated watch. "Remember how I ran home from this place, and I said I hit my head on the well and found my seeds had spilled? Well I picked up what I could and put them away in a little stinky sardine can which I hid under the floor boards of my room."

"Then one day after a very heavy rain, I was amazed to see a huge vine growing up beside the house. It was nothing like I'd ever seen before. The stalk and its shoots and tendrils were made from hundreds of fibrous strands clustered together and twisted, rope-like. Its entwined girth was much thicker than a pillar supporting a building. Standing at its base and looking upward, I could see it spiraling towards the sky. Impulsively, I scrambled up the branches of the stalk. The foliage was huge and mostly blocked my view of the ground, so I had no real idea how far up I'd climbed until I parted the leaves at one point and noticed I'd passed the peak of our roof. Scared out of my wits, I very slowly crawled out onto the shingles, hugging the sides of the chimney. It was like being on top of the world—a perfect place to sit and think on any other day.

"Anyway, true to what P. Pod had said, the vine kept growing and made outrageous beans. The wind-up is that I started studying plant life through correspondence courses by mail and came up with many different, er, botanical creations. It was only then that I became famous. People hunted me down from all over the world to be a keynote speaker at one academic gathering or another."

Jane was having a hard time trying to suppress a laugh. The story was getting more and more farfetched as John spoke.

"I prospered and remodeled the house at my cost just as you saw it, and I was thrilled to finally have the benefits of modern plumbing. Moan and Groan tried to be nice to me because of all the money I was bringing into the household. But it was too late for them to make up for all the years of nastiness I'd had to put up with. Frankly, they were fortunate that yours truly didn't throw them out, but the last thing I wanted was to hear them banging on the door all the time demanding to be let back in again.

"One day, by accident, my father sprinkled my patented plant hormone powder instead of confectioners' sugar on my mother's freshly baked upside down cake. Soon after, they kicked the bucket…" John managed to gasp "…the end" just before he took another deep breath. "Whew! Just under the wire. That took fifty-six seconds," John said, still looking at his watch. "Now come along. Let's move on. Keep a low profile and zip your mouth for beet's sake."

"*Beet's* sake? Hah! *Beet's?*" Jane parroted. "The right word is Pete's…" John was already out of earshot heading for the house. *What a dork he is,* Jane thought as she traipsed after him.

"Holy moley!" John whispered as Jane got to his side.

He continued to speak low. "Look how chunky the stalk and shoots are! And the tendril—they're like giant arms and fingers grasping at the wall. Why, the sinewy three headed dragon is even moving!"

Jane noted John's childish imagery and smiled to herself. She could see the vine clearly now. It was twisted and thick as a lamppost, rising above the roof of the house.

"Come on. Cup your hands and hoist me up to that first branch." John pointed to a point about three feet over his head. "This is all you have to do. And wait right here for me. Don't move. Even if I don't slip, I may need to make a fast getaway and skim down the vine very quickly. So I'll need you to help break the fall. I won't be long. Oh. I almost forgot. Here. Take the keys to the truck in case something happens to me and you have to get away." John handed them to her.

"I don't know … I … I'm very nervous about all this. We need to get out of here. What if they let the dog out? Then what do I do?"

"Tell it to sit or lie down."

"I'm serious."

"I'm John. Come on. As I said not too long ago, we're wasting precious time."

"Okay. Okay. Get it over with and be careful."

Jane compliantly bent down, John put his right foot in her cupped hands, and she heaved him upwards. With his other foot, he pushed off her throbbing head, annoying her to no end and causing her to let loose a grunt through her clenched teeth. He grabbed the branch above and after stabilizing himself she looked upwards as he continued to ascend among the shadows cast by the mysterious lights.

The flickering, strange radiance from the second floor windows piqued John's curiosity as much as it raised concern since it could have passed for a Halloween spook house. As soon as he got to the second floor window he ducked below the sill and raised his head slowly to peer inside. Grateful for the subtle illumination, he could see that the room was unoccupied. He stretched his left leg onto the ledge and remained awkwardly straddled between the window and the vine stalk while he lifted the screen and bottom sash. He figured it would take only one miscalculation to bring about his demise.

He grabbed the frame of the opening and pulled himself onto the ledge, sitting with his legs dangling over the sill. He then dropped into the room and waited a few seconds for his eyes to become accustomed to the pulsing yellowish glow. Much to his surprise, he saw that it emanated from a hoard of clear jars occupying every inch of space in freestanding narrow shelves that stood like sentries around the perimeter of the room. Despite his eagerness to inspect them, he paused and surveyed the rest of the surroundings before moving another muscle.

This must be the entire top floor of the house, he thought. He was standing near a super king-size bed positioned in the middle of what was one big room with three windows. A dark quilt was bunched up partially on top of disheveled striped bedding and otherwise draped onto a bulky wooden trunk at the foot of a concave mattress. The carvings on the trunk were typically Gothic: pointed arcs and horrific winged devils intertwined with snakes and other creatures. Several puffy pillows, haphazardly tossed against one of three carved hawks protruding from the massive headboard, supported the upright backs of two baby dolls dressed in plaid pinafores.

"Ah ha! Just as I figured. The first of the missing girl evidence," John murmured. "I'll make sure you pay dearly for this you monsters!"

Looking further, he spotted a long, ragged nightgown hanging over the edge of the bed and touching the floor near a rather large pair of grossly misshapen slippers.

Jumpin' Jiminy, those must be two big, ugly feet. He stroked his beard, perplexed over the incongruent discoveries. He snapped his fingers. *Of course! They keep her locked up here at times, and she plays with the dolls. Sure. That's what little girls do.*

A huge, grotesque cabinet and a large, matching, ornate, and imposing chest of drawers were the only other pieces of Gothic furniture in the room besides the shelves. Thinking of Jane's moat comment and observing the decorating motif on the furniture, it felt like he had been transported to the middle ages.

Now to examine those glowing jars. No, wait. Who cares about that? Is there a posse of concerned citizens out and about seeking this phenomenon? No. Every minute of my investigation is precious; there's no time to waste. *But like it or lump it I have to be prepared. After all, Jane will ask me about it, and the last thing I would want to report is that I didn't check it out. Oh, I would never hear the end of it. She would torture me with questions and berate me.* As John got himself riled up while processing this dilemma in his mind, he was already tiptoeing carefully towards the shelves. He could barely stifle a gasp as he got closer, and the force of it caused him to choke.

"Why, those brutes!" he whispered, still a bit agitated. *Is that what they make the poor little girl do,* he thought, *collect fireflies to light their house? Wait until Jane hears this. She'll never believe me. Who in the right mind would? But she's not in her right mind, so on second thought, she might believe me."*

Thousands of captive fireflies were presenting their flashing light shows in differing patterns of yellow and orange. *Jumpin' Jiminy, there are jars with green ones. There must be a new variety of species here, he thought.* He was dumbfounded. Each jar, and there were all different sizes, was set up carefully to sustain the insects. Inside, long pieces of grass gave them a place to hide as they would in the wild. Along with pieces of bark, moistened paper and a slice of apple were situated on the bottom.

There was clatter from downstairs. John jumped. He moved slowly across the room to the door, which was slightly ajar. It creaked as he gave it a slight push, and cringed as he squeezed through the opening. With only a bit of the eerie radiance seeping out from the bedroom, he found himself situated in the yawning darkness of a wide landing at the top of a winding staircase. He adjusted the door to the way it was. Grabbing onto the handrail with clammy hands, he proceeded to slowly descend into a sinister looking narrow hallway.

As he reached the bottom, he nearly tripped on what appeared to be an oversized stuffed animal of some sort, sitting upright on its haunches, its dark fur nearly camouflaged by the scant lighting. *What's this doing here? I could have broken my neck! Only a child would do something so careless. A child. Perhaps a young girl. I'll grab this telling evidence on my way back.*

He could smell the aroma of cooking. The growling in his belly, the only audible sound, made him realize how hungry he was; his trembling legs and racing heart made him realize how scared he was. First he took several deep breaths, inhaling through his nose and exhaling out of his mouth. Then he cautiously began to move, mindful of potential squeaks in the floorboards.

A shaft of light forced him to lean into the wall, almost knocking down a pair of mounted lion heads as he crept along. He followed the wafting smells to where the echoes of some awful singing were emanating from. He peaked around a corner through a colossal archway leading into the kitchen area of a great room where two softly lit medieval looking chandeliers hung from the high ceiling. He sucked in his breath.

Facing away from him was old Mrs. Ogar, standing on the brick hearth of a wide fireplace, stirring the contents of a kettle suspended over a roaring fire. Her long, wiry, blue-white hair was sticking out from her head as though it were electrified. With her free hand she was snapping her fingers to the beat of her off key voice and hopping around on her feet as though she were barefoot over hot coals.

With darting eyes, he quickly surveyed the surroundings to see if Mr. Ogar was there and to assess what was what in case he had to make a quick escape. It was an open concept design combined with the living room, which was farthest away beyond what he guessed was the front door. All he could see was a couch and a double glider chair, the kind that would normally be situated on an outdoor patio.

A long grimy porcelain sink, which reminded him of a trough, was on one side of the hearth close to a couple of long wooden work tables and a chopping block pierced by an array of knives and cleavers. Pots and pans were haphazardly stacked on the floor and filled with utensils. A variety of jars, cans, and gunnysacks took up space on several shelves above. A second look at the jars startled him, and he began to think that his imagination was running wild. It looked like they contained eyeballs, intestines, clumps of hair, bent nails and an assortment of other unidentifiable contents. Some of the jars had powders and shavings in them with a skull and crossbones prominently displayed on a label. He felt a shiver creep up his spine, which made him think this whole plan of his was not a good idea.

The tiled floor seemed like it had never been washed, and he was horrified to see a long brown streak leading from a closed door to the chopping block. He shivered again and this time the hairs on his arms stood up as he imagined it was dried blood, such that might occur from dragging a hemorrhaging body across the room.

Why would anyone cook in an ancient fireplace like that these days? he wondered. While observing the stone walls with creeping cracks and the rustic wooden furniture, again he recalled Jane's sarcastic comment about the whereabouts of a moat. *And what was the other thing? Um… Um… ah yes, a drawbridge. Ha! Not so farfetched, Jane! It was obvious this house has many medieval features. Holy moley!* Upon second look, the kettle appeared more like a witch's cauldron than anything else. His shoulders shuddered and his knees weakened as he heard the gurgling bubbles and saw Mrs. Ogar encased in a hefty amount of steam emanating from the boiling liquid. Wide-eyed, he watched her reach into the kettle with a pair of tongs. John winced in anticipation of seeing something gross come out of there. However to his relief, the woman extracted two large chunks of meat that she tossed on a platter and proceeded to bring to the long table where there were three place-settings but only one humongous chair. One of the plates had the bone remnants of an already consumed slab of meat. *Ah ha! Three! Another clue not to be overlooked.* A large pan on the floor by the sink caught his eye, but he was unable to see the contents. *Must be for the dog. Jumpin' Jiminy! Come to think of it, where was that mean dog?*

John quickly drew his head back and out of Mrs. Ogar's view. His heart was pounding, and he knew it was making so much noise that it surely would betray his presence. He pressed his body to the wall and beads of sweat continued to drip down the sides of his face as he calculated his next move. All the time he was berating himself for causing this predicament in the first place. There he was, caught in the inertia of an "if–this-then-that" decision making process. But what was done was done, and he had a job to do. He had to find out if there was a cellar. *But how? Where's the old man? For sure he'll be here any moment to eat.* He calmed himself down with ten deep cleansing breathes as he pictured himself on a parade float being the hero of the day for saving the life of a young girl.

Unable to stand the tension of inactivity any longer, he stretched his upper body forward to peek back into the kitchen. There was Mrs. Ogar bent over and rapidly beating the contents of a frying pan resting on a grilling grate over the fire. The next thing he knew, his rubber legs gave out causing him to lose his balance. Horrified as he fell forward into the room with a flare, he heard his own voice spontaneously breaking the silence.

"Hi there, Mrs. Ogar!" he shouted matter-of-factly as though he were making a routine visit.

The woman was so startled that she instinctively threw up her arms, tossing what looked like a glob of scrambled eggs and cheese towards the ceiling. The concoction then proceeded to land squarely on her head. She spun around to face him with the egg mixture dripping down her face. Simultaneously she reached into a holster belted around her waist and pulled out a spray bottle labeled "MACE" in large letters. As she pointed it in his direction her eyes were glazed over in a rage. She looked ghastly evil.

"Hi, Mrs. Ogar," he repeated, this time with a forced Cheshire cat smile and a wide arcing wave befitting a movie star.

Mrs. Ogar continued to stare at him, her eyes shifting nervously like a frightened child. She suddenly looked like she was about to cry.

"Ma'am, Mrs. Ogar," he croaked, his mouth parched. "I'm sorry I startled you—I…I…tripped. I'm such a klutz. Here, let me help you clean that off…I…"

"Don't touch me! Step back…step back or I'll spray you. I will. I will. I will." She grabbed a rag and wiped her face.

John looked anxiously around, anticipating a dreaded encounter: being torn to shreds by the ferocious family dog or by the monstrous Mr Ogar. *Come to think of it, where are they?* he pondered. As his teeth began to chatter, he concluded that this plan of his was not a good idea, and he had to complete his investigation much quicker than he thought.

"Well just who are you?" she gruffly said, her demeanor changing again.

"My name is John. I'm … I'm … er a termite inspector. From the Bye Bye Termite and Roach Service. I met your husband on the road one day, and he asked me to stop by when I was in the area. And tonight I was in the area." John approached her with his hand extended for a handshake.

In a deep hoarse voice she said, "My husband asked you to come here and check for termites? Hah! What a bunch of bull. We never have anyone come here. This is a trick. Step back! Step back!" She held the can of mace out in front of her, with her finger poised on the trigger.

"Easy. Easy. Put that away," John pleaded. He knew he was in over his head and needed to get out before Mr. Ogar showed up. "And besides, just how did you wind up here in my kitchen, John-the-termite-inspector?"

John stuck to his story. "I was driving by, heading home from a long day of work, and being hungry I was attracted by the savory smells in the air from your cooking—I see you made quite a feast—and I remembered that I promised your husband I would take a moment to look around the next time I was passing by. And so I came to the door, which was slightly open. Then I heard your beautiful singing, and since you didn't hear me calling out I invited myself in. I didn't mean to make such a grand entrance, which I deeply apologize for, and for interrupting your family dinnertime. So if you show me to your cellar, I'll do a quick check and be on my way."

"Cellar? What cellar? We don't have a cellar. It would have cost extra, and construction was already over budget."

"Well, then I'll be on my way." He glanced at the three settings on the table, secretly wishing he could have something to eat. It seemed like forever since he had his last meal. "Before your guest arrives."

"What guest? I told you, John-the-Termite-Inspector, that we don't have people come here."

"Oh. I thought...because there are three place settings and..."

"Well you thought wrong. My husband eats enough for three people. He'll eat you too if you get in his way. You should stick to your own business, not someone else's."

"Sure. Sure. Well, would you mind, since I took the time to stop by—kind of as barter payment—if...if I took a bit of your delicious meal with me to tide me over until I get home? Maybe you can wrap it up. I'm famished."

Mrs. Ogar stood with her mouth open wide enough to accommodate an apple.

"Why you little nervy runt. I doubt this is anything you would want to eat," the old woman squealed then began to laugh wickedly.

"It's Dopey Boy, not runt," John murmured under his breath recalling his mother's cruel words.

"What did you say?"

"Nothing. Forget it. Forget I ever asked for something to eat," John replied, very disturbed by this woman's lunatic behavior. "No strings attached. It's a free visit. No cellar, nothing to check, so I'm leaving now."

"You'd better leave," Mrs. Ogar continued, "and quickly. If you stick around another minute and my husband finds you here, then it's dinner *you'll* be. He likes to eat puffy doughboy types like you, grilled on toast, spread with Schmuck's seedless jam. As luck would have it, I shopped yesterday for more jam. The remaining contents of the last jar were eaten by my husband along with an ornery young fellow from the wrong side of the tracks." She cackled with laughter again. John's heart started racing. He wanted his legs to do the same, but instead they were nothing but dead weights.

Suddenly, the whole house shook as a door slammed, followed by fierce barking. Cutting through the noise, Mr. Ogar's voice bellowed out from the front of the house like a roaring lion. "Wife, I am hungry for the rest of my dinner and am coming for it now." John felt the hairs on his arms stand up. *He must have been out walking that dog.* He could hear the man's heavy feet stomping on the floor as he approached the kitchen. The dog continued barking and growling. *Oh no! It's coming closer. Shut up you vicious dog!* John's mind raced. *What to do?* He stood frozen in place. This scenario was far from how he had envisioned conducting an investigation. Mrs. Ogar's eyes widened like saucers, and she screamed, "Get out now wretched man, if you value your life. Husband, there's a termite inspector in the house."

Suddenly the dog became silent. John didn't waste a second. Faster than a magician's sleight of hand he seized a chunk of meat off the plate along with a dinner napkin as he darted towards the staircase with his heart in his throat. In one fell swoop, as he reached the first step he bent down, and with his free hand he snatched the stuffed animal he almost fell over before. The slight resistance took him by surprise causing him to stumble a bit into the next riser, still clutching the meat and napkin with his other hand. *Jumpin' Jiminy, this is heavy! What's it stuffed with, rocks?* He dangled it tightly from its floppy ears and, taking two steps at a time, he entered the bedroom and darted for the open window. John could hear Mr. Ogar clomping up the stairs, huffing and puffing, his deafening voice closing in on him.

"Wife! Wife! Get the gun and wait for me out front."

When he reached the ledge, John leaned out and hollered down, "Jane, heads up!" He jammed the napkin and meat down his shirt and tossed the stuffed toy out of the window before sitting on the ledge. At that moment he turned around to look back into the room. "Ich!" he gasped. In the light cast by the fireflies, he could see Mr. Ogar's hideous, hairy face and huge gawky body. He had lost momentum and was panting wildly while leaning on the wall by the doorway. *Lucky for me he's not in good physical shape.* "Nana

nana *naaa* na!" John taunted the humanoid with his thumbs in his ears and his wiggling fingers extended, resembling a moose.

John propelled himself off the ledge to reach the beanstalk, and slid down as though he were on a firehouse pole. When he hit the bottom, he called out, "Jane! Jane! Jumpin' Jiminy where are you? The monster's after me. I'm not waiting."

Jane was nowhere in sight.

John scrambled to recover the stuffed toy, yanking it by the ears and trailing it behind him as he ran. In the distance he could hear Mr. Ogar ranting out the window. His last words rang loud and clear: "You're a dead man!"

"Well, tough luck Jane, you nitwit," John shouted over his shoulder into the night as he made a beeline for his truck. *I'm not about to conduct a manhunt for her. She can like it or lump it. Oh no! The truck keys…she has the keys! What do I do? What do I do?* All of a sudden he heard the familiar ferocious growls and rapid barking so loud as to be practically at his heels. *The pet beast is loose. Mrs. Ogar let it out. I'm cooked!* Without sparing a second to look back, John never ran so fast or screamed so robustly in his life. It was a scream for help as much as it was a cry of terror.

THE ESCAPE

John expected that any moment the dog would pounce and maul him. "Go away. Go away. Go. Go away! Get down!" he screeched, his voice getting higher and higher pitched. He didn't dare turn his head lest he trip or run into something. As he passed the "outhouse" he sharply turned in the direction of a voice calling to him.

"John! John! I'm in the truck. Get in," Jane shouted from the open window on the passenger side.

Figuring he had no time to stop to open the door, he continued to run around the vehicle, kicking up a load of peanut shells strewn by the passenger side.

"John! What are you doing? What's with all the yelling? What's wrong with you?" Jane continued shouting as he passed by again. "Get in! Stop running around. Let's go. Should I start the engine? The key's in the ignition. I'm ready to go."

"No! No! It'll blow our cover. Grab this evidence. Quick!" John flung the stuffed animal at Jane's door, and it hit with a thud as it ricocheted away from the vehicle.

"What? What did you say? What was that noise?" Jane peered out into the darkness.

John remembered the meat he jammed down his shirt. *What dog wouldn't love a chunk of meat?* When he reached the driver's side for the fourth time, totally out of breath by then, he pulled it out and tossed it over the truck as far away as he could. The napkin fluttered to the ground.

"Fetch! Go fetch, doggie!" he shouted.

Realizing that the creature had stopped making its horrible sounds, John seized the opportunity to open the door on the driver's side and scamper onto the seat. In his mind he pictured the ravenous, man-eating canine tearing at the beef, thankful he had the food to give as a surrogate for himself. He sat shaking and gasping for breath, then, frantically began to fan himself with both his hands as though he had just bitten into a handful of jalapeño peppers.

As he looked around through the windows to survey the area outside, he expected to see a giant dog in the vicinity. A Mastiff or Great Dane came to mind. But there was nothing moving around as far as he could tell. *It must have taken the prize snack to its den.*

"John!" Jane poked him to get his attention. "Why were you acting so crazy running around the truck like that? What happened?" She could see John's angry face reflected in the moonlight. "Let's get out of here. Your behavior is scaring me."

"Oh…that's…very funny. I'm…scaring…you?" John asked between heavy breaths. "You're asking…what happened? You…want to know…why…I was acting so crazy…running around? Well…excuse me, missy…if my behavior…bothered you. I just had…the worst experience…of my life…which nearly ended by the way. I was all but devoured by…a monster…and his ferocious…colossal dog. I escaped…with my heart in my mouth…by sliding rapid fire…down the beanstalk…expecting to find you…where I left you…ready to catch me. But no. Oh no! You're not there. You're nowhere in sight. I scream your name. You don't answer…even when I desperately…yell for help…with a dog on my tail…viciously barking and growling at me…the whole way over here."

A dog was after him? I didn't hear any dog barking or growling. Jane felt that John's tirade was as implausible as his panting was dramatic. Being confined with him in the truck made her feel increasingly uneasy. She had to leave this strange place. But where to go? She was tired and her back was aching from being flung so hard onto the floor during the drive over. She intentionally didn't ask any questions because having the answers served her no purpose.

"Interesting play-by-play. But tell me, did you accomplish your mission?" Jane mockingly asked, sounding like a TV secret agent.

"Yup. Yup. Yup. I did what I set out to do." John was beginning to compose himself and emitted a loud sigh of relief. "I'll give you all the details engrained in my mind forever, every last one, as soon as we get on the road." Recalling Mr. Ogar's last words, he frantically surveyed the area to see if the man was approaching.

"And what's that stinky burnt smell?" Jane asked.

"Oh, that was only a slab of cooked meat I took from Mr. Ogar's dinner plate. Mrs. Ogar had just cooked it. I was hungry," John said plainly. "I had shoved it down my shirt, and then threw it at the dog to distract it from attacking me."

"What are you talking about? I didn't see a dog. Where did it go?" Jane tried to project as much calm as possible because judging from John's antics and outlandish stories, he could well be a psychopath influenced by figments of his imagination. *He could keep me prisoner forever in his botany laboratory, possibly feed me to a carnivorous plant, and from the way things appear around these parts, no one will ever know it. Ha! Furthermore, who's to say that he isn't the one who abducted the young girl? Ha! Jeez! I'm getting carried away.*

"I have now recovered sufficiently to depart," John announced in a very formal tone. "Jumpin' Jiminy! I almost forgot. Did you get the evidence I tossed to you?"

"No. Whatever you threw to me you weren't too accurate with. I heard something hard hit the door," Jane said nonchalantly looking out through the window. What was it? I'll go get it." Obviously it was important to him, and she didn't want him to have any excuse to have to come back before taking her to Hannah.

"No you're not," John commanded. "Obviously that horrible man-eating canine is still out there. On top of that, Mr. Ogar is probably on his way to hunt me down."

"So what is it that I'm getting for you?" Jane persisted, ignoring John's admonition as she shoved the door open and scooted out. *It's a good excuse as any to stretch a moment,* she thought.

"It's a big stuffed animal. Hurry up. This truck is about to leave here at any moment," John yelled after her. "I'm going to count to ten, and then I'll get going with or without you. Like it or lump it. One … two … three … four … "

"I found it," Jane cried as she came upon a furry mound. She stooped down to pick it up. "Jeez. What kind of stuffing's in this thing? It feels like a brick." Swinging it by the ears, she hastily skipped back like a happy child.

" … nine … ten. Time's up! Time's up!" John announced. As he looked to the left out his window, he suddenly spotted a flashlight waving about. He froze in fear, as the silhouette of a looming figure emerged, stomping toward them. A single gunshot rang out and the bullet splattered loosened dirt and pebbles in the air near John's door. It was followed by a thunderous voice.

"Here I come, you vermin. I can smell your blood. I'll rip you to shreds. I'll kill you and cook you for tomorrow's dinner!"

At that moment, another misdirected shot resonated in the night air. Without a moment for thought, John turned the key in the ignition and revved up the engine.

"Get in, get in, get in!" he repeated frantically as he leaned toward the passenger door to reach for Jane.

Jane flung herself on her knees inside the truck, tossing the stuffed animal on the floor and grabbing John's extended hand. He yanked her towards him with all his might, simultaneously jamming his foot on the gas pedal while throwing the truck in reverse.

"We're out of here!" John exclaimed over the racket of the exhaust system. Still accelerating backward, he cut the wheel sharply to face the direction they had originally come from, and as he did so, Jane's open door forcefully swung outward on its hinges.

Another shot rang out and blasted the bottom of the exposed door. It was immediately followed by a crisp thud and a booming, blood-curdling shriek from the rear informing them that Mr. Ogar had been hit.

John spontaneously slammed on the brakes and shifted the gears forward. As he gunned the engine, Jane, still on her knees, braced herself with both arms splayed outwardly, the left hand pressed against the back of the seat and the right on the edge of the dashboard. Picking up speed along the road heading the way they had come, John could see nothing in his rear view mirror but a thick cloud of dust.

John began to swerve the car violently from side to side. "What are you doing?" Jane screamed. The open door was swaying back and forth in rhythm to the vehicle's erratic movement. "Are you trying to toss me out of the truck? You're real lucky if your darn plant specimens in the back didn't snap in two."

"Hold on," John blared. "Haven't you ever watched science fiction films where people flee in a car thinking they ran over some ghoulish creature that was pursuing them? Then when they stop to chill out, the creature, which turned out to be holding on to the roof, breaks into the car and chomps on their heads. Well, I'm heading that off at the pass, in case Mr. Ogar scampered up on top of us."

"Why in the world would he do that even if he could, that is, assuming his legs weren't flattened out by your rear tires? It would make more sense if he were to grab onto the side and climb into the open cargo area and then..."

"Like it or lump it Jane. I wasn't taking any chances."

John assumed a reasonable speed to get the truck back on course. He slowed to a stop and with the engine idling, checked his side and rear view mirrors.

"We're alive and all is clear," John said matter-of-factly. He wiped the sweat off his brow with the bottom of his shirt.

Jane sat back in the seat. The swerving had made her nauseous. "Okay. Okay. Nice thinking. But quite frankly, the way I feel now with motion sickness and the horrific noise that comes from this truck, I would welcome having my head bitten off."

"Oh, come on. I bet all my priceless plant creations that that statement isn't true." Suddenly solicitous, he bluntly asked, "Do you need to throw up?"

"Thanks for asking. Close to it, but no. So where are we going now that I've fulfilled my end of the bargain? Are you taking me to see Hannah as you promised?" Tears welled in her eyes as she clutched the locket around her neck and pressed it to her chest. It was the best she could do to connect with the children she could not recall, but longed to see again.

"As to your first question, I'm heading for my home. As to your second question, I'll take you to meet Hannah—but certainly not now. No way. No how. I already said it will have to be in tomorrow's daylight. And so you know, when we get back I have a full plate of things to do first. I need to water the plants in my laboratory, feed the carnivorous specimens, and catch a few winks during what's left of this night. Like it or lump it."

Jane shook her head in frustration. She felt exasperated by John's outlandish statements. She didn't like the idea of going back to his house, but knew it would be worse to be out driving in these parts while it was dark, especially without having slept.

John turned towards Jane. "What do you think this is that I'm driving—an open-air shuttle? How about you shut the door now? Where did the bullet hit?"

"Now that's what I call a great idea," Jane said sarcastically as she pulled the handle towards her. "It caught the bottom corner. Nothing major—it's a little bent. It still shuts tight, thank God. We surely don't want any of those unidentified road fuzzies climbing in. You know, the ones you saw on the road and so adeptly avoided. Nor would we want your prize evidence to fall out considering all you went through to get it.

"Speaking of which, hold up a moment." Jane picked up the cumbersome stuffed animal. "I want to check this thing out." She held it up, catching its oversized body in the moonlight. "Behold the ratty looking evidence—whatever it's evidence of I don't know. It's what we came all the way out here for. It's why you put our lives in jeopardy climbing that freaky beanstalk and possibly getting yourself killed—getting us both killed by that madman?"

"So?" John asked defensively.

"So? ... you said so? So?" Jane continued to inspect the evidence using the opportunity to avoid looking at John. He was getting on her nerves again. "This is weird stuffing. Something is definitely inside of it. Do you have a flashlight?"

"No. What am I, a theater usher?"

"That's too bad," Jane said ignoring John's wisecrack. She was beginning to get used to them. "I wanted to check something out. I feel a zipper in its back. And I swear there's some kind of a block inside. Maybe it's gold bullion left over from the Ogars' renovation funds. Ha ha."

John didn't laugh. "Well today is your lucky day," he said seriously. "You would have known that sooner had you probed further with your questions. The fact is I don't have a flashlight, but I do have a camping lantern."

Jane rolled her eyes. "Oh yes. My lucky day. You already pointed that out earlier. Yeah, right. Some lucky day this has been for me."

"It's under the dashboard," John said. There's a charger connected to it. It's solar powered so it should work."

Jane located the lantern and flicked it on. John looked over her shoulder as she opened the zipper and removed an object. She burst into a fit of laughter.

"Hey John, your big evidence of an abducted child and giant attack dog is nothing but a tacky intruder alarm system. This is the vicious giant growling dog that was riding on your heels about to devour you." She held up a rectangular, metal box, somewhat bigger than her hand. "It's marked 'loud output speaker.'" Jane examined it further, turning it face up in her lap. "Hmm. It has a label on it that says 'Pet Sentry, Wireless Motion Detection System.' Ha! Ha! An alarm system! An alarm system!" she repeated. "You were running from a "canned" dog. What do you have to say for yourself?"

she asked, relishing the humor in John's idiocy while still feeling exasperated.

John began speaking as though nothing extraordinary had just happened.

"In answer to your dumb question about what I have to say for myself, the loud barking certainly gave me the sense the dog was giant sized, and you would draw the same conclusion if you heard the sounds that were coming from it."

"You know, you're even more of a lunatic than I figured you are." Jane responded with a giggle. "My point wasn't about the size of the dog you claimed was after you. It's that … Oh what's the use. Forget it."

John chose not to acknowledge Jane's snide remarks or her question, and instead responded defensively.

"Look, I can clarify what happened even though I don't owe you an explanation since you're not the boss of me."

Suddenly, three gunshots rang out in rapid sequence, and a deep thunderous voice permeated the atmosphere. "You vermin! You good for nothing punk! Wait 'til I get my hands on you! You'll be a nice feast for my dinner tomorrow."

"Mr. Ogar!" John and Jane screamed simultaneously as they locked eyes.

As John's body went rigid with fear, Jane instinctively turned around to look out the back of the truck. In the distance a massive looming figure was hobbling towards them. Two more gunshots resonated in the still air.

"You vermin! Punk!" Mr. Ogar bellowed again as he maintained momentum while dragging a leg behind him.

"John! John! Go! Go!" Jane shouted as she gave him a mobilizing shove. He pressed down hard on the accelerator and they shot off leaving a shroud-like barrage of airborne dirt and pebbles in their wake.

With his eyes glued to the road and after some moments of silence, John began to speak about his time in the house and his hair-raising escape. When he'd finished Jane said, "Humpf," and folded her arms in a huff. "In case you didn't notice I was preparing for us to make a quick getaway—a much more practical plan than standing by myself out there in the creepy dark because of your ridiculous notion that I could catch you if need be."

"Have it your way. I don't care." He said, "When this thing landed on the ground, a switch must have loosened because the barking started up *after* I retrieved it and was already bolting away from the house."

"What *I* think," Jane said, "is that while you were running, the motion sensor unit was tripped by one of the Ogars back at the house. That made the speaker play the barking and growling sounds. Then it stops by itself after a while, having accomplished its job of raising an alert."

"Hmm, you may be on to something," John remarked. "Very perceptive, Jane Doe. You make a good sleuth. It was probably Mrs. Ogar who tripped it, because I heard Mr. Ogar order her to grab the gun, and he'd meet her in front of the house. You have to admit. It's certainly a unique item. I imagine I could sell it for some good amount of money. Or I can use it as my own phony guard dog. Heh. Heh," John chuckled. "You know, to keep up appearances."

"Very funny," Jane said lightly. "But I think you need more than keeping up appearances at this point. Besides, you would have to get the sensor part of the system, and I doubt that in your spare time you would ever go back again to the Ogars' house to steal it."

She closed her eyes, determined to be patient and go along with whatever John wanted. She decided she would doze off during the rest of the trip back and remain in the truck when they arrived. The sun would surely wake her at daybreak.

"It'll be best if you don't wake me when we get to your house. Is that OK with you?" Jane asked.

"Whatever you say," John replied. "I'll keep your window open a bit so you don't suffocate. I have some chemicals stored out in the rear and the fumes might kill you if they sit and fester in the sun, especially if there isn't a breeze. And then what would I do? How would anyone identify your body when even you don't know who you are?"

Jane sighed and made a conscious decision not to ask John about the chemicals. At this point, considering her overwhelming fatigue, he could say she had sprouted five heads, and she wouldn't care. She stretched her arms and legs and then drew her body into a comfortable fetal position in preparation for welcome sleep.

"Oh by the way," John said, interrupting Jane's moment of bliss. "We have bonded together in conversation and experiences. Therefore I now want you to refer to me with my more familiar name, 'Jack.' Like it or lump it. Remember me, Jack Bean, the famous botanist."

Jane chuckled. "Surely I will never forget *you,* Jack," Jane mumbled derisively. "Wait—did you just say *Bean*—that your last name is *Bean*? When you introduced yourself you said *Beam*.

"So?" Jack said. "Things can't always be the way they used to be. Times change. You know, I just went through a hell of an ordeal, so I'm glad to have peace and quiet without your nagging me and playing a hundred questions. This is the perfect opportunity for me to ruminate about my experience at the Ogar house and plan my next move to find the missing girl."

"How absurd, changing your name like that." Jane stopped short. "Sure, John Beam, er Jack *Bean*. Whatever you say. In the meantime, my plan is, I'm going to put my obscure life into your little botanist hands and get some shuteye. I'll see you in the morning."

Jack's sudden shriek, "Whoa! Jane! Jane! Quick! Look! Look ahead!" was loud enough to pierce the din of the truck's exhaust system. This caused her to spontaneously bolt upright in her seat to face the windshield. Looking beyond into the darkness, she sighted the rear ends of three rotund animals snared by the headlights as they fleetly sprang across the road.

"It might be the same type of creatures that made me almost veer off the road on the ride in," Jack said. "Remember? You got so testy with me over that."

"Jeez, what were they?" Jane asked incredulously, ignoring Jack's huffy addendum. "Those certainly weren't a pack of dogs."

"How would I know? Have I ever professed to being a zoologist?" Jack asked.

Jane couldn't contain herself any longer. "Good grief, Jack. You're simply too much for one person to tolerate. What would being a zoologist have to do with knowing whether or not those animals were a pack of dogs?"

"I can't hear you!" Jack said as he covered his ears with his hands and used upward pressure from his thighs to steer the wheel. "La, la, la, la, la, la, la."

Jane let out a sigh of exasperation. She was way too tired to get caught up in more of Jack's ridiculous banter. She had an inkling of what they just saw, but she didn't trust her vision given the extent of her fatigue and the blinding sharp pains in her head that still kept appearing intermittently. She thought how much better it was to be dangerously careening along in the truck with the likes of Jack than being out and about by herself with the possibility of being ripped to shreds by the wildlife. She slid downward on the seat, rolled herself up into a ball and closed her eyes. The next thing she knew it was daylight, and a loud wail was rousing her from a deep sleep.

8

MEETING GOLDIE

As Jane slept, a seemingly random series of images flashed into her mind, each one prefaced by a searing light that made her headache worsen. The carousel of images seemed to be accompanied by the sounds of the world but in a distant and weirdly underwater kind of way. *Where am I?* she thought. There was a set of headlights rushing toward her, the burbling sounds of people talking urgently, which she tried but failed to understand—were they even talking in English?—a series of bright lights flickering in and out of phase above her, as if she were lying on her back and moving rapidly through a narrow corridor, as if on a toboggan going backwards down a snowy hill, *or like Alice falling headfirst through the rabbit hole,* she thought, feeling strangely calm about the observation.

Eyes floated in and out of view, hands pulled at her irritatingly and she tried to slap them away and tell them to leave her alone, but she belatedly noticed something in her mouth (*what is that?* she wondered) stopping her from talking, and found she was unable to move which caused her to start to panic before an unexpected sense of euphoria swept warmly through her, calming her. The eyes were in somehow blank, green and blue faces, strangely obscured with no hair and no mouth or nose. But they weren't frightening for some reason ...

Then she was in a room, filled with beeping flowers—was that possible? Do flowers make sounds after all? A voice droned beside her, rising and falling in the rhythm of storytelling, but she couldn't focus on what it was saying, or who it was. One sounded young, then it sounded older, then it all faded away as the headache became worse...

Jane awoke abruptly feeling thirsty and disorientated. The approaching high pitched scream that had awoken her grew louder. She had a piercing pain inside her head, and the sunlight stung her eyes as she tried to take in her surroundings. The first thing she noticed as she rubbed them into focus was that she was alone in the front seat of a truck. Then she remembered how she came to be in this place as her grogginess receded.

Jack was missing, obviously having stuck to their agreement not to disturb her when they arrived at his house. He had removed the hideous stuffed dog alarm and had left her window slightly opened, enough to let in the fresh morning air. A cool bottle of water was by her side and she drank it feverishly, grateful for Jack's thoughtfulness. She remembered what he had said about chemicals he was carrying in the back of his truck and worried what kind they were. She thought she detected a subtle medicinal odor. *Maybe it's disinfectant he uses to sterilize instruments in his laboratory when he does his genetic modification procedures,* she thought. She laughed as she pictured Monster Mouth, his giant mutated Venus Flytrap.

Jane got out of the truck carefully, feeling a bit dizzy. She turned to where she thought the scream emanated from, being sure to remain close by the vehicle with her hand securely planted on the door handle for balance and in case she had to hop in quickly to save herself. In the distant open field she saw a figure moving rapidly towards her in a zigzag fashion, arms flailing. The person appeared to be female, and considering her antics Jane thought she might be a victim of an attacking insect swarm. Although small in stature, her piercing voice was massive, resonating loudly in the otherwise silent surroundings and exacerbating Jane's jabbing headache. Jane soon found herself standing before a teenage girl, whose frizzy amber colored hair framed her face like a lion's mane.

Jane frantically scanned the area for the flying predators, but evidently nothing was pursuing this girl. Jane glanced nervously over her shoulder towards Jack's house, noticing that both halves of the Dutch doors were closed. There was no point in calling out. She looked back at the girl who was rather disturbed about something and was babbling on and on in between her gasps for breath. She was practically standing on Jane's toes, looking up at her with wide-open eyes while speaking.

"Not another oddball," Jane mumbled under her breath. Suddenly it dawned on her that this serendipitous encounter with another human being might evolve into an opportunity to get rescued without having to depend on Jack. Considering the potential for personal advantage, Jane decided to assume an optimistic attitude regardless of the negative initial impressions the girl had given her.

At first glance, Jane noticed that the girl's face was freckled. Then upon closer scrutiny through squinted eyes, Jane perceived that some of the freckles were situated in rows, lined up vertically and horizontally. They were connected with straight lines forming boxes here and there and each box contained a single initial in them as though the girl had played a game of Dots on her face. Jane closed her eyes and squeezed her head between both hands to get relief from another knifelike pain. *Oh God, make this go away!*

More startling to Jane than the sheer nonsense of her imagination was that a trace of memory had surfaced out of the blue. She couldn't remember important things like who she was or where she came from, or how she got here, yet she recalled playing Dots. In her mind's eye she saw a fleeting glimpse of her opponent—a child. *One of my children?* Jane squeezed her locket sentimentally. She couldn't quite make out the face before the image dissipated as circular flashes of lights occurred first in her left eye, then in her right. A sudden flush of warmth coursed through her body and the ordeal was over in what might have been seconds. Jane rubbed her aching forehead and temples. The girl was still chatting incessantly, and Jane made a concerted effort to pay attention to what she was saying.

"Those conservationists are the bane of my existence," said the girl. She kept chanting the same words as she paced in front of Jane. Jane detected a trace of a speech impediment.

"Did you hear what I said? Did you hear me? Huh?" the girl asked.

How impudent this person is, Jane thought. She didn't get a chance to answer.

"I can't stand them anymore!" the girl interjected as she looked intensely at Jane.

"What? Who?" Jane asked.

"Didn't you hear me before?" the girl responded. "I told you, "THE CON-SER-VA-TION-ISTS." She made rapid motions with her fingers while slowly enunciating the syllables.

Jane was taken aback. "Why are you talking to me like that?" she bellowed, ignoring the finger gestures. "What's your problem? We certainly don't appreciate hearing all of your screaming this morning."

The girl mimicked Jane in a bratty juvenile voice. "We certainly don't appreciate hearing all your screaming this morning. What do you mean, *we*? There's no one here but you. Oh I know! You're a wanna be Queen, and you're using the 'royal we.' Queen Victoria often ..."

"You're being obnoxious," Jane said. She had only just met this person and already Jane was out of patience. *So much for being positive*, Jane thought.

"Sorr—y!" the girl shouted. "Sorr—y! I'm just kidding around."

Jane nodded once in acknowledgment. "Why are you shouting? If you must know, there *is* somebody else I was referring to, young lady. Maybe you know him—Jack Beam—Bean, whatever. That's his house over there," Jane said as she pointed to it.

The girl frowned in thought and shook her head.

"Well anyway, I'm sure he was as sound asleep as I was when you came over here yelling like a banshee. He's quite eccentric and impatient—a very strange man. If you woke him up I would be concerned if I were you. Truthfully, he scares me at times." Jane's eyes darted about expecting Jack to materialize any moment. The odd girl just stood quietly, staring at Jane with a deadpan expression. She seemed to have short-circuited.

"Now exactly what's *your* problem?" Jane queried sweetly. "You obviously have a big concern, and I'm sorry we digressed." Being the adult in the midst, she didn't want to succumb to childish banter.

"What do you care?" the girl retorted with tears flowing down her cheeks. "But since you asked, it's the bears. This time, it's a family of bears. They are out to get me and ruin my life, and I can't do anything because of the conservationists. In fact, nobody was able to do anything about all the bears wandering around looking for food. Thanks to those conservationists a lot of people left this place."

Jane realized that the girl was obviously distraught about something serious, so she decided to cut her some slack. Her ears perked up as she thought about the unidentifiable creatures she and Jack had seen by the road during the night. So they may have been what she thought they were, after all! *If they're hungry there's no telling what they would eat.*

"Bears? Really? Out to get you? Jeez!" Jane said. "How awful. How about this? You can tell me the *bear* facts after you introduce yourself."

The girl smiled. "That's a clever line."

Jane chuckled. "I'll go first. My name is Jane."

"What's your last name?" the girl asked.

"Well, that's the million dollar question. I don't remember. I was in…I think I was in some kind of accident or I was assaulted someplace. I don't know who I am or where I came from."

"Maybe you were attacked by the blood-thirsty bears," the girl said. "I wouldn't put it past them."

"Hmmm, that's something to consider as a possibility."

"So how can you get by without having a last name?"

"That's seemed to bother Jack too. Actually he gave me a name. It's Jane Doe." Jane laughed thinking about the absurdity of it all.

"Oh how original!" the girl responded sarcastically. "I wouldn't go around using it if I were you. If you think about it, all the other Jane Does around are notorious impostors just like the guy, John Q. Public."

"I know what you mean, but Jane Doe is the best name I have to go with for now. But it's only very temporary. Jack was going to help me find my real name."

Well, nice to meet you Jane Doe," the girl said politely with a big grin. She curtsied.

The girl looked at Jane inquisitively. "Is Jack your father? Parents are the only ones who assign names to their children."

"Hell no," Jane exclaimed. "Jack is the first person I encountered after my trek from those mountains beyond." Jane pointed in the direction from where the girl had come from.

"That's very weird. Why would a perfect stranger give you a name?"

Jane started giggling as she spoke. "Good question. Get this. Jack said he couldn't talk to strangers, so he had to know my name. Since I don't know my name, he decided to give me one. Therefore by being able to call me 'Jane Doe,' in his mind I wasn't a stranger anymore, so he was able to talk to me. What do you think of that logic? Go figure."

The girl shrugged her shoulders and looking down, became engrossed in cleaning off what appeared to be a bird dropping on her shoulder. Jane found this to be very odd. *I don't recall seeing a bird anywhere in this vicinity. But why would I? They sit in trees, and there are no trees.*

The girl looked up at Jane. "Did you say anything? I'm deaf, in case you hadn't noticed. But I'm an expert at reading lips as long as I can see them moving of course."

Jane stared at her, completely surprised at the revelation. "No, I didn't notice. I'm very impressed. Now will you tell me *your* name?"

"What's so impressive about that?" said the girl, disregarding Jane's request for her name. "I've been getting along perfectly fine, living a regular life. I have a positive outlook on things, except about the bears trying to take advantage of me. I may not have my hearing, but not having a name is worse because without having your name you don't have an identity. I feel badly for you.

"Here you are trying to find yourself, and it's not your fault. People should have their identity figured out by the time they're well into their adulthood. I can't stand it when adults head off for Tibet to have an audience with the Dalai Lama in Dharamsala so they can find themselves. Or get this. My girlfriend's dad suddenly bought a used Harley Davidson motorcycle, rolled up his life into a backpack one day, and abandoned his family to head out across the country in order to find himself. What's with having to go far away in order to find oneself?

"Let me introduce myself," said the girl not skipping a beat and as though Jane had not already asked. "My real name is Goldie Hare. My nickname that other kids call me is Goldie Dreadlocks because I wear dreadlock extensions. The whole look is salon created. It only takes five hours to do every so often. I'm not a Rastafarian in case you are wondering. Not that there is anything wrong with that. I just like creative self-expression. There is nothing between the lines to read into, such as my being anti-establishment, rebellious, or that I am honoring some national heritage. I just like it. People can go overboard analyzing things to death, don't you think? Even Sigmund Freud said that sometimes a cigar is just a cigar. You can call me Goldie." All the while her attention was fixed on Jane's face.

"Shhh. Did you hear that?" said Jane.

"Hear what?" said Goldie. "I told you, I'm deaf! D-E-A-F," Goldie spelled out. "If I can't see your mouth, I can't know what it's saying."

Jane disregarded Goldie's curtness. "I don't know. I heard talk-ing—a din of voices, indistinguishable background voices."

"Maybe it's coming from a radio or TV inside Jack's house," Goldie suggested. "That is, if he has magic to receive airwave broad-casts. For the most part they are non-existent here. This is such a dead community. I hate living here."

"Hmmm. It stopped. Anyway I'm glad you finally told me your name, Goldie. The next thing is that I would love to go get help now. I don't want to have to count on Jack for that because it might never happen." She glanced at the door to his house. It was still shut. *This is my chance to leave unnoticed.* "Come to think of it, by any chance, have you heard any reports about a family looking for a missing woman?"

"Nope. I haven't *heard* a thing. Sorry." Her joke went over Jane's head.

"It sounds like you are more assimilated into civilization than Jack is. So can you to direct me to town—maybe to the police station? Or do you know somebody by the name of Hannah who lives near the road that leads to the town?"

"Forget walking to the town. That's like going to another state. But I know of Hannah and where she lives. She's near where we call "down road," a scary, steep road. That's the one that heads right to the town. But getting to her is kind of a trek too. I can draw you a map, but I'll go with you part of the way and steer you on the right course where it's tricky. By all means you should do it in daylight. However, for starters, although I'm scared to go back home, I need you to come with me so I can leave a note for my dad. We don't have phones up here either. He's on a business trip for a couple of days. I'm not sure exactly when he will return. Otherwise he might think I was kidnapped. You know how parents can get."

Jane mulled this over to herself. *No, I don't know how parents can get, because I can't remember mine, and I haven't a clue as to what type of parent I am.* She spontaneously touched her locket sentimentally. *Come to think of it, this could be a good opportunity for me to try and open this at her house. I'm sure there will be something more appropriate to use than a chisel!* She chuckled recalling Jack's outrageous plan.

"Hey, hellooooo Jane. Earth to Jane. Where are you?" Goldie asked.

"Oh—sorry. OK, sure I'll go with you," Jane responded, having some trepidation herself. "While we walk I'm very curious to hear what you have to say about these bears that are upsetting you."

"By the way," Goldie said with a sigh, "I'm a latchkey kid and pretty much take care of myself since my mom died."

"Oh, I'm so sorry to hear that," Jane interjected. The somber way that Goldie said this tugged at Jane's heartstrings. "That's terrible. If you don't mind my asking, was she ill, or did something happen...?"

Goldie brusquely interrupted her. "Thanks for your sentiments. No, she wasn't ill. She was never sick a day. It was a car accident...a serious car accident. I don't know the details. All I know is that it has made my dad and me very sad."

Jane could detect a lot of resentment in Goldie's tone of voice. She thought it was best not to probe further.

Goldie continued. "If you're going to be walking around these parts you should be aware that besides the bears, there's other danger lurking about too," Goldie continued, clearly avoiding further talk about her mother. "You probably don't know this, but a little girl from around here has been missing for awhile. We heard at school there's an Amber Alert out. You would be wise to never be by yourself."

Jane thought about telling Goldie that she knew about the missing child, and that Jack had a suspicion about who her kidnapper might be. However, Goldie didn't give her the chance to get a word in edgewise.

Goldie continued chattering. "Before we start walking, there are certain procedures we have to follow in order to communicate with each other."

"You mean there are *ground* rules?" Jane asked, amused by what she thought was another clever pun.

Goldie ignored Jane's quip and continued. "I need to look at you when you are speaking. So if you talk and don't let me know it, you'll be wasting your breath."

"Got it," Jane said. "The rule is that I must make sure you're looking at me when I speak. So, I'll tap you whenever I want to talk. We'll just need to be careful not to bump into anything when we look at each other while walking," Jane added in a teasingly tone.

Goldie let out a shriek and dramatically doubled over from her waist in spurts of laughter. Swiftly recovering, she stood upright and then pulled Jane by her wrist. "That's a laugh and a half, Jane. There's nothing around here to bump into! Let's go this way." Goldie pointed in the direction they would be heading. "I'll tell you about the bears."

Goldie got up on her toes and executed an elaborate pirouette. They moved onward.

9

BEWARE THE BEARS

The concept of direction was nil. All around her it looked flat and pale tan and homogenous with little in the way of landmarks. To Jane it was like starting out in the midst of a field of corn on a cloudy day. She looked ahead to the horizon and observed that they would be traversing a slight incline.

"This morning I left my usual oatmeal breakfast cooling on the ledge by the open window," Goldie stated. "There's a screen of course. My poor mom, God rest her soul, had always said, 'Eat oatmeal every day, Goldie. A meal of oats boiled in water is good for you.' Depending on one's heritage, some people call that porridge. Porridge is really thick and pasty. I have to add honey to it so that I can get it down my throat without gagging. It's called gruel if it's more on the watery side. I'm more of a gruel person, but that means it's super hot because there's more boiling water. You see, I don't put cream or milk in either porridge or gruel, so the bowl has to be set out to cool by itself.

"And here's a little tip I'll share with you, Jane. You don't go into a coffee shop or your local House of Pancakes and place an order for porridge or gruel unless you want to be humiliated. Once I asked for porridge. I heard the server call out to the cook, 'The young peasant over there wants a plate of porridge.' Everybody in the kitchen laughed. So, the lesson learned is only call it oatmeal in these parts, regardless of the cereal's consistency."

Jane rolled her eyes and clenched her fists from ediginess as she walked along side Goldie who kept talking and digressing endlessly. Was everyone around her as oddball as Jack and Goldie? God, she hoped not. Goldie still hadn't gotten past the oatmeal cooling on the ledge by the window, and not knowing what to expect regarding bears roaming around was making Jane tense up. *Enough with the oatmeal,* she thought.

"This morning, I made my oatmeal too thick so I added honey," Goldie said. "I had just put the bowl near the open window and..."

Jane heard a loud buzzing sound. She looked inquisitively at Goldie although she didn't expect to see a reaction.

"Oops! Wait," ordered Goldie, coming to a halt. "I have to shut this off. It's my vibrating watch. At home it tells me when the doorbell rings, and I can program it for wake-up times. I always have it set on strong in case I fall asleep. It's so I don't miss one of the Chinese cooking programs I like to watch on closed caption TV whenever I'm home from school. It's a good thing it went off because I forgot about my show. It will be on soon, and we can watch it together. There. It's off. Let's go."

"Wait a minute. You watch a TV show? You can get television reception?" Jane perked up. "I thought you said..."

"Yeah. What I said is true. This is the one and only show that gets through on a local government access channel. It's being relayed or something. Don't ask me how or why. And since it's my only source of TV entertainment, I live to see it. Plus I like cooking just like my mom. Let's keep going. I don't want to stand in one place too long."

Jane was miffed. She kept her legs moving at Goldie's pace thinking that the last thing she wanted to do was to sit and watch a Chinese cooking show. What would be a better alternative is that while Goldie watched the show, Jane would use the time to lie down. She needed a nap before the trek to meet Hannah, and at least that would be a way to turn this sojourn into something positive.

"The alarm is very loud. Why do you need the sound too?" Jane inquired. She thought that was strange. Goldie was still talking, naturally oblivious to Jane's question since Jane didn't let her know she had something to say. *This process of communication is going to take getting used to,* Jane thought. She let the question drop.

Goldie kept on talking as they walked on. "As I was saying, I had just put the bowl of oatmeal by the window, and my buzzer went off indicating that someone rang the doorbell. So I went to answer the door, I forgot that I had been taught never to answer the doorbell without asking who it is. I just opened it. Go ahead—crucify me. Anyway, nobody was there. I stepped onto my stoop and looked all around. Nothing. So I went back to the kitchen. I immediately noticed that my bowl of oatmeal was gone from the window ledge. The screen had a big hole in it. I asked myself, who would steal my oatmeal?"

"Well, I know who stole my oatmeal. It was three bears, and they are sly ones. They work as a team. Two act as decoys. One commits the crime."

This was definitely sounding far-fetched, so Jane tapped Goldie to get her attention. "Surely you can't be serious."

"Well, I am. Here's what else. There was a morning town hall meeting last week about all the happenings in the neighborhood. I went in late to school so that I could go to the meeting and didn't lock my door on the way out of the house. Hey, we have a low crime rate, so what the heck. I learned my lesson though. Stupid, stupid me."

"Through a sign interpreter I heard a lot of people reporting that they were missing things from around their homes. Four people lost all their food stored in garage freezers. Three bears had been spotted cavorting in a neighborhood swimming pool. Two large bears and a baby bear. Restaurants were reporting security video camera footage of nocturnal break-ins by the bears, despite the signs saying *no bare feet allowed.* Ha Ha. Get it?" Goldie slapped her thighs while consumed by a fit of boisterous laughter.

Jane snickered. She figured that Goldie had no idea how ridiculously loud she was at times. But more annoying to her was that Goldie was seemingly inclined to interject whimsy into the story, and it was turning out to be a bit too much of mixing fact with fiction. *I wouldn't be surprised if next she'll report someone heard that the three bears signed up for dancing lessons at some local Learn the Salsa Studio.*

"Everyone who lives around here is afraid," Goldie continued. "A mama bear with her cubs can be particularly dangerous. If you come near she will be ferociously aggressive. As to the males, that's a whole other story. They hang around all by themselves usually feeding, and what you have to do is be alert all the time, I mean ALL the time, so you see the bear before it sees you. You don't want to surprise it. Then steal away quietly—take a detour if you have to. Once I wasn't too far from my house and saw a bear stand up on its hind legs and look around with its nose up in the air. It was so big—it had to be over ten feet tall. I was so scared it would pick up my scent and charge at me, but I was lucky because it dropped back to all fours and continued doing what it was doing."

"Wow. I would have run away so quickly." Jane was feeling uneasy with all this talk about bears.

"You can't outrun a bear, silly." Goldie shook her head vehemently. "They bound or gallop at about 30 miles per hour. One of the conservationists told me that."

"Then in that case I guess you would have no other choice but to climb the nearest tree, to save yourself," Jane said.

Laughing hysterically, Goldie bent down and slapped her thighs like a "yee-hawing" cowboy.

Jane wasn't in the mood to have to deal with Goldie's antics. "What did I say that's so wildly humorous, huh?"

"Hey Jane, in case you haven't noticed, there's kind of a shortage of trees around here. That's one big problem especially as far as the bears are concerned. They prefer dense forests like we used to have where they can be alone and forage anytime for a variety of food resources like certain plants, nuts, fruits, insects, bird eggs, and small animals. They're ominie…omi…omniforous."

"Omnivorous." Jane interjected. "So that means they eat anything." She was horrified as she thought about her overnight sojourn in the woods and played it over in her mind.

"Yup. Thanks for the word. But that's all beside the point," Goldie added. "You never, I mean NEVER, climb a tree to escape from a bear. Obviously you don't know that bears have strong limbs and sharp claws, which make them expert tree climbers. They are especially skillful when there is something up the tree that they want. And I'm not just referring to the yummy, crunchy bugs or honeycombs they scoop out of bee hives, if you get what I mean."

"I see. So I drop to the ground and play dead. Right?" Jane asked imagining herself being caught any moment in a bear ambush.

"No. No. A big NO!" Goldie cried. "If the bear charges at you it's best to stay put. Often it's a bluff, and the bear will veer away. If you play dead the bear could turn predatory. If you run, it could decide to chase you. Once the bear leaves, back away slowly. Dropping to the ground, face into the dirt is a last resort. Grab the back of your neck and squeeze the sides of your face with your elbows and…and…I don't want to talk about this."

"Ok. Ok. Me neither," Jane responded. "But thanks for sharing your knowledge. It's all good to know since I'm traveling in the open around here."

"You're welcome. And one more piece of advice—don't do any traveling by foot at dusk, night or dawn."

"Is that your house up ahead?" Jane asked, anxious to safely get inside.

"No. But we're close. That's one of many that have been abandoned around here. They're all spread out so you can't see them from this spot. I'm sure we'll be leaving next. The bears are too much of a nuisance and danger. They got acclimated around humans as more and more trees were taken down where they used to hang out and eat."

Jane chuckled at the thought of bears hanging out like a group of young teens outside of a fast food restaurant in a shopping mall.

"What happened to the trees? Jane asked.

"What happened to the trees is that a builder came around out of nowhere and started clearing the forest for lumber. We didn't have laws to stop it, because the politicians never imagined anyone coming up here—to these hinterlands—to harvest wood. Unfortunately it was too late when the conservationists woke up. By then it was already the end of the bear dens in holes, under rocks, or in hollow tree trunks. So they migrated close to our homes, seeking shelter, and also lured by the smell of food. Now they come to rely on us humans for sustenance any way they can get it."

"The locals wanted animal control to humanely subdue the animals, capture them, and transfer them elsewhere. Others said they should be shot and made into rugs. Then there was a group of animal rights fanatics. They wanted to start a save-the-bears campaign. The whole meeting was getting out of hand. Oh no!" Goldie shrieked and stopped short. She pointed to the ground. "Bear tracks! Fairly fresh and different sizes. See? It must be the family that took my oatmeal. I can't tell which way they are going, though. That's not good given we're so close to my house. See?"

Goldie pointed with her right index finger as they rounded a bend in the road. Jane nodded. She could see it ahead in the distance. They still had about a quarter mile to walk, but at least an end was in sight, and they had picked up their pace. As usual there was nothing else in visual proximity, which was a good thing, because they could notice whatever might be lurking about. Unbeknownst to Goldie, she had supplemented the girl's rowdy behavior with her own intermittent bouts of clapping and shouting so as not to take the bears by surprise, especially if there was a cub in the mix. On the other hand, *where would we go if suddenly they saw the bears bounding toward us?* Her mind was racing faster than her heart. And there it was again— the awful knife-like pain in her head accompanied by fleeting dizziness and momentary fuzzy vision.

As she rubbed her eyes, Goldie's house came into focus. It was nondescript, and like Jack's, plopped in the middle of nowhere. Jane wondered how land was parceled out in this area and how many acres people owned. There certainly was plenty to go around. Gray clapboard covered the sides and the increasingly familiar indigenous stone made up the front. Three double hung windows were across the second floor with a corresponding window beneath each of them on the first floor. The roof peaked in the center and sloped to the left and the right. A very tiny brick chimney protruded from it.

Unlike Jack's house there were no flowers, but lo and behold, there, closest to them and off to the left side of the screened porch, were two tall trees between which a tightly slung hammock swayed in the light breeze. Jane was willing to bet that was the very spot where Goldie was when the bird dropping landed on her. A dirt driveway, perpendicular to the road, curved towards a dilapidated detached garage situated off to the right of the house. Other than that there was not much else to speak of except that the dismal property was a marked contrast to Goldie's flamboyant personality and appearance. She noticed a girl's white bicycle leaning up against the sliding garage door, which was partially open.

That's certainly very careless of Goldie, Jane immediately thought. *She complains about all this trouble with bears roaming around, and what does she do? She leaves an invitation for them to come and stay awhile in her free shelter.* The many paw prints they were seeing as they got closer to the house was not a good sign. *It almost looks like there was a scuffle of sorts. And there are trails of…*

"Blood!" Goldie screamed. "Oh no! They killed something, and that means they're hungry. We're doomed. This is a nightmare! Hurry, Jane. Get inside quickly. Those furry culprits could be in the backyard or on the roof—any place ready to attack us," Goldie shouted dramatically. "Hurry! Hurry!"

Goldie scooted on ahead towards the front door and to Jane's dismay, entered the house without having to use a key. Given that this girl was so concerned about her life, keeping the house unlocked when she was alone or out was dangerous, even under normal conditions. *Where's her common sense?* Considering that Goldie had also left the garage door open, Jane made a mental note to have a serious talk with her about taking appropriate safety measures.

Goldie's pleading and urgent tone caused Jane's anxiety level to escalate, and she felt as though her heart was about to burst. Not wanting to risk a moment of being outside by herself, she made a mad dash for the entrance while cautiously scanning the surroundings. She entered the house, slammed the door behind her, and leaned against it panting frantically as she clutched her locket for comfort. With a deep sigh of relief she reached behind to secure the latch.

"Goldie? Goldie?" Jane called out. Goldie was nowhere in sight. "Goldie? Goldie?" Jane's voice trembled as it declined to a whisper. "Goldie? Gold..." *I'm so dumb. Of course she won't hear me! But where did she go?* Jane took two small tentative steps into the room. A sudden thud and a scratch on the outside of the door caused her to freeze in panic.

10

AT GOLDIE'S HOUSE

*W*hat *if there are bears in here, and one or more are on the outside trying to get in? Jeez! I'm trapped!* Afraid that at any moment a bear could come charging through, Jane stepped to the side of the door and leaned against the wall for support. Her knees felt weak and shaky.

Her imagination ran wild as she pictured poor Goldie lying motionless on the floor somewhere, a victim of a bear attack. Her heart was pounding, and she could feel sweat emerging on her face and palms. *How did I ever get into this mess? Things keep getting worse instead of better. At this rate, I'll never get to Hannah. I'll never see my children, my husband, my family. I'll...*

Goldie startled Jane as she appeared almost out of nowhere. "Did you get a load of all those bear prints outside—there must have been some kind of a scuffle—gee whiz, what's the matter with you, Jane? You look like death."

"I saw them all right," Jane said nervously while she surveyed the surroundings. For the first time she noticed that she had entered directly into the living room. "I'm very tired, that's all," she sighed.

"Well you can rest a bit before we leave," Goldie replied. A holster dangled from a black fabric belt around her waist and tucked into it was a metal spray container that looked like a small fire extinguisher. "I'm so glad my dad still has a supply of this bear repellent.

I had to use our extension grabber in order to reach the cans on the top shelf of the mudroom. Of course, I first had to waste precious minutes scrounging around to find the tool. It's never in one place. We'll be safe now, especially when we get outside. This stuff is a hot pepper formula that shoots out over thirty feet and forms a fog around the animal. You hold it way out in front of you when spraying. Here—I got one for you," Goldie handed a can to Jane.

"Thanks." Jane took the item halfheartedly, feeling upset about being in this predicament in the first place. "I wish you had told me what you were doing instead of disappearing like that. I was imagining the worst had happened to you. Did you check around to make sure the house is buttoned up before we make ourselves comfortable? I think a bear was trying to get in at the door. It must have left."

"Did it ring the doorbell?" Goldie asked, ignoring Jane's question. "I didn't get a vibration signal from my watch."

"Of course not!" Jane snapped. "You can't really be serious asking that question, can you?"

Goldie raised her eyebrows. "I sure am serious. I'm surprised it didn't ring the bell like, if you remember what I had said earlier, one of them did this morning as a decoy so another could steal my cereal."

"Well, maybe the bear changed its mind because its accomplices showed up to go for a joy ride in their new convertible getaway car," Jane said sarcastically.

Goldie pondered that for a moment and then doubled over in hysterical laughter. "That's the funniest thing I've ever heard. So very funny. I'm thinking of it being a golden color—like honey." She continued to laugh, holding her sides as tears ran down her face.

Jane stared at Goldie incredulously, until Goldie calmed down after gasping for breath.

"Well, what are you standing there for?" Goldie asked with a wide leftover grin. "Go ahead and make yourself at home on the couch. The Chinese cooking show is about to start. I'm already boiling water to get us some herbal tea. Drinking herbal tea is calming and gets me into the right mood. I'll be right back."

Before heading for the kitchen, Goldie went over to the television and turned it on with the sound so loud that Jane thought her head would explode. From where she stood, Jane could see the closed caption text at the bottom of the screen.

Jane didn't ask Goldie what kind of mood she had to be in to watch a Chinese cooking show. She really didn't care. What mattered to her right now was taking a nap. She felt exhausted, and the couch was appealing, but first she thought she should go around and check the house. Judging from Goldie's carelessness about security, she didn't feel safe enough to relax.

Just as Jane lowered the sound level to nearly a whisper, Goldie let out a piercing shriek. Jane immediately started to run towards her, clutching the bear spray tightly and holding it out in front as instructed, ready to activate the trigger any moment. Goldie came running out of the kitchen in her usual, frantic way, nearly knocking Jane down.

"Oh my God what's the matter? What happened?" Jane asked.

"I don't believe this," Goldie shouted, jumping up and down in a tantrum. "I'm rip roaring angry!"

"Whoa, calm down," Jane demanded. "Jeez. What happened?"

"Ok, Ok," Goldie spoke excitedly. "I wanted to get honey for our tea. I always have a jar of freshly harvested honey on the kitchen counter. Anyway, the jar wasn't there. So I looked in the cupboards. Not there either. Then I went to the pantry where I keep a supply. This is an old house so it has a pantry. And a root cellar. Cool, huh? It doesn't have much of anything else, it's quite lacking charm, but it has a pantry and a root cellar of all things. Can you imagine? Awhile back I was reading about beekeeping and what a good thing it is for the environment, so I became interested in it as a hobby. I used to keep a lot of beehives in the back yard. I should show you what's left of them after being ravaged by bears, but you would have to wear protective gear since some bees buzz around quite angry over this. Honey infused with home grown lavender is my specialty."

Jane sighed. Goldie's tendency to digress from the issue at hand was so annoying.

Goldie continued. "So I looked in every cupboard for my honey and couldn't find it. But here's the worst of it—come let me show you. What an abomination!"

Goldie grabbed Jane's hand and pulled her through the kitchen into the adjacent pantry.

"Look! Look on the floor and the shelves. What do you see?"

Jane looked down and saw a hardened blob of golden goo with the partial impression of a bear's paw pad and two toes. It looked like a wax seal, the kind used on ancient documents or letters. As she looked up gradually towards the ceiling she spotted small claw marks on the top and underside of each shelf. Obviously a young bear climbed the approximately ten feet up to get the prize. A mature bear would have toppled everything. It made her skin crawl.

"Ick! How in the world did it get in? Jane asked. "Do you think it…they…

could still…"

"I don't know anything," Goldie interrupted. "And I'm not going to look any further for my honey pot. So let's forget the tea and watch the Chinese cooking show without it. At this point, I'm not in the mood for having tea. I'm sorry."

"Don't be concerned about the tea," Jane responded, wanting to be accommodating. "But would you mind if instead I took a nap while you watch TV? I'm very tired, and I have a dull pain in my head that's nagging me to no end."

"Fine with me. You can use the first bedroom to the right. I don't know about your body, but the sheets are clean." Goldie winked.

"Is that a hint?" Jane asked with a chuckle. "But it's not a bad idea. Would you mind if I showered?"

"Suit yourself," Goldie replied. "There are towels in the linen closet at the end of the hall. The bathroom is on the left of it. Now I'm going to watch my show. I'll wake you up later." Goldie turned away and headed for the living room. "Hey Jane," she yelled, "the chef is in the process of shopping for a five to a six pound duck in a Chinese open air market. I can't wait to see how he cooks it. Oops! The volume indicator bar is way down. I'll raise it so you can hear."

"Wow, that's great," Jane said automatically forgetting for a second that Goldie wouldn't hear her. She went to the closet and grabbed a bath towel and face cloth, and headed for the bathroom, thrilled to be able to take a shower and escape the blasting sound of the TV. The bathroom was fairly old but very neat and clean. Off to the left was a white enamel, free standing, claw foot tub. An oval metal shower curtain frame was suspended from the ceiling and supported by the showerhead which rose vertically from the faucet fixture. She couldn't help but laugh at the childish clear vinyl curtain speckled with little smiling bees hovering around cone shaped hives.

Before climbing in, she removed the chain and locket from around her neck, kissed it lovingly and placed it on the side of the porcelain pedestal sink. *Jeez! What a memory lapse!* With all the excitement, she realized that she forgot to show Goldie and see about getting it open. *I think a knife or a metal nail file would do the trick.*

The water pressure was weak, but nevertheless it was so enjoyable being under the hot shower that she could barely motivate herself to get out. The lemony smell of the soap bar made the experience all the more refreshing. As she dried herself she couldn't help but hear the Chinese chef talking about making Mandarin pancakes as a side dish to the duck. *It's beyond comprehension as to why Goldie would be the least bit interested in this. A meals-in-minutes cooking show would certainly be more practical for her.*

Groggy and very anxious to lie down, Jane wrapped herself in the towel and headed for the bedroom to the right. Heavy striped drapes were drawn over two windows, keeping the room comfortably dark and perfect for sleeping. It was impeccably neat except that the bed wasn't made. A quilt was bunched up on the floor. It looked like Goldie must have changed the sheets and then got sidetracked with something else. They appeared rumpled, but Jane didn't care. The thought of snuggling up in a bed after all she had been through was very enticing.

Now all she needed was something to wear. With the light from a little crystal lamp on the bureau, she fished around in drawers until she discovered a frumpy flannel nightgown. She put it on expecting it would be small for her, but surprisingly it actually fit her perfectly, almost reaching to her shins. She turned off the lamp, approached the bed and pulled back the covers enough to blissfully slide in. Lying on her side in the fetal position with her arms folded under the pillow, she yawned widely, gave out a big sigh, and closed her eyes. Before nodding off, she extended her arms and legs into a delightfully long stretch.

"Ew!" Jane screamed. "Ew!" Like a bug trapped in flypaper, her feet were immobilized by something thick and sticky. She rapidly drew them upwards and flew out of the bed. She turned on the bedside lamp and yanked off the bed covers, throwing them into a heap on the floor.

"Yuck!" Jane exclaimed. She looked at the bottom sheet, and saw it was covered by globs of a pale yellow sticky substance. She walked to the other side of the bed and spotted three familiar claw prints among some dribbles and little splatters of this stuff all over the floor. Several large shards of a broken brown jar lay in the midst of the mess. It must be Goldie's missing honey pot, she thought. Judging by the limited paw prints by the bed, Jane concluded that the bear licked all the honey off his paws before taking off. *Taking off to where?* She parted the drapes and checked the windows. They were shut tightly.

Jane was grossed out over the whole situation, especially having immediately convinced herself that the bed might now be infested with fleas or whatever other little parasites wild animals carried along with them. *I must advise Goldie to make sure everything gets fumigated.* After using the clean parts of the top sheet to wipe the honey off her feet and legs, she headed to the bathroom again to wash herself off.

This time she drew a bath and sat in the tub scrubbing and scrubbing herself with a handy loofah until her legs and arms were red.

Once she felt sparkling clean, Jane went back in the bedroom to check out the closet for something to wear. She found a light-weight cotton jumper designed with tiny little flowers and squares which came to the top of her knees and fit her as comfortably as a nightgown. By then she felt so lethargic that she longed for a nap.

Jane could hear the TV. No doubt Goldie was still contentedly occupied with her Chinese cooking show. She figured that if she were to tell Goldie now about what happened, the girl would get so freaked out they would have to leave the house immediately. Jane had no energy left, and the thought of being out in the open without the strength to run if need be frightened her. There was no question that she needed some sleep.

Jane decided she would go into one of the other bedrooms where she had seen bunk beds. This time she would lie on top of the bedspread of the bottom bunk. As she got into the bed she turned onto her back and looked up at the bunk above.

"Ew! Oh no! No! No! Not again!" Jane screamed.

Honey was dripping from the bedsprings. Some of it had crystallized like little stalactites descending from the ceiling of a limestone cave.

"Ick! Disgusting!" Jane cried. Judging from the smell it was more of Goldie's lavender honey. She bolted out of the bed, infused with adrenaline. There was no way she could sleep here. With anxious curiosity, she hastened to check out the space on the other side of the bunks and discovered several different sized bear prints memorialized in clumps of hardened honey. The tracks led to the double window similarly situated as in the other room. Hanging beneath the sill were the shredded remnants of a screen, its frame still in place beneath the raised lower sash.

Trying to look at the bright side of her discovery Jane concluded that it was good news the prints were leading outward and not inward. *Hopefully that's that with the bears.* She slammed the window shut, angry with herself for not checking out the house before, as she had wanted to. *This is further proof that Goldie is simply irresponsible when it comes to ensuring her safety. So typical of a young teen no matter how smart!*

All of a sudden, a searing pain shot through her head and dissipated, leaving her with residual dizziness. She stood still hoping it wouldn't recur. As she waited, she became engaged in a stream of consciousness. She had to get out of this place sooner than later and find her way home to her children, her family, one way or another. She had to reach that woman Jack mentioned, Hannah. *I better not forget the name. I should write it down in case. And what about Jack? Did I act too hastily in leaving? Maybe he's wondering what happened to me.* There was something about him that she missed, but she couldn't put her finger on what.

Jane ran to Goldie and plopped on the couch. Feeling queasy, she immediately put her head between her legs taking slow, deep belly breaths.

"Jane, now what? Are you ill?" Goldie asked. "You better not be. We don't have time to wait for you to recover. My show is just about over, and we'll have to get going. This is the part when the chef's family comes out with their chopsticks to eat what he made. Look. Doesn't the roasted duck on the platter look yummy? What presentation! Chinese cuisine is all about the art of presentation. I really like the garnishments. There. The show's over. I hope you got some sleep. Gosh, Jane. What's with your arms and legs? They look red. Whatever is the matter with you?"

Jane sat up slowly. "For a moment I felt like I was about to throw up, but I'm better now," she said, ignoring Goldie's callousness. "You're not going to like this. I have to show you something."

Jane led Goldie to the first bedroom and showed her the honey-coated mess. Goldie was stunned and speechless as she surveyed the bed and the floor. When Jane took her to the other bedroom to show her the honey dripping from the top bunk, the blood drained from Goldie's face.

"No, no, no, no, no, no!" To Jane's dismay, Goldie stormed out of the room and began running around the house like a lunatic, crying and screaming.

"They're missing. They're missing! Jeepers. They're gone. All disappeared into thin air: four 18th century antique Chippendale ladder-back chairs with claw feet that have been in the family for over 200 years!!!! How can this be? I've got a knot in my stomach. I'm going to faint. It has to be a nightmare."

Evidently, the whole situation with the honey was being over-shadowed by the fact that some chairs were missing. Jane followed Goldie as she ran into the kitchen and to Jane's horror, pinched herself with ice tongs. Goldie rubbed her eyes and then ran back into the bedroom to look again.

"No, it's not a nightmare. It's real. The chairs are still missing," Goldie cried out.

Goldie continued to run frantically about, and Jane heard her call out in tears from somewhere below.

"Gee whiz, Jane, I found them. I found them! I'm in the base-ment. Go to the pantry," Goldie sobbed. "You'll see the opening to the stairs right by the shelves."

Jane followed Goldie's instructions and found her with her head in her hands, sitting on a step halfway down in the midst of a pile of wood. Jane went down to her.

"What in the world happened?" Jane asked, totally mystified as she surveyed the scene.

"The good news is that I found them. The bad news is that I found what was left of them. Look at all this." Goldie pointed to the scattered pieces of wood. "I have it all figured out," she said forlornly. "At first, the three bears dragged my very valuable chairs here and stacked them up haphazardly to reach the jars of honey I had on the top shelf. I don't need a forensic reconstruction of the crime scene to prove that the bears' weight was more than the old chairs could handle. As the bears clambered up, the chairs broke, and everything toppled down the staircase. I can't express how vio-lated I feel because these three bears had invited themselves into *my* home and had eaten *my* oatmeal and honey, had been lying in *my* beds and had climbed on *my precious* chairs, breaking them to bits."

Jane looked at Goldie's pathetic face. There was something about her that made Jane feel a desire to comfort her, to smooth things over as a mother would do for a child.

"Aw, Goldie. I'm so sorry about your chairs. But I can't imagine bears planning such a thing. Maybe this is vandalism. Your front door was unlocked. Anyone could have walked in and..."

"No. It was the bears. I told you everyone has seen their behavior. They're very clever. Who knows, maybe they are a new breed, which learned from hanging around humans so much."

Jane didn't want to get into an argument over this. "Yes. You could be right. Do you want me to help you clean it up?" Secretly she wished to conserve her energy and hoped that Goldie would say no so they could leave quickly.

"No thank you. Let's go," Goldie sighed. "My heart weighs on me so heavily," she said with the drama of a Victorian letter writer. "I need to get away from here. I now have no choice but to go with you down road to report this atrocity to the police while you report your own predicament. If we happen to run into a forest ranger along the way I'll ask him to come over and investigate."

"A forest ranger? *Forest* ranger? But Goldie, there's no forest around here," Jane quipped.

"Why does that matter? I'm sure a person can be a ranger without a forest."

"Ok. Let's get going," Jane said, realizing it wasn't worth challenging Goldie on this either.

"Yes. Immediately. I'm glad you're better now, because we need to move on so that we can get to where we're going. If there's anything you want to help yourself to from the fridge, feel free. What's perishable will only spoil anyway. Who knows how long I'll be away."

"That's very considerate of you, Goldie. I wasn't even thinking of eating, but I know having food in my stomach will give me much needed energy."

While Jane hastened to wolf down American cheese slices and two apples, Goldie wrote a note for her father. She gathered bottled water, made up small zip-up bags of trail mix for each of them, and put it all into two canvas totes. Before they left the house to begin their trek, Goldie grabbed a broom from the mudroom.

"This broom may come in handy. You never know when we may need to whack something," Goldie said. "In the meantime I'll use it as a walking stick. I'll get my dad's bear spray holster for you to wear so you don't have to carry the can."

"Good idea," Jane said.

Goldie headed towards the kitchen to a closet where she removed a belt and holster from an inside hook and brought it to Jane.

"Here, put this on. It might be a little big on you, but you can knot it around your waist instead of using the buckle."

Jane secured the belt as instructed.

"Let's go," Jane said as Goldie opened the door a crack. They both held their breath as Goldie proceeded a bit at a time, ever so slowly opening it more, such that the eerie creaking of the hinges made them cringe in anticipation of the unknown.

11

THUNDERSTORMS

"Looks like the coast is clear," Goldie announced after tentatively stepping outside and looking around. "The bears are probably sleeping off all of my honey they ate. Either that or they're sick from overindulging. Not to mention I had added lavender and that's a soothing herb. Lavender produces a sedative effect that improves sleep quality. Speaking of honey—I never got to show you my bee hives. What's left of them, anyway."

"Another time," Jane replied absentmindedly. She was thinking about how much beyond her years Goldie often sounded, yet there were still the childish, if not bizarre, antics that emerged every once in a while.

Ever vigilant, they walked a half hour in silence, retracing their steps. Jane felt a major sense of responsibility since she was the ears for both of them. Any little sound caught her attention, and she couldn't stay calm. *I could sure use some of that lavender.* Her head was pounding again, and she noticed that when she turned to look at Goldie her neck felt stiff.

At one point Jane distinctly heard rumbling, which sounded like thunder, in the distance. She tapped Goldie on a shoulder and stopped. Goldie stopped and faced her.

"What?" Goldie's eyes were swollen and red.

"Are you crying?"

"It's nothing. Never mind," Goldie snapped. "What do you want?"

"I heard rumbling. Maybe it's thunder."

Goldie pointed upwards. "But there isn't a cloud in the sky. It's a beautiful afternoon. Perhaps it was your stomach telling you you're hungry." Goldie faced forward and continued walking.

Clearly Goldie was not in a good mood. Jane tapped her arm, and Goldie turned to look at her again.

"What?"

"Goldie," Jane said as she tenderly reached out to smooth the girl's hair off her face. "I just want to say that it's been a terrible ordeal you've had with the three bears. But running away won't undo all the harm that's been done. You need to go back home, safely, and confront it. You can always make more oatmeal and collect more honey from your beehives. You can always buy new bedding. You and your dad can save up money to replace the valuable chairs with reproductions. I know the chairs' sentimental value can't be reincarnated into something else, so you need to come to terms with that."

"Thank you for the thoughtful advice, Jane. It's the best ever. I will remember it always." Goldie gave her a hug and then curtsied.

Jane chuckled at Goldie's dramatically delivered compliment. *What a character!* She didn't think that she really did all that much to help her. It's become obvious that little favors and kindness make a big impact on her. Despite all her self-sufficiency, Goldie was a very needy person. *But who wouldn't be thirsty for attention being alone a lot in this secluded community? At least she attends school as a diversion and appears to be interested in a lot of things beyond her years…*

Jane's thoughts were interrupted by a horn behind them persistently beeping in the distance. She stopped and turned abruptly. The ground was vibrating ever so slightly and it became more pronounced. Goldie felt it too because she stopped to look around. A dark colored pick-up truck was barreling at high speed up the slight incline they had just walked.

The horn blared louder as the truck got closer.

"Oh my! It's heading right for us!" Jane yelled to the air as she yanked at Goldie who was staring at the approaching vehicle in dismay.

With nothing around to run towards for protection, all Jane could think of was to get out of the way and off the road in the opposite direction once the truck came closer. If it stopped ahead they could cautiously wait to see what happens. *After all, it could be a fortunate encounter—somebody who can give us a ride. We may be taking a risk, but on the other hand, walking a long distance in bear country, tired as I am, is not exactly a great alternative,* she thought.

The truck kept barreling towards them, and Jane started to run, motioning Goldie to stick by her. Goldie followed as if she were Jane's shadow. They both looked over their shoulders as the truck came to a screeching halt, kicking up so much dust that it enveloped them. Sprinting the way they did, clutching their paraphernalia, with bear spray cans bouncing in hip hugging holsters, had knocked the wind out of them. They tossed their bags to the ground and bent over at their waists, panting and coughing within the tornado-like swirl of dust.

Jane shouted, "Did you see what I think I saw?"

Goldie nodded. "Yup. There was no driver!"

The cotton jumper Jane borrowed from Goldie's closet had slid up to her butt, and she quickly pulled it down, feeling a twinge of embarrassment. In tandem, she and Goldie gasped for air as they brushed off their clothing in almost synchronized movements.

Goldie gave her a fleeting glance, and they both turned to look at the rear of what was a very dusty, black pick-up truck. Although it was stopped ahead, Jane could hear the engine still running. Her instinct was to bolt, but her legs felt nailed to the ground. Besides, she had no idea where they would they run to. Certainly not back to Goldie's house with those bears lurking around. *With the way my luck has been going, I could get trapped there and lose precious time getting to my children. They need me, and my whole family must be worried sick over what must have happened to me.* She felt a warm flush course through her body and her heart was palpitating. Fortunately, she didn't have a chance to dwell on her situation and become all the more despondent. Her ruminations were abruptly interrupted when Goldie began hopping like a jitterbug from one foot to the other.

"Let's rehash this," Goldie said, her voice quivering. "About that truck which was barreling down on us, and is now just sitting there up ahead, did you see anyone on the driver's side? 'Cause I for sure didn't, and it's so freaking me out."

Jane shook her head. "I didn't see anyone, and I don't like the way this looks. As much as I dislike the idea, we may be better off heading back to Jack's house, unless wherever we were aiming for is close by."

"Well, I vote for going to Jack's house," Goldie said. "We're not too far from there, and I bet we can convince him to give us both a lift down road. Is that a plan?"

Jane nodded. Besides, despite all of Jack's idiosyncrasies, there was a part of her that missed him. It was his kindness and scientific knowledge about plant remedies that had saved her life after all.

Jane continued to stare at the stationary pick-up as if transfixed. "OK. Let's just wait a bit and see what happens," she said. She had fleetingly noticed white printing on the trucks side as it passed them, but from where they were in relation to where it had stopped ahead, she couldn't make out the words.

"Fine," Goldie replied. "But if for some reason we have to run, do what I do—keep zigzagging. That throws the aim off of your pursuer in case, well, you know, in case we are barraged by arrows or gun shots."

Jane nodded. *That explains it,* she chuckled to herself, recalling the moment she had first seen Goldie approaching her in a similar fashion in front of Jack's house. *She applies that technique even when evading bears. What a character she is!*

Jane's musing was interrupted when all of a sudden the truck swiftly accelerated forward, the tires screeching and the rear body fishtailing, leaving another big spiral of dust in its wake. They watched in dismay as it disappeared into the distance.

"You creep!" Goldie shouted after the truck was safely out of view.

Jane tapped her gently on the shoulder. Goldie turned around, her face ashen.

"Let's get out of here now," Jane said. "Wow. You look awful."

"I got scared," Goldie declared. "I was thinking, what if that were the kidnapper I had mentioned to you? I could have disappeared off the face of the earth, and nobody would have known except people who read their milk cartons and see photos of missing and exploited kids. And what about you? Your family doesn't even know where you are now, let alone that you went missing again."

Jane took a moment to appreciate Goldie's last statement and felt a deep pang of longing to be home, safe and sound with her children and the rest of her family. "All the more reason for us to get rolling now and go back to Jack's house," Jane responded.

"Yes. Let's. We'll take a less traveled route than what we used to get to my house," Goldie replied. "I know my way around these parts like the back of my hand."

They picked up their canvas bags. Goldie pointed a few yards away where she had tossed the broom.

"I'm going back to get my broom. You can wait here if you want to."

"Forget that, Goldie," Jane told her. "It's really not going to help much if a bear is that close and you use a skinny broom as a club. It would splinter into smithereens once it made contact. Anyway, by then you should have already pulled the trigger on the bear spray."

"Well...I kind of like using it for support as I step along," Goldie said as though she were a feeble, elderly lady.

"Go on then and get it," Jane responded.

After Goldie came back, they took some sips of water and ate a handful of trail mix before proceeding. They ambled on in silence for a while until they came to a decrepit split rail fence, which surrounded a wide and deep field of low brush interspersed with wildflowers.

Jane noticed that the top of a stone chimney protruded above a cluster of pine trees that hid the rest of the house it belonged to. All the while she continued to wrack her brain for elements of her identity and people in her life. But it was futile and discouraging. There were certain things that came to mind but nothing helpfully enlightening. The more she tried, the more stressed out she became, which caused her head to pound and throb. For comfort she reached for the locket around her neck, at the same time realizing that she had forgotten to mention it to Goldie.

"No! No! It can't be! Jeez!" Jane screamed. She let go of the canvass bag and rapidly swept her hands around and up and down her neck and chest.

"Where—where—how could this be?" she cried. She felt the blood drain from her head. Feeling faint, she held on to a fence post as she let herself drop slowly to the ground in front of it.

"What's wrong? What's wrong?" Goldie asked nervously while watching Jane's frantic movements. "Did you get stung or something?"

Jane suddenly felt a sharp pain in her eyes while fleeting white specks scattered about her line of sight. As it dissipated, she looked into Goldie's concerned face all the while trying to replay what she did at the girl's house and during their walk up to this point. *When—when did I last touch the locket? How could the chain have come off? I'm totally losing my mind!* She thumped her head in frustration.

"Jane! What happened? Why did you hit yourself? Tell me!"

With tears welling up in her eyes, Jane told Goldie about her jammed locket, the inscription and how Jack said he would need a chisel to get it open.

"I was so looking forward to trying to open it at your house. For all I know about lockets, there could be photos of my children inside. I can't imagine how I could have forgotten something so important to me," Jane sniffled.

"Oh, I'm so sorry." Goldie knelt next to her and wiped the tears from Jane's face. "Think. Think. You said you were wearing it on the way to my house. So you probably took it off…"

"Yes! Yes! I remember," Jane bellowed. "Before I showered I placed it on the sink. But I don't know whether I put it on again after. Maybe I did, but not securely. That means it could be anywhere. Jeez, I feel like I am going backward, getting further away from my kids instead of closer. I can't imagine what's going through their heads, probably thinking of the worst scenario. And here I am plodding along, alive, and no one knows it."

Goldie patted Jane's hands soothingly. "Well, you know what we can do? We'll get to Jack and ask him to drive us to my house first. We'll watch out for signs of the bears, and if the coast is clear, I'll run in and check the bathroom. I bet it's still on the sink. But we better get going right now. It's nice and sunny now but look— the sky is getting cumulus cloudy back there, and it's common to have sudden storms around here in the afternoon. It's caused by the rapidly rising warm air. At our high elevation, condensation occurs when the dew point is reached and those kinds of clouds form. If the atmosphere is unstable and the air continues to up lift, the clouds grow into cumulonimbus. Then voila! We get thunderstorms."

"I don't mind a little passing rain," Jane said. "After what I went through the other day my skin could certainly use having more clouds around. Plus I would think that the rain will help cool things off."

"Well, that may be the case wherever you come from, but here a thunderstorm can get very bad. Sometimes along with the heavy rain we get lightening, high winds and dangerously huge icy hailstones. They may not hit the ground right away. Instead, the strong downdrafts and tilted updrafts keep on recycling the ice particles so they get bigger and bigger, accumulating more rain or cloud droplets which freeze until the ice chunks get too heavy to be lifted up anymore or the downdraft pushes them to the ground.

"Thank you for the meteorology lesson," Jane chuckled. "You certainly are a wealth of knowledge for your age. I bet you're a super student. I wonder how my own children are in school or if they are even school age for that matter."

Goldie gave her a hug and a big smile that lit up her freckled face. "Don't worry. It won't be long before you find out. Let's get going and try to stay ahead of this."

Jane looked up and was surprised to see that the sky had turned dark gray far behind them. She and Goldie picked up their things. They hadn't taken more than four steps when she heard rumbling. Her immediate thought was that the mysterious truck was approaching again. But rather than give in to her anxiety, she tossed that notion aside and assumed it was thunder. Suddenly she was jolted by a shrill holler. Instinctively she poked Goldie's shoulder to get her attention, practically knocking her off balance if it weren't for the broom that steadied her.

Goldie stopped walking and faced Jane. "Ouch! Gosh, that hurt! Whatever's the matter?" Goldie asked rubbing the ache out of the spot.

"Someone screeched something," Jane replied. "I think it came from behind us. There it is again!" They both turned around.

12

MEETING RUBY

"Hey s'up?...Hey there!...Um, like...can I come over to you?" a fretful female voice called out.

Jane waved her over. She and Goldie waited as a girl sauntered over to them dressed in an eccentric looking outfit with one of her hands pressed to her chest.

"EH MAGAWD!" she gasped. "I think...I like totally...freaked you out. Sor-eee! My name's Ruby. Ruby Ryderhud."

Goldie and Jane didn't know how to react to the woman before them. She'd seemingly come out of nowhere, clearly out of breath as though having sprinted for the finish line in a race.

"Ah, hi. I'm Jane, and this is my friend Goldie. She's deaf, but she lip reads very well as long as she can see your mouth. Is something wrong? Are you alright?" They couldn't help staring at the girl's bright red hoodie decorated with rhinestone flowers, layered sparkling red beads of different lengths, and mid-calf red leather boots. What appeared to be white, cake icing was smudged on her face and bangs.

"Um, I'm so totally pumped to like hitch up with you." She took a deep breath. "I like could really use some help—do you have a napkin or something to um, like wipe this grodie icing off my face? You know, this totally tard boy, Wolfgang, well, the dude made me fall into the cake I was carrying and got me totally messed up. Fer shur, I'm totally angry at him you know for like doing that to me. Plus I got so totally freaked out and like so afraid of what he would do next that I had to get away as fast as I could. Can you relate?"

"I don't *totally* understand much of what you're saying, so excuse me if I don't say, like, too much. Can *you* relate to *that?*" Goldie said sarcastically.

"Goldie! I'm surprised at you," Jane was taken aback at her rudeness. "I'm sorry for that, Ruby."

"EH MAGAWD! Um, like, don't go acting kind of weird and all. So, like do you think I would have bothered you if I didn't totally need help or something? As if!"

"Goldie, what Ruby is wondering is if we have something she can use to clean her face. Also she was running from a threatening situation."

"My bad," Goldie replied with a smile. "I didn't mean to be rude. I was a little frustrated. I'm finding it hard to read your lips. That's all."

"Sweet. Pay it no mind. Like, I totally get you. So, um, chill," Ruby said.

Jane had reached into her canvas bag and pulled out one of the paper towels Goldie had packed. She handed it to Ruby as she pondered that no matter what words Goldie understands, she certainly wouldn't be aware that Ruby strangely ends every sentence as though it were a question.

"Sweet! Thank you."

Ruby began to wipe the icing off her face.

"So, um, like did I get it all off?"

"Mostly. Let me help. I, um, like your red ensemble," Goldie remarked with a smile as she wiped off the remaining icing.

"Awesome. You know, fer shur, red happens to be my favorite color, and it's like totally a coincidence that it matches with my name. Um, nobody ever told me that um, just cuz my name is Ruby I have to love some other color like um, yellow or teal or purple or whatever, other than red. As if!"

"No. No of course not," Jane replied, recognizing that there was some sensitivity around the association of Ruby's color preference with her name. "We don't mean to stare at you. We're just very tired and surprised that you showed up. That's all. We thought we were the only ones around here and were in a big hurry to get to a particular place before the storm hits. Come to think of it, it's looking pretty bad. Say, you didn't by any chance see a dusty black truck driving around a little while ago did you?"

"Um, no. Fer shur. Like why?" Ruby asked.

All of a sudden, a loud crack of thunder caused Jane and Ruby to flinch. Jane pointed to the darkening sky for Goldie's benefit just as a bolt of vertical lightning flashed in the area of the thunderheads.

"Eh magawd!" Ruby screeched. "Um, so it looks like a killer storm is coming, fer shur," Ruby screeched. "Like, no way are you two going to get totally ahead of this, you know."

"Oh my. Oh my," Goldie shrieked as she dropped her bag and broom and began to wave her arms frantically. "We can't spend another second out here. We'll get electrocuted. We'll be blown away. We'll be bombarded with hail bricks."

Ruby looked at Goldie. "Eh magawd! Like, hey Goldie. S'up with you totally buggin' out like that? Chill!"

"Huh? What language are you speaking? I can't make it out. Jane, is she speaking English?" Goldie asked.

Jane nodded as she looked up at the sky. "Yes, but it's a different dialect. Anyway, we do have to get out of here. And quickly." As she looked around frantically a few raindrops fell on their face and arms.

"O. M. G!" Ruby screeched. "Um, fer shur it's going to pour down in buckets like in minutes. And Goldie's right about the danger—hail the size of golf balls and like sometimes oranges or bricks, falls from the clouds. But no worries, you two. Like fer shur you both can come with me. I'm on my way to see my grandma. That's where she lives."

Ruby pointed to the house that Jane and Goldie saw beyond the split rail fence.

"Come on," Ruby said, and waved Jane and Goldie to follow. "Um, we have to walk around a ways to like get to the entrance path. Um, the yard is like totally full of hidden grodie thorny things so no way would I ever climb over the fence and take a shortcut. As if!"

"Are you sure your grandmother won't mind us strangers barging in?" Jane asked as she and Goldie kept up with Ruby's rapid strides. "Of course we'll leave as soon as the storm passes."

"Like I said, no worries," Ruby replied. She picked up the pace and Jane and Goldie had to hurry to catch up with her.

Ruby turned to Jane. "Um, like, I've been meaning to ask. What's with the broom? Um, like, is Goldie going to be a witch?"

"Huh? What? What do you mean?" Jane asked, quite taken aback at Ruby's question.

Ruby laughed as she observed Jane's perplexed expression. "Like don't totally freak out. So um, you know, I'm just like asking. Like, I don't mean a *real* witch. As if! Jane, um, you know, I'm like asking cuz it's totally on my mind cuz like I'm going to play a part in a play. Um, that's why I'm on my way to see my grandma."

Jane looked behind to check on Goldie and saw that she had begun to walk backwards fully engrossed in observing the darkening sky and apparently not the least bit interested in anything that Jane and Ruby had to say.

"Any minute it's going to hit us with a vengeance," Goldie shouted. "The wind's even kicking up."

"Um, that Goldie's totally real, right? and she's way lucky that she can't hear those thunder booms. Sweet! We're like almost there."

Jane turned around again, to find Goldie facing forward and so close that she was practically on Jane's heels. She pointed ahead of them and Goldie nodded. Ruby continued talking as they maintained a brisk pace and turned onto the short path leading to the front of the house.

"So um, Jane, like you said, you were on the way to someplace. Um, like where? There aren't exactly destinations around here, if you like get what I'm saying."

"We're anxious to see a person whose house I suppose shouldn't be too far away. His name is Jack Beam or Bean, whatever," Jane laughed thinking of Jack's peculiar name change.

"EH MAGAWD! Like, are you totally serious?" Ruby asked. She had stopped so abruptly that Goldie knocked into her. Ruby turned around.

"Sorr-eee! Goldie said. "But I didn't expect you to stop short like —especially since we're being followed so closely by that thunderhead. What's wrong?"

"Oh, no bother, Goldie. I'm cool. Fer shur, it's totally my fault."

Ruby continued to hustle onward as she spoke. "Um, so Jane, do you mean that dude in the like burlap shirt who says he's like the greatest botanist on the face of the earth? Um, fer shur he's like missing some tools in his toolbox. Like, what I mean is that he's so totally strange."

"Ha ha. I think you mean he's not the sharpest tool in the box," Jane interjected. "But really, he's quite smart."

"Oh, whatever. Um, he talked at our school once about different kinds of energy sources he was inventing, like using plants for making cars run. And um, by the way thanks to him we hardly have any trees left. You know that's cuz for years his family used wood to like heat their place, my mom said. So, um, like, they totally cut down many of the trees around here. But so did other people for different purposes, like building things. Um, much later some conservationists like came around from down road and fer shur, put a stop to all that, but like it was totally too late."

Jane was glad that Goldie wasn't paying attention to Ruby when she mentioned the conservationists. It would have definitely set her off.

A clap of thunder and a flash of lightening along with a very strong gust of wind, spurred Jane and Ruby on to the covered front porch with Goldie a hair's width behind them just as a torrential downpour swiped at her back. They all stood there and looked out at the driving rain.

"Whew, that was close," Goldie exclaimed. She threw down the broom and canvas bag as she pushed back one of the wicker chairs and plopped onto its overstuffed cushion.

"Yes totally," Ruby responded. "You know, like, you wouldn't catch me being out in that. As if! You both can sit down and totally veg here if you want until it passes. Um, I'm like going to tell Grandma we're here so she totally doesn't get scared."

Ruby went to the corner of the porch and stooped down to lift up the edge of a floorboard. She removed a key and held it up.

"Sweet! It's still here."

As Ruby opened the door she shouted, "Um, hey there Grandma! It's Ruby. Like, where are you?"

"I'm in the bedroom at my sewing machine, dear," a sweet elderly voice called out.

Ruby turned towards Jane and Goldie. "Um, like, do you need to use the bathroom or get water or something?"

"No, thank you," they both replied.

"Ok. Um, wait here," Ruby said. "I'll be right back. I want to like wash my face. Um, some of that grodie icing hardened up, and it's so totally annoying. I really can't stand it another moment."

As soon as Ruby went into the house Jane and Goldie began munching on some of their trail mix.

"I don't get what that girl's saying half the time," Goldie remarked.

"Don't worry. It's not your fault. She constantly says *um, totally* and *like*—often in the same sentence. For me, the fact that she ends every sentence as though it's a question means I have to think twice whether she is asking something or telling something. I wish this rain would stop. I'm very anxious to get going."

It didn't take long for Ruby to return, looking refreshed with a scrubbed red face.

Jane continued to look out gloomily at the heavy rain. "So Ruby, why don't you continue your story while we wait here for the storm to pass? You were telling us something about being in a play and that you got into some trouble on the way here."

Ruby sat on the floor in front of Goldie with her knees bent and legs crisscrossed. She looked up so Goldie could see her speaking.

"Um, well I'm like named after my grandma who used to own an awesome store down road called The Party and Costume Emporium. She like designed and sewed costumes for cool theme parties and events. So, um, at school we're having like a little play about the fable called *Peter and the Wolf* —you know, about the really ditsy shepherd dude who wants people from his village to pay attention to him when he's alone with his sheep. So like he would scream for help saying 'Wolf! Wolf' when there totally wasn't a wolf around. Then, EH MAGAWD, the awesome villagers would drop what they were doing and run to him only to find that the dude was totally making things up. So, like they stopped listening to him, and then one day there really was a wolf which ate up all the sheep. The villagers were like totally bugged out over this and chased Peter out of town. Um, from this story we learned that when you're a liar like Peter crying wolf all the time, or whatever, then fer shur you can't like ever be trusted to tell the truth."

Jane and Goldie nodded their heads in agreement. At that moment, a flash of lightening lit up the surrounding area with such intensity it was as though someone had flicked a full set of ballpark stadium lights on and off.

"One, two, three, four, five…" Goldie counted out loud in rapid succession and stopped as soon as she felt the porch shake from the crack of thunder which followed.

"EH MAGAWD!" Ruby screamed. "You know, these storms are like major scary."

"Don't be scared," Goldie said soothingly. "I'm sure you already know it's very normal around here and also to see lightening that runs down from the sky to the ground like a silver pole. But it's OK as long as you don't go out and about in it. The good news is that it's just a mile away. It'll get here and be over before we know it."

"Sweet! Um, like how do you know all that?" Ruby asked.

"It's easy. I use the flash-to-bang method of calculation. What you do is start counting seconds as soon as you see lightening flash and then stop when there's thunder. I can't always feel it like I just did, but I always can tell from the reactions of people around me. Since I got to five seconds then that means the heavy rain and all has about a mile to go to get to us."

"That's news to me, Goldie," Jane said. "Then we won't have to wait as long as I thought we would. I'm kind of on edge because we've been so delayed, and we need to move on. That's all. I'm trying my best to be patient."

Jane pulled up one of the other chairs and sat in it with a sigh. "As long as we're waiting this out, Ruby, let's hear the rest of what you were telling us before about the play you're going to be in. I'm sorry for the interruption."

"Sweet. Um, anyway, some of the kids are like wearing totally awesome sheep costumes that Grandma made. And EH MAGAWD, get this, one of the girls is named Mary, and you know, of all things she's going to play a little lamb! Isn't that so totally funny?"

Jane and Goldie chuckled at the coincidence.

"Um, but the bad thing that I'm like totally bummed about is our teacher has me playing the wolf in a double costume with the class creep, and eh magawd, get this too—you know the dude I mentioned before? Wolfgang? Well, like his whole name is Wolfgang Putz—we call him Wolfie. Fer shur, I like think our teacher picked him cuz of his name. Um, he's even like a mean wolf cuz he's a total bully who picks on girls and little animals. You know, Grandma designed a real cool wolf costume, but the bunk is that it's um, made for the two of us to get into. Wolfie's like going to take the front part of the costume because you know the head's a bit heavy, and like I'll be in the rear end."

"Gosh, that's all very interesting, but how did you wind up with cake icing all over your face?" Goldie asked.

"Um, Grandma wanted me and Wolfie to come over to try the awesome costume on together. So like early this afternoon I told Mom that I was coming here, and like right before I get out the door she hands me a boxed cake, you know, the kind that has a cellophane window. So um, she says to me, 'Hey, Ruby, take this over to Grandma, and make sure it gets there all intact.'" Ruby scowled while recounting that comment.

At that moment a lightening flash and rumbling of thunder caused Jane and Ruby to flinch. The heavy rain that followed shortly, with strong winds and hail bouncing off the porch railing in chunks, forced them to move closer in towards the house wall.

Ruby continued. "So, like I was saying—um, on the way to Grandma's house I ran into Wolfie, and he asked a hundred questions like how much further was it to my grandma's house, and what did I have in the box. So, um I told him it was like close by fer shur, and that it was totally none of his business what was in the box. I then said, 'Hey Wolfie, like why don't you take a hike?' Well, um, that totally ticked him off you know, because EH MAGAWD, um, the next thing I knew the bully shoved me like totally hard to the ground."

"Aw, you poor thing," Jane interjected. "You must have been scared out of your wits!"

"EH MAGAWD, fer shur," Ruby remarked. "Um, like that ditz is nothing but trouble, totally. You know, I had to do all I could to like get my arms out to save my face from like hitting the sidewalk, and like wouldn't you know but as a result, well, I like dropped the cake box and EH MAGAWD, my face landed totally square into the cellophane widow of the box, um, crushing the whole thing flat."

"Jeez." Jane sympathetically shook her head. "You're lucky you didn't break your nose."

"Well, um, you know, the sides had like busted open, and pieces of cake were totally all over the sidewalk. Then in like a nanosecond I was so totally grossed out to see that an army of ants had mobilized out of nowhere to like attack the glop."

"Ew! Ew!" Goldie screeched, shaking her hands in the air as though she were trying to extricate flypaper from her fingers. "Were they red fire ants? I read that a swarm could cover a person with venomous stings in minutes, and the person could swell up and die from anaphylactic shock." Goldie shuttered. "What did you do?"

"Eh magawd, how grodie is that! Um, I don't know what like 'ana…fat…el' shock is but anyway, no they totally weren't like red whatever ants!" Ruby looked at Goldie with a scowl and shook her head. "Like, what do you think I did? Um, lie there on the ground and like watch the ants as they carted away tiny pieces of cake? As if! Um, fer shur I immediately got up and like ran as fast as I could with my face totally covered in cake glaze, which you know, like I was wearing when we met."

"Say look! The rain's easing up," Jane announced excitedly.

"Yeah, sure is," Goldie added. "The storms we get here stop as quickly as they come on."

"Sorry again, Ruby. Go on," Jane apologized.

"Shur. You know, the costume looks so totally cool! Um, when I went inside before, Grandma was like busy reinforcing one of the seams on the awesome wolf's head that she made. Um, lucky for me, you know, Grandma said that Wolfie had already tried on his front part and like—get this—um, she said he rudely rushed out as she asked him to um, wait for me. Whew! Um, like after what that dude did to me before, you think I would totally ever want to be in the costume with him today? As if!"

"I don't blame you, Ruby," Jane said distractedly. She got up and walked off the porch to the open air to assure herself that the storm had dissipated.

Goldie grabbed her broom and ran out shouting, "Wait Jane, there's still a chance of lightening."

Nah, it's looking good. I can't wait anymore." Jane gestured thumbs up with both hands as she passed Goldie and came back onto the porch. "I'm sorry Ruby, but we must go right away."

"Um, fer shur you both, I say *both*, must come to see my totally awesome school play. Like will you?" Ruby asked enthusiastically as she rose up from the floor.

Jane suddenly gasped. A trace memory—something embedded in the past—had emerged from the recesses of her mind. She was up front in an audience, watching little children cavorting on a stage dressed as little flowers. One child, whose blurred face was framed by a circle of white petals, was waving to her. *My child? A boy or a girl? Is it recent?* Her heart skipped a beat, and her breath was suspended as though she were on the cusp of making a discovery. Her chest felt heavy.

"Um, will you? Will you?" Ruby was standing before her in anticipation of a response.

"We'll see," Jane said, knowing full well that she didn't intend to stick around much longer, let alone to see a play. *Not to mention, come to think of it, that Goldie wouldn't understand one word the characters said, which of course is beside the point.*

"Come on Jane," Goldie shouted from the front yard, while leaning casually on her broomstick. "Why are you just standing there? I thought you wanted to get going. The sun's trying to come out. Good bye, Ruby. Nice talking with you."

Ruby waved back at Goldie.

Jane gave Ruby a tight hug and stepped down from the porch. She turned around to face her.

"Oh, and Ruby—good luck dealing with that bully. Thank you so much for letting us stay here during the storm."

"Um, I was totally glad you could come over and like talk with me. You know, I hope I see you again," Ruby replied.

Jane smiled and wiped a tear from Ruby's cheek. She walked over to Goldie and asked, "Do you know how to get back on track from here?"

"Yup-de-doo," Goldie replied as she began skipping. "Come on. Follow me!"

Jane laughed at Goldie's childish antics and caught up to her. They started walking at a moderate pace.

"What happened to you just before?" Goldie asked. "You sort of zoned out for a bit."

"I don't know. How very strange that was. It must have been triggered by Ruby's talk about costumes and her school play. I suddenly had a memory of watching a stage show of some sort," Jane replied. "A child dressed as a daisy flower waved to me, but I couldn't see the face. It was a blur. The whole image took my breath away."

"Wow, that's cool," Goldie remarked. "Maybe you're getting better."

"Oh, jeez, Goldie, I'm lost in so many ways I can't stand it anymore. And my head, it gets such sharp pains on and off. There's obviously something seriously wrong with my head. I've got to get help. I've got to get home to my children," Jane moaned. "And I so wish I knew their names and whether they are boys or girls or one of each." Tears welled up in her eyes.

"Aw, Jane, don't worry," Goldie said soothingly. "We'll be at Jack's house in no time, and he'll know what to do."

They walked along the dirt road past barren openness interrupted with only a smattering of oddly clustered dense groves of tall pine and aspen trees. With no sign of life about, Jane became engrossed in her thoughts, hoping to stimulate those parts of her brain that were dormant. She was so distracted that she put all of her trust in the fact that Goldie would get them to Jack's house. After what seemed to be about an hour trekking through deserted and unfamiliar territory in the late afternoon haze, she noticed that Goldie was chewing on her fingernails. This worried her.

As they approached another section of woodland, Jane tapped Goldie's shoulder to get her attention.

"How about we rest for a bit in the shade and have some water and trail mix? We could use a bit of a break from the heat," Jane suggested. She observed her bare arms. "Jeez, despite the haze it looks like I got a little sunburn. You sure do have erratic weather systems here." She gestured to the ground at the foot of a nearby tree. With nothing to rest on but a bunch of twigs, they plopped themselves down and sat cross-legged. Goldie began to sniffle.

"Goldie, what's wrong?" Jane asked.

"Don't be angry. Please don't be angry. But...but...we're lost!" Goldie blurted out. "I know we headed in the right direction because I tracked the sun when it first came out, but I think somehow we angled over too far when the haze set in. Oh my. Oh my," she whined in her usual dramatic fashion. "I've never been lost before."

"Oh, you can't be serious," Jane cried, shaking her head in disbelief. "Now what? I don't know how much farther I can keep going without an end in sight. And I certainly don't want to be caught out here at nightfall."

Jane closed her eyes and leaned against a knobby trunk. Her head was pounding again, so she pressed the front and back of it between her hands. The squeezing pressure gave her some relief.

"Hi. Hi there, Miss." In between Goldie's sniffles, a voice in the background startled Jane. "Miss, Hello…Hello," it repeated again.

Jane looked over at Goldie who had settled down and was munching on her snack, naturally oblivious to the sound.

"Hey there. Look behind you, Miss. I'm over here!"

Jane stood up quickly and turned around.

13

MEETING CINDY

"Who's there?" Jane exclaimed.

Goldie was startled by Jane's sudden movement and turned towards her. Jane pointed to a sparse grove of trees behind them.

Somebody was peeking out from behind one of several, skinny looking trees not far from where Jane and Goldie were situated. Jane couldn't make out the face in the shadows. Whoever it was, the person was slim enough that that the tree trunk camouflaged the rest of their body, giving the appearance of a head and neck floating in the air.

"Gosh!" Goldie screamed dropping her trail mix bag to the ground as she jumped up. She stood next to Jane while holding her broom out in front in a defensive position.

"Now that's downright freaky. What is it?"

"We can't really see you," Jane shouted. "Will you step out in the open? We're not going to bite you, you know."

Jane heard a slight voice, but she couldn't understand it.

"Please speak up," she said. She was clearly unnerved by this strange intrusion and tried to sound assertive. "I know you're speaking, but I can't understand one thing you're saying. Why don't you come out from behind the tree?"

"No. You'll laugh at me." The female voice trailed off.

"What did you say?" Jane asked. "All I heard was "no" and 'laugh.' You really have to raise your voice because this conversation is going nowhere. Better yet, could you please come over to us?"

"What's going on?" Goldie asked, nervously looking back and forth between the person and Jane.

Jane shook her head in exasperation. "I haven't the slightest notion. And whoever that is doesn't have much of a voice. Don't feel like you're missing out on anything."

Jane and Goldie watched intently as a petite young woman walked tentatively towards them, looking fragile as a porcelain doll. Her shoulder-length strawberry blond hair was held back by an aqua ribbon and wispy bangs draped over her forehead. She was wearing a ragged, knee-length, brown dress topped with a waist down white apron. Her tan bodice had puffy brown and tan striped sleeves, which extended to her elbows. She appeared to be limping or dipping lower to one side in her gait, possibly due to one leg being anatomically shorter than the other. But as she got closer, it was obvious that she was wearing two different shoes: a rubber flip-flop and a transparent sandal with a little heel.

She had stopped a short distance away, muttering incoherently and seemingly hesitant to approach.

Goldie looked back at Jane and whispered, "Has she said anything?"

"Yup. But don't ask me what. And what's with that get-up?" Jane whispered back. "She looks like a scullery maid or something. I know because I've seen servants dressed like that in old-time movies."

"Maybe she's a character in a local theater group and went to a costume rehearsal," Goldie suggested. "I know! She's in the same show as Ruby and is playing Little Bo Peep." Goldie laughed.

"Or she works in a theme restaurant or beer garden," Jane added with a chuckle.

She shouted with a smile, "Well hi there, young lady. I'm Jane and this is my friend Goldie."

"See, I knew you would laugh at me," the young woman said. As she approached Jane and Goldie she looked nervously behind her.

"Oh, no. Not at all. You misunderstood. We weren't laughing at you. It was about something else." Jane lied. "I'm sorry, but you were speaking so softly and standing so far away that I couldn't hear what you were saying. And so you know, Goldie can't hear anything anyway, being that she's deaf. Try to remember to always face her when you speak. She can read lips very well."

"Sure. Don't mind me—you said you are Jane and Goldie, right? Er...my name is Cindy." With a broad grin, she extended her arm, and they exchanged handshakes. "You can't imagine how much I'm pleased to meet you. And I, ah...don't know where to begin except that until I saw you both sitting here, I was running away, because I'm good as dead," Cindy said. She kept looking back, obviously very agitated.

What is it with this town? Here's yet another odd person with a personal conundrum, Jane thought.

"What's up with your shoes?" Jane inquired, choosing not to question Cindy's odd outfit lest she sound condescending and rude.

"I figured you would find this strangely comical. But it's a long story, and if I explained you wouldn't believe it anyway."

"Try me," Jane said. "I'm actually a magnet for people with troubles, and I'm especially adept at attracting my own."

"You think *you* have a long story? You should hear the likes of ours," Goldie chimed in. "I've had enough aggravation with three bears that wreaked havoc in my house and stole my honey, and Jane here—she doesn't even know who she is, so she's using a fake name somebody gave her to get by with temporarily as she sets out to find her family. And on top of that I got us both off course and lost on the way to a certain man's house here in Tree City where we were heading for help."

Cindy's mouth was agape. "Oh my. That's so incredible. It sounds like a horror movie. But Jane, what's that about your name and not knowing who you are?"

"Goldie's right. I seem to have been in some kind of accident. I can't remember much except that I was walking around and wound up at some man's house. He saved me and also started calling me Jane because I don't know anything about myself or where I came from. All I know is that I have at least two children because I was wearing a locket with an inscription and…and…" Jane's voice began to quiver, so she abruptly stopped talking. *Listen to myself! I sound utterly ridiculous.*

"And what?" Cindy asked, grabbing Jane's hands in hers for comfort.

"…and I misplaced or lost it somewhere," Jane replied. She took a deep breath and gained her composure.

"Whom were you trying to get to? Not too many people live around here and maybe I know where the person's house is."

Jane responded. "It's the man who saved me. I'm very anxious to reach my family so he was going to take me to see somebody called Hannah who may have heard news reports about my being a missing person. His name is Jack Beam or Bean—I don't know which is real—but he's kind of…"

"A strange little man in an Idaho potato burlap shirt and bib-top baggy cutoff pants who claims he's a famous botanist. Right?" asked Cindy.

"Jeez, you got that right," Jane exclaimed. "You know him? Do you know where his house is?"

"I sure do. And I know about Hannah too. You are quite out of the way—you're on the wrong side of the forest. But if you come with me and help me to sneak back into my house for something important, that would be wonderful. There was no way to do that by myself. I will direct you on the right course from there. You'll be at Jack's house in no time. Hannah lives several miles from here, and certainly Jack should at least drive you there, if not directly farther to our village, a ways down road from her. Hannah helps a lot of people."

Goldie looked at Jane with saucer-wide eyes. "This is so amazing—so very fortunate for us that Cindy popped out of nowhere.

Going with her is our best bet, Jane. We'll do her a favor, and she'll do us a favor. What do you think?"

"You're right. We've got to get on track and quickly while we have some time before it gets dark," Jane replied. "But Cindy, I thought you said at first that you were running away, didn't you?"

"Yes. I'm in desperate straits. Given my situation it's my only hope to end my misery and abuse by my stepmother and her two, creepy daughters. I'll tell you what I can while we walk to my house. It will take less than a half hour if we keep up a reasonable pace. It's not a waste of time for you, because you need to head in that direction anyway."

Jane and Goldie picked up their things.

"By the way, what's with the broom, Goldie?" Cindy asked.

"Well, it's…it's my walking stick. That's what it is," Goldie replied defensively.

"Cool," Cindy said. "But don't you think it would be better to remove the bristles part? You just twist that off like a screw. Believe me I know about brooms!"

Goldie shrugged. "I like it like this. It's a conversation piece."

"I see," Cindy said with an understanding nod. "Stay in the middle as we walk, and I'll remember to face towards you when I'm talking."

They hustled along with Cindy walking lopsided in her odd shoes. As the threesome crossed the perimeter of the forest, Cindy said, "My dear mother died three years ago when I was fourteen years old. I'm an only child, and took it very badly because we were always very close. I frequently visit her grave to kind of connect with her spirit and bring her only fresh flowers. Um, I just hate those tacky plastic ones."

"I know how you feel," Goldie said. "My mom is gone too."

Cindy patted Goldie's back sympathetically and continued. "Dad became depressed and started hanging out at King's Tavern every night after work. It's a bar not too far from here. When he was home he would sleep a lot so I was left on my own, except I had a friend whose parents let me stay at their house over the weekends. If it weren't for them I don't know what I would have done. Dad made a very good living and gave me a lot of pretty things to wear—whatever I needed—plus he hired a housekeeper to do the cooking and cleaning. He wanted me to study a lot and do well at school so I could get into a good college."

While they walked deeper into the woods along a wide, cleared path, the earth crackled under their feet. Jane was grateful for the shade provided by the towering pines whose moss-caked trunks towered like skinny high-rise office buildings. Alongside them the ground was choked with low thorny brush, fallen pinecones and interlaced branches that eerily poked and jabbed at her. Jane swatted at insects circling her excitedly, attracted to her sweat in the humid environment. She became distracted with her thoughts. *These bugs are driving me crazy. Jeez, this is like déjà vu all over again.* She tuned back to what Cindy was saying.

"Dad met this floozy named Letty, and they struck up a relationship. She looks like a pumpkin to me because she's round and squat with orangey hair and a little bun on top like a stem. Her ugliness is also reflected in her evil daughters, Zella and Asia. I don't know what Dad saw in her, but as fate would have it they wound up getting married, and Letty came to live at my house along with her girls. Collectively I call them, 'The Steps.' That day was the beginning of the end for me."

"Zella and Asia are both airheads and a little older than me—though not by much. Zella's a month older, and Asia's about a year older. Believe me, if they spent a day at a store cosmetic counter getting a makeover, that wouldn't put a dent in improving their sour looks. Letty turned out to be quite a shrew, and within the space of two years she had dominated Dad to such an extent that he had a fatal heart attack."

Both Jane and Goldie gasped.

"Oh, Cindy, that's awful—to lose both your mom and dad so soon," Jane cried. "I'm so sorry for you."

"Thank you, but you haven't heard the half of it." Cindy pushed aside a low hanging vine as they approached it. "Under Dad's will

Letty was named my legal guardian until I turn twenty-one, and all his money rolled into two trusts: one for Letty with income for life, remainder to her daughters, and the other income for me until I became twenty-one at which point I would get all of that trust's principal and interest outright."

"Almost immediately after high school graduation, Letty fired our housekeeper to save more money for herself and her daughters. Then she gave Zella and Asia all my nice clothes and designer shoes. Each day the three of them tormented me. Having no other place to go, I was forced to do the house chores like laundry, cleaning, cooking, and so on. To maintain my sanity, I would sing a lot, and since Letty would get so ticked off hearing me sound happy I sang even more for spite."

"Letty took my bed away, leaving me to sleep on an inflatable mattress in the cold and damp basement. I've been very afraid to tell anyone or to run away, because the old coot threatened to get her nasty brother to find me. He's the leader of a gang called the Devils. She said he would ruin my pretty face and hurt anyone who helped me. Well, the woman could steal a chunk of my life, but I was determined she would never take my soul."

"Gosh, this is so sad and awful for you," Jane said. She could see that Goldie was enthralled with the story.

"How much further do we have to go?" Goldie asked.

"We're almost there." Cindy replied. "Now get this. A flyer came in the mail announcing that King's Tavern was hosting a big Karaoke talent show and beer festival in two weeks, which is tonight. Everyone who comes whether to sing or not, is required to dress up especially nicely. Mr King said he would give $1,500 to whoever was crowned the winner, and I could surely use that money when I decide to get out of this place. Of course, The Steps got it into their twisted minds that one of them would win, even though they are all tone deaf, and that they would look simply fabulous in what were *my* beautiful clothes."

" 'Lots of luck, ugly duckling,' they all snarled at me after I said I would like to go. 'Looking the way you do you wouldn't get past the bouncers at the door,' Zella had said to me."

"I still remember how their scornful laughter echoed throughout the house. I hate them so much!" Cindy clenched her fists irately. "I want to make them eat their words, but I have a dilemma. I already have the voice, but I would need nice clothes and shoes if I were to go. Fortunately I had saved a frumpy, yellow, calico sundress I had worn in a high school play as one of the chorus singers in *Oklahoma!* I figured no one would care, and anything goes today anyway. But I absolutely could not walk into King's Tavern wearing the clunky sheepskin boots Letty had let me keep for the winter or a pair of shoddy flip-flops I wear in the summer.

"The good thing was that I had received an allowance from my dad until he died, some of which I had hidden away. So I snuck out today as soon as The Steps left to get their hair and nails done. Conservatively speaking, I had a window of two hours to get back and settled in before they returned. I put on my flip-flops and dashed as fast as I could to the shoe store.

Jane's ears perked up and she stopped walking. "Wait ... There's a shoe store around here? I didn't think there were any stores. There's barely anything. What else is there?"

"Ha ha. Well of course there are a few stores," Cindy replied. "Small shops. What do you think? We're not a hunter-gatherer colony, you know. We need to buy things. One is a convenience store. The owners either deal directly with local suppliers or buy items in town down road and then sell them up here for a little profit. Living here is like living on a small island. Maybe worse because we can't get phone or television signals.

"So as I was saying—the flips were super hard to run in, even though I'm in excellent physical condition. But they were a much better option than wearing my boots which would have slowed me down, although I have to say that the custom orthotics I have in them are great support for my feet. I grabbed the first pair of decent, inexpensive, open toe high heels I could find. The problem is that I have a very small and narrow foot that has always made it difficult for me to find shoes that fit. Plus, since I didn't have much time to fuss with trying on shoes, whatever first came closest to fitting I would have to make it work."

"There were no other customers when I got there, only a handsome sales associate whose name tag said 'Yung Printz.' After I told him where I was going tonight and what a rush I was in, he offered to help me find a nice pair of shoes. I told him my shoe size, five-and-a-half narrow, and that I wanted something inexpensive that would go with my yellow dress."

"Yung and I had a chance to chat a lot while I tried on the various pairs of shoes he brought me. Two pairs were very nice and fit okay, but I didn't have enough money to buy them, so I had to put them aside. Then the shoes I had my heart set on were not available in my size. They were much too big, and I would have had to stuff paper in them to keep them on. Anyway, they looked too clownish on my feet. So I had to go with a pair of clear plastic sandals which are a child's size large."

"Meanwhile, I had no idea that so much time had passed, and when I asked Yung what his watch said, I was shocked. I was behind schedule in allowing myself ample time to get back home. As I was paying, I noticed there was a red magic marker by the cash register. I asked Yung if I could have it to color my toenails with. He said sure, but otherwise he would lend me money to buy nail polish. I would have liked that, but unfortunately there simply was no time to go to the general store for a bottle. I thanked him for everything and bolted out of there so fast that I didn't have a second to turn around and answer his earlier question about where I lived."

"As I ran home like a lunatic, I felt kind of lopsided and looked down at my feet. To my horror I saw two different shoes! I had on a left flip-flop and a right plastic sandal. I freaked out. I realized I had left their mates in the store, and it would be a big risk to go back for them and safely beat The Steps home. Then to make matters worse, when I went to get the spare key that's usually hidden under a stone in the backyard, it wasn't there. One of those dreadful sisters may have taken it today or forgot to put it back another time. They are both very stupid besides being conceited, and believe me they have nothing going for them. And since I knew I couldn't get in through the cellar window by myself, it was a defining moment. I had no choice but to forget the Karaoke contest and run away from there forever. So here I am!"

"Yikes!" Goldie cried. "This is some blazing hot situation you're in, huh? Whatever you need us to do it has to be reasonable. I don't want to get involved in something that's illegal or risky."

"Not to mention that we're running out of time," Jane added. She winced as a stabbing pain shot through her forehead, and turned away reflexively feeling suddenly sick. Behind her, as if from another place and another time, she heard an echoing, loud, repetitive beeping. What she said seemed to have triggered a memory, or something, distracting her from the moment. "We're running out of time doctor," someone whispered urgently. "Her BP is crashing. Quick, help me get her up on her knees…" Jane's nausea grew worse…

"Jane, Jane are you ok?" said Cindy suddenly. She grabbed her arm and tried to support her as she sank to the ground. "You look as white as a ghost? Do you need to sit down a bit?"

Jane knelt, the world spinning, catching her breath and her wits. She waved a hand in an effort to look like she was ok but felt completely disoriented and weak-kneed.

"I'm fine. Really. So sorry." Slowly the world stopped spinning, the pain in her head lessened, and she came back to the present. She found herself sitting in the middle of the road, feeling exhausted, her nausea slowly receding, finally taking in what Cindy had been saying. It sounded so familiar somehow. In fact all of this sounded familiar, but she couldn't put her finger on why…

As Jane regained her presence of mind once her headache went away, she slowly and cautiously stood up, her maternal instinct spurring her desire to help Cindy.

Cindy started speaking again as if nothing had happened. "Don't worry. It's nothing illegal, and it's not going to take long," she said assuredly. "Listen. We're approaching the driveway to my house, and until I first check something out we all have to be quiet."

When they came upon an opening to a road, Cindy suddenly put her arms out to stop Jane and Goldie. She pointed to a barely visible string that was horizontally suspended between two little trees, about two feet off the ground.

"It's all clear," Cindy announced. "See it didn't take long, right? And the good thing is that The Steps didn't get back yet. Otherwise their car would have snapped the string. I hung that there so I would know what to expect if I came up with a solution and decided to return. Come on."

How really clever of her, Jane thought. She and Goldie stood still, dumbfounded. What they saw directly ahead of them was way beyond what they imagined. The typical dirt road was bordered on both sides by gray bricks and led to a huge, dreary, old stone house of Gothic design. It had four gables and three stone chimney stacks protruding through its steeply pitched slate roof. A row of five arched windows on the second floor were each broken up into three panes of yellow stained glass. They were repeated in clear glass on the ground floor, except one was replaced by a forbidding black double wooden door recessed in a portico supported by two columns.

Cindy looked back. "Why are you both just standing there?" she asked. "Never mind what you see. Stay with me."

Cindy led them into the rear of the house along a mossy brick path on the right side. It connected to a patio on which three wrought iron chaise lounges with garish red cushions were arranged in a semi-circle. The rest of the yard was covered in gravel and sur-rounded by tall dense evergreen trees. The rear windows were iden-tical to the ones in the front except that in the center and close to the ground was one small transom window divided into two panes of blackened glass.

"So now what?" Jane asked.

"What I have to do is remove a ground level window to get into my bedroom below. I already have it pried off. And when I say *below*, it's *way* below. It's not a typical basement. It's more like a dungeon, which means the window is very high off the floor. And I mean REALLY high."

Cindy grabbed one of the cushions and walked over to the window, placing the cushion on the ground next to it. "A dungeon? Cripes! Are you serious?" Jane asked. She right away thought of the missing girl.

"I said it was *like* a dungeon," Cindy replied as she worked.

She tugged on two cords that were tucked into the metal casement—one on the top and one on the bottom. Jane and Goldie watched as she grabbed the cords and wound each of them around her hands. She gave a tug and the whole window frame dislodged from the opening. She tipped it gently onto the ground, laying it to the side.

"By any chance, while you've been living in your like-a-dungeon quarters, did you happen to run across or hear about a little girl that has been missing from the area?" Jane asked.

"The one that turned up on some milk cartons, you mean?" Cindy asked.

"Yes, that one," Jane responded. "Why do you ask if it's that one? Are there others?"

"There have been, a couple of children, maybe over the last five years," Cindy said. "I know one was a girl who was found dead, the poor thing, and the other, a boy, was never found. Maybe the little girl you have in mind is the one who was here a few weeks ago. I can't say for sure because I tend to lose track of time. I never saw her myself. She was selling all occasion and holiday wrapping paper to raise money for her class trip. Letty, in a rare form of thoughtfulness, had invited her into the kitchen to place an order. She actually had the nerve to shout down to me to ask if I needed any. Then she said, 'Oh how silly of me—you have no friends and anyway, what would you ever have to wrap?' I remember Letty broke out in a fit of laughter as did Asia and Zella who were making their own selections."

"I went up the stairs to listen from behind the door. They ordered ten rolls in all. In fact Asia and Zella in unison confirmed the order extremely loudly so I would hear, just to be spiteful as usual. Later there was a lot of shuffling around overhead, like they were moving furniture. Whatever happened after the girl took down the order, I don't know."

"That sounds very suspicious if you ask me," Goldie said.

Jane nodded. "I'll be sure to mention it to Jack when we see him."

"There. It's ready," Cindy announced. "Next, I need us to form a human chain so I can be lowered in. My bed is right underneath the window, against the foundation wall so if I slipped it would cushion my fall. Once I get in, you can continue on with your journey. I'll tell you where to go. It's not far and is very straightforward."

"Oh, so let me get this all straight," Jane stated. "Your room is way underground, it's like a dungeon, and you left the house today and returned home with mismatched shoes. Now you're in a hurry to get back inside before your little escapade is discovered by your gross stepsisters when they return from their primping or else you'll be in danger. And all Goldie and I have to do is turn into a human chain, so you can literally drop in, whereupon at that point you will give us the directions we need. Yes? Am I right?" Jane was more inclined to forget about helping Cindy and immediately get on her way to find her family.

indy shrugged her shoulders, her eyebrows lifted and her eyes wide with hope. "Well I guess that just about sums it up," she remarked. She pressed her hands together in a praying gesture. "Please ... please won't you do it?" She anxiously looked at Jane and Goldie.

"Well, I don't know," Jane replied. "It sounds so complicated— so over the top to me. Why can't we just hold your hands and drop you in?"

"Because you simply can't. I need at least two other bodies in tandem so I can get lower. Otherwise I might bounce off the mattress as though it were a trampoline and break my legs if not my head when I land on the bare floor. I could be lying there seriously injured ..."

"Oh, Jeez!" Jane annoyingly interrupted. "Enough. This scheme of yours is very bizarre."

"I agree," Goldie added. "Can't we find a long branch or a rope for you to dangle from? We'll hold the other end and lower you..."

Cindy put her hand up. "Stop. Please. Please. We're wasting very precious time. Let's be realistic."

"Oh that's funny. *We* should be realistic, she says," Jane muttered.

Cindy kept talking. "There's no time for a scavenger hunt for items. Besides, the branch suggestion would never work anyway. It would be horizontal when it passed through the window, which does me no good for going downward close to the wall, not to mention that it would probably snap in two from my weight. Please. My plan will work. It's not as bad as it sounds. It will be very quick, and then you can be on your way in no time."

"I guess we'll give it a try and see how it works out," Jane said, emitting a sigh. "But under one condition: you'll tell us now, not after, how to get to Jack's house from here. What do you say, Goldie?"

"Yeah," Goldie replied, halfheartedly with a shrug. "Let's get this over with. But it sounds very weird to me."

"Oh thank you. Thank you. This means so much to me. As to the directions..." Cindy pointed. "Go out the way we came in over there and turn right onto the wide path we were on before. Walk a short distance, about 200 feet or so, until you come to a tree on your right that has three red birdhouses hanging from its lower limb. You can't miss it. You'll be able to see it from a distance. There's a narrow path of trampled woodsy vegetation beginning near the foot of that tree. Stay on it for about fifteen minutes, if you hustle, and it will take you out of the forest to open space. It's similar to the environment where I first came upon you except you will see tall rock formations scattered about in the distance. Walk in that direction. Get your bearings by looking for a solitary grouping of three flowering trees which have been shaped into what looks like to me as lollipops."

Jane let out a gasp. "This is bizarre. It all sounds so terribly familiar. I...I...don't know why...but..."

"I doubt you've ever before seen anything so ridiculous," Cindy said. "Before you get to the lollipop trees, which are near Jack's house, you can't miss a stupid sign hanging on a rock formation that says, 'Welcome to Tree City.' Got it?"

"Let me see," Jane said. She ran through the instructions again.

"You got it," Cindy said. "So are you two ready? We don't have much time, but this should only take a few minutes."

Jane and Goldie nodded.

"Here's how this will work. Both of you are going to lie facing down on the gravel, legs straight out towards the house. I'm going to go first of course, and partially extend into the opening. Goldie, you line up in front of me, and I'll hold onto your ankles. Jane, you lie in front of Goldie, and she'll hold onto your ankles. Then I will signal you both to slowly slither backwards in a snakelike motion so that Goldie will ultimately wind up extending more than half her body into the opening, effectively lowering me down about three feet. At that point, I'll be lined up with my bed below. I'll let go and drop. Then with Jane anchored in place, Goldie, you use her legs to scramble up and out of the opening."

"Wait a minute, Cindy. *Anchored?* Anchored to what? Just how am I supposed to anchor myself?" Jane asked.

"Ah, good question, and funny you should ask," Cindy replied. "Since you're the anchor person, you obviously need to secure yourself to something to create friction. I have just the right equipment for that."

Cindy shot off like a lightning bolt to one of the nearby trees and yanked out two objects from the back of its trunk.

Goldie made a circular motion with her index finger by her temple.

Jane mouthed to Goldie, "Crazy for sure. Let's do what we need to do quickly and get out of here. I'm having second thoughts about helping her with this, but she appears to be in such a quandary. I feel sorry for her. I never imagined we would be doing something so convoluted."

"Jeez, what have you got there?" Jane asked when Cindy returned. Jane and Goldie each took one item and examined it.

"They look like hammers of some sort," Goldie observed while folding her arms and making a face.

"Well, you're close," Cindy replied, ignoring Goldie's body language. "These are ice axes which belonged to my father. He was a mountaineer in his youth. As you can see they have a very sharp, steel spike, which has a remarkable bite. It easily penetrates hard surfaces on steep terrain. Jane needs to use these as ground grippers, walking one hand behind the other while slithering backwards. You don't have to use much pressure. Simply snap your wrists and it will dig in. Push forward and pull up to extract it. Do you get the picture? Try it out first."

Jane removed her bear spray holster and put it on the ground with her canvas bag of snacks. She extended her body facing down and slinked backwards using the tools to pierce the earth underneath the gravel. "I think I can manage this," she exclaimed, quite surprised at her dexterity. *This is absurd. What am I getting myself into?*

"Be extremely careful of the spike," Cindy warned. "Don't look back or away. I don't want you to hurt yourself. It's very sharp. Goldie, keep your body tight and your head facing forward for balance as you hold onto Jane's ankles. I'll signal you by tugging on your ankles when I want you to start moving backwards, and I'll shout *go* at the same time for Jane to hear. We'll start off close to the window and take it very slowly to give Jane a chance to securely walk her axes in baby steps. You'll slither one way to the right and then to the left and pause. Then again, slither one way to the right and then to the left and pause. So on—I think only a few times—until Goldie's legs are dangling inside at a right angle to her upper body. At that point I'll shout *stop* as I let go of you and drop to my bed. Got it? You'll see."

Cindy ran off without waiting for an acknowledgment. Jane and Goldie were so taken aback with this elaborate plan that they could only react with blank stares while Cindy proceeded to sit on the window ledge facing in. After removing her sandal and flip-flop and tossing them inside along with what appeared to be the red marker, she pivoted around to face them, resting on her knees. She pulled the lounge cushion towards her creating a soft bridge from the opening to the ground, which was a little lower.

After positioning herself Cindy shouted, "I'm ready." She gave a thumbs-up signal to Goldie and gestured that she come over to lie down in front of her.

Jane rolled her eyes as she looked at Goldie and said, "Let's get this ridiculous thing over with as soon as we can. Go as close as you can so she can grab your ankles."

Goldie nodded, and like Jane, removed her bear spray holster and laid it on the ground along with her broom and her own canvas bag They set themselves up in chain formation. As soon as she had a firm grip on Goldie's ankles she gave them a tug and shouted *go*. Immediately they started the slithering movements as planned. With all her might, Jane manipulated the ax blades into and out of the ground, one after the other, in a backward "walking" motion. Facilitated by the rolling action of the little gravel pebbles, she and Goldie synchronized their movements like partners in an ice dance performance. Holding tightly on to Goldie, Cindy descended into the dark abyss.

"Stop!" Cindy screamed.

The rest happened so fast.

Goldie shouted, "Jane, Cindy dropped off. Go forward. Hurry! Pull me out. My legs are dangling. Go forward. Pull me! Pull me out! Pull me now!"

Simultaneously Jane screamed, panicked and oblivious to the abject hopelessness of her commands falling on deaf ears. "Goldie, let go! The ax is slipping in the gravel! I can't get a good grip! Let go of my legs! Let go! Let go!"

If Jane were to assume that her pleas had emerged as spoken words, she recognized they were fruitless as she and Goldie became swallowed up by the void.

14

ESCAPE AGAIN!

Jane and Goldie landed hard on Cindy, in a heap on the mattress below. Once Jane came to she became aware of a heavy weight crushing her chest. Her shoulder was being shaken and someone gently tapped the sides of her face.

"Jane, wake up. Jane, can you hear me?"

She tried to respond, but no sound came out, and her eyelids were too heavy to lift.

"Come on. Open your eyes," the voice said.

Jane detected a radiance in front of her and when she was finally able to open her eyes, the shock of the glare of a flashlight caused her to reflexively shut them. She rested a moment, lying still where she was. Finally she tried opening them again.

"Where am I? What happened?" Jane murmured.

"Shhh. It's me."

"Who?" Jane asked.

"Cindy."

"And me, Goldie."

"Jeez. Who? Where the...?" She rubbed her head. "Ouch! Get that light out of my face. All I can see are white dots."

Just then a door slammed, followed by the sound of shuffling feet.

"Shhhh! It's me again. Cindy." She whispered, "You're on my bed in the basement. You, Goldie and I fell from the window high up there," she pointed with her index finger. "I have to talk very quickly. The Steps are back. We got here just in time!"

"Steps?"

"Jane. Get a grip. Keep your voice low so they don't hear us. You know—The Steps. My cruel stepmother and her two gross daughters. Remember?"

"Oh. Sure. It's coming back to me." Jane rubbed her head.

"The reason for the flashlight is because I don't want to turn on the lamp and give us away," Cindy said. "Fortunately, there's no switch at the top of the stairs, so it's better to have The Steps encounter darkness if the door is opened."

Jane touched her head again and could feel some soreness, not unlike what she had before. *Just what I need*, she thought. *Another blow to cloud my memory even more.*

"You were out cold for a couple of minutes," Cindy continued. "I think you hit your head on the wall, ricocheting off Goldie when you landed. We all crashed on top of each other. It's about twenty feet down, so it's a darn good thing my bed was right here to cushion the drop. What in the world went wrong up there?"

"Well, your grandiose idea didn't pan out," Jane replied. "I couldn't secure us into the ground. The gravel was too deep in one area, and of course Goldie couldn't hear me yelling so she kept wiggling and pulling. The next thing I knew I was through the window opening and..."

"Shh. Stay quiet. Get up. Quickly," Cindy spoke softly as she stood up on the floor in the midst of the faint light cast by the window above.

"Now what?" Jane asked. "I want to get out of here."

"Don't worry, you will, and I'm going to be prancing away from here with you. Keep your voice down. Both of you, get off the bed," Cindy ordered as she nudged Goldie. "Hurry!"

Jane grabbed Goldie's hand and signaled her to be quiet. They both rose and stood by Cindy.

Jane and Goldie looked up at the window above them and gasped.

"We came in through that? From all the way up there?" Goldie asked incredulously.

Cindy nodded. "Shhh. Quickly, take this," Cindy ordered while tossing a quilted coverlet to them. She pointed with the flashlight beam. "Go to that corner and cover yourselves up. I'll throw some clothing on top and make it look like a laundry pile in case someone comes down, which would be highly unusual. But I'll make sure this isn't one of those rare times. I'll let you know when the coast is clear."

"I'll give you a little jab to your shoulder once I hear that the coast is clear," Jane said to Goldie who nodded in acknowledgment.

Stepping into the shadows, they went over to the designated spot and lay down back to back, close to the wall, tightly folded in fetal positions. Jane promptly pulled the quilt over their bodies and assumed the outside position that gave her the possibility of peeking into the room. She lifted up a corner and stared into the dimly lit area just as the sound of footsteps above got louder. When the door creaked open at the top of the stairs, she watched as Cindy rapidly slipped on her boots and threw the red marker, the sandal, and the flip-flop under her mattress. She then sprawled out on her bed, and within seconds, a recognizable gruff voice called out from the landing at the top of the stairs.

"Hey you, Miss Ugly."

"What is it, Zella?" Cindy asked weakly followed by a contrived moan.

"What are you doing down there in the dark at this time of day? Resting? Loafing around? Suffice it to say, obviously not doing your household chores. Typical! From what we can see, you haven't made a dent in getting them done. For one thing, the crystal drops on the dining room chandelier are not glimmering like they are supposed to, had you cleaned them."

"That's because I'm sick and puking all over the place," Cindy feebly responded. "I have a bad stomach bug. I wouldn't come down here if I were you unless you want to catch it. And make sure you tell that to your mother and sister."

"Yuck. And take a chance that you might sneeze and get snot gunk all over me? Ick no. What a shame that we three have to bear the brunt of your uselessness because of your unhealthy state," Zella croaked. "Well dear girl, while you waste time recuperating that means you'll have all the more to do to catch-up as soon as you feel better. And here's the list of extra things that Mother noted for you to do tonight. I'm tossing the notepaper on the staircase. No doubt you'll be a very busy little punk over the next couple of days. Too bad. Tsk tsk. And I hate to put a crimp in what I bet is a vicious trick to contaminate us, the weasel that you are, but I'll be sure to disinfect the door knob on both sides and my hands as well. Don't think for a moment that I won't tip off Mother and Asia to your sneaky biohazard scheme."

Jane and Goldie remained still and quiet under the coverlet, breathing as shallowly as possible.

"For your information," Zella continued, her voice resonating loudly within the room, "Mother and Asia are getting dressed now and putting on the finishing touches as I already did, and we will very soon be on our way to King's Tavern for the Karaoke contest. Each of us had a mud facial at the spa, and our nails and hair done. Oooh la la. Too bad you couldn't come along. Oh well. You would have loved it, and I must say we all look quite stunning with our makeovers. We'll be sure to take many photos and share them with you so you can see the fun you missed. Tough luck for you, little runt, that you can't join us tonight, not that you have a snowball's chance in hell to win anyway. Got to go." Zella howled in laughter as she left, slamming the cellar door behind her. The sound of her heels click-clacking on the bare floor receded as she moved away.

After a few moments at a level of silence so thick it could be cut with a knife, they were jarred by the loud thump and click of the front entrance door and the revving-up and ebbing of the car engine as it took off.

"It's all clear to come out now," Cindy announced as she turned on the light. "I'm getting ready quickly so that we can scoot."

"I'm certainly for that," Jane said. "This detour that we took is way beyond what I bargained for."

Jane poked Goldie's shoulder to let her know that it was safe, and they both threw the coverlet and the stack of laundry off to the side. It took a bit of time to get used to the glare at which point they could see Cindy standing by the illuminated bedside lamp with her foot raised on the nightstand. She was coloring her toes with the red marker.

"Charming. Very charming," Jane chuckled.

"Well, you may think this is funny, but of course the bigger joke will be on The Steps, as I'm going to King's Tavern no matter what," Cindy resolutely remarked. "I can't wait to see their faces when I walk in, let alone appear at the microphone to sing." Cindy let out a hearty laugh. "I picture myself winning the $1,500 and running away from this rat hole forever. But even if I don't win, I'm out of here. I could care less that Letty's connected to a bunch of thugs who will hunt me down. It can be a hundred thugs she knows. A thousand thugs. I'm not spending another moment in this place. No more washing dishes, getting on my hands and knees to scrub floors, cooking meals and taking a myriad of other orders from the Steps at their whims."

Goldie sat motionless and disinterested on the bed. As Cindy was engaged in her ranting and primping, Jane looked around and got a view of her dreadful and meagerly furnished sleeping quarters. Sinewy roots climbed stone walls that oozed a slimy dripping substance that ran along the perimeter of the wavy brick floor. Cobwebs dangled on the rafters of the high ceilings, and a skewed wooden staircase directly ahead led steeply up to the door to the main part of the house. Jane thought that without a doubt this deep cellar, probably constructed centuries ago, must be bone chilling in the winter months. The only elements that suggested an iota of potential warmth were the huge furnace across from where Cindy slept and a little tattered area rug near her bed. The other squalid details she noticed for the first time were a small, round, wooden table and an old metal chair. The room reeked of misery.

She watched as Cindy walked over to a shabby chest and opened one of the drawers.

"Hey Jane, can you help me get this on?" Cindy asked as she pulled out a flouncy, long, yellow dress.

"Sure," Jane replied, "I'll do anything to move things along quickly. I must get out of here, like right now, before something else bad happens. I've had enough excitement. My heart aches for my family and my head hurts." Suddenly she heard a loud snort and looked over at Goldie who was sound asleep on Cindy's bed.

Cindy peeled down to her underclothes, and, after quickly passing a few strokes of a brush through her hair, she tied on a delicately sequenced ribbon. "It will only take a minute, and then I promise we'll go. I'm going to hold my arms up over my head. All you have to do is align the armholes with my hands."

Jane gathered up the bottom of the dress to its middle and did what she was instructed to do. Once Cindy's arms were through the armholes, she let the dress unravel by itself over the rest of Cindy's body.

"There," Cindy said, while smoothing out the material over her tiny hips. "Would you please tie the long streamer into a bow in the back?" Jane complied, noticing that the glittery material matched the band in her hair.

Cindy checked herself out in a cracked mirror that hung over the chest. She turned around. "So, how do I look?" she asked, raising her voice over Goldie's echoing snores.

Jane stepped back to get a better perspective. She gasped, being quite captivated by Cindy's transformation and glamorous appearance. The dress was fitted with a tight bodice and the fabric flared out somewhat below her waist, dropping to just above her ankles. Her flowing hair was swept back off her face with the sequined ribbon that matched the bow on the back of her dress. She looked like a princess. The only thing missing in the picture were her shoes.

"You look absolutely beautiful, Cindy," Jane exclaimed. "But what are you going to wear on your feet?"

"No problem," Cindy replied. "I'm going to wear my flip-flop and sandal as before and stop into the shoe store on the way to the Tavern to pick up their mates. It's open late tonight, thank God. I think the new sandals will complete the ensemble perfectly. Ready to go? Go wake up your daughter."

"You bet, I'm ready, except Goldie's not my daughter," Jane replied. "We only recently met. Don't take this personally, but I won't feel relaxed until I'm far away from here. The last thing we need is for The Steps to come back and then we get trapped in this dungeon. I don't know how you lasted here all this time. Really. I admire your courage."

"Well to tell you the truth," Cindy replied, "I cope as well as I do because I dream a lot. I'm fascinated by what my mind produces whether I'm daydreaming or asleep. Everything seems lifelike and vivid, yet gets so twisted up at times that I can't make sense of anything. A good thing is that I'm always freely out and about in my dreams looking for something. I don't know what it is I'm after, but I never give up. On the other hand, I sometimes dream I'm in a hospital room looking at someone lying in bed motionless, like in a coma or something, and at other times it's me that way, except I can see and hear what's going on, but people don't believe that I can because I can't talk to them. They come in and read to me and talk to me and play music or other soothing sounds, and then suddenly they all leave and I'm alone and I can't talk or move or do anything…" She paused in her chattering, her voice catching as emotion overcame her. "No matter, though. Because tonight I can be free of it all."

Jane wasn't sure what to say in response. Goldie was still snoring peacefully in a deep sleep, and Jane shook her awake.

"Mom?" Goldie murmured as she awoke.

Jane was taken aback. *How weird that Goldie was calling out "mom" and Cindy just referred to Goldie as my daughter.* Tears welled up in her eyes as the motherly words plucked at her heartstrings.

Goldie sat up fully alert and looked at Jane, then at her surroundings and then back at Jane.

"Goldie, "I'm sorry to wake you, but you have to get up. We're getting out of here now...quickly...before The Steps have some reason to come back."

Goldie screeched when she saw Cindy.

"Wow!" Goldie cried. "What a transformation! You look gorgeous! Did you get tapped by a magic wand? Except apparently it missed your feet because you're still wearing those mismatched shoes. What's up with that?"

Cindy laughed. "Thanks. I've been wishing for a magic wand for a long time but no such luck. I'm going to the shoe store to pick up the other sandal on my way to King's Tavern, but first I'll get you both on the road that will take you back to Jack's house. Then I'll be on my way. Come on. Follow me, and tip-toe as we go up."

Cindy headed for the stairs with Jane and Goldie practically riding on her heels. She stopped abruptly and turned to face them. "Sorry. I forgot something."

Cindy went over to the dresser and grabbed a black valise stuffed beneath it. "I wouldn't want to leave this behind. It has a change of normal clothes, my boots and a 32-ounce bottle of pepper spray. I mean hot, hot, very hot pepper spray. I made it myself after I got the urge to leave here, before I even had a plan."

Goldie smiled. "Hey. We think along the same lines but for different purposes. Jane and I each have bear spray. We put it down outside with our other stuff."

"Cool. We'll get it later," Cindy responded. "If it stops wild bears, then it'll certainly stop any human wild life that might stand in our way."

"How did you make it?" Goldie asked. "I love creating concoctions."

"It's simple," Cindy said. "I used stuff found in the house and collected the ingredients over many months so The Steps wouldn't notice. The mixture includes ten tablespoons of Cayenne pepper, two tablespoons of finely minced garlic, two tablespoons of baby oil, and fourteen ounces of white vinegar. I strained the mixture using a piece of discarded stocking so nothing can clog the spray holes, and mixed it all together and poured it into this all-purpose spray bottle. I've been keeping it cool in the basement, which makes it stronger.

"Off we go," Cindy said as she headed for the stairs.

When she reached the landing at the top, she very slowly turned the knob and opened the door a crack. Jane could hear a beeping sound.

Cindy softly shut the door, until the bolt clicked. When she turned around, Goldie and Jane saw horror written all over her face. She gestured for them to be quiet and to go back down the stairs

"Oh cripes!" Cindy whined when they got to the bottom.

"What? What is it now?" Jane and Goldie asked anxiously.

"It's a trigger trap," Cindy said. "A signal. Those rat-faced Steps have a line hooked up from this door to something out front. My guess it's to alert someone when the door opened. I wouldn't be surprised if it's one of Letty's big thugs standing guard. Argh!"

"Now what? What should we do?" Jane questioned in a trembling voice.

"The only option we have is for me to bring out the heavy artillery—the hot pepper spray," Cindy said as she rummaged through her valise for the item. Once she had the spray securely in her hand, Cindy turned to Jane and held out the bag. "Here, you take this, or better yet, have Goldie carry it, at least until we are out of the house and in the clear."

Cindy led them up the stairs again in single file. Jane's head started pounding and adrenalin coursed through her veins. She had to get out of this place and reach Jack, no matter what. *Somewhere my children are calling for me…* She sighed mournfully.

As they neared the top landing, Jane heard approaching footsteps that sounded like squeaking tennis shoes. A lump formed in her throat, and she could barely breathe. She turned to hand the bag to Goldie and signaled to her to stay back. Goldie retreated two steps and crouched down in the darkness. Jane could barely see her form, now camouflaged by the black bag she had placed on the step ahead and in front of her face.

"Listen carefully," Cindy said directly into Jane's ear. "The guard is right outside this door. I'll go out nonchalantly since he won't be surprised to see me. I'll leave the door open a bit so you can see what's going on, but stay low to the floor so you don't attract any attention. I'll distract him so he won't look down. Now listen carefully."

Jane summoned up as much power of concentration as she could as Cindy continued with her instructions. "On the far wall to the right is an archway alongside the refrigerator. That leads to the dining room which is adjacent to the living room, and we will be heading left through there towards the front door. As soon as I spray the pepper concoction in this bad boy's face and he's disabled, I'm going to the fridge to grab a large can and will turn to give you a high sign. That's your cue to come out. We're going to bolt for the archway. Every second counts so you have to react quickly. Make sure that Goldie has the bag and is right on your heels like a fly to sticky paper. Got all that? Ready?"

Jane's throat was so dry that she could barely emit a sound. Instead, she nodded and dropped backwards to reach Goldie and grab her hand. She led Goldie to the step directly below the landing, and winced as the tread creaked from their weight. She signaled her to crouch down just as Cindy twisted the knob and peeked into the room. Looking up from below Cindy's feet, Jane watched as she then pushed on the door, revealing a husky man standing and facing the opening, alertly posed in anticipation of something about to happen. From her viewing position at floor level she observed his mid-topped sneakers with open laces and his low-ride black jeans with a bit of his rounded midriff exposed beneath a white tank top.

Head to waist, the man was covered in gaudy bling. His thick, bulldog neck was draped with multiple gold and silver chains of varying lengths, and a large black cross dangling from one of them. Adding to that a thick gold braided bracelet, gold watch, and diamond rings, and he was a living poster child for conspicuous consumption. A red bandana encircled his head over slick-backed hair and was tied into a knot, fastened in the front. A light blinked underneath the band at his right ear. Jane could barely contain her astonishment at the variety of prominent tattoos on his face, upper arms, and neck. Completing his ensemble was a puffy silver jacket, casually thrown over his left shoulder.

Everything about this person was menacing. *No wonder Cindy is so intimidated by the possibility of being tracked by one of these tough guys,* Jane thought. She could feel her anxiety mounting and an adrenalin rush began to course through her body, causing her to quiver. Just as the anticipation became too much to bear, Cindy stepped forward and quickly swung the door behind her, making sure she left it ajar for Jane to see through.

Cindy called out, "Hey there!" The man raised his eyebrows in surprise and stepped forward. Cindy held one hand down to her side, carefully positioned over the pepper spray.

"Yeah?" the burly man gruffly responded, clearly taken aback by Cindy's glamorous appearance.

"Who are you?" Cindy asked.

"I'm Toro, one a Letty's boyz. Where d'ya think yaw gawin', ma lidda hotty?" He assumed an aggressive stance as Cindy approached him.

"Why, I'm going right here," Cindy coquettishly remarked, quite startling him. "See anythin' ya like? Wan me to give ya somethin'?" The man's face lecherously lit up as he simultaneously smacked his lips.

"Ew, gross!" Cindy squealed, and in one fluid movement, she extended her arm out in front and sprayed the pepper solution into Toro's eyes, taking him completely off-guard.

He screamed in pain, "Ya lidda bitch!" and began to wipe his eyes frantically with his fingers while screaming louder and louder. Cindy quickly sprayed his hands as an added irritant, getting some on his ear as he turned.

Seizing the opportunity of Toro's incapacity, Cindy made a bee-line for the refrigerator and removed a large coffee can from the rear of the bottom shelf, after strewing all the contents onto the floor. She waived Jane and Goldie out whereupon Toro blindly lunged for

Cindy, incredibly managing to grab her wrist tightly as she darted past him. In desperation, he continued to rub his eyes with his tainted free hand, making the intense burning all the more acute.

"Let go of me!" Cindy shouted, dropping the can while trying to push him away.

"Yaw done faw babe," Toro said to Cindy, pulling her so tightly towards him that her compressed lungs emitted a rush of air. "My awdas wa ta snuff ya out if I had ta. An believe me, I'll do it very slowly and painfully, I might add. So in case ya have it in dat pretty lidda head of yaws dat you'll be carrying out yaw escape plans, well, lem me jus say dat reinfawcements are on da way. Ya can bet ya won't get outta dis alive." Toro, blinded as he was, was still ignorant to Jane's and Goldie's presence.

He used his free hand to reach into a back pocket, but Cindy twisted herself away, and Jane instinctively inserted herself between them. Still holding on to Cindy's wrist while she was screaming and clawing at him, Toro reacted with a miscalculated punch at Jane's face while yelling a sequence of very foul expletives.

Jane spontaneously moved one step to the right and swiped the punch away from her body with an open hand. Then without a second of hesitation, she performed a sequence of moves that came naturally to her. She grabbed Toro's free wrist and pushed his arm upwards, twisting it backwards and downwards as he gasped. The horrendous pain inflicted on him by this action forced him to let go of Cindy, who spontaneously crumbled to the ground. Goldie helped her to her feet.

As Toro dropped his upper body to follow his wrist, Jane gave him a head butt to his nose, stomped on his instep and used her palm to shove his face upwards from beneath his nostrils. A loud crack and a gush of blood gave her a clear indication that she had broken his nose. Barely able to see, and holding his damaged face, Toro began writhing on the floor and screaming like a toddler throwing a tantrum.

"Good grief, Jane. That was simply amazing action!" Goldie exclaimed.

"Ditto. Thank goodness that you're so skilled in martial arts," Cindy cried.

Jane stood motionless with her mouth agape, stunned by her apparent expertise. "I didn't know…I could do that…I…I…" she stammered.

"Here, take this, you brute," Cindy bellowed as she quickly bent down and sprayed some more of the pepper liquid into Toro's eyes and face. "Not so tough now, after all are you, Mr. Hulk, Huh?"

In rapid sequence, Cindy smoothed out her hair and dress and picked up the can, which had rolled under the table. Then she turned to Jane and Goldie.

"Come on! Time is precious," Cindy yelled. She began to run, leading them through the other rooms and out the front door as planned.

Suddenly Cindy froze in place, which caused both Jane and Goldie to nearly knock her over. Cindy's bag flew out of Goldie's hands as Goldie extended her arms in front of her for balance.

"Oh no! That creep, Toro, wasn't bluffing. We've got company. Look!" Cindy cried and pointed to a commotion on the road.

15

REINFORCEMENTS

"Duck down here behind the hedges," Cindy commanded. "Obviously Toro wasn't lying about the reinforcements! His buddies are swarming all over the place, and I bet they've set up a blockade on the road."

Goldie said, "He must have signaled for them somehow."

"They use walkie-talkies since there's no phone service," said Cindy.

Jane added, "Maybe he pressed some speaker or panic device in his pocket when he put his hand there. I noticed a blinking light by his ear. What do you think that was?"

"It's probably a two-way radio ear piece like the secret service people use," Cindy replied. "By the way, I can't thank you enough for what you did. You know, you saved us all with those neat self-defense moves. You really were amazing, but you seemed kind of hesitant. Why?"

"Surprised is more like it. I'm astonished and perplexed, to say the least. I didn't know I had martial arts skills. They just came out of nowhere. It was like an old habit. I have to assume I must have trained hard to get something like that embedded in my brain. It's yet another question about myself for which I have no answer. Speaking of which, I want to get going. I'm anxious to find my children, my family, and especially to find myself."

Cindy watched tears wend their way across Jane's cheeks and drip off her jaw. She nodded and gave Jane a quick hug.

"Change of plan! We'll have to go a different way," Cindy said. She picked up her bag and inserted the can. "Follow me. Stay down, and don't make a sound in case Toro is up and about. We're cutting through the back of the house so now's the chance for you to get your things that you left outside on the ground."

As Cindy led Jane and Goldie around the side of the house, Jane heard male voices yelling in the distance, giving orders to spread out. Without losing momentum, Jane and Goldie each grabbed their canvas tote bags and bear spray as they traversed the familiar back yard to its perimeter. Goldie decided to leave her re-purposed broom behind and have one less item to carry.

They arrived at what first appeared to be a dilapidated garden shed that Jane realized was actually an abandoned child's playhouse. It was made of weathered pine board siding, and what must have once been a charming gabled roof was now rotted and gnawed at. A single, large, semi-circular chomp in the ridge of the steeply pitched roof caught Jane's eye, and she surmised it was the work of a large wild animal. She chuckled to herself because it reminded her of the impression left after taking a big bite into a slice of watermelon. An empty and peeling pink window box was under each of the two boarded up windows to either side of the flaking white and pink door, which Cindy opened. A strong musty smell wafted into the fresh air.

"Eek! Help! I'm getting attacked by bats!" Goldie screamed, jumping up and down while shaking her arms in the air, as several birds flew out past her head. Cindy grabbed her arm and dragged her inside.

"Gosh, Goldie, what's wrong with you?" Cindy asked angrily. "Those were birds, and all they did was fly out of here. When you carry on like that, making such a ruckus, you can draw attention to us. Good grief!"

Goldie began to cry.

Jane went over to her intending to calm her down, but Goldie walked away to the far wall, sulking.

"She's a bit eccentric, I know," Jane remarked to Cindy after they were out of Goldie's view. "She's deaf, as you know, and apparently can't tell when she's being loud. What *is* this place?"

Cindy responded, "It's a playhouse that Dad built for me back in the good times, when I was little. Eventually he converted it into a shed to store the lawn furniture and cushions, but it fell into disrepair so we left it empty. Fortunately for us now, The Steps never bothered to have it taken down although they did have the floor boards removed because they were infested with termites. They're not much into aesthetics as I'm sure you've noticed. In a second you will see that I made an alteration anticipating that one day I might need it."

Cindy walked over to where Goldie was already calmed down and was lingering about. She gave a comforting squeeze to her shoulders. At the wall, Cindy put the fingers of both hands into two open knotholes and pulled upwards. The wall disengaged, and she put it to the side in the room.

Jane and Goldie gasped in astonishment.

Before them was a long cylindrical tunnel shaped by a continuous canopy of vines and branches. Sparse beams of light penetrated the living ceiling and created a dappled effect that made it an enticing sanctuary in what would otherwise be most ominous. Far ahead there emerged a white circular light, piercing like a laser in the contrasting deep shade. Jane squinted her eyes. It was so mesmerizing and beckoning that in an instant she felt an energy drawing her to it like the undertow of the ocean. Trancelike, she proceeded towards the light, feeling as though she were floating.

Suddenly a voice pierced the ethereal silence. "Jane! Jane! No. Don't go. Please don't go. Come back! We need you."

Jane abruptly stopped walking and turned around. She could see Cindy standing with her hands on her hips and Goldie alongside her, poker-faced.

"Whatever are you doing going off like that?" Cindy said when Jane returned. "I need you and Goldie to help me put this part of the wall back."

"I … I don't know. I felt so strange. I saw that light ahead and … it was pulling me … it was so welcoming … like … I don't know … how to explain …"

"Jane, it's just the sun peeking in at the other end," Cindy remarked. "It's low in the sky, and the glare is strong in the heavy shade. Sure is nothing magical about that."

"Well, you know what I think?" Goldie added. "I think you hit your head quite hard before, and you're having some after-effects. Nice running off from us like that."

"I'm so sorry. I don't know what came over me," Jane replied.

"Forget it," Cindy said. "Let's not waste any more time. Here's what I need you and Goldie to do."

Cindy showed them two loops of rope fastened to the outside part of the section of wall that she had removed earlier. As she slid it over to the opening she and Jane each took a loop and with Goldie's help, dragged the piece towards them, putting it snugly back in place.

"OK. Let's go quickly," Cindy ordered as she picked up her valise. "I hate to tell you, but this detour will take us out of our way. However, at least it will be safer through another part of the countryside. I can assure you we won't encounter any roadblocks that Letty's men may have set up. Once we are out in the open, I'm going to set you on course for an alternate route to Jack's house, and I'll go in another direction to the shoe store before heading to King's Tavern."

Jane and Goldie nodded in agreement, and they all began walking as briskly as they could, giving consideration to Cindy's personal limitations from wearing two different shoes. When at last they reached the light at the end of the tunnel, Cindy took the can out of her valise and removed the snap on lid. She put her hand inside and drew out a rolled up clump of paper money.

"Here, you two," Cindy said. "I want you to take this. Even if I don't win the $1,500 I will have plenty for myself to live on for months and months, courtesy of The Steps' slush fund for vacation spas and beauty treatments. I wish I could see their looks of horror when they don't find this can in the fridge." She laughed heartily. "I can't ever repay you for all that you've done for me in the little time we have known each other. Giving you a share of this stash is the best I can do. Oh, wait. I almost forgot. I also have these for you to remember me by."

Cindy reached into her valise and pulled something out.

"They're called friendship bracelets, but I made them for myself using rows of different colored fabric scraps from my old worn out clothes. I wanted to have something pretty to wear when everything else around me was so dreary. Here you go. One for each of you."

"Wow!" Jane cried. "Thank you so much. This is lovely. You don't have to do all this, Cindy. We were glad to help you out, and it's been quite an experience we will never forget. Right, Goldie?"

"I'll say," Goldie replied, her eyes wide as saucers upon seeing all the money that Cindy had confiscated. "But to tell you the truth, it was a crazy idea—not exactly anything I would want to re-live. I love the bracelet though. It's real cool!"

"But how will we ever know what happened tonight and whether you got away from The Steps safely?" Jane asked.

"Well, let's throw it out to the universe to think of a way. Come on now," Cindy sniffled softly, deeply touched by Jane's concern. "Let's do a group hug." They all held on to one another tightly for the last few moments they had together.

Once they separated, Cindy continued talking and pointing ahead. "What you can do is follow a path on the inside edge of the clearing over there. It will take you out of public sight into a wooded area and eventually to desolate open space. There it intersects with a road, if you can call it that. Go left. It's really a commonly used narrow strip of land that's been worn down over many, many years—probably from use by horses, covered wagons, stage coaches, and more in recent times by cars and trucks. It's actually like a lot of roadways around here. Otherwise the whole area is extremely rocky with tall rock formations about.

"Remember what I told you earlier: Nearby, you'll come upon a sign—the only sign there is, by the way—that says, 'Welcome to

Tree City.' Get your bearings by looking for the cluster of what to me look like lollipop trees. From there you don't have much farther to get to Jack's house. I don't know exactly how long you'll have to walk, but it's in the vicinity. I'm going to backtrack a ways in the opposite direction." Cindy looked at her watch. "There's still plenty of time before it gets dark so you'll be fine. Remember, head left when you get to the open space."

"I think I know exactly what you mean if that's the only sign of its kind," Jane remarked nodding in recognition.

"Yup," Cindy replied. "There is only one such sign. Jack's father put it there years ago."

"Take care Cindy and good luck winning the Karaoke contest," Goldie said. "I wish I could see The Steps' faces when they discover you there and how beautiful you look. That will be a priceless photo opportunity."

Cindy chuckled. "Yes it will be priceless, and the thrilling memory of it will stay in my mind forever. Jane, I hope you find out who you are and where your family is very soon."

"Thank you. Me too," Jane sighed. "I'll never forget you Cindy. I hope you get all the good things you deserve."

Jane and Goldie dropped their bracelets into their bags and waved goodbye as they turned towards the area Cindy had pointed out to them. They both shuffled in silence along a path weaving through the woods, and Jane thought about what Cindy had said. Her words rang persistently in Jane's ears, and she yearned to have those well wishes come to fruition. It was only gradually that she became aware of a growing din of voices, although she couldn't make out any words. *Perhaps my intense thoughts are stimulating my memory banks,* she thought.

The walk was secluded and serene. Lush towering shrubbery to their left shielded them from view of the open field. In the absence of any breeze, the tall deciduous trees were perfectly still, though speckled light glimmered across their faces. Except for the sound of crunching leaves and snapping twigs beneath their feet, it was utterly quiet. Occasionally an acorn dropped around them, likely disturbed by perching birds or scrambling squirrels. Other than that and a few scurrying salamanders, there was no sign of life. Eventually the trail began to gently curve inward, and Jane began to worry that Cindy's directions were off the mark. *Where's the open road? How much further do we have to go?* They were being led deeper into the forest, possibly somewhere too remote for comfort.

"Hey Jane, look over there," Goldie said, jolting Jane out of her ruminations. She was pointing a short distance ahead to a sign mounted on a red and white candy cane post. As they approached, the delicately scripted words, "Sweets Stop" came into view. An arrow pointed to a location off the path and deeper into the trees where they spotted a little gingerbread house nestled within the shadows.

"How cool is that?" Goldie exclaimed, her eyes as wide as saucers. "Why don't we get something to eat there?" Goldie suggested. "Our supply of snacks is running low."

"Not a bad idea," Jane responded, feeling curious. "Let's do it and do it quickly!"

It was so long since they had their snacks that Jane figured they needed to take a break and get something to eat and drink. Besides, it was truly serendipitous that they should come upon this store and with money to spend. After passing under an archway of stacked yellow, orange, and red plastic candy Lifesavers, they came upon a trail of colored round pebbles, which to Jane resembled jellybeans.

They stopped for a moment to examine the shop, which had an astounding although very tacky thematic appearance. Its faux thatched roof was made of imitation straw that looked more like rows of plastic fringe. The tan facade was dotted with artificial gumdrops hanging on little cup hooks, and the trim was painted in swirls of mock icing in hues of lime green, pink, and white. Each of the three windows to the right of the chocolate wafer door were outlined in imitation red licorice swizzle sticks. The dribbled stucco chimney was coated in faux icing dappled with round, flat stones appearing to be chocolate chip cookies.

"Golly!" Goldie exclaimed. "What a masterpiece of creativity, don't you think?"

"That may very well be," Jane replied, "but it's too unreal. I can't imagine such a business establishment thriving in the middle of nowhere. I'm not getting a good feeling here. On second thought, let's get out of here before anyone sees us."

Goldie nodded and they turned to leave. But it was too late. Jane jumped, totally rattled by the unexpected greeting that shattered the pervading silence.

16

AT THE SWEETS SHOP

"**H**ello there! Don't go. Come in. Come in," a deep and husky voice called out loudly.

Jane tapped Goldie to get her attention.

"Let me handle this."

Goldie nodded and they both turned to face the store.

"Oh, I'm so sorry. I didn't mean to startle you," said a tall, striking young man who had emerged from the doorway. "Can I help you?"

"No...well actually yes!" Jane replied tentatively. She was captivated by the man's attractive dark features, curly hair, and tanned olive skin. "We didn't think anyone was around. It looked like the store was closed. Hi."

Given all that happened at Cindy's house and not knowing if he was connected in some way to the gangsters, she didn't want to make him suspicious of anything.

"We're er...er kind of running late on our way to...er...a friend's house for dinner, where a lot of people are expecting us," Jane lied. "We were passing through and saw the store sign and er...er, thought we would buy something to bring as a gift to our host. We would need to make a selection...er...very quickly so we don't keep everyone hungry and waiting to eat. Otherwise they'll send a search party out for us."

"Sure. Have a look around," the fellow said. "You may want to select a variety of sweets—cake, candy, pastries, breads, and the like. That's what most customers do, because they get overwhelmed by all the choices and just stand at the counter unable to make a decision. To save you time, I can put something together for you according to how much you want to spend." He held the door open for them invitingly.

"Ok. That would be nice," Jane responded, entering the store with Goldie in tow.

The sweet smell of cinnamon sugar, vanilla, and the buttery hint of home baked goods pleasantly bombarded them.

"Gol-ly!" Goldie blurted out, standing still in awe. "This is confectionery heaven."

The interior was painted in pastel colors and was surrounded by shelves filled with large jars of different candies. Trays of cookies, pastries, breads, and little cakes were displayed in a long glass case beneath the counter. On the counter top was a framed photo of the young man with his arms around a German shepherd.

The man went around the counter and pulled out a pink cardboard box and unraveled some white and red ribbon imprinted with the shop's name.

"I see you noticed the photo. That's my dog, Greta. I'm Hansom," the man said with a charming smile.

"You sure are," Goldie blurted out loud to Jane's embarrassment.

"Goldie!" Jane screeched. "I'm so sorry. She sometimes says things without thinking, and since she's deaf, the tone can be kind of loud. As you heard, she's Goldie, and I'm Jane."

"Oh, pay it no mind. Comments like that don't matter to me anymore. It's the story of my life. I hate my name, and I hate my parents," Hansom said glumly.

Seeing that Jane and Goldie were staring at him, clearly dumbfounded over this harsh revelation, Hansom continued chatting non-stop as though he hadn't spoken in days.

"I can see you're shocked at what I said. My bad. I shouldn't have said that to you about my parents. But I'm sure you can appreciate how I feel about being called Hansom, which by the way is spelled H-a-n-s-o-m. There's no "d" in it if that's what you thought. Well, it's been awful. You can imagine, there has been no end to the jokes and ridicule I've had to endure. My parents thought they were being so original by coming up with that name. You know how it happened? They'd been to a wedding and decided to take a ride in one of those fancy horse-drawn covered carriages—the kind that go in and around city parks. It's called a hansom cab named after an architect who designed it in the early 19th century.

"My mother was eight months pregnant with me. Everything was going fine until one of the carriage's two wheels hit a pothole, and my mother was tossed out of her seat onto the pavement. To make a long story short, she went into labor. The driver and my dad lifted her back into the carriage, which is where she gave birth to me. There were all kinds of newspaper headlines like, 'What a Hansom Baby!' 'This Hansom Baby Has Big Apple Cheeks.' 'Mayor Welcomes Hansom Family.' 'A Hansom Little One!' On and on. I know this, because I found all the news headlines stuffed in a scrapbook. So you see that's how they got the idea to give me that name."

"It's obvious that your name has been a sore point for you, and you're bursting with resentment," Jane said sympathetically. "But we need to pick out some goodies in a hurry and get moving. By the way, you don't have to shout. Goldie is completely deaf, and I'm not hearing impaired. All you need to do is make sure she sees you speaking, because she can read lips, expertly."

"Right-O! I beg your pardon," Hansom interrupted in a softer tone. Disregarding Jane's request, he continued with his story. "But my name has been the least of my problems. In the early days, as I was growing up, we were very prosperous because my father had inherited his family's wood cutting and logging business. He had quite a monopoly in the village, which was surrounded by a very thick forest. The never-ending job of cutting up huge felled trees for firewood and local furniture production always put his skill manipulating a chain saw to the test.

"Then one very windy day my father was in the forest on one of his *'chopping* sprees'—ha ha—as my mother called it. Well, he got his skull fractured by a rotten tree limb that fell on top of him. He was never the same after that and required a lot of care by my mother. He couldn't even look straight because his eyes wobbled and rolled outwardly."

"Hey stop! Stop! Listen, Hansom," Goldie interjected. "Things may have been awful and all for you, but we weren't expecting to hear your life story. You seem like a nice guy, so maybe we can meet another time to chat. For now, we would really like to buy something dessert-like from you to bring to our host as Jane said, and we wouldn't mind having a little treat to take with us on the way to nibble on. We haven't eaten in a while." She was becoming agitated, shuffling her feet on the saw-dusted floorboards.

"Why sure. How inconsiderate of me," Hansom said contritely. "I don't know what came over me. I'll get you some freshly homemade mint chocolate chunk cookies and milk to wash them down. How's that? You can dunk them. They're delicious. In fact, I'll join you if you don't mind."

Jane was starting to feel a bit dizzy. All the sweet smells around her blended together, almost to the extent that she had absorbed them and could taste them. However, the fused flavor was unpleasantly medicinal. Her head had begun to hurt and throb, and the swishing sound of her own heartbeat was resonating in her ears.

"Would you mind if I sat down? I suddenly don't feel well," Jane asked. She looked around the room anxiously for a seat.

"Whoa," Hansom replied. "Let me get you a chair. You're turning green."

Hansom ran into the back of the store and brought out a foldable camping chair. Jane sat down and put her head back. Within moments, she felt suspended in time, like she was either fading away or otherwise coming to. She could hear echoes of her name being called from far away and could sense movement around her.

Jane's eyes fluttered open and out of focus. An indiscernible face was hovering over her and a man's voice addressed her as she felt her hand being stroked and patted.

"Hey, Jane. It's me. Hansom. Remember? What's wrong? What happened?"

Jane squeezed her eyes and blinked several times to clear her vision.

"Jane! Jane! Are you ok?" Goldie asked, shaking Jane's shoulders with alarm.

"Yes. I'm better now. How weird that was," Jane murmured. "It came on so quickly."

She massaged the sides of her temples.

"You need to rest a bit," Goldie said. "I don't want you to pass out on the path while we're walking. Do you want something to drink?"

Jane nodded.

"Hansom, would you please give Jane and me something to drink? We'll pay you of course. We'll get going as soon as Jane feels alright."

"Sure," Hansom responded. "Water or milk? It's all I have."

"Either will do," Goldie remarked.

"OK. I'll fetch both for you, and the cookies too," Hansom said enthusiastically. "I keep the cookies in the refrigerator. The cold gives some zing to the mint chocolate chunks. And don't be silly—it's no charge."

Hansom returned holding a cold metal baking tray of cookies, a large water bottle, and a container of milk. He grabbed three plastic cups from behind the counter, and he and Goldie sat on the floor near Jane's feet. He offered the cookies to Goldie and Jane.

"Thank you," Goldie said as she helped herself first then held out a cookie to Jane. "Jane, do you want one? A drink?"

"No, nothing to eat, and just a little water to drink, thanks," Jane replied. "Oh and Goldie, if you don't mind my saying so, only have one cookie yourself or you'll ruin your appetite for the dinner we're having shortly."

I sound like the mother that I am, Jane reflected with a chuckle. Immediately she felt a sharp pang of separation anxiety, of a desire to hug her children—to reach Hannah and plead for help in finding her family. *Jeez, why in the world are we wasting time here?* The minty smell of the cookies was disturbing her senses even more and the mere suggestion of eating one exacerbated the awful taste lingering in her mouth. She looked over at the milk container and noticed it had the same sketchy picture of the missing girl that she had seen at Jack's house. She poured herself a cup of water, hoping some sips would cleanse her palate.

"So, Hansom, see the missing child's face on that milk container?" Jane asked. "Have you ever seen her?'

Goldie stared at Hansom in anticipation of his response.

"Huh? What are you talking about?" Hansom asked. He lifted up the milk container to scrutinize it, and turned it in his hands until the photo was apparent.

"To tell you the truth, I never noticed that before," Hansom remarked. "Well anyway, I don't know who she is. In the first place, I'm not too good at remembering faces, and secondly who could tell from this bad image anyway? From that picture somebody is supposed to recognize the kid? Tell me, did you ever see 'Wanted' photos in a post office and laugh at how bad they were or how ridiculous, especially if the person was wearing a ski mask?" Hansom chuckled. "It reminds me of that."

"Well, did a little girl ever stop here by herself that you can think of?" Jane asked, ignoring Hansom's quip.

"Come to think of it, only once. Not too long ago, a young girl came by to sell wrapping paper for her school."

Jane and Goldie's eyes lit up.

"She had a wagon full of different kinds of wrapping to choose from. I felt sorry that she came so far out of the way, so I bought a bunch to use in the store. In fact, I'll wrap the box of desserts for you to bring as your gift. I have a nice glossy paper with a paisley print."

"Did she have braids?" Jane inquired, stepping into the role of detective.

"I don't think so," Hansom responded. He looked up pensively at the ceiling. "Let me see—she had on one of those knit pull-down hats that covered her ears. As she was talking to me I couldn't see her hair. Wait—yes. She had braids. When she walked out the door I saw one big plaid bow down her back. It looked like two braids were twisted together and tied with a ribbon. What are you, some kind of private investigator?"

"Oh, no. There's a whole story behind how I got involved in this, and it really doesn't matter," Jane responded. "Let me just say that a friend of mine had a hunch that the girl was kidnapped and that he knew who might have abducted her. We went on kind of a bizarre expedition to explore that and see if perhaps she was being held captive, but it didn't pan out. Did she say where she was going next, or could you venture a guess?"

"No. She didn't say," Hansom said. "As to a guess where she might have gone next—maybe she went to my parents' house, which is the closest residence, but I know for a fact that neither of them would ever get up to answer the doorbell."

"How can you be for sure?" Jane inquired.

"Oh believe you me," Hansom emphatically said. "And if you bear with me for a minute or two while you rest and pull yourself together, I can explain why, so you don't waste your time thinking about this and getting on the wrong track. Are you sure I can't offer you some cookies?"

Jane shook her head. "No thanks. Really. I don't feel like it. Plus I would rather hold off since there will be lots to eat for dinner as usual."

Hansom continued with his story. "After my father's accident, he drove my mother crazy being out of his mind and home all the time since of course he could no longer work. She went off the deep end having to take care of him in addition to me. I don't know how this all started, but at some point both of my parents began taking drugs, the hallucinogenic kind, and they flipped out. When they became all frenzied and out of it from taking LSD or mescaline they would often grab me and lock me up in the root cellar with lots of food and water. Sometimes it would be three days before they would let me out. I felt like a caged animal."

"What do you know?! Another kept-in-the-cellar story!" Goldie exclaimed.

Hansom looked at Goldie inquisitively, and Jane glared at her with a shut-your-mouth look.

"Huh?" Hansom remarked.

"Sorry for interrupting. Don't mind me," Goldie said meekly. "I was thinking of a story my mom used to read to me."

"Wait—hold on," Jane cried. "You said there's a cellar in their house, and they used to lock you up in it? Is there even a remote possibility they could be keeping a little girl there?"

"Yeah," Goldie added. "How would you know unless you checked it out?"

"No way. That's impossible," Hansom responded. "In the first place, as I said, they would never answer the doorbell. Hear me out. As time went by, gradually all their savings dried up, so they had to go on public assistance. They were always craving sweets because of the drugs, and after cashing their monthly welfare check my mother started giving me money to pick up lots of goodies for them at this very store. Since I had grown to despise both of them, I came up with a scheme to make sure they became so obese that they would be unable to get around the house much or out the door to track me down once I left the house. I wanted them to really feel what it was like to be a prisoner. So I made sure I brought home high-calorie candy, buttery cake, and zucchini bread so that they would become grossly fat."

Jane could hear the bitterness in Hansom's voice. She shook her head partially in sympathy and partially in exasperation for having to listen while she recuperated. She was getting anxious over all the time that was passing, and she had no idea how much farther they had to go to get to Jack's house.

"Well it worked. My patience paid off. I would say that they're over four hundred pounds by now."

Jane and Goldie gasped.

"Yup. That's the God's honest truth," Hansom added. "They've been hobbling around with bamboo canes, which was the only wood I could get that was strong enough to withstand their tremendous weight so that they could at least get to the bathroom. My mother developed diabetes and lost most of her vision, so I got a Seeing Eye service dog to help guide her. That's Greta, in the photo up there. We're very attached to one another. She's such a devoted dog, yet my mother has been awful to her too. Can you imagine— she hits Greta with her cane when it's her own fault for frequently tripping over her two fat feet!"

"Jeez, how cruel!" Jane remarked. "I'm surprised that Greta doesn't bite her."

"I wish she would, but Greta's a very gentle dog," Hansom said. "However, who knows, maybe one day soon her canine instincts will take over, and she'll attack that nasty witch. So, you see, there's no chance my parents could kidnap a child. Plus, I'm the only one who regularly goes in the house, and I would know if someone were being held there."

But that doesn't rule out Hansom from being involved. The thought gave Jane goose bumps.

"How did you wind up working here?" Goldie asked.

Hansom said, "I became friendly with the owner of Sweets Stop; his name is Sinbad. One day I told him my plight. He felt sorry for me, and as soon as I could get working papers he gave me a part-time job as a baker. My parents didn't care where I was or what I did, so I started coming here right after school. Soon, this store became my sanctuary. I now sleep here and get up at 3 a.m. to do the baking, but the downside is that I miss Greta terribly. Whenever I plan to check in on her I always bake extra that morning for my parents, adding more sugar, butter, and even lard to the batch of dough. I also bring them an ample supply of leftovers and broken peppermint candy sticks. I'm pleased that these two have become fatter and fatter. My fantasy is that soon they'll explode." Hansom chuckled in an unpleasant sort of way.

"What?" Goldie asked, crinkling her nose in disgust. "How gruesome."

"Aw, it's just a figure of speech. Didn't you ever stuff yourself during a nice dinner and say you're so full you're ready to bust?"

"I'll say. My mom was the greatest cook on the face of the earth. I loved eating the meals she made and especially the desserts. They..."

"Well, on that note, it's time for us to get going to our dinner engagement," Jane said firmly. "I'm feeling much better now. Hansom, if you don't mind, please put together a nice mixture of pastries in a bo—and yes it would be nice if you wrapped it with the paisley paper. Can you do that quickly? I'll leave it up to you to make the selections."

"Righto. I'm on it!" Hansom responded as he got up off the floor and headed for the bakery counter.

Suddenly there was a harsh pounding at the door. Goldie's arms spontaneously shot upwards in surprise as she was startled by the vibrations. Jane, already sitting on the edge of her chair, fell off with a grunt.

Hansom spun around and signaled Goldie and Jane to be quiet. He hurried over to them and grabbed their hands, practically dragging them and the chair to a room behind the store.

"Whatever was that? What's going on?" Jane asked. She noticed that he was sweating profusely from his brow.

"Coming! Coming!" Hansom cheerily bellowed as he opened a closet door and shoved Jane and Goldie into the space. Their intrusion triggered an overhead incandescent bulb that instantly went on to reveal a small storage room full of boxes and baking supplies.

"Listen both of you," Hansom ordered. "Stay here. If you value your life, don't make a sound. Not a cough. Not a sneeze. Nothing. I'll explain later. Trust me. Please. Trust me. Not a sound. OK?"

Jane detected the fear underlying Hansom's speech and the terror plastered on Goldie's face. She signaled to Goldie to make sure she complied with Hansom's directions. Goldie nodded and Jane put her arm around her as reassurance. They looked up at Hansom.

"Good," Hansom replied. "It'll be quick. I promise. I apologize for all this. It was entirely unexpected."

The pounding got louder and more relentless, revealing the degree of impatience on the part of the individual outside. Jane and Goldie watched in horror as Hansom unbuckled his belt and unbuttoned the waistband of his pants. Noticing their reaction, he stooped down towards them and whispered, "I'm sorry. It's only to give the impression as to why I'm taking kind of long to answer the door … like I was … ah … ah … indisposed, if you get my drift."

Hansom unscrewed the bulb and handed it to Jane. "You need to keep it dark in here. This fixture has a sensitive sensor and your slightest movement would keep the light on."

He closed the door behind him and ran to the front of the store, his shouted words trailing him, "Coming! Coming! Coming!"

It only took a moment before Jane heard a muffled gruff voice. It sounded familiar and instantly made her flesh crawl. *No, no, it can't be!*

"Hey you—what the f***!, Hansom. Whaz up wit da locked daw?"

"Oh. Shucks. Give me a break, Toro. I was indisposed. Kind of … ahhh … ahhh … not to be gross or anything … but … I was … ahh … sitting on the throne, if you know what I mean," Hansom stammered.

"Well get yaself pulled togetha and buckled up. I need ya ta do a run."

Jane gasped. *Toro? It can't be!* Jane felt the blood drain from her face.

17

A CLOSE CALL

"What's wrong?" Goldie whispered.

Jane patted her head reassuringly, realizing that it was too dark for Goldie to read her lips. Jane strained her ears to catch the bits of conversation.

"Now? You need me to do a run right now?" Hansom asked.

"Yeah. Da big boss needs ya ta do dis right away. Here. Drop it awf at da usual place," Toro replied.

"Oh. Sure. No problem. I'll go get my knapsack." Hansom's tone was upbeat. "Hey man, what's with the bandages? What happened to your face?"

"It's nothin'," Toro briskly answered. "I got inta a brawl defendin' da boss, is awl."

Jane chuckled to herself upon hearing Toro's blatant lie and relished knowing she was the cause of his misery.

"Gee! You're so brave," Hansom exclaimed obsequiously. "I hope it doesn't hurt much. Be back in a jiffy. I know exactly where the knapsack is."

Jane was stunned over Hansom's coincidental connection to Toro, and the fact that he was in such close proximity made her heart pound with fear. *Yet another dreadful situation I'm entangled in. I'll never get to talk to Hannah at this rate. When will I ever find out who I am and be reunited with my family?* Tears welled up in her eyes and she wiped them away with the back of her hand. Her nerves were shot and despair was taking over her.

Jane listened as squeaking footsteps thumped about while at the same time the muffled sound of a voice increased as it approached where she and Goldie were hiding. By now her heart was racing and she held her breath.

It was Hansom's voice. "Do you want anything to munch on, Toro?" he shouted.

"Nah. I jus hatta smoothie," came the distant response.

"Psst. Jane. Don't say a word now," Hansom whispered after he opened the storage room door. "I have to talk quickly. This is very serious stuff. These are dangerous people. Stay put and absolutely silent until I get back. It shouldn't be longer than an hour. Take this little lantern. It has fresh batteries in it. Use it sparingly, though. Sorry. It'll be ok." Jane heard his footsteps recede.

The front door slammed so hard that it shook the floor and the vibration made Goldie flinch. Jane soothingly patted her head. She was glad that Hansom had given her a flashlight. Otherwise, sitting in the dark she had no way to communicate with Goldie. *It's better that I don't tell her about Toro right now. Besides, I have no idea if we're the only ones in the store.* She was petrified, based on what Hansom had said and already having encountered the likes of Toro. Thankfully, Goldie had fallen asleep judging from the rhythmical snoring and snorting Jane heard in Cindy's house. Jane poked her, and Goldie quieted down.

Jane listened intently for any sounds. All of a sudden light filtered in under the door casting eerie shadows on the wall and making her feel all the more terrified. At the same time, Jane detected movement in the room based on the telltale squeaks of rubber soles on the floor. She became stone still not knowing who might be roaming about or whether it was more than one person, because noises seemed to be emanating from different directions. The trepidation over the possibility that somebody might engage in exploring the back room and discover her and Goldie caused Jane to suck in her breath and tense up even more. Her worse fear was that it might be Toro. In a few moments she heard the flush of a toilet and the sound of running water. Taking advantage of the commotion and the radiance slipping into the space where they were huddled, Jane woke Goldie and immediately signaled her to be quiet.

Soundlessly Jane mouthed the words, "I hate to tell you this but the person who was pounding on the door before was none other than Toro!"

Goldie's eyes opened wide with terror. Jane patted her reassuringly.

"Hansom had to leave for about an hour to run some kind of errand for the man. Somebody was walking around on the other side of this wall and used the bathroom."

Jane frantically looked around in the dim light to see if there was anything she could use as a cover or something large they could hide behind. To her disappointment, apart from the supplies on the shelves, there were four empty milk crates, two sacks of flour and a white baker apron hanging on a hook. The reality was they had no alternative but to lean into the wall, as far back as possible into the corner, like flattened out cartoon characters.

"If someone were to open the door and look in, I don't want us to be in the direct line of sight," Jane mouthed.

In a few moments the light went out, and Jane could hear the footsteps fading. She spontaneously emitted a big sigh of relief and gave Goldie's hand a comforting squeeze in the darkness. Jane tried to relax by counting slowly to herself and focusing on the process of inhaling and exhaling air. She was up to number twenty when she heard a distant voice. It was Hansom's.

"Oh, Toro! You're still here? Well, the job's all taken care of. I didn't think you'd be waiting. Is there something else you need me to do?"

"Nah. Not now. Maybe layda tanight. Stick aroun' in case I cawl ya. I was jus hangin' out faw a lidda while. Da boss and da otta boyz are on a client job lookin' for tree gals. By da way, ya didn't happen ta see dem aroun' dees parts recently did ya?"

"Hell, no. I haven't seen anyone yet today," Hansom lied. "But I'll keep my eyes on the lookout for them."

"Yeh. Lemme know," Toro said. "Dare's a nice rewawd fa ya—a finda's fee if yaw tip leads us ta capture dem alive."

"Well I sure could use the money. I'll be sure to call you right away," Hansom replied. "What do they look like?"

A loud bleeping sound abruptly interrupted their conversation. Toro reacted by speaking into a small walkie-talkie he had pulled out of his pocket.

"Yeah? Dis is Toro. Whatda you want? Yeah. Yeah. I'm wit him now. He did it already. No. Nobody. Any luck? Yeah boss. I'm comin' now. Sure. Seeya Hansom, I gotta go."

"But wait, Toro, what do the girls look like?" Hansom shouted after him. The door slammed.

Jane was on edge. Her anxiety escalated as she strained to hear the banter taking place in the shop. Time seemed to stand still with the sound of footsteps approaching. The door to the storage room opened. Jane held her breath and clenched Goldie's arm, anticipating the worst.

"Phew. You can come out. The coast is clear," Hansom said to Jane and Goldie. They didn't move a muscle.

"Ahem. I said you two can come out now. I'm sorry for all this. I didn't expect it."

Jane and Goldie stood up slowly, hindered by muscle stiffness. The space was stuffy, and the cool air sifting in from the room felt good as they took a moment to stretch. They emerged from the darkness squinting into the light.

"Wow, Jane! Your face is ashen," Hansom cried. "Are you OK?"

"I've been sitting with pins and needles in a dark room barely able to breathe. Take a guess as to whether I'm OK," Jane snapped. "Can you tell us what's going on? That guy sounded very tough. What's his name? *Oro?*" she asked feigning innocence. "I could only hear bits and pieces of what you both were saying."

"No, Toro, T-O-R-O" Hansom replied. "Toro. As in Spanish for "bull." It's his nickname. He's in a gang, and they all have nicknames like Beast, Billy Gotee, Hook, Stilts, Pinhead, to name a few. I figure it's because his neck is thick and short like a bull's and he's likewise very dangerous. His whole gang is dangerous. I'm sure you heard Toro say that they're looking for quote: 'three gals.' By any chance that wouldn't have anything to do with both of you, would it?"

"Heck no!" Jane exclaimed. "Do we look like a threesome?"

Goldie scowled, waving Hansom's question away with her hand. "Hey, we don't want any trouble. We have enough problems to deal with already. Jane doesn't know where she came from or who she is and my home was wrecked by three bears who also spilled all my honey." She let out a dramatic sigh.

Hansom frowned. "What, may I ask, are you talking about?"

"Oh, never mind. It doesn't really matter. We should be going," Goldie replied. "We're running very late, and I bet our friends are already looking for us. Right, Jane?"

"This whole situation is very disturbing, to say the least," Jane said. "Goldie's right. We'd best be on our way and not push our luck any further. When you were running your errand somebody was walking in the back room, and used the bathroom. That was a close call. Do you think it was Toro?"

"I bet it was. There was no one else with him when he came by," Hansom replied.

"What if he started snooping around looking to see if you were hiding whomever that gang is hunting for?" Jane asked. "I can't imagine what the consequences would have been if he had discovered us in the storage room—not only for us, but you too."

"Yup. That was a close call alright. I was so relieved when he had to leave after getting the call. It certainly wouldn't have been safe to have him lingering around here."

"Oh yes—I heard several bleeps. He has a phone?" Jane asked.

"Phone? Oh no. Unfortunately, there's no phone service around here," Hansom remarked. "We use two-way radios instead. You know—long range walkie-talkies. The bleeps are how it sounds when a call comes in. Some of the guys use the earpiece accessory when they're out in the field, 'on assignment' as they call it. They think they're cool. Look, I don't blame you for feeling upset. In the first place, I didn't expect Toro to stay here when I was gone. He never does. He's always occupied on some...er...assignment, like he's on now. That's why when I got back I was very shocked to find him still here, but I had to remain calm and act indifferently. Something happened to his face in a fight, so he was taking a break."

Jane and Goldie surreptitiously caught each other's eyes knowingly.

"Before you go, let me explain what's going on," Hansom said. "I want you to be informed so you can better watch out for yourselves when you leave here."

"That would surely be very helpful, but please hurry if you don't mind," Jane said. "This detour has already become more than we bargained for. We'll make our purchase and get going."

Hansom nodded and began talking as he put a variety of pastries and candy in a pink cardboard cake box. Jane noticed that an enchanting graphic of the store along with its name was imprinted on the cover. He grabbed the ribbon he had unraveled before.

"I'll wrap it in the paisley paper and tie it with our usual white and red ribbon," Hansom said. "How's that?"

"Yes. Yes. That would be nice," Jane replied. It made her think of the missing girl. *Poor thing. I wonder if she's the one who went house-to-house to sell wrapping paper.*

"I'll be quick," Hansom said as he cut the paper to size. "Before Toro arrived I was telling you I got in good with Sinbad, the owner, who gave me a job as baker. The more time I spent here, the more I discovered. Of all things, this sweet shop is actually a front for a drug cartel. Drugs! Can you imagine? Right up my parents' alley. I couldn't escape the drug scene, even in a sweet shop."

"No wonder the store is in such a secluded area," Jane said. "You have to get yourself out of this situation as soon as possible because drug traffickers are a rough and tough crowd. Everyone is dispensable, even their own flesh and blood. They may like you today, but tomorrow could be a different story."

"Don't you think I know that?" Hansom said with a sigh. "You're right about why this place is out of the way, although we do get some regular customers, mostly on Sundays. However, the bulk of activity happens here in the middle of the night. This way nobody would ever notice. I realized that the more I knew, the more dangerous it was for me. So I never asked any questions. Before long I got sucked into doing the cartel's dirty work by dropping off some parcels here and there on my way to school. Sinbad always instructed me to keep moving after I made the drop and never to look behind me. I was so scared of being shot that I carried several of my big textbooks in my backpack thinking they would deflect a bullet or two."

"I can't believe you're telling us this!" Goldie exclaimed. "I learned about drug cartels. It's so bad in some countries that even people in the local government are afraid to stand up for the law. Even if they try to get in the way, they're easily bought when it comes time to hearing threats of danger to their family members. Hansom, you're as good as dead if you turn on them. They'll sniff you out and hunt you down no matter where you go."

"Gee wiz, Goldie. Could you be any more blunt?" Hansom remarked with a laugh. "While I realize the peril, I play along, since my ulterior motive has been to bide time to fatten up my parents. The good news is that my patience has paid off according to plan. Nature took its course, so I'll be sneaking out of here in a day or two, and I'm taking Greta with me."

"Well, good luck," Goldie said, looking at him askance. "I have to say, it's one bizarre story—stranger than fiction, as a matter of fact."

"Well, truth is often stranger than fiction, and I tell the truth," Hansom added.

He tied up the cake box and handed it to Jane. "Here you go." She slipped her fingers under the ribbon bow and held it securely.

"I hope you and your friends enjoy these. No charge. It's on the house for all your trouble."

"Why, thank you Hansom, that's so *sweet,*" Jane said, chuckling at her pun. As Hansom opened the door to let them out, Jane turned to him and asked, "How far is it out of these woods and to the roadway? We go left at that point and were told that nearby it would bring us towards a 'Welcome to Tree City' sign. What do you think?"

"I would say you have about a fifteen minute walk to the outer road," Hansom replied. "But I have no idea where that sign is. I've never heard of it."

"Eh, we'll find it, I'm sure. Please stay safe and out of trouble. I wish you luck in finding a much better life than you've had," Jane said to him as she and Goldie went out the door.

"Bye Hansom!" Goldie said with a big grin and dramatically swooping wave.

Jane watched Hansom wave back and display a warm smile as he stood in the entranceway. She was pleasantly struck by the picture postcard image of Sweets Stop and Hansom's boyish charm. The enchanting impression remained with her as she and Goldie started strolling along the colored pebble path to the trail they had been traveling on since leaving Cindy's house. Just as they turned onto the trail, the echo of the loud, familiar bleeping sound disturbed the quiet atmosphere. Jane sensed this meant trouble so she turned to let Goldie know. They picked up their pace, and within moments her apprehension was validated.

She heard Hansom screaming behind them in the distance, "Jane! Jane! Run! Run! Toro called me. He's on his way here with the other men to search the area. He wants me to help."

Jane grabbed Goldie's arm to stop her. Goldie spontaneously looked over her shoulder.

"What? What? What's wrong?" Goldie stammered.

"We have to get out of here real quickly," Jane relayed. "Toro and the gang are coming to search the area."

"Yikes!" Goldie sprinted away like a racer in a fifty-yard dash, flailing her arms in her usual dramatic fashion and dropping her tote in the process.

"Get away. Quickly. Run! Run!" Hansom's booming voice continued to echo about. "They'll be here any minute. I'll stall them."

"Thanks for the warning," Jane hollered back as she raced to catch up to Goldie. Without missing a beat, she scooped up Goldie's bag with her free hand and continued to run like her life depended on it, which it likely did.

18

MEETING NAPOLEON

By the time Jane and Goldie reached the clearing, Jane was gasping for breath and collapsed to the ground. Goldie wanted to take advantage of her second wind and keep moving, but no amount of encouragement could get Jane up and running.

She came to with a panicking Goldie shaking her. "Jane!... Hey Jane! Come on. Come on. Open your eyes. Take some slow, deep breathes."

Who is that? The voice Jane heard was faint.

"Jane! Do you hear me? Come on. We have to get going. I don't want Toro or the other guys to find us."

"What did you say?" Jane asked as she looked up at her blurry surroundings. She was feeling queasy and the familiar jabbing pains in her head were back.

"What's wrong with you? Toro. Remember Toro? I don't want him to track us down. Let's go. I'm afraid."

"I...I...Who are..."Jane stammered.

"Jane! Look at me. Hurry up. We have to get out of here. Fast." Goldie cried.

"Jeez, I don't know what happened," Jane said. "I must have passed out. My head hurts."

"You were practically choking to death. For a moment I thought you might need mouth-to-mouth restitution," Goldie replied. "I once saw a Red Cross training video on that in school."

"You mean *resuscitation*," Jane laughed. "Not *restitution*. And no, I don't need that. I'm OK now."

"Whatever the word is! Who cares?" Goldie yelled while impatiently jumping up and down like a child throwing a tantrum. "Come on! We have to keep going. It's getting late, and I'm scared. I don't know this area," Goldie whined. "Cindy said that the 'Welcome to Tree City' sign we first have to get to is nearby. I hope she's right and that her idea of 'nearby' doesn't turn out to be 'far' for us doing the walking. Those are such subjective concepts. I wouldn't want us traipsing around lost in the dark."

"No. No of course not. I'm okay, I think," Jane said, hiding her amusement over Goldie's comments. "I'm sure we'll be there in no time flat."

"Thanks for rescuing my tote. Want a snack to give you energy?" Goldie asked. "You didn't have anything to eat before when Hansom offered it to you. There are still some munchies in our bags. And we also have plenty of sweet stuff to eat if you want to dip into the cake box, since we really aren't going to anyone's house for dinner. Yoo-hoo. Jane! What's wrong with you? Earth to Jane!"

"Huh?" Jane responded. She could hear Goldie's babble, but her mind was elsewhere.

"You're drifting away." Goldie held up the nicely wrapped cake box that Jane had dropped. "You know—these baked goodies and candy that Hansom gave us to bring as a house gift? Remember? And the phony story you came up with about the house dinner we were supposedly on our way to?"

"Of course I remember all that." Jane said. "Thanks, but I don't feel like eating a thing right now. I'm a little nauseous. My mouth is a bit dry, but I'll wait to get water at Jack's house."

Jane felt déjà vu. When she first arrived at Tree City after her harrowing descent down the rocky slopes it was with her parched tongue sticking to the roof of her mouth. And it would be Jack's house where she'd wind up again, looking for a much needed drink of water. *Full circle.*

"Well, in case you want it, don't forget that we have the water bottles I packed," Goldie said. "You can dip into your tote bag too. If you drank something it would even help to lighten the load."

"I know," Jane replied. "And it's so sweet of you to be concerned about me. Don't worry. I'm okay now," Jane replied. "Let's move on."

Jane took the cake box from Goldie and they started walking.

"Jane, I don't like this at all. It's so strange—this dirt roa—it's in the middle of nowhere. And there's all this empty, open space. No trees, no anything but stones and dirt and those weird tall rock formations." Goldie demonstrated with a broad sweep of her arms. "Who would travel along here? You know what I think? I think this must have something to do with those drug runs Hansom was telling us about. I don't know where I am—I'm out of my element, and I'm afraid of those bears turning up."

Bears! I almost forgot about the bears. Jane's mind reverted to when she was riding in Jack's truck, and he had seen some creatures crossing the road. Remembering the sighting gave credence to Goldie's expressed fear, which made Jane feel uneasy as well. *Could those have been Goldie's bears?*

"I promised I would help you get on your way to Jack's house, and we got so sidetracked that now we're lost again." Goldie began to cry.

Jane gave her a consoling hug. "Don't worry, dear. I'm sure we'll get to Jack's house very soon, and then we'll be safe. He said he would take me to that lady, Hannah, for help. All I want is to be with my family. If you feel lost being out of your element, can you imagine how I feel? I don't know who I am, where I am, or how I got here. I'll make sure Jack takes us to your home first, and you can decide if you want to stay or come along to report the bears to the police, but in either case I can check if my locket is in your house. That's the plan, and we have to have faith that it will all work out."

Goldie simmered down and wiped her eyes, but it was very obvious to Jane that she had lost a lot of her spunk. They continued to trudge onward, together as a team, but alone in their thoughts.

It wasn't too long after that they felt a subtle tremble underfoot and they both flinched. Simultaneously, Jane heard rhythmical beeping coming from behind. She grabbed Goldie's arm with a sense of urgency and pointed over her shoulder to alert her.

"I hear a horn blaring," Jane exclaimed.

They abruptly stopped and turned around. Goldie swiftly glanced over at Jane with fear etched on her face.

"Oh jeez," Jane exclaimed. "Not again! It looks like the same truck that terrorized us earlier!"

Jane covered her ears from the continuous beeping. As it became evident that the vehicle was descending upon them, they had no other recourse but to hasten sideways off the road to get out of the way. As it got closer, the truck slowed down and passed them, leaving behind a trail of smelly exhaust that dissipated slowly in the still air. It came to a stop ahead of them but not before sending up a spray of road dust that made them cough. They turned their faces away, waiting a moment for the loosened dirt to settle.

"There was no driver at the wheel," Goldie cried. "How could that be? This is really freaking me out again!"

"Me too" Jane said. "Let's stay put a moment and see what happens. We should have our bear spray ready, just in case."

Jane's instinct was to run, but the reality was there was nowhere to go. Her anxiety level was high, and her heart was racing. She took several deep breaths and held on tightly to the spray canister with one hand and to the tied ribbon on the cake box with the other hand. Along came the lightheadedness. Next thing she knew a voice was calling out, seemingly from far away, and she could feel jabbing on her shoulders and arm. Someone was patting her hand.

"Jane! Jane! Jane! Open your eyes! Come on. Open your eyes."

Jane found herself lying on her side. The crushed cake box was under her head serving as a pillow, and as her eyes came into focus she recognized Goldie on her knees and hovering over her, concern plastered on her face.

"You fainted again," Goldie said. "Whatever is wrong with you? I think you should have something to eat and drink."

"I'm OK," Jane said as she remembered the driverless truck and where she was. She got up slowly and turned to look at it about a hundred feet ahead of them. The atmosphere was quiet once again.

"The engine isn't running," Jane remarked.

"No kidding," Goldie said. "I figured that out considering those black exhaust fumes stopped spewing out of the tailpipe. I don't like the way this looks. There's still a kidnapper on the loose and at least one missing child we know of, maybe more. I don't want to be the next one."

Jane spoke. "I don't like the way this looks either, Goldie. But I think we should be doing more than just standing here talking about our impressions. Let's get a bit closer."

Goldie picked up the slightly squashed cake box and unsuccessfully tried to stuff it in her tote. Instead she carried it sideways under her arm.

"Oh well," Goldie said. "No sense fussing about this, now that it has your head impression in it. And anyway, we're not really bringing it anywhere. Some ruse you told Hansom!"

Jane chuckled. "Well you have to admit, it was a good excuse for not having to linger around there. Plus it was better for us to give him the impression that people were expecting us shortly."

Goldie nodded although Jane wasn't too sure she was completely focused on the conversation.

They cautiously maintained their distance walking parallel to the road until they were several feet from the rear side of the truck. They paused and stepped into the roadway to assess the vehicle. Part of the cargo area had a covered section constructed of wood, and across the side metal panel Jane noticed the large words, *Snoe's White Glove Cleaning Company,* poorly hand printed in white. She couldn't help but smile at the absurdity which was at the same time welcome comic relief that helped to diffuse some of her tension. There was dust all over its black body, which looked like that of an old model pickup truck. Someone had traced the words, "The Snoe flakes" and "Neat Freaks" in several places amidst the considerable number of dents she could see. The driver's door was twisted inward, and the shattered window glass was being held together by duct tape.

Just then the front passenger door slowly opened. Goldie stiffened up and grabbed Jane's arm. She was wide-eyed with fear.

"Stonewall it," Jane said. "Keep smiling. Appear friendly and confident."

Jane's heart was racing again. Suddenly, she felt a slight sting in her upper arm and instinctively slapped it. She looked as she removed her hand, and thought she noticed something drop off. Curious as to what it might have been, she checked the ground near her and saw nothing.

"What's the matter now?" Goldie asked.

"Probably got away, gosh darn it," Jane cried. "I got stung by something. Again. I hate these insects around here." Her attention returned to the truck.

By now a pair of very pale little legs was visible beneath the bottom of the door. The sandaled feet were groping for the running board and then hopped down to the ground. A little man not more than four feet tall, emerged from behind the door and immediately started hobbling towards them. He was dressed in clashing colors—a multicolored tie-dyed tee shirt cut at the bottom and ragged madras plaid shorts reaching to the tops of his knees.

It struck Jane that he looked like he was caught in a time warp being that his attire was right out of a distinctive era gone by. The man was clean-shaven, wearing oversized dark sunglasses with black and white striped frames. His black baseball cap had the word *Snoe's* printed in white on the visor, and his long white hair was gathered into a ponytail protruding through the opening of the back band. Over his shoulder swung a badly stained, bulky, leather satchel, which reached to his calf. The tan leather was worn and peeling on the side as though it had been dragged along the ground.

"Hey, what's wrong with you two gals?" the man shouted. "What kind of pedestrians are you?"

Jane faced Goldie to relay what the man said. Goldie's brows turned deeply furrowed as she stared at him.

"Are *you* the driver?" Goldie asked.

He nodded. "Of course. Who else? Say, do you both want to get yourself killed? I almost ran you over," he said without pausing for a response. "Huh? Why aren't you wearing high visibility safety vests? They come in orange and bright yellow, and you can get them in mesh, which is cooler material. Thank your lucky stars that this is a dry road and that the truck has reliable brakes."

Jane smirked as she digested the preposterous admonition. She and Goldie didn't move a muscle. Both had one of their hands poised over the trigger of their bear spray.

"But regardless of how good the brakes are, the laws of physics never change," the man continued as he came closer. "It takes many feet before a truck can come to a complete stop after applying the brakes. I was following the city speed limit of 30 miles per hour and that means it takes me 30 feet to react and then another 45 feet to completely stop. That comes to 75 feet total stopping distance. If I were going 40 miles per hour it would take 120 feet for me to stop. You would know all this if you took a defensive driving class."

Despite the little steps he took, the man walked with determination, his hands threateningly on his hips which was the way he kept them as he stood right before Jane and Goldie. Jane's impression was that his aim was to appear tough through his body language to over-compensate for his small size. Not perceiving this stranger as being much of a threat now that he was out in the open, she and Goldie remained in place. As he peered up at their faces, Goldie had a better view of his mouth, but for the most part she was looking down at the top of his cap while he spoke. Jane knew that lip reading was going to be a real challenge for her.

"Hi," Jane and Goldie said in unison.

"Hi? I saved your lives and all you can say is *hi*?" the man replied.

Jane ignored his zany comment. Suddenly he reached into his bulging satchel. Jane sucked in her breath. Not knowing what to expect, her nerves instantly got the better of her. Within those few seconds, she convinced herself there was a weapon in there and that they were going to be harmed on the spot. She held Goldie's hand. Like her own, it was clammy.

Instead, the man withdrew a little wooden board that Jane perceived to be about six inches square. She expelled a sigh of relief. There were two hinges on one side, which he proceeded to unfold making the object double its length, forming a rectangle. After laying the board on the ground, the little fellow flipped up four wooden spindle-like legs that were somewhat shorter than the sides of the square parts. He turned it over to set it upright in front of them.

Jane was aghast that the item was splattered with deep red stains the same color of the blotches on his satchel. Having become dramatically on edge and thus fallen victim to macabre thoughts, she couldn't help but presume they were traces of dried blood. It wasn't until the man climbed onto it that it became clear it was functioning as a portable stool. Standing on it he was no higher than Goldie's chin and Jane's chest.

Goldie stubbornly stared him down and didn't budge. "Yuck," she said.

Being as close as the little man was, Jane detected a faint odor of mint around him; probably from the gum he was chewing. She noticed that his skin was very pale and his eyes were pinkish. She didn't say a word, preferring to see how this all played out. He got off the stool, backed it up a little, and placed it where he could climb up and have a different vantage point.

"There. That's better," he said. "Now I know what you gals look like up close. You're both very dirty and dowdy, aren't you?" He pointed to Jane. "Your dress has no style. Kind of just droops on you like a sack. I suppose a belt might help relieve the desperation. Accessorize! Accessorize!

"And you, my dear, all that wild curly hair," pointing at Goldie. "You look like you were raised by animals in the woods. It's so matted it's all but screaming for help. Shampoo, shampoo! A shaping! A shaping! Anyway, who cares? Let me introduce myself. I'm Napoleon Snoe at your service." He bowed, nearly tipping the stool.

Jane nearly choked trying to suppress her anger. "Well la-di-da, Napoleon Snoe," said Jane. "My name is Jane, and this is Goldie." *Here's this little bully, walking and talking the way he does, and of all things he's named Napoleon. How perfect!*

Jane was flabbergasted that she had wound up in yet another peculiar situation with another peculiar person. Was she as crazy as all the people she had been meeting recently? Almost nothing this man said made any sense or was worth dignifying with a response. Plus, she despised being called a *gal.*

Goldie was visibly upset. She stood face to face with Jane and whispered through gritted teeth. "I have to calm down or I'm going to jump on this guy's head. Considering this new predicament and my experience with the three bears, I'm having a terrible day. Here's this little sample of a man named Napoleon, standing there on a tiny folding table no less, the self-proclaimed wardrobe and beauty critic, impolitely speaking his mind about our looks after he nearly ran over us. How dare he! And furthermore he's a menace to society, a lethal weapon on the road, driving with impaired vision. As soon as I have a chance, like when I tell the police about the bears, I'm going to report him before he seriously hurts someone."

"Are you done with your private conference?" Napoleon asked as he stepped down to the ground. "I think you gals need a good scrubbing and cleaning, and fortunately for you, you came to just the right person."

Jane recovered her voice and said. "Listen, Napoleon, do you think you're addressing a set of dentures in a jar? For somebody we don't know, you've come across very offensively. Furthermore, we didn't *come* to anywhere, least of all, to you. Goldie and I were in the process of *going* someplace—to meet up with our friends who are probably wondering by now what's taking us so long. You then rudely intruded and scared us out of our wits. So why don't you pack up your stool, get back in your truck and be on your way?"

Napoleon wasn't paying attention. He was wearing a frown while rummaging through his bag. Goldie was observing him intensely, and again Jane held her breath in anticipation of what he might pull out this time. *Perhaps I pushed his buttons too far.* She wanted to kick herself because by behaving like that she could have put their lives at risk.

"Hey Napoleon, what are you looking for?" Jane asked, switching gears by trying to sound friendly and casual.

Napoleon stopped what he was doing and looked up at her and Goldie. "My six brothers and I are in the business of cleaning. It's a business we inherited from our old man. We can clean anything. In fact, you're looking at the creator of a comprehensive stain removal chart. *Show me a stain... Then watch it wane.* We clean floors, furniture, clothing, anything around the house. *It's a crime to have grime.* We are qualified, reliable, and courteous."

Jane and Goldie listened in bewilderment to Napoleon's canned sales pitch. "That's all well and good, but what are you looking for?" Jane repeated.

"I'm going to clean your grimy faces and arms while I'm at it," Napoleon proclaimed. "All that's needed is a mixture of liquid castile soap, olive oil, and granular sugar as a scrubbing element. I can add almond extract if you like the aroma. I have those ingredients with me, and I'm looking for the measuring cup and mixing jar."

"Whoa, like heck you will," screeched Goldie on the verge of tears. "You'll keep your own grubby hands off of us."

"Fine, suit yourself." Napoleon's face had flushed beet red in anger. "I repeat: *it's a crime to have grime.* If you want to be an outlaw, that's your problem, Miss Goldie."

In a huff, Napoleon quickly gathered up his folding stool and satchel and began to shuffle in the direction of the truck as Jane and Goldie stared after him.

"Eureka!" Napoleon blared. He stopped abruptly and turned around. His face was back to its pallid color.

"I had a thought," Napoleon said as he snapped his stubby fingers. "I could give you a lift further up the road, but only as far as I'm going." His whole demeanor had surprisingly softened.

Goldie and Jane looked at each other.

"Excuse us while we have a short conference," Jane remarked.

"Er, I have a bad feeling about him," Goldie whispered. "He's very creepy. What do you think those reddish-brown stains on the satchel and stool are?"

Jane nodded her head with understanding and mouthed her response to Goldie. "I've been wondering too, and I know what you mean, but we don't have much of a choice. Let's think about it. The alternative is being out here on our own, in open space, potentially alone with roaming wild animals, not knowing where or how far Jack's house is, and aimlessly wandering about as daytime fizzles out by the minute. In addition, I have stabbing pains in my head again and two glaring flashes of light momentarily blinded me. If you didn't see them then there's something going wrong with my vision, and that scares me too. I'm so afraid I'll pass out, which means I could be lying here helpless and where would that get you? Are those reasons enough?"

"Well given how you presented the options so bleakly," Goldie remarked, "then apparently we could be as good as dead either way. Humph! I'll leave it up to you. Just be ready with the bear spray in case things get out of hand."

"That settles it then. Let's go," Jane said. She signaled to Goldie to stay by her side as they approached Napoleon.

"Well if it's not too much of a bother, Napoleon, we'll take you up on your offer considering that it's getting late. It will give us a chance to hear about your fabulous cleaning tips," Jane remarked, stroking his ego. "In exchange for the favor, I can give you a terrific referral. There's a man I met recently who was covered in greenish dust. He said it's pollen from working in his laboratory with plants, so just imagine how filthy his place is. You and your brothers will be kept very busy there. Goldie and I are actually on the way to visit him, but he apparently lives much farther away than we were led to believe. If you help us out in getting there, when we reach his house I'll introduce you. How's that?"

Napoleon's eyes lit up like a little child's. "Nifty. I'm always looking for new business. Hop in the truck. Use the passenger side. The door on the driver's side is jammed."

Nifty? Jane laughed at his expression and beckoned Goldie to come along to Napoleon's truck. They watched as he made numerous attempts to toss his satchel up onto the seat.

Jane could tell that Goldie was tense. As she got closer to the truck, Goldie hesitated and made a comment, lowering her voice. "I can't get my mom's advice out of my head. She said I was to never get into a car with a stranger, and considering that we don't know much of anything about Napoleon, I'm going against her wishes. But you're right. There's no other alternative. Night time is approaching and we'd be out walking all by ourselves, possibly lost."

Jane and Goldie watched as Napoleon was finally successful in getting his satchel into the truck. He scrambled up after it.

"I'm in," Napoleon shouted. "Both of you gals get in from this side too and sit beside me on this bench seat. It'll be easier for Miss Goldie to climb in if she first pitches up that there bakery box she's got. I'll put it somewhere for safe keeping."

Jane relayed what Napoleon said, and Goldie did as she was instructed. Napoleon grabbed the cake box as soon as Goldie tossed it. He sniffed it and broke into a big grin before gruffly shoving it under the seat. Jane boosted Goldie in first and followed after her. No sooner had Jane closed the door than to her consternation she heard a loud click. She immediately tested the handle and it didn't budge. Napoleon had activated the door lock.

"Why did you do that?" Jane asked, looking past Goldie, who was watching him. There was no answer. "Napoleon, why did you lock us in?"

Napoleon gave her a deadpan look. "Why not?"

Before Jane could respond, Napoleon had already put on the most ridiculously thick goggles she had ever seen. He looked like a pilot about to fly an open cockpit plane. As he settled himself behind the steering wheel, it became evident as to why they hadn't seen anyone driving. Napoleon's head was below dashboard level. There were extensions on the foot pedals for his little legs, but that only solved one of his challenges.

"Put on your seat belts and let's rock and roll," Napoleon said. Jane tapped Goldie and repeated his words.

"There's that annoying echo again," Napoleon commented. "Echo! Echo! I hate echoes."

"Napoleon, Goldie is deaf," Jane told him, mustering up all the sweetness she could. "But she reads lips very well as long as she can see your mouth when you're speaking. When she can't see your lips, then I have to repeat what you're saying."

Napoleon was expressionless and silent, appearing deep in thought. Suddenly, as though sparked by a jolt of electricity, he reached under the seat and pulled out a tubular leather case about two feet long. Jane felt the blood drain from her face as she pictured a shotgun. *So, this is how it's going to end.*

19

UP PERISCOPE

With her anxiety mounting, a sharp stabbing pain in her head caused Jane to suck in her breath and momentarily squeeze her eyes shut. As the pain subsided a little she imagined Napoleon a ritualistic killer with some nefarious plan ready to implement. He would be methodical in his approach, having first gained trust from her and Goldie and then waited for the right moment to subdue them. At that point, while donning a gas mask and layering it over the goggles, he would simultaneously release poisonous fumes from the contents of the leather case he was fiddling with. It would immediately disable her and Goldie, and maybe even kill them.

As the acute pain waned, Jane put her right hand over the bear spray trigger and resumed watching Napoleon intensely and mentally prepared herself to make a move whenever he attacked.

Goldie looked at Jane with an inquisitive expression. Jane shook her head and shrugged her shoulders to make it clear that she had no idea what Napoleon was up to. In an effort to try and put her at ease, Jane pulled Goldie closer to her side. She kept her eyes fixed on Napoleon and her hand on the bear spray. Her head still hurt, but she was pleased that at least she was able to get a grip on herself.

The steering wheel hampered Napoleon's movements, and twice he hit the top of his head on the underside of its rim. While fumbling with the object and cursing under his breath, he was finally able to remove a rusty metal cylinder from its leather casing, which he quickly stuffed back under the seat. Once the cylinder was finally extricated, he held it in a vertical position to the right of the steering wheel column, in front of the dashboard. It wasn't until Jane saw him look into the bottom of it from where he was sitting so low that she had a shocking inkling as to what it was.

"Jeez. Don't tell me that's a friggin' periscope!" Jane shouted. "Surely you're not going to drive the car by relying on mirrors in a tube, are you?" She pointed to the apparatus.

Napoleon ignored her and maintained his position.

She watched as he put the key in the ignition and started the engine. Feeling the truck shake as the motor revved up, Goldie looked over at Napoleon and gasped.

Goldie exclaimed, "You're crazy if you think you're going to drive like that with us in the car. No way. I want to get out. Now! Let me out!"

Goldie started to cry and pound on her thighs. Jane attempted to quiet her down.

Napoleon paid no attention to their protests and except for a grunt here and there, didn't utter a word. Instead, as if in defiance, he stomped on the gas pedal extension. The engine raced and the truck bucked forward. A cloud of dust was left rising into the air behind them.

Goldie quieted down and Jane decided not to pursue the issue any further. *The less said to Napoleon, the better.* The last thing she wanted to do was antagonize him. The idea that she and Goldie might be left by the road to fend for themselves as darkness set in was, relatively, more frightening. She knew they were stuck with him as being the better chance of reaching Jack's house other than walking around without any sense of direction.

"Er… Napoleon? I didn't mention the landmark we have to look for by the road," Jane said. "It's a cluster of rock formations with a 'Welcome to Tree City' sign. Are you familiar with that?"

"No," Napoleon mumbled.

"Well, I bet it's rather noticeable so I'll keep my eye out for it. It's important for finding the house we're going to."

"Then you look for it since you have nothing else to do. I keep my eyes on the road, the safe driver that I am," Napoleon replied.

"Could this perhaps be the wrong road?" Jane asked.

That depends on the perspective of the one traveling on it," Napoleon said. "For me, this is the right road. For somebody else it could be the wrong road. There's not just one road in the world."

"Well, no but…" Jane left the conversation at that.

As they moved forward in silence, Jane glanced back and forth at Napoleon and the desolate landscape she scanned intermittently through the grimy windshield. *Where's the "Welcome to Tree City" sign? Where's Jack's house? Are we on the wrong road?* Small clusters of pine trees began to appear here and there along the road, adding a pleasantly soft touch to the otherwise harsh geography. *I know this isn't right. I just know it. It was desolate where Jack lives.* Jane looked over at Goldie and noticed she was sleeping. She figured that the side-to-side subtle swaying of the truck caused by Napoleon's periscopic driving soothed her like a baby in a cradle.

As she watched Goldie sleep, Jane thought she looked so vulnerable in her peaceful state. Even more than before, it stirred up maternal feelings, and tears came to her eyes as she thought of her own children and family she hoped were looking for her. *Oh my. I've never known what it means to be homesick until now. When will all this craziness end? I've got to get help.* She closed her eyes hoping that when she opened them this experience would be wiped away like chalk on a blackboard. Fearful of confronting reality but with wishful thinking yet in her heart, Jane squinted, as though in anticipation of a gruesome scene in a horror movie. Suddenly for a fleeting moment, Goldie's face appeared different though unidentifiable, much like special cinematic effects of one image seamlessly morphing into another. Jane cried out at the unexpected surprise, unnerving Napoleon to such an extent that he dropped his periscope and veered sharply off the road. He abruptly came to a stop.

"Good Grief!" Napoleon exclaimed. "Whatever was that all about? You could have gotten us all killed. Lucky that I have excellent reaction time and was able to save our lives." Napoleon removed his cap and wiped his brow above the goggles before picking up his periscope from the floor.

Goldie continued to sleep undisturbed by the ruckus.

"I'm sorry. I … I … er … er … I saw …" Jane stammered not knowing what else to say in offering an explanation.

"What? Where? I didn't see anything. Did I hit something? A person? An animal? What a mess that would be."

"Calm down, Napoleon. I'm sure it's nothing. I made a mistake. I'm sorry." Jane was still stunned over the apparition. "I must be low in sugar and badly dehydrated, and that's affecting my vision. It's ok. Sorry." She grabbed a bottle of water from her tote and between gulps munched on a handful of trail mix that Goldie had packed.

"Well, at least it's not road kill that I would have to clean up," Napoleon morbidly replied. "I don't have a chemical that takes out blood stains." He turned to face front, got into position as before, and started the engine.

Could that explain the reddish brown color on the stool and satchel? But so what? It may or may not be dried blood. Maybe Napoleon is a clean freak but a sloppy painter. Jane wished that her negativity would go away. It only served to make her more agitated.

Napoleon got back on the road, not exactly staying on a straight course, but not recklessly swerving either. In this area, the surface of the dirt road was as smooth as glass, sweeping out before them on an upgrade. Taking advantage of the absence of dust, Napoleon opened the window on his side a few inches.

"Napoleon, so, far I haven't seen the 'Welcome to Tree City' sign or anything else that's familiar," Jane blurted out. "That landmark shouldn't be this far away from where we met up with you."

"Maybe the sign fell down or was stolen," Napoleon replied. "If you don't mind I would like to concentrate on my driving. I've put up with enough distractions already."

Jane saw that Goldie had awakened. She was staring at Napoleon intently and was wringing her hands as though she were expecting to be in an accident any moment.

"What?" Jane inquired out loud.

There was no answer.

"What? What did you say?" Jane asked again.

Napoleon replied curtly, "What, what? I didn't say anything. I didn't hear anything."

Jane turned to Goldie.

"Did you say something, Goldie?"

"I didn't say anything," Goldie replied. "My heart is in my mouth, so how could I speak?"

Napoleon chimed in, "Hey, nobody said nothing! Give it up."

"Well I heard a voice," Jane snapped. "It wasn't clear but definitely there was something."

"Could have been puffs of wind whistling through a grove of trees, or through the little opening in my window," Napoleon said. "Or maybe it's the tires screeching on the filthy, slimy oil slick. The highway department comes around here and puts oil on the dirt for traction on upgrades and steep hills. It messes up my tires so I had to concoct a special degreaser to clean them."

Jane was exasperated and felt motion sickness coming on. She sighed deeply and shook her head. "Beyond that, unfortunately, it doesn't look like we're where we need to be. How much farther will you be taking us?" She was concerned because the sun had dropped low in the sky, and before long it would be dusk. *Maybe he knows where Hannah lives and can get us there instead.*

"Questions, questions, questions," Napoleon exclaimed. "For your information, we're going to my cottage which is up that steep hill in the distance ahead of us. That's where you can spend the night."

"Your cottage?" cried Jane as a knot developed in her stomach. *How novel that* he *actually calls it a cottage.* "To spend the night? But I thought you were going to drive us as far as where you were heading."

"Yes. Exactly. That *is* where I'm heading," replied Napoleon. "So that's as far. Humph."

"But you didn't say that."

"You didn't ask about specifics," Napoleon quipped.

"Well, I hardly think we should stay at your place when we barely know you. Ah...ah...I mean, Goldie and I wouldn't want to intrude. So, after you let us out, we'll be on our way." She poked Goldie who was nodding off to sleep again.

"I have a news flash for you," Jane said to Goldie, raising her voice for Napoleon's benefit. "We didn't spot the sign landmark; so our plan didn't happen. Napoleon had *kindly* said that if we didn't find the house we were looking for, he would drive us only as far as he was going, and it turns out it's to his cottage as he calls it, just minutes away—as a matter of fact, right up at the top of that highest hill ahead. As you can see it's getting dark so he *very thoughtfully* invited us to spend the night there. I think we shouldn't...ah...ah...you know, be an imposition on him any longer, not to mention his family. Therefore, we should be on our way. At least we had a chance to rest. OK?"

"Be on our way? By foot? Again? Tonight? To Where?" Goldie asked.

"I think we should head directly to Hannah and not risk being detoured by some other extraordinary encounter. Maybe, just maybe, Napoleon can do us one more *tremendous favor* and drive us to where Hannah lives," Jane said keeping her voice raised.

"Not a chance," Napoleon interjected, obviously taking note of Jane's words. "Tonight, I'm not going to where anybody lives other than to my own place. I've been out cleaning all day, and this is the end of the road for me. Actually it really is. Ha Ha. You'll see." He gave the truck more gas as he approached an incline.

"Then no way am I going anywhere," Goldie somberly told Jane. "Right now all I want is something to eat and drink and not to walk any more. Plus it's almost dark, and I'm certainly not trekking outside with the insects, wild things, and Toro and the other creeps like him scavenging about who knows where. After all, since three bears showed up in my house and are prancing around in the neighborhood, there must be more where they came from. They've already eaten my cereal, taken my honey, lain in my beds, and broken my chairs, and I'll certainly not give them an opportunity to take my life."

"OK Goldie," Jane remarked with a sigh. "We'll wait until daylight. It's a good thing you packed the snacks and water. I had some before in the car while you were asleep. I obviously went too long without giving myself some nourishment." She was too exhausted to insist upon leaving right away, and Goldie was right about the dangers they could encounter. *How much worse could it be to wait it out at Napoleon's place?*

For the next few minutes, they traveled in silence on the road, which inexplicably alternated between curves and straightaways. Jane couldn't fathom why, in all this open space, the road was so circuitous. But regardless of what the explanation might be, she perceived the sinuous design as being very symbolic of the twists and turns she had been experiencing ever since she first found herself wandering amidst the craggy cliffs overlooking Tree City. The whole experience seemed somehow dreamlike.

Along the last straightaway, the level road began to incline in a series of dips and rises. When they reached the foot of the longest hill, Napoleon shifted gears for traction. The truck crawled upwardly, coughing and sputtering until just beyond the crest where the road leveled off and Napoleon continued driving for what Jane figured could not have been more than ten seconds. The dispersed radiance from the high beams revealed to Jane that the place they had come to was devoid of civilization. And except for the few little pine trees scattered about accompanied by their shadow partners, there was no sign of life. *Where's his so called cottage?* Jane's eyes darted back and forth with anticipation between the dusty windshield and the passenger window. She saw nothing and was getting more and more anxious. At last she couldn't contain herself any longer. "Napoleon, where… where's your…"

"Eureka! We're at my destination," Napoleon suddenly exclaimed and turned off the engine. "This is as far as I go, and anyway it's the end of the road for real. A few more yards and we'd be over the cliff. Ha Ha. You gals can get out." He deactivated the door lock and packed up the periscope in its case. Jane and Goldie were in the process of sliding sideways to get out of the truck on the passenger side when Napoleon started yelling impatiently "Hurry up! Hurry up."

As Jane and Goldie gingerly hopped down and stood outside, they watched Napoleon swiftly grab the squashed Sweets Stop box from under the seat. He removed his goggles and hung them on the rear view mirror as he slid over to the open passenger door. Once there he vaulted his little body to the ground in a dramatic drop and roll manner, nearly knocking them over with his satchel swinging behind his back. He quickly popped up and ran to the right, shouting, his voice trailing behind him.

"I have to use the john. No time to put out the welcome mat, so it's up to you to show yourselves in."

By then night had fallen, and the moon's thin light had changed places with that of the faded sun. Jane and Goldie stood still in the isolated place and observed Napoleon disappear fairly quickly. The sound of a latch and the creaking of hinges informed Jane that he had passed through a gate. It was momentarily followed by the slam of a door, which resounded in the otherwise intense silence.

Jane tapped Goldie for her attention. "Napoleon invited us to follow after him and show ourselves into the house. He rushed off because he had to use the bathroom," she relayed.

"So do I, come to think of it," responded Goldie. "Plus I want to wash my filthy hands and refill our water bottles." They stretched their arms and legs. "You know he took our cake box. Who said he could have it? I think that was very nervy."

"I'll say!" Jane chuckled, thinking of how little this mattered in the scheme of things. "But apart from that, my instinct is that he's not someone we should be with. First of all besides his satchel, I think there were dried bloodstains on the top of his folding stool.

That kind of freaked me out. Secondly, he's downright weird and said he lives with six brothers. Luckily, he left the truck unlocked. For the night I would rather stay safely locked inside the truck as I did at Jack's house. Since Napoleon said this road ends nearby at a cliff—the very word *cliff* makes me cringe—we'll head downhill when the sun comes up. Although we don't know the way to Jack's house or Hannah's, I'm sure we'll manage somehow. We're bound to meet up with someone along the road who can help us."

"Do you really think it's blood?" Goldie responded. "It could have been used as a cutting board for meat. Or maybe it's just paint. And anyway, so what?" Goldie was swinging her foot nervously skimming the hard packed dirt.

"I don't know Goldie, I'm probably just overreacting. I simply don't want to take a chance. I thought Jack was very strange, especially at first, but he's relatively tame compared to Napoleon. And who's to say this man's six brothers aren't like him or maybe even worse? Seven all in one place! Jeez! Let's both clean up in the bathroom. Then we'll wait out the night in the truck."

Goldie nodded in agreement. They both proceeded slowly past the rear of the truck, along the way that Napoleon had run off. Their feet crunched beneath them with each step as though they were walking on crushed eggshells. Jane was grateful for the faint moonlight. Otherwise her trepidation would be much worse. At the spot where they last saw Napoleon, they stopped before a wooden gate coated in high gloss white paint. Alongside it and perched on top of a post, was a matching mailbox with "SNOE" printed in gold letters on the sides. A polished brass "7" was nailed to the drop door.

Jane and Goldie stared ahead. As their eyes adjusted to the scene before them, their mouths dropped open in wonderment.

"Oh my gosh!" cried Jane, unabashed at shattering the silence.

20

THE COTTAGE

Before them, with the backdrop of a fresh, round moon and true to Napoleon's description, was a charming cottage—quaint, old-world, and thatched. The entire picket fence, on either side of the gate and surrounding the cottage, was bordered on the inside by meticulously trimmed little hedges. Beginning at the gate, a winding, silvery, textured path led to the front entryway, and it struck Jane that the dim in-ground path lights installed along its edges gave the appearance of a mini airport runway. Darkness loomed behind each of the four up and three down casement windows whose diagonal muntin bars separated diamond-shaped panes of glass.

"Look at that roof!" Goldie exclaimed. "What's that all over it?"

Jane shrugged her shoulders.

The peaked thatched roof, steeply slanted on the sides, was made of what appeared to be dried reeds. It was dribbled with a thick glistening substance that reminded Jane of sprinkled glitter encased in streaks of hardened glue on arts and crafts projects. The whole setting smacked of a sparkling and pristine world.

Jane tentatively opened the gate, and she and Goldie took a few steps inside as it swung back and latched shut. Goldie shook her head in awe. "This is a magical wonderland," she said with the child-like enthusiasm of being in a toy store. "I never *ever,* saw anything like this before."

Along the path and covering the entire front property was an iridescent granular white substance that looked like a winter snowfall. They bent down and scooped up a handful to examine it closer in the slight light. Looking at each other with quizzical expressions they exclaimed in unison, "Pearls?" They stood up and surveyed the area again.

Goldie shook her head in disbelief. "But they can't be real. No way. There are a gazillion of them. I know! I'll test one with my teeth to see if it's gritty. I learned that in a magazine about gems. It's a way to tell a real pearl from a faux pearl." She started to bring one to her mouth, but Jane knocked it out of her hand.

"Goldie, are you nuts? We don't know for sure what they are or where they came from. Considering Napoleon's penchant for cleaning things, they could be contaminated with bleach or some other industrial chemical."

"You know what, Jane?" Goldie asked. "You're one paranoid person. I like you a lot, but sometimes you say things that scare me."

"I'm sorry, and yes I may very well be paranoid," Jane snapped. "But I only want to keep us safe long enough to get help. I want nothing more than to go home—wherever that is—and sweep my children up into my arms. So I can tell you one thing. If I had found some white beads in my mom's jewelry box, I might be inclined to rub one across my teeth out of curiosity. But picking them off this alien looking ground and performing that test? No way."

"You're probably right," Goldie muttered.

"Forget it," Jane replied. "It doesn't matter. Whatever happened to that little rug rat, Napoleon? Let's find out where he went. Come on."

Trying not to appear even more paranoid and upsetting Goldie further, Jane hid her lingering apprehension about entering Napoleon's house. She and Goldie glided along the pearly path to a glossy white door. Hanging from the knocker and haphazardly tied with a white bow was an ostrich feather duster.

"Some host he is," Jane said. She knocked timidly at first, even though the door was slightly ajar. She knocked again and then a third time, each time progressively louder. Losing patience over the lack of response she pushed the door ajar, and she and Goldie peeked in.

"Psst. Napoleon? Psst. Napoleon, are you there?" Jane whispered. The outside path lights cast shadows in the otherwise empty room, its darkness framed by the doorframes. There was no sign of him.

"I don't like the looks of this," Jane said.

"What should we do?" Goldie asked in a quivering voice.

Jane could tell that Goldie was on the verge of tears. She was considering the prospect of leaving right then and there when all of a sudden she was startled by strange noises.

"Wait." Jane put her hand on Goldie's arm. "Do you hear that?" Jane asked, feeling quite on edge.

"No. I don't *ever* hear," Goldie replied. "That's not funny. What's up?"

"I'm so sorry, Goldie. I said it out of habit," Jane apologized. "I heard groans—some murmurings."

"Are you sure?" Goldie seemed distracted. "This is too eerie being here in the dark," Goldie said. "I'm going to turn on some light. She groped around by the doorframe until she found a switch.

The single big, round, overhead light was at first blinding. As their eyes got accustomed to the light, it revealed a stark white pristine room. Jane tapped Goldie who was shielding her eyes with the side of her hand like a lookout scout.

"Jeez. It's like a movie set for a surgical suite," Jane said as Goldie turned to face her. "This is incredible, especially since they're so stingy with lighting in the rest of the place."

Goldie exclaimed, her voice cracking, "I'm getting goose bumps. Let's leave."

"Oh—now suddenly you want to scoot out of here," Jane remarked. "A little while ago you could care less. Besides, I thought you had to use the bathroom and wanted to wash up and all."

"I do. I really do," Goldie replied. "And fill the water bottles. We can't be hiking tomorrow and not have a supply of water."

"Napoleon said it's to the left," Jane added.

"Okay. Come with me, Jane. Be ready with the bear spray."

"Of course. We'll stick together." Jane called out in a whisper, "Napoleon? "Napoleon?" she raised her voice a little bit. There was no answer. *Wherever is that strange little man?* She motioned to Goldie as they tiptoed further in. Her eyes rapidly darted around the premises. The room was very simply furnished and astonishingly immaculate. A long, low, metal table was surrounded by little, white, wooden chairs and was set with plain white placemats topped by a small, white bowl and three utensils over a neatly folded white, cloth napkin. A white refrigerator and an old-fashioned porcelain sink with a step stool in front of it were a few feet away from the table.

"This is too peculiar," Jane muttered to herself. She turned to face Goldie. "Look at all the place settings ready and waiting for the next meal."

Jane spotted a case of bottled spring water at the end of the table, and alongside of it was a stack of clear plastic cups with "Snoe's White Glove Cleaning Company" printed on them. The visual suggestion of water made her realize how dry her mouth was.

She said to Goldie, "Wait here a moment. I want to check out the water supply over there." She pointed the case out to Goldie and walked over to it. Unfortunately, except for a few drops in one of them, the bottles were empty. She chuckled. *Just my luck. No matter. Tap water will do.*

"Forget it," Jane said as she came back to Goldie. "We'll fill the bottles in the bathroom as you said before. I'll go in first, and you stand guard by the door. Let's be very quick."

The bathroom, adjacent to the kitchen, was easily visible due to a hideous, little, clown nightlight inserted into one of the wall sockets. Jane peered inside and detected a lavender fragrance emanating from a basket of potpourri placed on top of the toilet tank. While taking several deep calming breaths and enjoying the aroma, she looked around in amazement at the chic appearance afforded by gray and white marble tile extending from ceiling to floor. As she headed for the sink, the stall shower off to the right caught her attention for a moment and she paused, almost as though to worship it. *Oh, to be able to enjoy that invigorating spray right now!*

Instead, Jane thoroughly scrubbed up and splashed cold water on her face at the sink, heeding the amusing hand printed sign, "Remember to Wash Your Hands." *They surely have an obsession with cleanliness and order around here.* She dried herself with a white towel from a neatly folded stack on a stool in the corner. A used towel hanging on the bar was too damp.

After they were done in the bathroom, Goldie hurried over to the refrigerator and opened the door.

"Gee Whiz. Look at all these jars of applesauce! And there are some squashed pastries too," Goldie exclaimed. "I can see the tops of milk containers stashed way in the back. Another one or two may be orange juice."

Jane looked over Goldie's shoulders at the familiar contents. "Those pastries must be what came out of the box that Hansom gave us," Jane said. "I think I'll have one. I'm starving."

"Me too," Goldie said as Jane stuffed a flattened creampuff in her mouth.

They each helped themselves to another as Goldie checked out the freezer compartment.

"Will you look at that!" Goldie said with her mouth full. "These people are like kids."

Other than some frozen candy bars and a container of vanilla ice cream, there were several boxes of frozen fruit pops. Suddenly a loud snorting sound came from behind them. Jane jumped.

"What happened?" Goldie asked. "What's up?"

"I heard a loud snort. At least that's what it sounded like," Jane replied.

"A snort? Golly, I hate to tell you, but that might be a wild boar," Goldie exclaimed. Her eyes widened into the shape of saucers. "Once I watched a nature show about wild boars. They're also called feral hogs. These grumpy porkers are nocturnal animals, and well, last time I looked, it *is* nighttime. Right? They can weigh as much as 250 pounds and are very aggressive and dangerous. Since they eat almost anything, we better watch out we're not gored by their ugly, razor sharp tusks. Those are really their canine teeth that curl out of their mouth. We better get out of here right now."

Jane pictured a boar suddenly bounding out at them from one of the cabinets, before getting a grip on herself. The absurdity of the suggestion and the fact that she would even give that possibility some thought made her laugh.

"Go ahead. Make fun of me," Goldie snapped.

"I'm sorry Goldie," Jane responded. "I'm not laughing at you. I appreciate the wealth of knowledge you have for your young age. But while we don't know what the sound is or where it's coming from, I'm sure we can be certain there is no wild boar in this house."

Goldie smirked and dismissed Jane's comment with a brusque wave of her hand.

The sound came again even louder, and Jane shuttered. It was definitely close by, and this time Jane could tell the direction from which it came. Goldie saw the fear on Jane's face and remained motionless.

"Again? You heard it again?" Goldie asked.

"Yes. Snorts and grunts. Some murmurings," Jane replied. "Much louder and it came from behind us. In fact, they're still going on." She pointed in the direction of the sounds. Unable to stand the uncertainty any longer and experiencing a burst of bravery, Jane decided to take a moment to track down the suspicious noise to its source. She motioned to Goldie to come along with her as she followed the sounds emanating from the other side of the kitchen, beyond the table. They gingerly crossed the room as though they were walking on eggshells. The far wall turned out to be a flimsy, free standing, space divider. Using her hands, Jane mimed to Goldie that the sounds she had heard were coming from here. They walked to the edge of the partition and peaked around it. Jane and Goldie gasped in unison.

In an area revealed by faintly diffused light reflected from the horrendous kitchen ceiling fixture, was a row of little beds, each covered in a white sheet. Rhythmic snorts and grunts were simultaneously being emitted from the sleeping occupants whose little heads were resting face up on fluffy pillows. Somebody was babbling gibberish. Jane and Goldie moved closer in to get a better look and stealthily proceeded down the line of seven beds to look at the faces. Each one was a man with white hair in varying degrees of baldness.

"They're practically clones of Napoleon," Jane mouthed to Goldie.

However, unlike Napoleon who didn't have any facial hair, the others had a white beard or mustache, and no two were the same style. Jane and Goldie continued on down the line of beds to see if they might spot Napoleon. Sure enough, they recognized him in the last bed without his cap on, his worn out leather satchel hanging on the metal headboard. His long, untied, white hair was splayed out on the pillow like an opened Chinese folding fan. Jane could hear him snoring and snorting like all the others, very soundly asleep. Jane did all she could to not jump on him and pound on his little head. She nimbly tiptoed out quickly to the kitchen, followed by Goldie.

"Why, that little bean brain!" Jane cried. "He invites us to stay overnight, ditches us as he races out of the truck to use the bathroom, and then goes to bed without saying a word."

"Hey, calm down Jane," Goldie admonished. "I didn't think Napoleon was the type to show us any semblance of hospitality. We knew he was strange from the get-go, but we used him for our purposes at the moment in getting out of the predicament we were in. Remember, all we wanted was not to be left in the open over night, nothing more. Creating a clamor over him will only wake everyone up before we have a chance to think this through."

"Well aren't you the voice of reason! You're right," Jane admitted with a chuckle. "Let's get out of here, hole up in the truck and leave at the first sign of daylight before anything else happens to us. I hope by this time tomorrow, I'll be with my family. That's my goal, and also to make sure you will get back home safely to your dad. I'm trying to stay positive. I can't imagine how sick with worry they all are."

Suddenly, a piercing pain shot through Jane's skull and the room began to spin around her. She pressed the front and back of her head with her hands for some relief.

"Oh, jeez, I have to sit down. I...I...feel like I was hit with a hammer," Jane said.

Goldie ran and grabbed one of the kitchen chairs for her. Jane plopped into it and closed her eyes.

"Are you OK?" Goldie asked.

"I just have to wait until this passes in a moment," Jane replied. "The lighting is bothering my eyes."

"Do you want me to turn it off?" Goldie offered

"No thanks, Goldie. It's otherwise way too dark in here. We could trip over something, and besides, you wouldn't be able to see what I was saying if necessary. Let's just go. I'll be fine in the truck."

As they both crossed through the kitchen, intending to leave as quickly as possible, Jane's attention was startled by thumping and clanging coming from beneath the floor. Goldie flinched simultaneously upon feeling the vibration.

"You felt something, didn't you?" Jane asked.

"Yes," Goldie replied. "It's underneath us. What did you hear?"

"A persistent thumping and clanging sound," Jane said. "There it goes again."

They looked at their feet and noticed there were little tiny spaces between the floorboards. Upon getting closer, to the extent that they pressed their noses flat over the cracks, they could see something flickering underneath. In the brightness of the overhead light, this would have otherwise gone undetected. The knocking began again. It was no accident. It was a deliberate pattern. Three times.

Jane looked at Goldie and said, "Somebody's in the lower region of the house."

"Yup," Goldie nodded. "There's definitely a slight vibration as though something heavy is being dragged around."

Goldie slithered around like a snake with her open hands palming the impeccably clean floor. Jane respected her keen sense of vibration that compensated for her lack of hearing.

"Here. It stopped here." Goldie pointed to the spot. Almost immediately, three thumps came again from below. Goldie tapped the floor three times with her knuckles. There were thumps back.

"Jane, put your ear to the spot. Do you hear anything else—a voice maybe?"

Jane did as Goldie suggested.

"Oh my. Yes," Jane replied. "It sounds like, 'Help me. Help.' It's very faint." There were more thumps. Jane tapped in response.

"Goldie, look!" Jane motioned to a short, linear gap, about a quarter inch wide in the floor under the table. She could hear the pleas again, and she tapped the floor in acknowledgment. She heard a thump back. She tapped two times. There were two thumps in response.

Jane looked up at Goldie. "Something is definitely amiss down there." She crawled under the table and continued to follow the outline of the gap.

"I think there's a trap door under here," Jane said after crawling back out.

"Then let's move the table so we can get to it," Goldie suggested.

Jane and Goldie quietly moved the chairs away and took opposite ends of the table.

"Wait." Jane signaled to Goldie for her attention and pointed to the case of empty water bottles. Goldie came over to her.

"We wouldn't want them to tumble off and wake everybody up," Jane said.

"Quick thinking," Goldie replied.

Together, they placed the bottles on the floor then proceeded to carefully move the table. They took special precaution not to tip it and have the plates slide off. Sure enough, on the floor where the table had been, was an outline of a trap door.

"Goldie, this was obviously intentionally hidden, and I think it was more than for aesthetic reasons. I wonder what those two big iron eye bolts are for. They're solidly secured into the floor beams." Jane was kicking them with her feet.

"Goldie, look, here," Jane said. "There's a long sliding iron latch on this end. I got it opened. Help me lift the door up."

The thumping and muffled cries for help were getting more and more frenzied. Jane decided it was best not to call out, and in case Goldie was thinking of doing that, she gave her the 'shhh' sign. Together they grabbed the door handle and pulled upwards. Dank air wafted past them as they peered into the void. Once the kitchen light permeated the darkness, it revealed wooden steps speckled with mold, pitched steeply towards the bottom.

"I'm going down to look," Jane gestured to Goldie. "Something's very wrong, and I can't leave not knowing what. If it's bad, we'll get out of here real fast and get help somehow."

"Be careful. It's probably slimy and slippery. I'll call out if anything happens up here, and I'm ready with the bear spray in case."

Jane could feel the cool moisture on the makeshift railing. Her eyes got accustomed to the pitch-black darkness the further she descended into the cellar.

With her tension mounting, she called out in a subdued tone, "Hello! Who's here? Where are you?"

A weak, sobbing voice responded, "Please help me, miss. Please. I'm over here. Look. Look!"

Jane turned towards the direction of the sound. Immediately, the hairs rose on her arms and the back of her neck. Her blood felt like it had turned to ice, and she froze in place.

21

MEETING PEARL

A short distance away from the stairs, a small girl was shining a flashlight on herself. It cast a looming shadow on a wall behind her and crawling insects, disturbed by the glow, scurried in all directions.

"Oh no!" Jane cried, totally stunned. "I can't believe this. Oh no," she repeated. "Honey, it's okay. It's okay now. I'm here to help you. What's your name?"

The girl astutely turned the light towards the very low ceiling to diffuse it. Even so, Jane flinched, as the shock of the illumination in the otherwise abject darkness stung her eyes.

"Pearl. My name is Pearl," she sniffled. "I'm nine and a half, and I was kidnapped by these bad men—*very* bad little men."

"Kidnapped? Kidnapped! Oh my," Jane exclaimed. She suddenly felt sick to her stomach. She realized the danger they were in and how deranged Napoleon Snoe and his brothers must actually be to do something like this. *Pearl could be the missing girl Jack was looking for. I have to find help. I have to find Jack.* Her mind was racing.

"Oh you poor thing," Jane said. "What do these awful men keep you here for?"

"They make me clean their dirty mops and rags every day," Pearl whimpered. "Who are *you*? Are you really and truly going to get me out of here?" she asked between sobs. "I want to go home to my mommy and daddy."

"Of course I'm going to help you, Pearl," Jane said sweetly. "You're going to be okay. My name is Jane. I'm...I'm...I'm...a mommy myself," she said, choking back tears and emitting a sigh. "Come over to me. I don't want to hit my head on the ceiling. I can't stand up down here." *The last thing I need is another injury.*

Jane could hear something like heavy metal sliding along the floor.

"What's all that clatter?" Jane asked.

"It's a heavy chain. My ankles are chained and locked together," Pearl replied. "See?" She pointed to them with the flashlight.

Jane was shocked at what she saw and felt like she was gong to vomit.

"Are you the police? It seems like forever since I was taken, and I've been waiting to be saved. I don't know how long it's been. I've lost track of time."

"I'm not a police officer, honey," Jane replied. "I just happened to wind up at this house. It's been a very long and crazy day. But never mind all that now. We're in a big hurry. Listen. The men are sound asleep. Upstairs is my friend Goldie who's being the lookout. We'll get you out of here." Jane hoped her voice did not betray the doubt she was feeling.

"Hurry is right!" Pearl cried. "They all take sleeping pills every night exactly at the same time, and depending on when that was, might wake up soon, and then you and your friend will be caught, and it will be hopeless for all of us because there are plenty of chains down here for them to use."

Sleeping pills? No wonder Napoleon conked out so quickly, Jane thought. *How bizarre. He leaves Goldie and me at the truck, makes a beeline for the house, and then pops a sleeping pill right away.*

"Jane. Jane. Psst Jane," Goldie softly called from above, breaking Jane's train of thought. "Are you OK? What's going on? Stomp hard on the stairs if you're OK."

Jane did what Goldie asked her to do.

"Thanks for sparing a few seconds of your time to let me know," Goldie sarcastically remarked. "Do you think you could come back upstairs and let me in on the secret as to what's going on down there? I'm real scared. Time is ticking by, and I want to get out of here before the men wake up."

"Pearl, that's Goldie, who's a few years older than you. Don't mind her. She's on edge too. She's deaf. She gets by with incredible lip reading, and she feels sounds by their vibrations. I promise we'll get you out of here. I have to go up quickly to speak to her and calm her down. In the meantime, can you hobble over to the stairs?"

"No!" Pearl replied in a high-pitched nervous tone. "I can move around but not as far as the stairs." Pearl's voice sounded breathless as though she were exerting herself. "Why do you think I'm still way over here? My ankles are chained together with a padlock, but it's not only that. The chain is shackled to an even heavier chain that's attached to the wall with another padlock." Pearl pointed to it with her flashlight. Jane gasped.

"Yeah, horrible, huh?" Pearl said. "Both padlocks have to be unlocked, and one of the brothers—one of the seven of them—has the key that opens both padlocks. Each day a different one wears it around his neck when sleeping. You'll have to find it. PLEASE. I have an escape all figured out. You've got to listen to me." Pearl's pleas were frantic.

Jane's immediate reaction was that any attempt to rescue this girl alone would be futile. *The whole idea is ludicrous.* She was also concerned about protecting herself and Goldie. *Goldie and I could run for help much quicker than it would take for us to hunt down the key to the lock—not to mention the risk that would entail.*

"And just how are we supposed to accomplish that, Pearl? Plus it's wasting precious minutes, especially considering the likelihood that one out of the seven will wake up. The best thing may be for Goldie and me to leave and return with the police."

"Police?" Pearl was becoming hysterical. "Reality check! There are no police around here for miles! No! No! Don't leave me. Nobody else will help. Believe me. Believe me. I know what you and your friend can do. I have a plan. Please don't leave me here." She started to cry.

"Alright. Alright, dear. But we're racing against time. I'll hear what you have in mind, but first I have to get up to Goldie to quickly tell her you're here and what the situation is," Jane said. "Like I said, she's deaf and has to be able to read my lips. I'll just quickly climb back up ..."

"No, No, No," Pearl frantically interrupted. "Listen, listen," she sniffled. "First things first. Please. Pretty please! See that spot over there? I want you to go over there." Pearl was shining her flashlight light to mark where she wanted Jane to go. "There. Go over there. I'll guide you. The room is empty so there's nothing to run into. But first as you get off the bottom step, put your arm up and feel for the ceiling beams so you don't hit your head. Then you'll be able to tell how far you have to bend down to come over to me."

"Psst, hey psst, Jane, I'm leaving without you," Goldie called down again in a low voice. "Bye! It's been great knowing you. Have a nice life, I'm serious. Very serious. Whatever are you doing? I can hardly see you it's so dark down there."

Jane asserted herself. "Pearl, you'll just have to wait a minute. I have to go up to Goldie to let her know you're here. I have to. I'll be right back. I promise."

"No, No, No. No. Don't leave me!" Pearl wailed.

"Gosh! Calm down. I'll be right back," Jane cried.

Jane carefully climbed the steep stairs.

"There you are," Goldie said snidely. "What's wrong with you—disappearing like that? First Napoleon vanishes—then you."

"Goldie, hold on. Hold on. Heck! It was only a couple of minutes. Sorry, but wait until you hear this. There's a little nine-year-old girl down there. Nine and a half, to be exact. She said she was kidnapped by the Snoe's. She's tied up in chains heavier than she is, and she didn't want me to leave her for a second. She's hysterical and all."

Goldie's eyes were wide and her mouth remained open in astonishment as Jane rambled on.

"She has this little flashlight, and she points the light around. Otherwise it's pitch black in there. It's cold and damp, and I can't imagine anyone putting a child in that situation. These men are crazy. We have to get out of here…"

"That's exactly what I've been saying all along," Goldie said. "This is all so incredible. We have to get her out of there. Do you think she's the missing child that Jack was looking for—the one whose sort of picture is on the milk containers?"

"Possibly," Jane replied. "I couldn't see her that well to tell if there's a resemblance. Her name is Pearl."

"Wait—did I read you right—you said *Pearl?*" Goldie asked. "Wow! That's an awesome coincidence!" Goldie exclaimed.

"Yes. *Pearl,*" Jane responded. *"Pearl.* Oh!" She laughed. The connection finally sank in as she pictured the ground cover on the approach to the cottage. "You're right, Goldie. That's a clever observation—and yes, I'm sure it's purely coincidence."

Persistent thumping resumed beneath them.

"Jane! Jane! Jane! Are you there?" Pearl's frantic little voice called out from below. "Don't leave me."

Jane faced downwards to the basement, and, against her better judgment about not making noise, she responded, "I'm still here, Pearl. I'll be right down."

Jane turned back around towards Goldie.

"Pearl was calling out. She's scared to death that I'll leave her. I'll go back down and see what it is that she was going to show me about a plan for escaping. Oh, and there's more." Goldie watched her intensely. "Pearl said that the men take sleeping pills at the same time every night which puts them into a very deep slumber. It explains why they didn't even know we were near them. That's a lucky break for us since it buys us some time."

Goldie frowned. "You mean Napoleon ran into the house and took a sleeping pill right away? Why would he do that and leave us just standing around?"

"Well, it's yet another indication that he's crazy. Seems like the men's obsession with order and cleanliness includes another obsession of having to be asleep in bed at an appointed time," Jane remarked. "So the clock was ticking for him to stay on schedule."

"He's weirder than we thought," Goldie said. "Not to mention he and his brothers kidnapped a little girl and are holding her prisoner in horrible conditions for who knows what reason. Hurry up and go see what Pearl has in mind."

Jane slowly started down the slimy steps.

"Pearl. I'm coming downstairs," Jane said. "Please shine the light as you did before so I can see a bit of where I'm going."

"Okay," Pearl responded. She did what she was asked, aiming the flashlight towards the ceiling.

"That's very helpful, honey," Jane remarked. She felt for the first overhead beam as she approached the bottom and stepped onto a concrete floor. "So where do you want me to go?"

"Over there. Go over there. It's around there."

Jane ducked as she proceeded to the spot that Pearl was pointing to with her flashlight.

"Stop there!" Pearl exclaimed. She pointed the light at the ceiling.

"Look up at the beams," Pearl instructed. "Grope for a piece of cloth and grab it with your hand. It's a little tied sack. I hope... I hope it's still there."

Jane fumbled around. "I have it," Jane announced.

"Yay! Bring it to me," Pearl said pointing the flashlight at herself.

Jane carefully kept her upper body low as she approached Pearl. As soon as Jane reached her, she knelt down to Pearl's level, and they gave each other a big hug.

"So what do I do?" Jane was feeling very anxious about whether she would ever get out of this place alive. *I'm about ready to jump out of my skin.*

"Listen to me very carefully, and the plan will be easy to pull off," Pearl said. "We'll be out of here in no time."

"Go ahead. I'm all ears," Jane replied.

Pearl explained, "Inside the sack is a container of applesauce and about 30 drug capsules. They're filled with some powdery stuff, which is the sleeping medication that the men take. I was able to accumulate the capsules a little bit at a time so no one would notice. One day I was going to figure out how to put it to use so I could escape from here. Take my flashlight—you'll need it for later—and all this stuff upstairs into the kitchen. First grab a spoon from one of the table settings. Then open the applesauce jar. Take each capsule, every one of them, twist it open and shake all the contents into the applesauce. Stir it all up very well, and keep the spoon in the jar.

"Oh, I almost forgot, and this is extremely important. Before you open the capsules, grab one of those folded cloth napkins from one of the place settings, wet it, and tie it on your face over your mouth and nose. You know, like a bandit. There's a chance that some of the very fine powder will pouf up into the air when you're dumping it, and this will prevent you from breathing it in. Also, tell Goldie to stay away when you make the mixture, and do *not* touch your mouth, nose, or eyes with your hand after you handle this or it might get into your body and affect you. That's what I learned in school about preventing germs from getting in, so I figured this would apply to the powder."

"I wonder if it could get absorbed through my skin," Jane remarked. "I'll be sure to scrub my arms and hands immediately."

"Ooh. Maybe. I never thought of that. So as I was saying: After you have the mixture ready, go into the bedroom where the little men are sleeping in their little beds. The men snore all night because they lie face up with their mouths open. I saw that once. Have Goldie aim my flashlight towards their mouths so you can clearly see what you're doing. Start at the bed farthest away so you can work backwards in case you have to escape for some reason. Quickly drop two spoonfuls of the applesauce into each of their mouths. After you're done, wait a couple of minutes while the medicine takes effect. Then go back and get the padlock key, which will be around the neck of one of them. Grab Napoleon's satchel because he keeps the truck keys in it. Come down here to me and free me up. Then we'll run out of here, start up the truck, and be gone in a flash. That's my plan. Did you get all that? I want to know if you got it all. My teachers always ask to repeat instructions back to them. It's a teacher thing."

Jane was astounded by the details of the well thought out scheme and all the directives Pearl threw at her. She repeated the instructions.

"You got it all!" Pearl exclaimed.

"I'm on the case," Jane replied, like an experienced law enforcement officer. "Don't worry."

They hugged each other again. Pearl handed Jane the flashlight, and after planting a kiss on Pearl's forehead, Jane headed for the stairs and climbed up.

"Oh, and Pearl?

"What?"

"I meant to ask, and I didn't notice, but ah…ah…do you happen to have braids?" Jane asked tentatively.

"Yes as a matter of fact," Pearl answered. "I have them clipped up over my head. Why?"

"Were you selling wrapping paper?"

"Yes! How did you know?" Pearl asked.

"I'll tell you later," Jane acknowledged with a nod and a smile. *Bingo!* She went up the stairs, leaving Pearl with the pitch-black as her only companion.

"It's about time," Goldie said. "I was beginning to think you were liking it down there."

Jane ignored the snide remark and, after grabbing a spoon and a cloth napkin from the table, signaled Goldie to follow her to the bathroom.

"Guess what, Goldie! Pearl is wearing braids!"

"Jeepers. No way!" exclaimed Goldie. "Could it be…?"

"And she was selling wrapping paper," Jane added. "I don't want to speculate at this point as to whether Pearl is the missing girl on the milk cartons, but based on the facts, it's seems rather clear to me that she is. We have some very critical business to conduct rather quickly. First, I'm going to moisten this napkin and cover my face with it for protection while I prepare a special mixture. While I do that I need you to stand a safe distance away so you don't inhale the powder." Jane explained the rest of Pearl's plan.

"So first let me get this straight," Goldie said. "Before we go back to find the key and grab Napoleon's satchel, all I have to do is shine the light on each man's mouth so you can drop the mixture in?"

"That's right. We're going to start at the far side which begins with Napoleon."

Jane tied the wet cloth over her face. Goldie left the bathroom and waited by the door as Jane prepared the concoction. She carefully completed the task in a few minutes and then cleaned up, leaving the soaked napkin and the spoon in the sink.

"It's all ready. Let's go!" Jane mouthed to Goldie.

Goldie smiled and raised her hand to execute a high five gesture with Jane. Amidst all the snoring and snorting, they tiptoed to the far side of the bedroom where Napoleon was sleeping. Jane felt her heart pounding, and the more she focused on it, the more it seemed that the beat was in syncopated rhythm with the men's sleep sounds. She was sweating so much that the hairs at the nape of her neck were already dripping wet. Goldie followed her and pointed the flashlight towards Napoleon's chin so as not to shock his eyes with the brightness. His mouth was wide open just as Pearl predicted. Jane wished she could stuff her hand down into it and choke him, but instead she gritted her teeth in her rage and stuck to the plan.

Before she moved on with Jane, Goldie decided to grab Napoleon's satchel while she was there. To her surprise it was much heavier than expected, and then she recalled the stool they had seen him take out of it. So instead of slinging it over her shoulder she dragged it along the floor. Down the line of beds, one by one, with trembling hands, Jane dropped two spoonfuls of the tainted applesauce into each man's open mouth, illuminated by the flashlight Goldie was holding. She watched the men's faces contorting into varying expressions as reflexes kicked in and as they spontaneously swallowed the slippery substance once it slid to the back of their throats.

Everything was going well until they got to the sixth bed. This man's head was turned sideways, so Jane had to think of a way to get him to face upwards. She motioned to Goldie to skip him and move on to the last bed. After spooning in the requisite two portions, they returned to the sixth bed. Jane had an idea. She went to the opposite side of the way the man was facing. Carefully she tickled his exposed cheek hoping to cause him to turn in that direction. It worked.

As he turned towards her, Goldie pointed the flashlight towards his chin, and Jane quickly shoved a spoonful of applesauce into his partially open mouth, forcing it wider. Just as she started to withdraw the spoon, the man clamped his teeth down on it. Jane and Goldie watched in horror as his eyes flew open. In rapid sequence he pulled out the spoon and grabbed Jane's arm, violently twisting it behind her back while squealing like a pig. She was scared to death that his noise would be enough to waken all the others. By then he was sitting up, and Jane was trying with all her might to use a self-defense move to extricate herself from his grip.

"Take that you miserable little runt!" Goldie yelled. Suddenly there was dead silence. As the man lost hold of Jane's arm, she pulled away and turned to see what happened. She was aghast seeing him lying on the floor.

"What the...?" Jane shrieked as she looked at Goldie.

"I hit him over the head with Napoleon's satchel! Boing!" Goldie exclaimed enthusiastically. "Remember the cruddy board he used for his step stool? Well it's obviously still in here. It knocked the guy out. Look!"

Jane didn't know whether to laugh at Goldie's answer or to cry because the pain in her arm and shoulder was excruciating. She decided instead to give Goldie a big hug. Then she knelt down next to the man and shoved the rest of the applesauce into his mouth.

"That should do it," Jane announced emphatically. "He'll be out cold for a long time."

"I saw who has the padlock key around his neck," Goldie said. "It's the man sleeping in the bed next to Napoleon's. I'll get it."

As Goldie went about retrieving the padlock key, Jane hurriedly pulled the truck keys out of Napoleon's heavy, cruddy bag before flinging it on the now empty bed. Having accomplished Pearl's plan, Jane and Goldie left the room.

"We did it Pearl! We did it! I'm coming down," shouted Jane gleefully at the top of the cellar stairs. There was no response.

Jane turned to Goldie. "You stay up here. Let me have the flashlight and the padlock key. Here. Take the keys to the truck."

Goldie did as she was asked.

"If you want to get my attention for some reason, bang on the top step," Jane instructed.

Goldie nodded.

Jane faced the basement opening. "Pearl! Pearl! We did it," she announced again. There was no answer. *Now what?* Jane crept down the stairs using the flashlight and bent over to protect her head. She approached Pearl, finding her asleep in a heap against the wall. She tapped her face gently to revive her.

"Pearl! Pearl!" Jane whispered as she unlocked both padlocks and freed Pearl from her chains. "Wake up honey. It's Jane. We did it. We did it! Goldie and I followed your plan to a T, and the men are all in a deep sleep now. Stand up and try to move your legs as best you can. We're going upstairs now."

Pearl opened her eyes and yawned. "Really? Really? You did it? I'm free?" she murmured groggily. "I'm so tired, Jane. I usually sleep when the men sleep. They always get me up early to clean up after breakfast."

"Well, Pearl, that's not going to happen anymore," Jane responded. "This horrible experience is over, and you're safe with me and Goldie. We're all getting out of here, and once we're in the truck you can sleep peacefully, dear. All I have to do is make sure you get safely up the steps."

Pearl and Jane carefully made it to the top of the stairs. Pearl plopped onto one of the chairs and let out a tremendous sigh of relief while Jane went over to the sink to wash her hands of the slime on the railing. Goldie followed behind them and sat on another chair next to Pearl.

"Hi Pearl. My name is Goldie. You had such a great idea about how to put those creeps out. It worked like a charm. You're brilliant." Goldie and Pearl hugged each other.

"I'm thirsty. Do either of you want anything cold to drink from the fridge before we leave?" Jane asked. She went to the refrigerator and grabbed two of the containers she saw before. "One of these is milk, and the other is orange juice. Hey Pearl. Look. This may be of interest to you." She handed Pearl the milk container.

Pearl opened it and poured it into one of the cups on the table. "Thank you."

"I don't want any milk," Goldie said. "I'll have the orange juice." Goldie poured the beverage into three cups, and drank them all like a fiend.

"Pearl, I meant that you might be interested in the milk container itself," Jane said. "Take a look at the sides of it. Do you notice anything?"

Pearl took the container and turned it around in her hands.

"Shoot! There's a picture of a child on it, and it looks like me in my braids!" She read the caption out loud. "Have you seen this missing child?"

"That's why you asked me about braids, huh Jane?"

Jane nodded with a smile.

"So it's *you*! Wow!" Goldie interjected. "It's odd that there isn't any information with it. What's your last name?"

"White," Pearl responded.

"Hmmm. Pearl White." Goldie repeated. "Do you know what's all over the Snoes' front yard?"

"No. What?" Pearl asked.

"You'll see when we get out of here," Goldie replied. "It's kind of weird-funny. Speaking of getting out…" She glanced at Jane.

Jane couldn't speak. The pervasive starkness and sterility of this white themed environment were getting to her. She winced as razor-sharp pain shot through the side of her head and quickly dissipated, unlike the many lingering episodes she had experienced before. Her vision clouded as though a veil had been draped over her eyes, obscuring the two people in front of her. The din of voices around her was nothing she could make sense of. As she emerged from her state of oblivion and confusion, her surroundings became increasingly distinct.

"Jane, are you sick?" Pearl asked on the verge of tears. "What's wrong with her, Goldie?"

"I haven't the slightest idea. She has these sort of crazy episodes here and there. Jane, Jane. Are you there? Earth to Jane," Goldie called out. "Yoo ho. Are you in there, Jane?"

Jane blinked several times, and saw Goldie and Pearl staring at her intently.

"Come on! Come on!" Goldie yelled. "We've got to get as far away as possible from the Snoes while they're sleeping."

"OK girls. Head for the truck!" Jane exclaimed as though nothing had happened to thwart their momentum.

They exited out the front door, with Pearl a bit wobbly as she shuffled along contending with her painful legs and ankles. She stopped and took a deep breath of the fresh night air. As an afterthought, Jane darted back inside, ignoring Goldie and Pearl's protests.

"Two minutes! This won't take more than two minutes. Start counting if you want to," Jane yelled.

Goldie started counting out loud as she jumped with flair onto the pathway illuminated by the high moon directly overhead. When Jane returned she had scooped up in her arms four empty water bottles and the containers of the remaining orange juice.

"You never know when we will next have an opportunity to drink something," Jane said. "It's better to be prepared."

"I got up to 114 seconds," Goldie announced as she came back to where Jane and Pearl were standing. "You had six more seconds to go. Pretty close."

"Thanks for the feedback," Jane said with a chuckle.

Goldie laughed as she handed the keys to Jane, who ceremoniously jiggled them in the air with a sense of defiance. Pearl took the opportunity of the door being open to take one last peek inside the cottage. She slammed it shut as hard as she could as though she were punctuating the last words of her gruesome story. "I'm so happy you were able to rescue me," Pearl exclaimed. "I can't wait to see my mommy and daddy."

"You will. We'll make sure of that," Jane said. "Come on."

With an encouraging touch from Jane, Pearl smiled. Elated with the prospect of making their escape but weary from their whole ordeal, the three of them cautiously trudged with uncertainty along the winding crunchy path towards the gate.

"Be careful, Pearl," Goldie said. "It's slippery. See what we were referring to about this ground cover? Don't all these tiny white balls look like pearls?"

"They do and they're so sparkly," Pearl exclaimed. "Why is all this here?"

"I guess we'll never know or care," Jane replied softly. She noted how nothing in the outer appearance of the pristine residence even so much as hinted at the horror within.

They opened the creaky gate and paused outside by the mailbox, trembling with overwhelming joy and anticipation of driving the truck far away from there. Jane and Goldie instinctively faced right towards where Napoleon had parked the truck earlier. Spontaneously they stopped walking and let out a shriek in unison as they frantically looked in all directions and then at each other.

"Where's the truck?" they bellowed.

22

THERE'S NEVER A CAB WHEN YOU WANT ONE

"Jeez! That's impossible," Jane cried, slapping both hands to the sides of her face in dismay as she observed the silent, deserted street.

She and Goldie ran straight out beyond the gate and with incredulous eyes panned the limited landscape slowly as one does with a video camera. From what they could see of the roadway, stretched out pale white in the moonlight, the truck was nowhere visible.

"What's wrong, Jane?" Pearl yelled.

"We don't see the truck, dear," Jane responded. "Napoleon stopped the truck over there, and that's the direction where we had walked from." She pointed to the right. "Don't worry. I'm sure we'll find it."

Tired and with her ankles very sore, Pearl sat on the ground and leaned against the mailbox post. She yawned and stretched her arms out.

"Now what? I feel like I'm going to conk out, and I can't even walk well. Those cuff locks rubbing over my anklebones were killers. If you don't find the truck and have to go on foot for help, leave without me and send my mommy and daddy to get me. I'm waiting right here." Pearl began to cry.

"Aw, sweetie, there's no way we would leave you like that," Jane said. She stooped down and gave Pearl a hug. "Let's not panic. There has to be an explanation. It has to be nearby."

"Well look at the bright side," Goldie interjected, trying to lighten things up. "At least there's all the money that Cindy gave us. We can always hail a taxi and take it to wherever we want to go in the whole wide world." She chuckled.

"Yeah. Except too bad all the taxis have already been hailed and taken by the horde of people around here," Jane quipped, followed by a nervous laugh.

Despite the moment of levity, Jane and Goldie looked around in utter disbelief, as though this were an illusion and at any moment a magician would emerge from hiding to make the truck materialize.

"This simply can't be," said Goldie. "We were standing right by the truck immediately after Napoleon got out and headed for the house. And we know for sure that he took the keys. Then we went inside and found everyone sleeping. Pearl, has there ever been anyone else around besides the Snoes?"

"Not that I know of," Pearl replied. "I never saw anyone else during the times when I was allowed out of the basement."

"Hey, this is interesting," Jane said as she tapped Goldie, who was facing another direction. Goldie spun around to look at Jane. "May I have the flashlight?" Jane inquired. Goldie handed it to her.

Jane flashed the light back and forth to the right along the dirt road.

"Look Goldie, a short way uphill. I'm sure that over there was about the very spot where the truck was parked."

She made a circle to mark the spot with the light beam.

"Come on with me," Jane said while beckoning to Goldie. "Let's quickly investigate this. We'll let Pearl rest. Pearl, we'll be right back."

They both began to stroll with their heads looking down like farmers and carefully examining the dirt for tire patterns as Jane swept the light beam back and forth.

Jane stopped abruptly and tugged at Goldie's sleeve.

"Gosh! Look," Jane screeched, pointing to the fresh tire marks in the dirt. There were two pairs of them, close together and they appeared different. They crouched down to look closer and then got up, retracing the path of the tire marks until they reached the point on the hill where they believed Napoleon had stopped the truck when they arrived. Goldie watched as Jane did a quick visual survey of the area with the penlight.

"Hmm," said Jane, once she had Goldie's attention. "Look. There are no tire tracks leading from this point forward so we have to assume this is where the truck was last situated and where we got out. Say, how about this? There are tracks swinging away from where the truck was and going across a little ways and back, which suggests to me that a turn was made. But they don't match the tire tracks on Napoleon's truck, which means his truck didn't turn around. It couldn't because it would have to be running, and Napoleon had the ignition key. I think that someone put the truck in neutral and pushed it backwards down the hill. In that case, my hunch is that it would follow the contour of the road, picking up some momentum on the rolling hills, and ultimately would have stopped at a level point."

"Gee whiz," said Goldie with a dramatic jump and clap of her hands. "That's a very clever assumption. But we won't know one way or the other until we check it out. Let's hurry. We'll get Pearl and head downhill."

Jane and Goldie walked back towards the house. Pearl was sound asleep where they had left her, sitting on the ground and leaning on the mailbox post. Jane gently shook her, and Goldie tapped her on the head.

"Pearl, Pearl—wake up—wake up," Jane said softly so as not to startle her. "It's Jane."

"Huh? Huh? Who? What?" Pearl opened her eyes and rubbed them to gain focus. She looked up at Jane and Goldie.

"Pearl?" Jane whispered into her ear.

"Yeah?" Pearl closed her eyes.

"Pearl, are you awake?" Jane nudged Pearl's shoulders. "PEARL!" Jane bellowed, losing patience.

"Yeah. I'm awake," Pearl mumbled. She opened her eyes barely.

"How long do you think the men will be sleeping given the extra dose of sleeping pills they got?" Jane asked.

"Oh, they'll be sleeping for a long, long time, Pearl replied. "You can be sure of that. Maybe for days. Maybe for weeks. Maybe for a hundred years."

"Ha! I'm asking because Goldie and I want to head down a ways and see if we spot the truck." Jane explained to Pearl what their findings and hunch were. "Do you feel up to coming along?"

"No. I told you I don't want to walk anyplace," Pearl whined. "I want to stay right here. I'm very tired. For one thing, I'm supposed to be sleeping now, and on top of that I had to rinse out and clean so many mops for the men yesterday. You'll come back quickly though, huh?"

"Alright Pearl. I'm worried about leaving you here," Jane said, although it was against her better judgment. "But I guess we have no other choice. Of course we'll be very quick. I promise. However, I want you to try and stay awake and alert. As a matter of fact I'm going to give you this bear repellent spray. Goldie has one too. If you're in danger from an approaching animal or a person, all you do is press on this trigger handle and take aim. Like this."

"Sure, I can do that," Pearl murmured after observing Jane's demonstration. She took the canister from Jane and put it in her lap.

Pearl's eyelids became heavier and heavier. Jane and Goldie watched sympathetically as she flopped forward into a slumbering heap.

Goldie shrugged her shoulders and began to tap her foot impatiently. "Leave her alone. Come on Jane, we're wasting time. Check your tote first to make sure you have the keys."

"I have the keys," Jane responded as she gave the thumbs up signal. She dangled them in the air for Goldie to see. "And the money Cindy gave us is safe and sound with me too, by the way."

"Let's first take a minute to go back to where the truck was," Jane said. "Since there's a little more light coming up, maybe we'll spot something we missed before. Come on."

Jane and Goldie returned to where they were certain Napoleon had parked his truck just a short distance away. Although they looked around and didn't observe anything new, from that vantage point they paused to gaze outward into the distance. With the exception of some deep shadows cast by trees, the flat land Napoleon had driven them through was encased in the fading moonlight. She and Goldie did not speak, preferring to respect the pervading silence as they trudged along downhill on their quest. The only sound that Jane perceived was the synchronized thumping of their feet.

As sluggishly as Jane propelled her legs, lead-like from physical and emotional fatigue, in contrast her mind was racing. She began to dwell on how lost she felt in this alien place without even a clue as to who she was. She stopped abruptly. She felt isolated. That is, until the stillness in the air was interrupted by a muted voice which encircled her like stereophonic sound. The jabbing and pounding in her head and the adrenaline rush ignited by her heightening anxiety was getting the better of her. Her chest tightened and she was suffocating, gasping for breath. Someone was pulling on her arm and patting the back of her hand, but she couldn't see who it was.

"Jane! Jane! Whatever's the matter with you?" asked Goldie snapping her fingers and glaring into Jane's face. "You're freaking me out again. It's Goldie. Remember? Goldie?"

Goldie's face came into focus. "I don't know. I...I...I," Jane stammered. "I heard a voice, but I couldn't make anything out. Was it you? Oh jeez. I can hardly breathe. I feel dizzy."

"Golly Jane! We don't have time for this! All you're doing is hyperventilating and making things worse for yourself. Relax," Goldie cried. "It's bad enough we've been traipsing around in the dark, stranded in the middle of nowhere, with our only hope for transportation having disappeared into thin air. These weird episodes of yours are a thorn in my side each time. If I could pull it out of me, I would stick you and snap you out of it. I think the jolt would do you good."

"Very funny," Jane said.

As Jane paused for a split second to take in a breath, Goldie did a ballet pirouette followed by a leap into the air. Then with a loud "humpf" and a left to right sweep of her head, she proceeded to walk on ahead in giant steps away from Jane towards the next hill.

Jane couldn't help but laugh heartily at Goldie's antics. She was grateful for the resulting release of tension and for having someone like Goldie as a companion. Deciding that she was wasting valuable time standing by herself, Jane tapped into her reservoir of energy to mobilize and catch up to Goldie, who had stopped to rest, huffing and puffing from taking those big strides. They gave each other a supportive hug.

Judging from the tire marks, so far the vehicle had stayed on a steady course, not veering too far off to the left or right. Jane looked out at the undulating road. If her hunch was correct, at some point where the road levels off they should find the truck. With nothing to stand in its way, Jane surmised that the momentum it would have picked up going down the hill near the cottage could have carried it quite far.

Sure enough, they saw what appeared to be the outline of a vehicle, turned sideways on the level road ahead. Instinctively, Jane clutched the truck key tightly as though it were a precious diamond in her sweaty hand. Giddy with anticipation for the prospect of escape, and pumped with adrenalin, both Jane and Goldie picked up the pace and elatedly sprinted to the vehicle. After all, they would have lots of time to relax and recoup their energy once they were seated and driving back.

"Gosh! Gee whiz!" Goldie exclaimed. She stood so still that anyone would think she were a shop window mannequin.

"No way! It can't be. It's impossible," moaned Jane, who felt like she was about to faint from what she saw.

The truck's wheels and tires were gone, and the chassis was mounted on two overturned wheelbarrows and two tree stumps.

The keys spontaneously dropped out of Jane's hand, and at that moment being so flabbergasted, she didn't have the wherewithal to stoop down and pick them up. She stayed in place, closed her eyes, and tilted her head back facing the sky in utter hopelessness, feeling as though she were drifting away on a cloud. She burst into tears. "I'll never get home. I'll never see my children. I'll never find out who I am. Never!"

Seeing Jane so emotionally distraught and sensing her despair, Goldie came over to comfort her.

"Don't cry Jane," Goldie said gently. "It'll be alright. You'll see. Sit down with me for a moment. We have to be strong and get back to Pearl quickly. Then we'll figure something out."

They both sat on the ground, leaning back-to-back so that they propped each other up. Remembering she had dropped the keys at that very spot, Jane swept her hands around on the dirt and recovered them. The fact they were now rendered useless was irrelevant. They were all she had to cling to as a symbol of hope for being united with her family.

"Jane, are you OK? Do you want to get up now and take a closer look?"

"We may as well since we're here," Jane responded with a heavy sigh.

She rolled onto her knees and rose slowly. She watched as Goldie popped up with such flair that the fleeting moment of whimsy reminded her of a child's wind up jack-in-the-box toy. They ambled over to examine the truck using the aid of Pearl's flashlight. The first thing they noticed was the white print on the side panel of the cargo space that said, *Snoe's White Glove Cleaning Company*.

"That certainly clinches its identity," Goldie announced.

They continued to scrutinize the vehicle. What had been the wooden covered section of the cargo area was smashed to bits. The front passenger door was gone, and as they circled around they noticed that the familiar twisted door with its taped window glass was still there on the driver's side. The body was dusty as ever with the familiar scrawled words: "The Snoe flakes" and "Neat Freaks" still intact. A multitude of scuff marks and wheel tracks surrounded the vehicle.

Inside the front cab section, everything was as it was before, except there was a ragged, gaping hole in the dashboard where a piece of it had apparently been sawed out, possibly where the radio had been. Napoleon's foot pedal extensions and his homemade periscope were stashed under the seat. His aviator goggles were still where he left them, dangling from the rear view mirror.

After completing their inspection, Goldie and Jane stepped back a bit as one would do to scrutinize a large painting. Together they absorbed the scene before them set in the midst of nature's vanishing nightlight as the sky prepared to make room for the emergence of dawn.

"Well that's that for us," Goldie said dejectedly. "Now what? I never imagined vandals would be lurking around the area waiting for a truck to appear so they could strip it. Did you? What should we do next?"

"I can't think—I can't imagine anything right now." Jane solemnly replied. "Let's get out of here. As you said, we'll head back to Pearl and later move on by foot. With the sun soon coming up, we'll be able to see things clearer in the distance, especially from the top of the hill. There have to be other homes out here, Jack's being one of them."

"Yeah, you're probably right," Goldie exclaimed in an upbeat voice. "I'm willing to bet there will be some signs of life not far off-road."

Together they commenced the gradually inclining trek back, not speaking but rather conserving what energy they had for their legs. Jane was convinced that with the approaching dawn, they would have a better perspective regarding their fate.

As they reached the steep hill leading to Napoleon's cottage, an increasingly loud chatter emanating from the distance behind them disturbed Jane's ruminations. *Not this again!* She immediately clasped her hands over her ears, all the while maintaining her pace alongside Goldie. She resolved to ignore the indistinguishable sounds, which she assumed were nothing more than a recurrence of her wild imagination. Almost immediately, she heard a loud rumble and the trembling ground caused both her and Goldie to abruptly stop and turn around.

Beep! Beeeeeeeep Beep! Beep! Beep!

The blaring sound of a horn, and a chugging, backfiring engine practically knocked Jane off her feet. This was one time she wished she were deaf like Goldie, who had no idea of the horrendous clatter she was missing. As the glare from the headlights of an approaching vehicle shrouded them, Jane tugged on Goldie's arm, signaling her to run. With adrenalin pumping wildly throughout their bodies, and with nowhere else to go, they scrambled as fast as they could towards the top of the hill with the vehicle trailing behind them. Then suddenly the engine noise stopped.

Hearing indistinguishable words calling out in a deep voice, Jane glanced sideways over her shoulder. To her horror, her peripheral vision revealed someone on foot, gaining on them quickly, only several yards away. While maintaining momentum as the road leveled off, Jane desperately signaled to Goldie for her bear spray. Goldie pulled the canister out of her holster and handed it to Jane who positioned her sweaty hand over the trigger. Intending to take their pursuer off guard, Jane stopped abruptly before reaching the Snoes' cottage. She turned around, assumed a wide stance for balance, and aimed.

23

WELL MET

Jane felt her heart pounding as the stranger also stopped running and stood motionless, still yards away. In the dim light and shadowy context, she was unable to make out a face.

"Jumpin' Jiminy! Wait! Wait! Dang it! Put that thing, whatever it is, down. This isn't a Wild West hold up or something. I'm looking for someone, and last I read in the local ordinance, that's no crime."

A nicely dressed man with short-cropped hair was glaring at them, having raised his hands up, palms facing forward in a gesture of surrender. Jane instantly recognized the distinctive voice and expressions, but the individual before her wearing a short sleeve shirt and tie appeared unfamiliar.

"Jack? Jeez, is that you Jack?" Jane asked tentatively. "Is that really you? Come up closer so I can see you better."

"Well, what serendipity this encounter is! It's the very Jane Doe who I've been knocking myself out searching for, and it's an unknown other person. Yup. It's me in the flesh," Jack replied as he reached them. "Underneath my clothes, that is. What are you two doing here wandering about town at this time of day? It looked like you were up to no good."

Jane's heart continued to beat wildly and a flush of relieving warmth flowed through her veins as she signaled to Goldie that it was alright. Jane felt like asking what town, but that was really so beside the point. She couldn't figure out if she was very happy to see him or not, given how he just scared them half to death. Goldie stood motionless, unable to see the conversation going on.

Jane turned to Goldie. This is ... It's Jack. The very person whose house we were heading to."

"Wow! What luck!" Goldie said with a big sigh and a dramatic clap of her hands.

"Jack, you ... you cut your hair!" Jane commented. "And your beard is gone. You're ... all dressed up. You look so ... so ... different."

"Holy moley, really?" Jack retorted. "That was me I saw in the bathroom mirror today? No kidding. So what if I cut my hair and shaved my beard? Like it or lump it. And since when did you become my stylist?" Jack retorted.

"Well, I didn't mean anything by it. I was just saying," Jane said. *He looks like an entirely different person—quite handsome in fact.* She decided to change the subject.

"Jack, this is my friend Goldie. I met her just about when I woke up in your truck. She can't hear, but she's a superb lip reader and speaks very well. You need to face her when you talk."

"That's right," Goldie added. "I always tell people, if I can't see your mouth I don't know what it's saying."

"I accompanied Jack on an investigation he was doing regarding a missing child and ..." She abruptly paused. *Oh jeez. What am I doing chitchatting; we have to get back to Pearl.*

Frantic, Jane turned to face Jack and said, "We're in a big hurry. Someone very special is waiting all alone over there, expecting us back any minute." She pointed ahead of them. "I have a surprise for you. Wait 'til I tell you about ..."

"Not now!" interrupted Jack. "Goldie what? What's your last name? I want to know who you are, because I don't talk to strangers which means we would otherwise have to put an end to this conversation immediately."

Pretending to sneeze, Jane turned her back to Jack. She faced Goldie mouthing the words, "Please humor him, because he could be our only chance out of here. He's definitely nutty, but harmless." Goldie nodded her head in understanding.

"My last name is Hare," Goldie responded. "Now how about you introduce yourself to me, because I don't talk to strangers either. Never. Not even to stray bears that come around my house."

"You're very wise," Jack said matter-of-factly. "My name is John Bean, and since we have just bonded in conversation you can call me by my preferred name, Jack. I'm a famous botanist in the process of formulating new strains of vegetables and other types of plant life."

Jane chuckled at the familiar pitch.

Jack glared at her.

"That's nice," Goldie said curtly, not caring to engage in any chitchat with this apparently peculiar man. She faced the ground and began making circular motions in the dirt with the tip of her shoe.

"Jane, listen up," Jack said. "This is what's happening. I'm on my way to Levi's Town this very early in the day to deliver some special giant bean and tomato plants and guess to whom? To Hannah! Didn't I already tell you that Hannah's a very important customer of mine? I'm quite sure I did so I won't repeat myself. She makes fabulous sauce. If you still want to see her, this is the only time to hitch a ride with me. You'll have to sit with me up front or in the back of the truck with the plants. It's either now or a probably very long time from now. Like it or lump it. I'm already off schedule waiting around and looking for you since yesterday. I made a deal to take you, and I'm a man of my word. Or did you find yourself already?"

"Find myself? No, unfortunately not," Jane replied. "Of course I still want to see Hannah. I'm sorry Jack for disappearing. Believe me. So much happened, I can't even begin to tell you. It's all been ah…ah…strange. The fact is, Goldie and I were trying so hard to find your house and got very lost and almost killed. We needed your help. But wait until you hear what we happened upon."

"First things first," Jack said, again uninterested in what Jane had to say. "Quickly, are you coming along? End of discussion. I'm tired of talking."

"Yes!" Jane exclaimed, disregarding Jack's curtness. "Absolutely. Right now."

"What about Goldie Hare?" Jack asked.

Jane paused. She thought about the plan that Goldie and she had to ask Jack to first drive them to Goldie's house to look for the locket.

"How far are we from your house, Jack? Goldie lives a short distance away and since I think I left my precious locket there— remember it? Maybe you..."

Jack cut her off. "In answer to your question, which has nothing to do with your motive for asking, the fact is that as the crow flies we're not far. But by road trip it's too far. I'm already out of my way and behind schedule."

"Then Goldie will have to come with us straight to Hannah's, if it's not too much trouble, Jack," Jane replied. "But... but... well, we have another person—a young girl—I was trying to tell you."

"Stop! I don't want to hear. I have a lot on my mind," Jack said.

"Well aren't you the ornery one!" Jane replied. "Then have it your way! In a nutshell, we have to take her along too."

"Another girl? A young girl? Do I look like a school bus driver? I'll have to think about it," Jack responded. "You know, this is all putting a kink in my plans. It wasn't a part of my agreement with you that I would take additional passengers to Hannah's House." Jack paused and briefly gazed upwards in contemplation while tapping his foot and stroking his chin. "Hmmmmm." He looked back at Jane. "I've just been in the process of thinking about it and decided it's okay. But since I'm not a logistics consultant, you'll have to figure out the seating arrangements among yourselves. I don't want to have anything to do with that. I only specialize in plants, not seating."

"Oh, thank you. Thank you," Jane said sweetly, stunned at Jack's sudden pleasant change in demeanor. "Wait until you hear..."

"Where did you say this other girl is?" Jack asked impatiently.

Jane pointed in the direction of the Snoes' mailbox.

"We left her to rest right over there. She was very tired and has trouble walking."

"We'll drive over to her together so I don't get lost and waste more time," Jack said. "Get in the truck now or never. It's growing later by the minute."

Jane and Goldie humored him. They got in on the passenger side and squeezed into the front bench seat. Jane went in first and sat next to Jack. As soon as he started the familiar, noisy engine, the radio immediately began blasting. It was somebody talking.

Jane tugged on Jack's shirt and shouted, "Please, please lower that!" She noticed a vintage radio/cassette player secured in the dashboard by masking tape. It looked vaguely familiar.

"Since when did you get that piece of electronic equipment put in? I don't remember seeing it in here before," Jane asked.

To Jane's dismay, Jack immediately turned down the music without protest, but he ignored her question. It took them but a moment to drive to Napoleon's cottage.

"Looks like there's a body over there." Jack spoke as though reporting something as trivial as a bird sitting on a fence. The headlights caught Pearl on the ground leaning against the mailbox, still sound asleep despite all the ruckus coming from the engine.

"That's Pearl. She's the girl we're picking up," Jane said. "Pull over here, and I'll wake her up. It'll be quick."

"Pearl who? What's her last name?" Jack inquired as he turned off the ignition. The truck backfired. "I have to insist on an introduction."

Having become accustomed to playing along with Jack's idiosyncrasies, Jane succinctly replied, "It's White. Pearl White."

"What?" Jack called after her. "What did you say?"

Jane ignored him. Goldie had already opened the passenger door and was on her way out. Jane lost no time in sliding over and joining her.

"I have to move my legs," Goldie announced as though she had been sitting for hours.

Jane went over to Pearl and gently shook her shoulder. "Pearl. It's Jane. Pearl. Wake up. We got lucky and have a ride to somewhere so we can get help. Come on, wake up."

Pearl moaned a bit. She opened her eyes and stretched her arms up and out to her side. "What?"

"I said wake up, sweetie. We can get out of here. We luckily found someone who is going to give us a ride. But we have to leave right now. Come on. You can sleep some more once we get going."

"Hey, hurry it up. I have to go now," Jack shouted out to them through the open passenger door. "You better get moving, or I'll take off without you. It's no matter to me."

Pearl stood up and squinted at the person in the driver's seat. She winced as she put pressure on her sore foot

"Who's *that*? Who are you?" Pearl asked with some trepidation.

"Well since you inquired, my name is John Bean. I'm a famous botanist in the process of formulating new strains of vegetables and other types of plant life. Once we bond together in conversation you can call me by my familiar name, Jack. And to make it even, now you must tell me who you are although I already know your first name."

"Pearl. P-P-Pearl White." She stammered.

"Pearl White? P-E-A-R-L W-H-I-T-E?" Jack spelled out. "Like the look people want for their teeth?"

Pearl simply stood there not knowing what to make of this person or what to say. She noticed Jane roll her eyes and exhale a huge breath of air out of her mouth in exasperation.

"Pearl, don't mind Jack. It's his way, but he means well," Jane interjected.

"Yes, that's my name, if you must know. What's it to you?" Pearl snapped back, having gained some gusto in her approach.

Jane realized she had better diffuse the brewing antagonism. She caught Goldie's attention and addressed her and Pearl.

"So girls, since it will be rather tight if we all sit up front with Jack, do either of you prefer to ride in the outside cargo area with some plants?"

"I will! I will!" Goldie yelled, while jumping up and down. "There's no way I'm going to be wedged between all of you on the front seat. I'll catch a few Zs while I'm at it."

Jane called out, "Hey, Jack, Goldie is going to stay in the cargo area. Is that ok? Is it safe?"

"Wahoo! Jack cheered. "That's one neat seating plan. It'll give me some elbow room."

Apparently not wanting to give Goldie a chance to change her mind, Jack got out and ran to the rear of the truck to drop down the tailgate. Goldie and Jane went over to him, and as Jane helped Goldie scramble up, Jack tapped her leg to get her attention. She turned around on her knees to see what he wanted.

"Here's something for you to lie on and cover yourself with," Jack said as he handed Goldie some cruddy, bunched up burlap sacks.

"Ew!" Goldie exclaimed with a grimace as she took it from him and shook out the dirt particles. She noticed it had 'Idaho Potatoes' printed on it. "Where did you get this yucky stuff from?" Goldie asked. "I'm not using that, thank you very much."

"Well sorrrrr-y I don't have my plush feather bed with me today for your highness," Jack said sarcastically. "Like it or lump it. If you don't care for the accommodations you can go find yourself a hotel. By the way, since Jane is concerned about your safety, I suggest that you stay down between the plants so you don't fly out of the truck if it happens to hit a bump—like should it run over something in the road that I didn't notice in time."

Goldie glanced at some giant bean and tomato plants and saw that they were all harnessed to eyebolts attached to the back of the cab. Clumps of hardened soil were scattered about the metal floor. She did a double take, spotting four old tires on rims, stacked on their side in pairs.

"What about those tires over there?" Goldie asked as she pointed to get Jane's attention. Jane looked in and nodded to Goldie.

"What about them," Jack snapped. "Are they in your way?"

"Where did you get them from?" Goldie asked suspiciously.

"Who made you a C.I.A. interrogator? You sound like Jane. Are you related?" Jack responded.

Goldie glared back at him. "Never mind," she muttered while clenching her teeth.

"That's what I say," Jane chimed in, not wanting to get into an altercation over this. "Jack, let's get going. You'll have to help me lift Pearl into the truck. She has a sore foot."

"What's wrong with it? Is it contagious?" Jack asked. "Some sores are infected and some are contagious lesions like chicken pox and shingles."

"No it's not contagious," Jane responded. "It hurts her. I said it's a sore foot, not that there are sores on her foot."

"Well, if you say so. I'll inspect what she has and give you my assessment. I may be able to save her."

"Oh my, Jack. You're too much," Jane remarked. "I didn't say it was a fatal injury." She and Jack walked over to Pearl who was sitting on the ground again, rubbing her ankle and calf.

"Pearl, before we get you into the truck, Jack wants to see what's been bothering you. OK?" Jane asked.

Pearl looked up and nodded as she extended her leg. Jack stooped down to see it better, and Jane used the flashlight to give him a better view.

"Jumpin' Jiminy that's some mean swelling you've got there, Pearl, along with an abrasion of some strange origin," Jack said as he examined the bruise. "How did you get that?" Before she could answer he continued. "But I can give you something to put on it while we're on the road, if we ever get going that is. I'm already *way* behind the schedule I planned for this morning."

"Like what? What would you possibly have with you now that would help her?" Jane asked nicely but with some skepticism.

Jack rose up quickly and scowled at Jane, face to face, as he ranted. "What's this, a job interview? I told you before that I'm a famous botanist. I know about many things that have to do with plants, from microorganisms to giant trees. I do research, scientific studies, and experiments in my laboratory. I figure out how plants convert simple chemical compounds into more complex substances. Lately I've been studying how genetic information in DNA controls plant growth. Do you need to see my resume?"

Jane didn't respond and chose to simply glare back at Jack. She knew it didn't take much to rile him up, but that he would quickly calm down if she didn't say anything.

True to form, Jack faltered, lowered his voice, and mellowed. "I always travel with a special liniment I compounded out of thyme and marjoram mixed into olive oil. It's soothing and healing for arthritis, muscle soreness and spasms, bruises, and sprains. Sometimes I use a raw onion or a sliced potato if I have one, which I don't. Do I look like a green grocery store to you? Marshmallow root would be good because it releases a gummy substance that can be applied to inflamed or sore areas of the body, but I haven't found it growing any place around here. Other than that, apple vinegar is an old standby for the same thing. So now I will get the liniment to put on Pearl, and we can hit the road. What's that loud noise?"

Jane listened to the gurgling sound. "Oh that? I think that's Goldie snoring."

Jack went to the truck and returned with a little red cookie tin that said Merry Christmas under a picture of a decorated Christmas tree. He flipped off the cover and removed two cotton puffs and a small case with the liniment. After applying the substance to Pearl's ankle and lower leg, Jack and Jane lifted her into the truck, sliding her to the middle, and Jane got in next to her. Once in the driver's seat, Jack started the engine.

"Everyone, fasten your seat belts, and let's rock!" Jack shouted as he released the clutch and floored the gas pedal. The truck lunged forward, leaving a cloud of dust in its wake. Both Jane and Pearl were frantically fumbling around for their belts.

"So just where *are* the seatbelts, Jack?" queried Jane, clearly unnerved by Jack's reckless takeoff. "And watch how you're driving or you'll toss Goldie out of the truck."

"Oh please. You always take me so literally," Jack snapped as he took his eyes off the road to frown at her. "It's just a figure of speech. There are no actual seat belts. What would we need seat belts for? Do you ever see anything around that we could hit, like other cars on the road, or walls to crash into? As to Goldie, she's tucked between my amazing plants, which are secured tightly to the truck. She would remain in place even if we soared off the top of Mount Fuji."

"Lighten up, Jack," Jane retorted. "Be nice. You're getting Pearl upset. Hey. Watch where you're driving! It's not a figure of speech when we're sitting in a vehicle and you say 'fasten your seatbelts.' I don't like the fact that there are no seat belts. What if we skidded and rolled over, or blew a tire and you had to stop short, or if a deer ran into the road before us? I don't feel safe riding unprotected like this, and even if Goldie doesn't get ejected, she can still hit her head. Arghhh!"

"A deer? A *deer*?" queried Jack with a smile. "Ha ha. There are no *authentic* deer around; just *you* Jane *DOE*. Have you ever seen even one deer in these parts? If I said, 'Hold on to your hats' instead, would you argue that since you aren't wearing hats I must be out of my mind to say that? Give it up. If you don't like the seating conditions, then find another form of transportation."

"You don't see the difference between referring to seat belts and referring to hats given the context of the situation we are in? Oh, forget it, Jack. It doesn't matter," Jane responded calmly with a wave of her hand. She could have kicked herself for losing her cool and inciting the discussion that was irrational as usual. She resolved that for the rest of the trip she would keep her mouth shut and not allow Jack to suck her into his illogical verbal warfare. This next leg of her journey was all about the joy of getting closer and closer to discovering who she was and finding her family.

Jane kept her eyes fixed straight ahead. Traversing the sparse countryside was uneventful as Jack kept the truck on course over the bizarre winding road. Given the fact that the shortest distance between two points is a straight line, Jane thought the many twists and turns were very inefficient. She could think of no particular reason for it other than perhaps to break the monotony and help to keep the driver awake.

Thinking about keeping the driver awake prompted Jane to break her silence and ask, "Say, Jack, don't you want to listen to your chatty radio program? I don't mind as long as you don't blast it like you had it before."

"Radio program? Ha ha," Jack chuckled. "Radio? Not here. Never. No way, no how. There are no radio airwaves of anything in these parts, no radio transmitter towers of any kind. All I can receive are certain television shows that are locally broadcast—some boring public access channel. Did you ever see me use a phone? We don't have phone service up here. Believe me, I would have picked up a phone a long time ago and called the police to get you. For the most part we communicate with neighbors by foot or car. I listen to both radio talk shows and greatest hits from the past, all on audio-cassette tapes. Nothing is live."

"So all you play are the same conversations and music, over and over again, on old cassette tapes?" Jane asked in surprise. "Good grief. I can't remember when I last even saw a cassette, let alone played one. You're living in a time warp."

"Yup. What of it?" Jack snapped. "Who are you— the road trip media director? Humpf. You don't have to listen. Cover your ears."

Jane laughed, and in being true to herself, she suppressed her natural inclination to lash back with an equally nasty quip. Instead she turned toward her side window and looked out at the surroundings. As her mind began to wander, she became faintly aware of background chatter interspersed in the midst of chirping and rattling from the grease hungry chassis and the noisy engine.

Before long, dawn's muted orange rays drove out the darkness and welcomed her like the outstretched arms of a mother beckoning her child. Jane noticed that the landscape was changing and becoming more alive with vegetation, including a smattering of fir trees. With nothing else of substance to see except the fading outline of the moon, the rising sun's emerging ambiance took on a life of its own. To her bewilderment, the more she intensely stared trance-like into the beyond, the more the shadows before her cast by the trees appeared to be human. Startled at first, Jane rejected the illusions and quickly turned away. She glanced over at Pearl, glad to see that she was sound asleep. With a sigh, Jane closed her eyes and relaxed, relishing in the anticipation of getting help for herself and ultimately being reunited with her children and the rest of her family in a familiar place.

No one had uttered a single word since the initial banter between her and Jack. Then, at the crack of dawn as though the rising sun's rays had ignited his vocal cords, Jack suddenly stopped the truck and cut the thick wall of silence between them with a boisterous announcement.

"Pay attention!" Jack suddenly called out.

Profoundly startled, both Jane and Pearl shrieked, as they were nearly jolted off the seat. Jane watched as Pearl's arms spontaneously flew upwards, like a newborn's Moro reflex.

"Pay attention," Jack demanded again, like a drill sergeant, oblivious to the degree of disturbance he had just caused. "You should always know something about where you're going before you get there. So I'm going to give you a little local history lesson since we are about to enter Levi's Town where Hannah's compound is. She runs a working farm, which is actually a safe house, the likes of which you've never seen. She helps everyone that shows up. The settlement is coming up around the next bend, and you'll be able to see a welcome billboard shortly."

"Good grief! What's with you? Did you have to shout like that?" Pearl asked, her voice quivering.

Jane gently squeezed Pearl's shoulders to calm her down and was about to explode at Jack, but instead decided to get out of the truck.

"Well Jack, you'll just have to wait. Like it or lump it yourself for a change. Now that you stopped the truck, I'm going to check on Goldie first," Jane said as she flung open the door and jumped down onto the road, not giving Jack a chance to say another word.

Jane walked to the cargo area, and standing on tiptoe, looked in from the side. Goldie was scrunched up in a ball, wrapped in burlap and lying between the plants, still sound asleep.

"How can someone sleep as deeply as this girl does?" Jane muttered to herself. She shook her head incredulously as she walked back to the front of the truck. *Her silent world must be more conducive to sleeping and for longer stretches,* Jane thought.

"I guess being deaf sometimes has its advantages," Jane remarked as she climbed back into the truck. "Goldie's still zonked out. How does your ankle feel, Pearl?"

"It's much better, thank you. It feels kind of numb which is good. Are we almost at that house you're taking us to?" Pearl asked as she turned to look at Jack. "I want to get home to my parents so badly." She started to whimper, and Jane took her hand to stroke it.

Jane looked at Jack to observe his reaction. She figured this would be the perfect segue for him to ask about Pearl's situation, if he had even an ounce of curiosity in him. Regardless, she was dying to tell him. However, she concluded that it was for the better not to resurface it in front of Pearl. *She's been traumatized enough over her ordeal and doesn't need to hear it rehashed.*

"That's the benefit of my ointment," Jack replied, oblivious to Pearl's emotion. "And yes, we are very close to our predetermined destination although the E.T.A. is not according to my original plan due to circumstances beyond my control."

"What's an E.T.A.," Pearl asked between sniffles.

"Estimated time of arrival," Jane responded with another squeeze of Pearl's shoulders. "It's more commonly used by pilots." Jane glanced at Jack with a smile. As frustrating as he is at times, Jane couldn't help but feel there was something endearing about the man because of his pure quirkiness.

"What? What's so funny?" Jack asked.

"I don't know. Maybe the way you say simple things. You sound so formal, like you're reading an official proclamation."

"Who made you my public speaking advisor?" Jack quipped with a chuckle.

"Oh boy!" Jane grinned and brushed him off with a wave of her hand. "You have a captive audience here, so go ahead with your history lesson since you think it's important for us to know about this Level Town."

Jack burst out laughing as he started his discourse. "First of all Jane, it's not '*Level* Town.' It's '*Levi's* Town.' After the war came to a close there was a boom in home building all over the country. One day, I read in the newspaper that a local farmer, a loner named Levi, saw this as a perfect opportunity to get out of the agricultural business. He grew potatoes and corn on a 4,000-acre farm handed down to him from his paternal side of the family.

"The neighbors said he was starting to behave more strangely than usual. When he would meet up with people in the general store, all he would ever talk about was how he was sick and tired of dealing with the high turnover of migrant workers, year after year. He wanted to get out of farming and head for an extremely cold location where he could fulfill his dream of buying a commercial fishing boat to do king crab fishing—blue, red, or golden—whatever he could catch. Nobody was able to talk him out of such a lame idea, even though he knew he was likely to die by drowning, or from hypothermia, or become accidentally maimed from the heavy fishing machinery on board."

"Wow. I can't imagine anybody wanting to do such a risky thing," Jane interjected.

Jack continued. "One day while Levi was getting his truck-loads of potato harvest weighed, luck would have it that he was approached by a wealthy real estate speculator, whose name escapes me right now. The two men struck up a conversation and before the last truck was weighed, Levi had a buyer for his farmland, which was to be developed as a residential neighborhood of affordable housing. The only condition Levi required for the sale was that the new community be named after him."

"No sooner had Levi left to start his new life crab fishing, than the bulldozers appeared to break ground on the farmland. Immediately a small three bedroom model home was erected, and a sign was posted designating the location as the future site for *Levi's* Town."

"OK. I got it; I got it," Jane interjected. "*Levi's* town," she emphasized."

Jack nodded and smiled. "A prospectus with a map showing the parcels of land available for purchase was supposedly on hand for inspection. Years went by and there were no takers, actually because no one could locate the developer to get the prospectus. As a matter of fact, I think he was one of America's most wanted criminals. But the developer was no match for the IRS that caught up with him and threw him into prison. It turned out that the agency discovered that Levi's Town was an investment scheme for illegally sheltering income. The developer had been taking tax write-offs on what he said was unproductive farmland."

"So what does this all have to do with the person whose house—a safe house you called it?—is where we're going to?" Jane asked impatiently. "What's the safe house all about, anyway?" She noticed that Pearl was fidgeting. "By the way, can't you talk and drive at the same time so we can move on?"

"Stop with the 20,000 questions," Jack replied. "I'm getting to the part about Hannah. So as I was saying when you interrupted me—in the meantime, the lone house in Levi's Town, together with 4,000 acres of land thrown in as an inducement, was up for grabs. It was eventually sold at auction by the IRS to a young, devoted, Morman couple, Hannah and Ethan Gooz, who were the only bidders. They took pride in their vision of breaking away from their religious community and creating their own fiefdom out of this isolated turf. Drawing on their farming experiences growing up in large family compounds, Hannah and Ethan had an innate ability to live off the land which, because it produced more than they could consume, they generously shared with town folks. Now here's the kicker. Their nurturing skills evidently crossed over from the growing things in the soil into their home, because they also maintained an enthusiasm for procreating. Eventually this resulted in their having fourteen kids, so the locals nicknamed the house, 'Rabbit Hut' and called Hannah 'Mother Gooz.' In fact, Hannah had so many children she didn't know what to do." Jack laughed heartily. "I couldn't wait to get to that part. It's my favorite."

"Fourteen kids?" Pearl was utterly flabbergasted. "Wowie."

Jack continued. "Yes, that's what I said. And if you can believe this, they were all crammed into the little house unable to afford any improvements while it turned shabbier and shabbier over the years. Well, once their plight became known and was broadcast on local radio, some volunteer building crew came in to help the family. They poured cement slabs upon which they built a series of extensions to the house. You'll soon see what I'm talking about although it's much more grandiose now since she shelters so many people. Most stay once they get there, but some are only passing through temporarily for one reason or another."

"She sounds amazing," Jane commented with hope in her heart. "I can't wait to meet her."

Jack started up the engine. "That's all I have to say; I'm not saying any more about Hannah since I was not hired to be her biographer. You'll have to wait to hear the rest directly from her."

With a roar of the engine the truck took off. It didn't take long for them to reach the billboard that Jack had mentioned. The hand painted sign, mounted high on two posts along the road said: "Welcome to Levi's Town. *Previous* Population 16." The word "*Previous*" was carefully printed above a caret symbol inserted between the words "Town" and "Population." It reminded Jane of the sign she had encountered not too long ago, welcoming travelers to Tree City. Minutes later, Jack reduced speed once he came to a "Village Speed Limit" sign which restricted driving to 10 mph. After that they rounded a bend that brought them to a ridge.

"Down there, look," Jack immediately shouted as he slowed the truck to a crawl and vigorously pointed ahead towards the end of a long gently sloping and winding road. "That's where we're headed— Hannah's House—to see the one and only Mother Gooz. Ha ha.

That's so hilarious. Isn't it? Gadzooks! The place has expanded even more since I was last here. Hannah must be prospering. Well, lah-de-dah. On second thought, that's good for me since it means more business."

"Oh my God!" Jane exclaimed, drawing her hands to her face as she observed the site sprawled out below them.

24

SANCTUARY

"Golly!" Pearl exclaimed. She turned to look at Jane with her eyes wide in surprise.

"This is beyond comprehension," Jane muttered under her breath as she surveyed the compound from their high vantage point.

"Jack, it would be wonderful if you would stop the truck for a minute so I can get a better look at this place. I've never seen anything like it."

Without a word, Jack brought the truck to a standstill whereupon Jane immediately opened the door and exited. Pearl hobbled after her.

Jane turned back towards the truck and shouted, "Jack, please go wake up Goldie and help her out. She has to see this from here. It's too astounding to miss."

Jane was mesmerized as she stood at the ridge alongside a yellow, metal sign marked "vista point" and experienced the panoramic view. In the flat light cast by the morning sun was a sprawling ranch house. Wildly spinning wind turbines stood on an array of distinctly outlined rectangular plots of cultivated land that stretched out every which way far into the surrounding land. Each plot was connected like tiles in a game of dominoes. Each one had vegetation planted in a different design that was clearly discernible from their overhead position. Leading beyond the perimeter of the farm and dipping towards the horizon amidst a vast wasteland speckled with a smattering of trees, was a continuation of the same kind of absurdly winding dirt road they had been traveling on.

Jack and a groggy Goldie came over to where they were standing. "Well look who's here!" Jane said, giving Goldie a hug. "Why, it's Sleeping Beauty who slept for a hundred years. What do you think... Do I look very old since you last saw me?"

"Ancient is the word," Goldie chuckled as she rubbed the sleep from her eyes. "I'm afraid to hug you back or you'll crumble to dust."

"Look at this place!" Jane exclaimed. "We're about to arrive at Hannah's House. That's her compound down there. Our salvation."

"I admit it's a cool view not to be missed. But how would you feel after sleeping for 100 years and then being gruffly awakened?" Goldie responded, noticeably grumpy. "And certainly not by any semblance of a Prince." She scowled at Jack who shrugged his shoulders. Jane laughed.

"Jack, all that way out there—" Jane made a wide sweep of her hand. "Is that the undeveloped parcel of Levi's Town?" she asked. Its barrenness was a stark contrast to the fertile property adjoining Hannah's House.

"How would I know," Jack replied. "Did I ever profess to be a surveyor?"

Jane ignored his trite sarcasm, in keeping with her new resolution.

"Oh my God, all of you—look carefully at the different planting designs—the checkerboards and mazes, the stars, the polka dots!" Jane cried. "How creative!"

"And swirls like dribbled icing!" Pearl chimed in.

Like a patchwork quilt, a kaleidoscope of colors permeated the land in hues of orange, yellow, green, brown, and red. Rows upon rows of parallel zigzags, diamonds, and crisscrosses were laid out resembling the ribbed shapes on a cable knit sweater. A section of greenery of some indeterminable acreage spread out behind the house arranged in concentric circles, each defined by a red border.

No doubt some very productive farming techniques are applied to turn so much of an otherwise barren landscape into such fertile ground, Jane thought.

As the four of them stood enthralled and in silence absorbing the magical scenery, Jane was consumed with nostalgia. It was as though, like a family, they were sharing a special moment together, perhaps a similar experience she had etched in her mind, yet to be retrieved. She looked over at transformed Jack with feelings of affection and gratitude, and was pleasantly struck by his burgeoning smile as he looked out at Hannah's settlement. Judging from what she had discovered at Jack's house and his knowledge about this place, Jane began to wonder if his proclivity for creating horticultural phenomena had something to do with this. She concluded that it was a feasible premise, especially considering the fact that Jack was transporting those huge vegetable plants to Hannah whom he said was a very important customer of his.

"So did you all have enough of the view?" Jack asked. "If not, it's fine with me if you want to stay here your whole life, but I have to make a planned delivery, and I want to get to Hannah in time for her breakfast feast. So I'm now going back to the truck to be on my way. If I happen to see you in the truck when I turn on the ignition you can come along."

Pearl started to cry. "I don't want to stay up here all that time. I want to go home. I want my parents! Please Jane, I want to go home."

"Oh jeez! Nice going, Jack," Jane shouted. "Pearl doesn't know that you don't really have it in your heart to leave us. Now, now, Pearl, don't be upset," Jane replied, giving her a kiss on the top of her head. "Don't pay any attention to him. He doesn't mean it. It's only a silly joke. Of course he's taking us along. That's the whole point of coming here. Hannah is going to help us. We'll get you to your mom and dad. You'll see. Come on you two. Goldie, I'll give you a boost into the back of the truck."

After assuming their places, Jack turned the ignition key and with the usual rumbling fanfare they made their way along the sloping road and reached level ground. Just yards away, a metal gate supported by wide stone pillars automatically opened for them. Jack whipped a right turn onto a long driveway leading to the house.

"This is downright amazing," Jane exclaimed as they drove through the gate. "It's as though we're arriving at the last remaining stronghold of a cattle ranch in the Old West."

"Didn't I tell you this place would be nothing like you could ever imagine?" Jack asked.

Immediately ahead they passed under a weathered, carved sign saying, "Welcome to Hannah's House." It dangled precariously on thin, rusty chains attached to a horizontal beam mounted on tall tree trunk posts on either side. *This archaic structure must have been the original entrance predating the automatic gate,* Jane thought.

Jane was in awe of the fastidiously cultivated lush greenery rising above the soil at various heights. Bales of hay were stacked neatly in front of two tall silos alongside a big gray barn. Close by in one designated area under cover, the yellow painted wheelbarrows, wagons, and carts lined up in corrals reminded her of a supermarket parking lot.

To their left they came upon a billboard mounted on a single wooden post.

"Jack, slow down—stop—look at this!" Jane cried. "Why it's like a shopping mall directory! With a map, no less."

On display was a numbered grid of the farming subdivisions and an expansive list of produce items, each with plot location numbers. She read: Lettuce #12, Broccoli #9, Spinach #27, on and on and on.

"Oh my!" were the only words Jane could express after reading the expansive list.

"Hey Jack, aren't those railroad track symbols weaving in and out on the map? There's a train here? A train? That would be wonderful. Why, it could be the way for me to get to the town!" For the first time in days, she felt as though she were about to burst with enthusiasm. *Surely a sophisticated place like this will provide me with the means to get home.*

"Dang it, Jane! You're getting carried away," Jack exclaimed. "In answer to your question, yes there's a train here. But I hate to disappoint you. The twenty miles of track only weave throughout the compound, picking up and dropping off things and people in connection with their work. It's not a passenger train. It has a narrow gauge track, the kind that's used for transportation at theme parks, zoos, and places like that. In case you're interested it's twenty-four inches between the rails whereas the rails for a passenger train track are four feet eight and a half inches apart. At first I was going to order an even smaller size train commonly used as an amusement park ride, but that's more suitable for children, and the guests at Hannah's House are usually grown up."

Jane was dumbfounded not to mention disheartened. "What do you mean *you* were going to order a smaller size train?" Jane asked. "You had something to do with this?"

Jack's face was so vibrant with excitement and pride that it glowed around him like the aura of a halo. He responded. "I helped construct it, and if I say so myself this is a very sophisticated system. The wooden ties were made from our local trees and everything but the locomotive was custom built: the flat cars, freight cars, coaches, and the caboose which is actually a replica of this very truck."

Jane burst into laughter picturing the likes of Jack's truck bringing up the rear of the train. Jack ignored her.

"And here's the clincher; I left the best information for last. The locomotive was originally a steam engine, but it runs on plants now, combined with solar power. Does that sound familiar?"

"Hmmm. Let me think a moment," Jane replied playfully sarcastic. "Oh yes! I know! And does it clang and roar as it chugs along?"

Jack didn't utter a sound as he picked up his driving pace. They passed fields that were ripe red and glowing green, an agriculture paradise of berries and vegetables. Jane took in a deep breath as a very pleasant smell wafted through the air. It hinted of freshly baked bread or muffins, and was the most welcoming sensation.

The cinnamon and butter aroma was so delightfully pungent that she could practically taste the food.

"Yummmm-my!" Pearl shouted. "I'm so hungry, and that smells so good."

Jane looked at Jack who was beaming ear to ear.

"What's up?" Jane asked staring at Jack's elated expression. "Am I missing something funny or are you grimacing from the sun glare?"

"I'm fascinated seeing all the results of my botanical research, is all I have to say, since you asked."

Just then, Jack proceeded to honk the horn annoyingly as he pulled up in front of the house along a line of sun-bleached, mission style benches. The truck backfired as usual when Jack turned off the ignition, frightening some roaming chickens and inciting a symphony of cackling as they scattered.

"How's your ankle?" Jane asked Pearl just as the truck came to a stop.

Pearl smiled and gave a thumbs-up over the racket. As Jane helped her out, Pearl turned around and yelled through the open door, "Jack! Thank you so much for making my ankle all better!"

"I'm glad I was able to apply my knowledge and skills to help you," Jack responded in a formal tone as he walked around the vehicle to where Jane and Pearl had alighted and were standing tentatively in place.

An abundance of lavender plants surrounding the front porch exuded a familiar scent dispersed by the gentle breeze.

"Ooooh. How nice," Jane remarked, getting a whiff of it. She closed her eyes as she took in another deep breath.

A thin woman, quite spunky for what apparently was a ripe old age, emerged from the entrance to greet them. "Hannah!" Jack called out as he scooted over to her, past Jane and Pearl, and bowed with flair. "I'm so happy to be here! It's been a long time, and I hardly recognize the place. It's really grown hasn't it? Gadzooks what a farm!"

Pearl stood tentatively by Jane's side as Hannah approached them.

"Jack Beam! Hallelujah. I am so ripping glad to see you again," Hannah exclaimed. Jack shook her hand in a very businesslike fashion. "Yes there have been some extraordinary additions to the compound, and that's because my place has become quite popular far and wide."

Jack interrupted. "Um, er, correction, Hannah. It's *Bean*. My last name is *Bean*, not *Beam*. B-E-A-**N**. That's what I go by. It suits me better."

Jane's ears perked up with interest. *So it's what I thought. He switched his name! What a character he is!*

"Oh, I'm sorry I … er … since …" Hannah stopped and shrugged her shoulders.

"Jack! Jane! Somebody! Hey, somebody help me get out of here!" Goldie screeched from the truck's cargo area. She was leaning over the edge waving impatiently for attention.

"Excuse me." Jack said to Hannah. He ran to the rear of the truck to lower the lift gate and hurriedly helped Goldie down.

Hannah craned her neck to see around the truck as Goldie approached from the cargo area. "I see you have these nice friends with you. Are they refugees of some sort?" With a big smile and a wink, she looked wonderingly at Jane, Pearl, and Goldie.

"Yes, um … maybe … Well, I don't know what they are … um, what to call them, actually," Jack replied. "But they aren't staying here for long. Jane is anxious to get home, and she reminds me incessantly about that. But she doesn't know where that is, and worse yet, she doesn't even know who she is. I actually named her myself."

Jack noticed Jane shaking her head in exasperation.

"What? What? But it's true, isn't it?" Jack asked Jane. He didn't wait for a response. He continued. "The one who was in the cargo area with the plants is Goldie. She's deaf but can read lips extremely well as long as she can see your mouth when you speak. Somehow she got hooked up with Jane after she escaped from some bears that broke into her house, and they've shared some adventures. She wants to report the bears to the police down road and needs a ride back home to look for some locket that Jane lost. This little one, Pearl, well, come to think of it, I never found out what her situation is, did I?" Jack looked at Jane. "She's like a hitchhiker of sorts whom I heard wanting to call her parents."

Jane laughed at the description of Pearl as hitchhiker. "I tried to tell you before, Jack, and now's not the time for it," Jane remarked. "We'll talk about it after."

"Fine then," Jack replied. "So Hannah, there you have it as far as introductions go."

"Ah." Hannah paused. She stood befuddled, not knowing what to say next about Jack's introductions. "Oh Lordy. Are you joking around with me Jack?"

"No, I'm not joking," Jack replied. "What am I, a court jester? If anything sounds outlandish, Jane will tell you herself if you don't believe me. Won't you Jane?"

"And just what is it that I'm supposed to tell Hannah?" Jane asked. "After all, you presented us so eloquently," she said snidely.

Jane extended her hand. "Hello Hannah. Never mind all that. It's very nice to meet you," Jane glanced around. "You have a fabulous place here. The lavender smells so wonderful. I don't know what's most pleasing: that herb's soothing scent or the mouthwatering aroma of freshly oven baked goods."

"Lavender grows wild around here, dear," Hannah proudly responded. "We use it for different things, especially for its aroma. It has quite a calming effect. If you like I will give you some sachets for your lingerie or to put by your pillow."

"Um that would be very nice, Hannah, I'm sure," Jane replied, wondering if it will ever come to pass that she would be able to put them to use. "As Jack said, this here is Pearl."

"Hi Hannah," Pearl said timidly with a little smile.

"Hello Pearl. Welcome to my home. If there is anything you need I will help you as best as I can." Hannah bent down and kissed her on the forehead. "That's such a lovely name. It's very pretty the way you wear your braids tied up on your head."

"Thank you ma'am," Pearl replied.

Jane continued. "This young lady, Goldie, with the dreadlocks and shuffling her feet in the dirt, is deaf as Jack mentioned. But she's excellent at reading lips if you face her when you speak. That takes a little getting used to."

"Welcome to my house, Goldie," Hannah said, making a point of facing her directly.

"It's so cool being here. I can't wait to look around some. Thank you for having us," Goldie replied as Hannah gave her a hug.

The four of them stood there silently waiting for cues from Hannah as to what they should do next.

Hannah gave a single clap of her hands for their attention. "I have twenty-two people permanently living here and several newbies as well."

"That's quite a guest list," Jane commented.

"Yes," Hannah replied. "And a very cohesive one, if I say so myself. More settle in forever than those who come and go, but everyone who stays over no matter how long has to sign a charter agreement which outlines the basic beliefs and practices of our community. The bountiful farm and mature gardens are of course thanks to Jack's miraculous seeds and plant specimens we added years ago. We rotate our major field crops with legumes to sustain the soil with ample nitrogen. I believe that vegetarianism is a lifestyle that's most beneficial for our planet. Everybody who lives here, praise the Lord, pitches in to help with the sowing, planting, maintenance, harvesting, and hauling.

"Um...Well, you folks came at a perfect time, and I will do all I can to make your visit as pleasant as possible. But I must first ask for your kind patience and indulge me for some time this morning in following house rules. Praise the Lord, all my residing guests are going to assemble in the great room within five minutes to enjoy a farm fresh buffet breakfast and personally welcome our new arrivals who are already in there. I require guests to introduce themselves to the other residents and if they want, to share their tales of why it was that they came here. It fosters camaraderie and understanding. So come along! Sticking to the house program is very important."

Jane took Pearl's hand and along with Jack and Goldie, followed Hannah up the three steps to the large wraparound porch leading to the front door.

"How charming!" Jane exclaimed, as she noticed an array of rocking chairs and little tables neatly organized in conversational seating arrangements.

"Hmmm." Jane pointed to a bronze plaque by the door and read the statement out loud. "'Hannah's House: An Environmentally Conscious Community for People of All Ages.' This is really quite an impressive enterprise you have here, Hannah."

"Sure is, if I do say so myself," Hannah responded. "No God-given natural resource is overlooked. We have aquifers that collect rainwater for irrigation, solar and wind power supplies our energy, and oil made from our vegetable plants is used for fuel. Oh, Lordy, excuse me, won't you, please? How could I forget!"

With that, Hannah ran to the far side of the porch where a tarnished cast iron bell was mounted on one of the ceiling support columns. As she rapidly whipped the clapper rope back and forth, people began coming from all directions around the compound. The clanging ruckus was deafening except for Goldie, who stood stoically. Jane, Jack, and Pearl grimaced in pain as they covered their ears and ran as far as they could to the opposite side.

"Goldie's got an advantage," Jane said to Jack with a laugh. "I'm willing to bet that Hannah has a hearing impairment from routinely ringing this bell. Don't you think?"

"How would I know," Jack replied with a chuckle. "She certainly doesn't look like that Notre Dame character, Quasimodem…you know, the bell ringing hunchback. And besides, when did you become an audiologist?"

Oh jeez. "The name is Quasimodo." Jane giggled and brushed off Jack's comment with an air swipe of her hand as she and Pearl walked back to the doorway where Goldie was standing. Jane noticed that Hannah was already occupied waving to everybody approaching and giving each person a hug or a high five as they went into the house, all very congenial and enthusiastic. Although she was intrigued with Hannah's House and how it evolved into such an elaborate sanctuary of sorts, she was more anxious to get help for her and Pearl. As her frustration mounted, so did an emerging knife of pain in her head. She began to feel dizzy and urgently needed to sit down.

Pearl tugged at Jane's wrist. "When can I call my parents? I want to call my mommy. When? When?"

"Soon, Pearl. I'm sure it'll be very soon."

Since it appeared that everyone had arrived into the great room, Jane quickly took an aisle seat in the back row, along with Jack, Goldie, and Pearl, just as Hannah went up front to a podium. Her head was throbbing and she leaned over to rest it on Jack's shoulder as it dissipated. Jack gave her a reassuring pat on her thigh.

Hannah attached a little microphone to the collar of her blouse and then clapped her hands several times to signal the start of the program and get everyone's attention.

"Welcome to Levi's Town! Welcome all newcomers, visitors, and curiosity seekers—whoever you are, whatever you want to call yourself, it's fine with me. Welcome to Hannah's House, my house! I'm Hannah Gooz, your hostess for as long as you want to stay here. I'm affectionately known as Mother Gooz by the villagers because I raised fourteen children here in Levi's Town...like the brood in the nursery rhyme about an Old Woman Who Lived in a Shoe."

A smattering of giggles arose in the audience.

"Anyway...By way of background, this place wasn't always so magnificent. If you can believe it, at one time it started as a very tiny house, about as big as a bread box I used to say, and we were busting at the seams as the family kept on growing. If you're interested, you can read about the history of Levi's Town and this settlement in the scrapbook in our little library. There you can also buy souvenirs like tee shirts, mugs, saltwater taffy, and various other items you may be interested in." Hannah held up a green tee shirt with a picture of the house and the letters HH on a flag hanging from the top of the porch.

"What the..." Jane muttered under her breath, instantly visualizing a gift shop on the premises with a tour group wending its way through it. *Is she serious? Who here would be in a position to buy those things?* That thought reminded her about the money Cindy had given her and Goldie, which was still tucked away in her shoe for safekeeping.

"Shhh," Jack murmured as he lightly tapped Jane's hand. "Don't embarrass us."

Jane was relieved that her head pain was gone. She did all she could to smother her burgeoning laughter when she saw Hannah hold up the mug and saltwater taffy box.

Hannah put the items down and continued. "I'm sure the newbies of sorts are wondering how Hannah's House came about. So I'll give you the scoop in a nutshell, and then we can get on with the more important meet-and-greet part of the agenda."

"My husband Ethan and I were the first to buy into the community. Well, actually we were the *only* ones who bought here. That's a whole other story. Because of some snafu with the government authorities, no other homes were built, and as a result we got it for a steal at auction."

"Time passed. Our children grew up and eventually left the nest to begin lives of their own. As did Ethan, who had a mid-life crisis, bought himself a motorcycle, and took off never to be seen again. So one day I was sitting by myself as usual, near our electric faux fireplace enjoying the warm amber glow from the realistic looking flames. Well, I got into a melancholy mood and began thinking about what a waste it was to have all this space just to myself. I was lonely and imagined how great it would be to hear the sounds of voices again—to have commotion around. Besides, I figured I could use the exercise of bending at the waste to pick up clutter, cooking, changing beds, so on and so forth—doing the many vigorous activities that had made up my daily routine for most of my life. Then I had a come-to-Jesus moment—a revelation!

I realized that having domestic responsibilities was a major part of who I am—it was my identity. What I once thought was not having a life, actually *was* my life.

"I became inspired. I said to myself, why not open my home to others? I envisioned it as a bed and breakfast for travelers in need of a temporary place to stay while passing through. Or it could be a safe haven for victims of abuse, or law abiding citizens in hiding, or what not. After all, with plenty of rooms to share and chores to do, I imagined I could operate on the basis of a barter system. All I would require from guests in exchange for room and board would be help with daily chores, repairs as needed, and farming to keep up the food supply. I was very excited about this new idea. I pictured this as being the best self-sufficient community of its kind, ever. And oh Lordy, look at the results! The best thing is that it's all here for each and every one of you to enjoy."

"Those who've heard my story many times before, thank you, dears, for your patience in listening again. Now it would be nice if our new staying guests would come up front and introduce themselves. If you wish, you can come up to the podium and share your story with us in no more than three minutes, but there's no pressure to do so. Then we'll get on with the breakfast during which you all will have plenty of time to mingle with one another."

With that invitation, several people stood up and approached the front of the room. Jane extended her torso and leaned into Jack to see over the head of the person seated before her. As soon as the individuals turned around, she felt the blood drain from her face.

25

SURPRISE ENCOUNTERS

Indistinguishable voices caught Jane's attention in her semi state of unconsciousness. Through blurry eyes that were mere slits under heavy lids, she could detect the forms and shadows of faces hovering over her. They were so distorted and ghostly that they appeared extraterrestrial. She was frightened and struggled unsuccessfully to get away, but her arms were pinned down. She screamed for help to no avail. Frustrated and disoriented, she closed her eyes to clear her mind, as though she were resetting an electrical device. The placement of an icy wet cloth at the back of her neck shocked her into wakefulness. Jane shook her head to find her bearings. Judging from the hardness under her back she guessed she was sprawled on a floor.

Slurred voices called out, turning into echoes and then gradually distinct. "Jane, Jane, wake up! Wake up! Jane, Jane! That's it. Come on, open your eyes! Jane!"

Jack's fretful face hovering over hers was the first thing that came into focus. "You fainted. I thought you were dead as a door nail," he said.

"What happened?" Jane rubbed the front of her head where it hurt and detected a bump.

"You suddenly passed out and on the way down hit the back of the chair in front of you," Jack said.

Just then a voice called out, "Please everyone. Give her some breathing room. Back away. Everything is ok. She's fine. I'm sure there's nothing that a good meal and some hot tea won't fix."

Hannah bent down next to Jack and replaced the ice pack on Jane's neck with one over her forehead. "There, there, dear. You're fine. You look much better already. Lie here and rest just a tad more." She lifted Jane's head and placed a pillow under it.

Jane could see Pearl standing near her feet, sobbing. Goldie was trying to comfort her.

"Pearl, she's okay. Look. Don't worry," Goldie said soothingly. "Please stop crying. See, she's OK. See?"

"But Jack said she was a dead door nail," Pearl whimpered.

"Huh? Oh, never mind whatever he said," Goldie replied flippantly. "He got you upset over nothing. See? Jane's okay. Don't listen to him. Forget that!"

"Jane! Now that you're awake, boy do I have a surprise for you," Goldie cried as she nervously twirled some strands of her hair with her finger. "You'll never believe this! Never in a million years! Not even in a zillion years!" Goldie started jumping up and down with glee, like a young child walking into an amusement park.

"What? What?" Jane asked with a giggle, finding Goldie's behavior quite comical. She held the icepack on her forehead as she sat up. "Jack, please help me up. I'm fine now." Jack grabbed her extended free hand and pulled her to her feet. She felt a little wobbly at first but she steadied herself holding on to the back of a nearby chair. "How did this happen? I was fine and then..." Jane stopped short and gasped. "Oh my! Now I remember!" Her eyes widened. She scanned the gawking faces with anticipation as she smoothed out her clothing.

Goldie turned her head towards the others behind her. "Now's the time for the surprise," she yelled excitedly as she extended both her palms facing up and made brisk beckoning gestures with her fingers. "Come on! Come on! Hurry before she faints again."

The group parted and several voices called out her name as Jane was practically swept off her feet with hugs, totally stunned. Jack and Pearl spontaneously jumped out of the way and looked on.

"Unbelievable! Ah ... ah ... What a coincidence! To put it mildly," Jane cried. "Ruby! Cindy! Hansom!" She was overwhelmed. In a matter of seconds, a litany of questions queued up in her head, and she didn't know where to begin. Back and forth she scanned their faces looking directly at each of them. Cindy's flowing, strawberry blond hair and flouncy long yellow dress with the tight bodice were still very striking. But unlike before, her look was now complemented by transparent sandals on both her feet that revealed her red marker painted toenails.

"Jeez, Cindy. I can't believe you came here, and I'm seeing you again. I thought I never would," Jane cried. "I remember you said you knew about this place, but how did you get here?" Jane asked incredulously. "When ... Why ... w-what happened?" Jane thought she was sounding like a bumbling idiot and was relieved when Goldie interrupted her.

"Didn't I say you'd be surprised?" Goldie said proudly as she enthusiastically hugged each of them one by one. "Don't forget to close your mouth, Jane, or I'll stuff one of Hannah's big tomatoes in it." She laughed.

"I'm more than surprised. I'm astounded!" Jane exclaimed, while relaxing her jaw. "And I'm anxious to hear ..."

"Wait," Hansom interjected. "But how did *you* get here?" he asked, bubbling with excitement. "And how do you happen to know these two other new guests? He turned to Ruby and Cindy with a grin. "Hi girls. I'm Hansom."

"Why yes you are," Cindy replied with a coquettish giggle. "I bet you never heard that line before," she joked.

"I said the same thing when I first met him!" Goldie exclaimed. Hansom laughed.

"Pleased to meet you. I'm Cindy."

Hansom glanced at Ruby who acknowledged his eye contact.

"Sweet! Um, that leaves me. Hey s'up! I'm Ruby," she said. "Eh magawd! I'm like so totally pumped over this."

"Hi Ruby," Hansom responded, looking somewhat befuddled over Ruby's dialect.

Hansom turned to Jane and Goldie. "I'm so happy you're safe. I was very worried about you two once Toro came around. But I...I...don't get it—what are you and Goldie doing here? You never said..."

"Hold on," Cindy screeched. "Did you say "*Toro*?...*Toro*?"

"Yup. Why?" Hansom asked. "Do you know h...?"

Just then Hannah clapped her hands to get everyone's attention. She was back at the podium with her hands clasped together at her chest, smiling and beaming at her many guests. "Everybody, brunch is being served. As we share our blessed God-given meal, be sure to remember your manners and introduce yourselves to all the newcomers. Enjoy!"

"Ahem! Ahem!" Jack yelled for attention, waving his arms like a flagman as Pearl eyed the food on the buffet table. "Could somebody please tell me what's going on? Jane, do you mind getting me in on the group secret as to who these people are? I'm not a psycho, and you certainly know I don't talk to strangers. I need to be introduced."

Ruby, Cindy, and Hansom looked at Jack with quizzical expressions.

"Hey dude, like fer shur you can't be totally serious, um, right?" Ruby remarked.

Jane chuckled at Jack's malapropism. "Oh you're a psycho alright, but what you're not is a *psychic*."

Everybody laughed except Jack.

"But you're right," Jane replied. "I'm sorry. Where are my manners? Jack, meet Ruby, Cindy, and Hansom. You guys, these are my friends Jack, and over there next to Goldie is Pearl. And oh, you may not be aware that Goldie is deaf, but she is an amazing lip reader, so be sure to face her as you speak."

Jane looked behind her and saw that everyone else in the room had headed for the elaborate buffet that was set up on the tables in the back of the room. At Hannah's insistence, each person grabbed a large plate and lined up to serve themselves.

"Why don't the three of you go grab some food? Then we can sit together and catch up while you're eating," Jane suggested to everyone. "I'm not a guest planning to stay here much longer. Neither are Jack, Goldie, and Pearl. This is only a stop along our way. As you all know I'm very anxious to reach town for assistance in being reunited with my family and finding out who I am. This quest of mine has twisted and turned in so many unbelievable ways that relatively speaking I now feel as though my children are only an arm's distance away from me."

"I think getting some food first and gathering together is a swell idea, Jane," Hansom said. "Being that you have time constraints we'll be quick."

Ruby and Cindy nodded their heads in agreement, and the three of them proceeded to the buffet line.

Jane turned to Jack, Goldie, and Pearl. "I feel it will be presumptuous and rude if we helped ourselves to the meal ahead of any of the guests. After all, we're just passing through. Let's wait a little."

The three of them half-heartedly nodded.

"Oh, Lordy! Now don't you all go and hurt my feelings by not eating anything," Hannah said while striding over to them. "Why are you standing here? What about the young'un? Pearl dear, aren't you hungry?"

"Yes ma'am," Pearl quickly replied. "I'm actually super famished."

Hannah laughed at Pearl's bluntness. "Well, then what are you waiting for? Go girl—git! There's plenty to go around and then some. The same goes for the rest of you."

Jane watched as Pearl headed for the sideboard to grab a plate and hurried over to the end of the line. She stood on her toes, craning her neck to see the buffet selections and then enthusiastically signaled to them to come over.

"Hey, you guys—wait 'til you see all the food that's here," Pearl called out. "I've never seen anything like this. Ever!"

Hannah stood there beaming. "See? Now you all go help yourselves. There's plenty of seating inside and outside."

"Hannah, don't forget we have some business to conduct," Jack interjected. "And I'll need help with getting the plants out."

Hannah put her hand up and interrupted him. "Don't tell me about business doings while you and your friends here are suffering with empty stomach syndrome. And besides, nobody here is helping with anything until all bellies are filled to the brim and the meet-and-greet is over. After that my plan is to talk to Jane about how I can help her and Pearl."

"Why thank you, Hannah," Jack responded with a bow. "That's very nice of you."

Jane, Jack, and Goldie joined Pearl who was already filling her plate. There were ample helpings of hash brown potatoes and scrambled eggs, along with strawberry crepes, cranberry and blueberry biscuits, and chocolate chip croissants. Thinly sliced tomatoes the size of Frisbees were on the side, next to a large bowl of colorful garden fresh salad mixed with an array of beans, sliced cucumbers, and shredded carrots.

Pearl turned her head around to speak with Jane who was right behind her. "Who would eat lettuce for breakfast? Yuck. Um, do you see a pitcher of milk anywhere?" Pearl scanned the table looking for it.

Jane responded. "Well, first of all, this is a brunch which means that it's breakfast-lunch. Get it? So that's why there's also a salad selection. Second, I bet the milk is on the table over there where the juices and the coffee urns are." She pointed to their left. "I suppose one of those is for coffee and the other is hot water for tea. I'm heading there myself. Come with me."

Pearl sauntered over to the table, trying to carefully balance a dish of muffins and crepes along with an extra plate filled with sliced watermelon and cantaloupe.

"Hey Pearl, you forgot to take a napkin and utensils," Jack said as he came over to the beverage table. "I'll hold them for you until you sit down."

Jane was occupied with pouring herself some tomato juice.

"So, Pearl, do you drink tea or coffee?" Jack asked. "Let me pour it for you so you don't spill it and burn yourself."

"Gosh thanks," Pearl said softly. "Neither. I'm just getting some milk. I don't drink coffee. My mommy says I'm too young for that." She spotted a milk container and suddenly she shrieked. "Eek!"

Jane turned and saw that Pearl's face was stamped with horror. There in plain sight was a picture of her on the side of the container. In a heartbeat, and in one slick movement, she grabbed it quickly and dumped the contents into a nearby empty carafe. As she threw the container away in a nearby garbage can, she glanced around the room sheepishly to see if anyone was looking at her. She was relieved to see the other guests hadn't noticed since they were engaged in eating and socializing. That is, except for Jack.

"Whoa, missy Pearl," Jack shouted. "What was *that* all about?" Jack bent down and reached into the can to retrieve the milk carton.

"Have you seen…" Jack read the familiar missing person print out loud. He took one look at the photo and then at Pearl, back and forth several times. "It sure looks like you if in real life you were in black and white."

"Yeah, I know," Pearl curtly replied as she poured herself a cup of milk from the carafe. "I don't want to see it. Jane and Goldie saved me from those awful little men and it's over and done with, and that's that."

"*Little* men? Were they leprechauns?" Jack asked, attempting to lighten the conversation and ignoring Pearl's personal sentiments.

"Maybe. But not green ones," Pearl replied with a frown. "I don't want to talk about it." She looked away in an effort to end the conversation.

Jane stepped away from the table and gestured to Jack to be quiet and follow her. He immediately complied, practically on her heels, his eyes wild as he approached her face to face.

He spoke softly. "How come you never told me? Huh? Jeepers creepers, Jane. You knew I was looking for her. You even came with me to the Ogars' house for my investigation because I thought those monsters were the kidnappers." Jack's voice began to quiver.

"All along I've been thinking about this missing girl and wanting so much to find her. It's been haunting me every day. Every day! But you never said a word to me about this. How come? Jumpin' Jiminy!" A tear dropped down his cheek.

"Jack, calm down. Calm down. Get a hold of yourself. You're over-reacting. Listen," Jane said, patting his shoulder and feeling badly about his obvious distress. "OK? Can I talk? Can I explain?"

Jack nodded like a contrite child.

Jane continued. "I'm very sorry. I was waiting for the right private moment and it's been one thing after another. Perhaps you forgot, but after you found Goldie and me, you were consumed with being off schedule and hell-bent on hurrying to leave, even if it meant without us as you said. You rudely cut me off when I started to tell you about Pearl. You said you didn't want to hear my news. Do you remember?"

Jack nodded, appearing glum.

Jane continued. "Great! I thought you were going to deny it. When we reached Pearl she was very upset and hurting. That wasn't a good time to resurface the horror of it all. Then it was one thing or another in the truck. Remember? But anyway, she's been significantly traumatized so I didn't feel we should talk in front of her during our ride over. It's been on my mind all along to tell you, the first chance we had to talk alone. Really. In fact, I couldn't wait to tell you! I was so excited. I was aware how much finding this child meant to you. Go ask Goldie about that if you don't believe me. Are you all calmed down now?"

"Yes. I've fortunately had time to recover while you were babbling on," Jack replied softly with the hint of a smirk.

Jane gave him a kiss on his cheek, regretting the extent of hurt he felt and relieved over his quick flip to a non-confrontational demeanor. She felt like she was dealing with yet another adolescent.

"Look, I know you are upset, but I've got a perfect idea." Jane said to Jack. "Play along." She looked over at Pearl who was still absorbed in selecting food at the table.

"Pearl, honey," Jane called out. "Would you please put down what you have and come here for a moment?" Pearl waved in acknowledgment and came over to where Jack and Jane were standing.

"I was saying to Jack that it would be wonderful if you and he would sit down by yourselves somewhere while you eat. Jack would love to hear all that happened to you. Would you tell him? Only if it won't upset you, of course."

"Fine. I guess," Pearl answered tentatively. "But... but after that when are we leaving? I want to go home." Pearl's expressive face revealed her longing.

"Very soon, Pearl. I promise," Jane said, planting a kiss on the forehead. "Don't forget I want to go home too as much as you do, which is why we came here. I'll talk to Hannah about that after she stops scurrying around. Jack, while you and Pearl chat, Goldie and I will sit with Ruby, Cindy, and Hansom and hear what happened to each of them after we went our separate ways. What do you say?"

Jack was all smiles and enthusiastically replied as he snapped his fingers. "Hey Pearl, come on. Let's go sit outside on the porch. It's a nice day, and it's way noisy in here. I'm using too much energy trying to speak over all the yammering. Maybe by the time we finish, a couple of Hannah's guests will be available to help move the plants out of the truck."

"Go ahead, Pearl" Jane instructed. "You can see Jack's just dying to know what happened to you. You don't know this, but he's been looking for you for a long time." Pearl's eyes lit up.

"Jane's right," Jack said. "For a long time I've been emotionally invested in finding you, and I risked my life at the Ogars' house..."

"Jack!" Jane interrupted. "Put a lid on it! Why don't you go on ahead and find some seats and a table for you and Pearl. Give us a wave, and I'll help her carry her food over."

"Since when did I become an usher?" Jack asked, sounding like his old self again.

Jane laughed at his silliness, now more endearing than it had been.

"I want to go home," Pearl whined.

"I know you do," Jane said gently, understanding that the girl had only one thing on her mind. "And I will make sure you get home very soon. You have my word. You can tell Jack your story while Goldie and I spend a little time with our friends Ruby, Cindy, and Hansom. I promise we'll be quick." As Jane turned her head she noticed the group in a far corner of the room with Goldie jumping up and down and flailing her arms to get her attention. Jane waved in acknowledgment.

"I'll be close by—over there. See?" Jane said, pointing towards Goldie.

"Let's go Pearl. I'll help you carry something," Jack said.

Jane watched as Jack and Pearl went back to the buffet table for food and drinks. Jack made his selections and then headed toward the doorway with his own brimming plate in one hand and Pearl's cup of milk in his other hand. Pearl looked back at Jane and smiled before proceeding to follow him.

There was something about Pearl's look that touched a sensitive chord in Jane's heart and took her breath away. It was for but an instant, like the single spark from a struck match before the birth of the flame. She closed her eyes and stood motionless as she wandered aimlessly with her mind's eye into the closeted recesses of her mind. A memory was emerging and she intensely bore down on retrieving it, but her ruminations were harshly disrupted by a piercing scream.

"Wolf! Wolf! Everybody run for your life!"

Jane remained stone still. She watched in horror as Jack barreled back into the room, nearly knocking Pearl over as his plate of food and Pearl's milk splattered onto the floor.

26

FRIENDS

No sooner had people turned their heads towards the ruckus, than Jane heard a dog's high pitched yelp followed by feverish barking. She looked beyond the doorway, and saw the animal kicking up a swirl of dirt as it bounded up the road towards the porch, its nose rapidly moving back and forth in the air. Once it reached the steps and stopped, Jane could see that it was a German shepherd. The dog let out another yelp and began browsing the porch floor eagerly for scent. Then, with nose sniffing and twitching upwards, the dog entered the house and began to consume the food that Jack had dropped on the floor.

"Greta!!!! Greta!!! It's my dog, Greta!" Hansom cried as he ran towards the big German shepherd who in no time had inhaled every crumb and drop of liquid on the floor. Immediately Greta jumped on Hansom, frantically licking his face, both of them obviously happy to be reunited with each other.

"Hey girl. Where did you go, huh?" Hansom asked as he playfully rubbed the dog's belly. "I've been worried sick that you would never find me. You have a remarkably keen nose!"

"Well, well, what do we have here?" Hannah asked with a huge grin as she seemingly glided into the room carrying a tray of cookies.

"Oh thank God she's OK. Greta, sit! Stay!" Hansom commanded as he affectionately ruffled the fur on her neck. Greta obediently sat at attention. "That's a girl. Good dog. Hannah, this is my dog, Greta. May I let her stay in? Please? She'll be good."

"Sure. By all means. This is a pet friendly home," Hannah said. "But to be honest, she's the first four legged visitor I've ever had here."

"Well, Hannah, I know that Greta will set a fine example, and everyone will love her," Hansom said as he hugged the dog. "This is a very happy day, more than I could have ever imagined."

"Would she like a couple of freshly baked double chocolate chip cookies?" Hannah asked.

"Let me say this," Hansom replied. "She eats anyth ..."

"No! No! That's poisonous," Jack chimed in as Hansom and Hannah stood there speechless. "Dogs can't have chocolate. It contains theobromine, a toxic substance that metabolizes very slowly in their system. During that time it interferes with the heart, central nervous system, and kidneys, and can cause cardiac arrest or respiratory failure. The caffeine element in chocolate is no joke either. To save your dog, I would have to induce vomiting with syrup of Ipecac or a solution of hydrogen peroxide, water, and a touch of honey supplemented later with activated granular charcoal or very charred toast—assuming of course that all those items are available."

Jane and Pearl stared at Jack. "What? What?" he asked as he looked at Jane and Pearl with exaggerated intensity. "Did I suddenly sprout four heads or something?"

"Nothing. It's nothing," Jane said with a smile. "You two go ahead. I see that Goldie is getting very impatient standing over there." She gestured acknowledgment to Goldie and headed in her direction to join the group already engaged in chat and laughter as though they were old friends.

An astonished Hansom and Hannah silently watched Jack nonchalantly shuffle back to the table to fill another plate of food for himself and get some more milk for Pearl.

"It's about time!" Goldie said as Jane approached. "We've been waiting for you. We got you a chair. What the devil got into Jack? He's sooooo strange."

"Yup. He is," Jane replied as she sat down and patted Greta's head. "He's quirky and amusing at that. But the more I've come to know him, the more I've seen a whole different side of him. He's got a very big heart, and after all I can't ever forget that he's the one who saved my life."

"So Jane, how did Pearl get into the mix?" Cindy asked. "She's so cute. I love the way she wears those braids tied on top of her head."

"Well, it's very good news, and I won't take up the time giving you all the details," Jane replied. "She was the missing child whose sketchy face was on our local milk containers. A family of brothers, little men, had kidnapped her and held her against her will. Goldie and I happened upon her by coincidence after meeting one of the brothers on the road who gave us a ride as far as to their cottage. The poor thing. They treated her like a slave and kept her hidden and chained to a basement wall in the dark."

The whole group gasped.

"How awful! Was she the girl who was selling wrapping paper?" Hansom asked.

"I was wondering the same thing," Cindy added.

"Yes," Jane responded. "She's the one."

"Eh magawd. Like how totally gross that is that they would do that to Pearl," Ruby chimed in. "So, um, like how many little men were there and um, like what, um, happened to them?"

"There were seven in all," Jane responded. "Enough said. It was a very disturbing situation." She wanted to quickly change the subject before there were more questions so she looked at Cindy and Hansom. "Oh—before I forget, Cindy, you and Hansom should get together later and talk about your mutual acquaintance—that gangster, Toro."

"We sure will," Hansom replied. "Gosh, and will we ever have some stories to share about him!"

Jane noticed that Goldie's edginess had risen to the level of twisting her hair around her fingers and shifting her weight from one foot to the other.

"So, I see that Goldie is chomping at the bit to hear what happened to you all, including how you wound up here, and I'm as anxious to hear as she is."

"Um, Goldie—s'up with you?" Ruby asked. "Um like, won't you sit down and chill some? Besides it would like make it totally easier for you to see what we're saying. You want to like totally miss out on our stories? As if!"

"Fine!" Goldie shouted and immediately plopped down in the chair she had gotten for herself.

Jane spoke first. "As I mentioned before, we'll be leaving shortly. I came here hoping that Hannah would help me connect with my family who are no doubt looking for me. I also promised Pearl we would bring her to her parents. My memory is blank so I know nothing about myself, but because of an inscribed locket I was wearing, I'm sure I have children. I can't imagine what they're going through wondering what happened to me and if they will ever see me again." Tears welled up in her eyes and Jane briskly swiped them away. "Well…so given the time constraints for us, I hope you all don't mind telling the tail end of your stories from the point Goldie and I parted company with you. After we leave, you'll have plenty of time to fill in all the blanks with each other. How's that?"

They all nodded their heads.

Goldie gave a double thumbs up.

"So who wants to speak first?" Jane asked.

"I will," Ruby said.

"I'll talk next," Cindy offered.

Hansom shrugged. "And that leaves me for last." He leaned down from his seat and gave Greta a belly rub.

Ruby started talking. "Um, like, after you and Goldie went on your way, grandma totally wanted to test the awesome wolf costume with two people in it. So eh magawd, she like made me get into the rear part while she um, got into the front. Um, both parts had their like own zipper. So then we like zippered ourselves up from like the inside. Fer shur, it fit me perfectly, and I totally got the hang of um, moving in it with grandma like in the lead. I was so amped! So, like when we were um, ready to get out of it, that's when, eh magawd, the trouble started. The zippers were totally stuck! Um, we tried everything we could to like split them open. You know, we like twisted and turned to um, tear ourselves out of the costume, but fer shur, it was made too well. Um, like, it was very stuffy in there, and I was like totally sweating buckets. It was a killer! Can you relate? Um, in total panic, grandma and I like began screaming. You think it's nice being stuck in a wolf costume with the heat rising like, um, in a desert? As if! And um, so grandma like accidentally kicked me in my head with um, the heels of her shoes which totally knocked me like unconscious.

"So eh magawd, I like later found out that the um, nearby park grounds keeper, Mr. Hunt, had like heard our screams. Um, not knowing what to expect, he like grabbed his totally big hedge shears and like bounded into grandma's house. By then not only was I totally out of it, but like grandma had um, passed out from like heat stroke, being how it was so like an oven in there. Can you relate? So, um, Mr. Hunt said he like became hysterical when the first thing he like noticed in the bedroom was, eh magawd, the totally motionless form of a grodie wolf on the floor. Like, can you relate? So um, because it was so totally lifelike, he was ready to um, stab it with his sharp shears when he like got suspicious over seeing a zipper on the body. So um, Mr. Hunt like stopped himself totally just in time and like used his shears to um, cut me and grandma out of the costume. So like then he fanned us with like some cardboard that grandma had lying around for um, making parts of costumes stiff, whatever. Um, he like totally cooled us down and um, drove us to his sister's place to be like you know, examined. Um, like she's a nurse—a middlewife, something or other."

"Midwife! The word is midwife," Goldie interjected. "She delivers babies."

"Whatever. But like, um, thanks for the info, Goldie. Anyway…um, she said we were like dehydrated, so she um, made us rest there and like drink gallons of water, and she like iced up the top of my head where you know, grandma had accidentally kicked me.

"So while I was like chilling out, whatever, and running back and forth to the bathroom from like drinking all that water, I um, thought about how I like totally hated being with my mom for a whole laundry list of reasons, and like how Wolfie would keep on bullying me at school. Like I should have to totally keep putting up with that ditz? As if! So right after my um, last trip to the bathroom, I like gave my sleeping grandma an awesome kiss, um, got dressed, grabbed a bunch of like, you know, custard pudding snacks from the refrigerator, wrote like a thank you note on a napkin, and um, strolled out of the house.

"Then, eh magawd, you won't believe it, but I was able to hitch a ride with like a bunch of people on a church bus heading for a prayer meeting not too far from there. Fer shur, it was totally cool, um, singing with them along the way. So, I like told the driver, um, how I totally needed a place to stay to like do some more chilling out while I like get my head together. Can you relate? So um, what he did was like drop me off at the very edge of like a hill overlooking a totally awesome farm, and um, he told me that if I kept on walking along the road I would fer shur come to this place, Hannah's House. And sweet! Here I am. I'm so totally amped! The end."

"Thank you, Ruby. That's some story!" Jane exclaimed. "What a close call that was with Mr. Hunt. You and your grandma could have been killed. But you may also have suffocated had he not found and released you. You were twice lucky!"

Jane nodded at Cindy who began speaking.

"As you know I was going to go back to the shoe store to get the mates to my

flip-flops and sandals. I was hoping that Yung would be there, however it turned out that he had already gone home, and the sales help there couldn't find the shoes. Well, I had no choice but to wear what I had on. When I got to King's Tavern, there was a large crowd lined up at the door and a few people stared at my feet and laughed, but I didn't care.

"Inside, DJ music was blasting, and many people were dancing so I kind of hung out around in the crowd by the dance floor waiting for the Karaoke contest to begin. When I looked beyond the clusters of people I noticed The Steps sitting by themselves, as ugly as ever, by the far wall. They hadn't recognized me.

At last, Mr. King came up to the microphone and said he wanted the Karaoke contestants to line up because the singing was going to start momentarily. When it was my turn and all eyes were on me, I heard several loud gasps and cussing. I glanced over in the direction of the sounds and saw that The Steps' mouths were open, and their jaws had dropped down to their ankles. Then just before I was about to begin, I heard someone shouting, 'Wait! Wait!' Within seconds Yung Printz came running up to me with the mate to my sandal in his hand. In front of everyone, he got down onto his knees, removed my flip-flop, and slipped the sandal onto my foot. He got up, bowed and gave me a kiss on the cheek as the crowd cheered.

"Well, I'm proud to say that I was crowned the contest winner with only three votes against me."

"Way to go, Cindy!" Goldie shouted as she jumped up and clapped energetically. The others cheered.

Cindy giggled. "Why thank you, Goldie."

"Congratulations. That's terrific news," Jane interjected. "In retrospect, what we went through with you yesterday was all worthwhile."

"And I can't thank you both enough," Cindy said. She continued.

"So... when Yung came over to congratulate me I whispered to him that I was running away because I feared for my life at the hands of Letty and her dangerous henchmen. That's when he told me to go to Hannah's House, that I should take refuge here for a while, and he would be sure to come for me once things settled down. Yung gave me the mate to my flip-flop and got me a large carton to sleep in behind the shoe store after the contest. He secretly borrowed his mother's car later in the night and drove me here before the sun came up so he would have time to get back home before his mother woke up. And here I am. Ta da!"

Goldie clapped again, and Cindy curtsied.

"Way to go, Cindy! What a happy ending," Jane exclaimed. "Goldie and I were very worried about you, and now you are in the safest place ever, thanks to Yung. You should be very proud of yourself that you persisted with your plan despite the setbacks and the odds against you. So Hansom, that leaves you."

Hansom looked at Jane and Goldie. "After you both left I had to help Toro search for you which of course proved to be fruitless. Afterwards, I went to my house with the usual sweets, including some hamburgers for Greta. Greta, who usually runs to greet me at the door, was nowhere to be found, and I instantly became worried. I called out to my mother, but there was no response. My first thought was that she too might have passed out after stuffing her face since she had done that before after overindulging. At that point I was relieved to hear Greta barking from somewhere in the back of the house and went to get her. As I walked towards where the sound was coming from, I came upon my dad passed out cold in the hallway near the dining room. There was drug paraphernalia strewn about on the table: little scales, spoons, plastic baggies, dishes filled with ashes, pipes, and some fine white powder spread on a piece of glass. I couldn't believe my eyes.

"When I reached the kitchen I was first horrified at the mess. There were crumbs and chunks of cake and bread all over the floor along with shredded paper bags and crinkled aluminum foil. The bottled water dispenser had toppled and a jug-load of water had spilled on the floor. I concluded this was all Greta's doing."

"Then, looking beyond the chaos in one fell swoop, I saw my mother face down on the floor of the mudroom, near the pantry, making odd snorting sounds. Greta was lying on her side, barely able to move, her leash ensnared under my mother's body and pulled so taut that there was no way I could get enough slack to pull off her slip collar. So I went to the garage and got out the tire jack set. Once I was able to raise my mother up slightly I pulled her chubby arm out from underneath her and released Greta's leash from her hand. Nice guy that I am, I decided to put a pillow under her face and laughed at how hideous she looked with jelly and confectioner sugar all over her mouth and nose. As soon as Greta drank water and ate the hamburgers I had brought her, she was back to being her spunky self."

"I couldn't waste any time. I had to run. This would be my only chance to have a head start escaping from the drug lords. I grabbed my mother's hidden cache of $100 bills still stuffed in an old boot and packed some essentials like water, bread, and cold cuts. Then I took off with Greta into the thick of the forest. I remember hearing once that there was a clearing on the west side and a long winding road down to Hannah's farming settlement.

"One thing I recalled from reading about orienteering was that I should mark my route so that I don't wind up retracing my steps and going back to where I started. So as I hastened through the forest, I left some large crossed twigs along the way as markers. Greta and I walked so much that we both got extremely tired at which point we settled down and huddled together for warmth at the base of a large tree. When I woke up, Greta was gone. I called for her, but there was no response, so I figured she went on a hunting expedition for herself. I made myself a sandwich, anxious to be on my way and figuring that Greta would eventually pick up my scent. I also dropped bits of cold cuts here and there to keep her on the trail. This morning I made it out of the forest into the clearing I was told about. I walked and ran, walked and ran, and was ready to drop. When I got here I kissed the ground."

Goldie got up and gave Hansom a big embrace.

Jane rose from her chair. "Hansom, you're very lucky to be safely away from the drug scene forever. I'm sure you and Greta will fit in perfectly here."

Jane looked at her contented friends with tears in her eyes. "I'm so sorry. Goldie and I have to leave you now." It was a bittersweet moment.

That was all Jane could bring herself to say expecting, unlike Goldie who lived in the area, that it was highly probable she would never see any of them again. If she stayed a moment longer it would only make it more difficult to walk away. Goldie got up from her chair to stand with Jane, and after the well wishes, hugs, and final goodbyes to Ruby, Cindy, and Hansom, with heavy hearts they parted ways.

27

FAREWELL

When Jane and Goldie left the house, they saw Jack by his truck, speaking with Hannah.

Jane nudged Goldie to get her attention. "Where's Pearl?"

"I'm sure they know. If she's doing something fun, I'm going to join her," Goldie said, making a pirouette.

"Hey, Jack ... Hannah," Jane called out. When they both turned around, she gave a big wave, and Hannah beckoned them over. Jack simultaneously gestured for them to go away, but Jane ignored him.

"Hi my dears," Hannah said as Jane and Goldie approached, much to Jack's annoyance. "Jane, I didn't forget about you of course. Did you enjoy the meal?"

"Oh my, yes," Jane replied, thanking her profusely, as Goldie supplemented Jane's response with a two thumbs up and a huge smile. Jane looked around to see if she might spot Pearl.

Jack gruffly interrupted. "Dang it, Jane. Hannah and I are conducting important business right now, and since I'm continuing with our conversation you'll be bored listening. So how about you come back in a few minutes?"

"I'm sorry to intrude," Jane said politely to Jack, ignoring his terseness. "I wanted to let you know that we're done with our little reunion and goodbyes. And if you don't mind, I'd like very much to speak with Hannah. Do you know where Pearl is?"

"No," Jack said emphatically. He looked around from where he was standing, glancing at the sky and under the truck. "No. I don't see her. And since I'm not on a reconnaissance mission today, I don't have any radar equipment with me. I would hardly know if she were in the vicinity."

"Jack! What kind of an answer is that?" Hannah exclaimed with a frown. She looked at Jane and Goldie, who had detached herself and was busy etching her initials into the dirt with her feet.

"Don't mind him, Hannah," Jane said with a giggle. "I'm used to it. I've come to believe that it's his wry sense of humor and nothing else."

"Oh my Lord," Hannah exclaimed, glaring at Jack. "Then you're such a dear to overlook it."

"Well, you got that right!" Jack exclaimed, glaring back at Hannah. "She *is* a deer. A *doe* as a matter of fact. Jane Doe. I named her myself."

Jane spontaneously burst out into laughter, fully recognizing its antithesis in Jack's straight face.

Hannah sighed and shook her head, obviously perplexed. She turned to Jane.

"Pearl is over at the hen house collecting eggs for me. We raise free-range chickens here. I'm sure you came upon some stragglers cackling around along the driveway. She asked if she could help while Jack and I spoke. Lordy, she got so excited when I made the suggestion and gave her my egg basket. It made her feel important. The poor baby. I was with her and Jack when she was talking about what happened to her. Awful. Simply awful. There she was selling the giftwrap to make money for her school trip and Mr. Snoe grabs her as she was riding her bicycle…has the gall to knock the bike down with his truck, no less. How frightening that must have been for little Pearl to see a truck tailing her! It tore my heart out so I offered to buy fifty packets of cellophane paper after she gets settled in at home. I can use a supply to wrap souvenir gift baskets."

"That was a good idea to give Pearl something to do, and it's very thoughtful and kind of you to buy the wrapping paper," Jane commented. "She needs every chance to help build up her self-confidence and trust in people after what she's been through."

"By the way," Hannah added, "I know Mr. Snoe, er, Napoleon. He's done some hard-to-remove spot cleaning for me from time-to-time. I hate to admit it, but he does impressive work. Very meticulous. Humpf! However, now I have it in mind to use my influence to help Pearl's parents make sure that he and his brothers are brought to justice for this horrible crime. They can keep busy cleaning their prison cells."

Jane chuckled. "If I say so myself, you're a saint on earth!"

"Now, now. I'm only doing what is my calling and giving back my blessings," Hannah replied.

"Ahem!" Jack shouted for attention. "Hannah, your sainthood is all well and good, but I want to finish up with the transaction we were completing before Jane and Goldie interrupted us."

Hannah disregarded Jack's comment and turned away to tap Goldie, who after marking her initials, had made impressive outlines of three bears in the dirt.

"What about you Goldie?" Hannah asked in an effort to diffuse the bit of tension in the air. "Did you eat enough? Do you want more? I can scramble some eggs for you. Oh, I also put out freshly baked zucchini bread and carrot cake sandwich cookies. The cream cheese icing is in the middle. Yum!"

"No scrambled eggs for me, thank you, ma'am," Goldie replied. "I'm very full. But what you baked sounds super. If it isn't asking too much, would you wrap up a selection? I can save it in my tote for a snack later."

Jack sighed loudly for Hannah's attention. "First I need some guys to go into my truck and remove the plants you ordered. And here's your C.O.D. invoice. I hereby confirm that I cultivated your plants and duly delivered them on time and in good order."

"Thank you Jack," Hannah replied, ignoring all the hype. "I'm anxious to see the results. I'll have them taken out immediately."

Hannah dug into her pocket and pulled out a wad of bills. "Here you go. It should all be there as we agreed."

Jack counted the money dreadfully slowly and then lost track of what amount he was up to. He had to start all over, and much to Hannah's chagrin, he came up with the wrong number again.

"Oh Lordy, please let me do it, Jack," Hannah said. "I have to get to my guests."

He gave her the bills, and she counted the money out loud herself, placing bill by bill in his hand. Jane attempted to disguise her laughter by feigning a coughing fit, but the resulting squeal caused Jack and Hannah to glance at her quizzically.

"Yikes. He can't count," Goldie muttered under her breath facing Jane but out of Jack's earshot.

"Shh," Jane motioned with a grin.

"I'll go in and get some people to help unload the plants," Hannah announced as she began to walk away. She snapped her fingers and turned around. "Oh Lordy, Lordy. How rude of me, Jane. I almost forget—you wanted to speak with me?"

"Yes," Jane replied in the sweetest voice she could muster up. "I was wondering, does anyone here have a car and might be heading down road? Pearl, Goldie, and I need a ride to the police station since obviously we can't catch a bus or train from up here. Also, do you recall hearing any news about a family looking for a missing woman?"

"Oh, my dear Jane," Hannah replied as though she were composing a letter. "To answer your first question, I remember vaguely hearing something about a news bit like that, but unfortunately I don't recall any details. I'm always flitting about, and anyway my mind is not as sharp as it used to be. As to your other question, I'm truly sorry, but there are no cars and no drivers here." She raised her voice. "ON SECOND THOUGHT, THE ONLY PERSON WITH A VEHICLE IS JACK. SO I'M SURE, YOUR, ER, TRAVEL ARRANGEMENTS DOWN ROAD CAN BE WORKED OUT—ESPECIALLY SINCE I HAVE TO PLACE A BIG PLANT ORDER TODAY WHEN THINGS QUIET DOWN HERE LATER IN THE AFTERNOON. THE TIMING

WOULD WORK OUT PERFECTLY FOR ME TO GO OVER THIS WITH JACK ON HIS WAY BACK."

Hannah privately caught Jane's eye and winked.

Without waiting to hear if Jack had any comment to make, Hannah continued talking. "I'm happy you enjoyed your visit, even though it was so short. Feel free to stay longer if you want or come back any day in the future." She glanced at her watch. "Oh Lordy. My apologies but I have to get back inside. I must give the Hannah's House New Arrival Orientation to my newbies in exactly twelve minutes."

Hannah headed up the steps of the porch and looked back to wave at them before she entered the doorway.

"Jack!" she yelled, "I appreciate your coming all this way to deliver the plants. I really do. They're perfect specimens. I'll line up some men to come out and remove them right away. And make a note to include thirty more of those in a very large order I *must* place with you later today. It's very important to me, and I don't have time to do that now. When Pearl comes back would one of you please ask her to bring the eggs into the kitchen?"

Jack acknowledged Hannah's remarks with a salute.

Jane nodded and sighed as she took a deep whiff of the lavender in the adjacent flowerbeds and closed her eyes. She was especially anxious over what was to come and hoped that the relaxing benefits of the fragrant herb would do her some good.

Within moments, Hannah returned. She was wearing a wide smile preceded by three loud claps of her hands. Jane stood at attention like military recruit facing a drill sergeant.

"Jack! Task completed!" Hannah yelled. "Those plants will be off the truck in no time."

Jack sauntered over to the rear of the truck to drop the lift gate.

Hannah lowered her voice. "Psst, Jane, dear. I bet my life that Jack will be driving you all to the police station down road. The town's not far from here, only about a thirty minute leisurely drive. Can you believe that it's the first point where there's phone service?

You'd think we were living in a third world country up here, the way we are out of touch with the rest of the world."

Jane and Goldie watched as three men removed the last of the plants and placed them in wheelbarrows. Jane noticed many new huge tomatoes, which had to have emerged just in the short time they were on the road.

Jack lifted up the gate to the cargo area of his truck. He walked over to Jane and Goldie carrying a clipboard which he was perusing.

"Jack I have something to ask you that is extremely important," Jane said.

"Now where is this? Where is this?" Jack mumbled as he ignored Jane and continued to turn pages of paper on his clipboard.

"Jack! Please!" Jane screeched.

Jack replied, "I have to first find where I have the Hannah's House project and all its related parts on my to-do list, so I can check them off as completed."

"Can't you work on that another time?" Jane asked. Her head was beginning to throb.

"No," Jack responded. "Simply not. Like it or lump it."

Jack continued to focus on his clipboard.

"There! I'm done," he announced. He looked up. "What is it?"

Jane took a deep breath, with trepidation over the answer she might get from Jack.

"Can the girls and I count on you to bring us to the police station right now? I ... I ..." She felt weak and began to take a sequence of deeper breaths to try and calm herself down. "Oh. Oh. I feel dizzy."

"No kidding. You're making yourself dizzy doing that hypervention," Jack remarked.

"You mean hyperventilating," Goldie said.

"Whatever word it is," Jack replied. "Who do you think you are, Noah Webster's sister?"

Goldie disregarded Jack's comment. "There's Pearl!" she called out as she saw Pearl coming up the road. "Hey, Pearl, we're over here!" Goldie screamed as she waved jubilantly to her.

Pearl picked up her pace. As she approached them she proudly displayed her basket brimming with eggs.

"Excellent! Excellent!" Hannah exclaimed.

Goldie remarked, "Hannah said to bring the eggs into the kitchen, and while you're there, gather up some of those carrot cake sandwiches she just baked."

"Yup," Pearl replied. "Will do!" Her voice trailed behind her as she ran towards the house.

"And make it quick," Jack snapped.

"Jeez, what's up with you talking to her like that?" Jane asked.

Jack responded with a twinkle in his eye. "Hannah's not the only one who has lots of chores to do, you know. I have a new order to take from Hannah later, and back home I have plants to water and a load of research to get on with," he raised his voice, "AFTER I DRIVE YOU DOWN ROAD TO THE POLICE STATION!"

Jane was overwhelmed with joy and relief. "Really? That's ... that's ... that's wonderful! I ... I didn't think you would drive any further. I was almost resigned to the fact that Hannah's House would be the end of the line for us. Are you sure? I realize what a big inconvenience this is for you. I feel bad this will take you so far out of your way. You can't imagine how much I appreciate it ... I ... I ..."

"Oh, Jane. Shut your gaggle!" Jack exclaimed. "I said before that I was going to take you to town. You definitely have a deficient memory. That was the deal when you went with me to the Ogar's house. You don't remember? I'm a man of my word, and as a famous and respected botanist I stick to my deals like pollen sticks to my face. The best is that I'm getting a big order from Hannah out of this! I know she was scheming to get me to take you, bless her heart. So we'll let her think that she had something to do with this. Alright?"

Jane was dumbfounded over his astuteness and sensitivity. *He's surely a complex character.*

"Listen up. I'm about to announce my plan. You can tell Pearl yourselves. I will take you all to the multipurpose police station/ post office/jail house. I will leave Jane and Pearl there in good hands.

Goldie, I'll give you some time to file a complaint about those bears that broke into your house. But understand that I'm not waiting around too long for that. Maybe only ten minutes and if you're not back in the truck I'm leaving. Like it or lump it."

"That's a terrific plan," Goldie cried as she performed her usual pirouette. "Will you take me home after you're done with Hannah?"

"Of course, even though it's going to delay me even further from all the work I have lined up."

Jane could taste and feel her imminent rescue within reach at last. She closed her eyes and imagined what it will be like as she ran into the open arms of her children and her husband. *Their faces. What do they look like?* She envisioned forms. She couldn't capture features that were firing off and on in her mind, and she strained to bring them into focus. Yes. Yes. The promise of recognition was there—scattered bytes pushing out of the deep pockets of her memory bank. Like within the bud of a rose, there lies the mystery of its inner intricacies and the promise of eventually revealing itself with time and patience. She could hear them calling out, stroking her arm.

A man's voice: Jane! Jane! She opened her eyes and there was Jack peering into her face with a broad handsome smile. "Good, you're back with us. I'm going to start the truck."

Goldie and Pearl were rubbing her arms and gently slapping her hands and cheeks while talking to her. "Come on. That's it. That's it. Good."

"I'm fine," Jane said righting herself on her feet and dusting herself off, not admitting that she felt a little tipsy. The throbbing pains in her head were lessening.

"You blacked out again," Goldie exclaimed. "Good thing Jack caught you. The last thing you need is to fall on your head. You know, you're not right. You should see a doctor about your blackouts."

Pearl was in front of Jane, holding a cookie up to her nose so close that she could smell the pleasant baked fresh aroma and almost taste it. "Do you want this?" Pearl asked. "It's a carrot cake sandwich cookie that Hannah made. It's scrumptious and will give you energy."

Jane shook her head. "No thanks, honey. It's very enticing, but I can't eat another thing."

"I'll take it, if you don't mind," Goldie said, reaching out to Pearl.

"Then here," Pearl replied. "Hannah gave me a whole bag full of stuff she baked. We can share it."

"Hey you three," Jack shouted impatiently from the truck. "Are you coming? Now or never!"

Suddenly the engine backfired. Jack intermittently revved it up before letting the truck roll a bit to antagonize them.

"Yes, yes! Coming," Jane responded although she doubted that Jack could hear over the resounding noise.

The three approached the truck.

"I want to sit in the back like before," Goldie said.

"Me too!" Pearl exclaimed. "I want to sit there with you. It would be such fun."

"That's alright with me," said Jane. "I'll get Jack to help you both in."

Goldie and Pearl waited while Jane ran over to the driver's side and shouted to Jack over the noise.

"Do you mind helping to lift the girls into the back? Pearl is going to sit there with Goldie."

Jack emerged from the truck with a groan, seeming to feel imposed upon.

As he and Jane boosted the girls up into the cargo area, Jack said, "You both should bolt yourselves in tight with the straps that secured the plants. If the ride gets super bumpy for some reason, I'm not stopping for either of you if you happen to be tossed out."

Pearl and Goldie laughed at the absurdity of Jack's statement.

"Humpf!" Jack replied. "Like it or lump it."

With nothing more to say, and leaving Jane to make sure the girls strapped themselves in, Jack walked back to the driver's seat and turned on his cassette player for some music.

Goldie and Pearl dutifully walked across the truck bed to where the giant plants had been. As Goldie passed the four tires still in the same spot, she pointed them out to Pearl.

"What? What about that?" Pearl inquired.

"Never mind now," Goldie replied with a chuckle. "I'll tell you after. It has to do with something you missed while waiting for us at the Snoes' house when we went to look for Napoleon's truck." She turned to Jane who couldn't help but find that quite amusing herself.

"Yes. It's a funny and very strange story," Jane added. "I'm sure you both will have lots to talk about during the ride. Be sure to tie those straps tightly around you. Let me see you do it."

Jane watched as Goldie and Pearl wound the straps around themselves and fastened the hooks to the sidewalls. Satisfied that they were secure, Jane lifted and latched the tailgate. Then she went up front and climbed into the truck.

"Eureka! *Finally*, we're off!" Jack shouted over the rumble. "Wee-ha!"

With his typical outlandish flair, Jack gunned the engine before throwing the truck into gear and letting out the clutch. As Jane was roughly tossed sideways, outside she heard "whoa!" and "yikes!" followed by hearty laughter and giggles, but she failed to see the humor in Jack's recklessness. Furthermore, she felt particularly vulnerable riding without wearing a seatbelt, given Jack's heavy foot on the accelerator. She was determined to say as little as possible to him during the journey so as not to distract what little attention span he usually had while at the wheel.

The mid afternoon sun was directly above them, which was fortunate for minimizing glare. Jack made a right turn at the foot of the driveway after passing under the familiar cross beam with the dangling sign that from this side said, "Go with God. Come Again." They headed on the sinuous dirt road, along Hannah's cultivated area and continued through the vast barren part of Levi's Town. It was absolutely astonishing to Jane that anyone could turn an arid region like that into a viable homeland.

Before long, they passed a sign that said, "Farewell. Leaving Levi's Town." Compared to the message they read upon leaving Hannah's settlement, the curt and foreboding tone of this message disturbed Jane. She instantly glanced towards the left side of the road, expecting to spot a marker for entering Levi's Town that would be visible to those approaching from the opposite direction. But there wasn't one, and she thought this was also very peculiar. Perplexed, Jane ruminated about a possible explanation for this and the more she thought about it the more convinced she became that the road was only one-way, the way they were heading. This anomaly didn't sit right with her. She hesitated to strike up a conversation with Jack about it since it would mean competing with the blaring music and engine ruckus.

Jane's obsessive thoughts were interrupted when the winding terrain began to assume a gradual downward pitch before leveling out and becoming much narrower. At that point the topography changed, and based on the crunching sound of the tires, Jane concluded that they were rolling over a gravel-like substance. She was very curious about that, and if Jack were a more patient person she would have asked him to stop so she could get out and take a closer look.

Here and there the road circumvented towering buttes that appeared as though they had been plopped down in a contained area like a baker drops chunks of dough on a baking sheet. As they traveled in silence along the harsh and solitary landscape, Jane likened the conditions to her own personal feelings of emptiness and loneliness she had felt over the past several days. She pondered other parallels such as how much trepidation she had been experiencing about resolving her predicament, not unlike her uncertainty about what was lurking around the bends of the winding road.

The ride was monotonous, and Jane was glad it was going to be a short one. She was beginning to feel lightheaded, which she attributed to the pointless zigzagging they were doing. To help remedy this awful sensation she kept her eyes steadily focused straight ahead of her as though she were the one doing the driving.

As soon as the vehicle started lightly bouncing along irregularities in the road, Jack screamed out, "Wahoo! Weeha!" and began to pick up more pace.

"Hey Jack, slow down!" Jane screamed over the noise. "I guess you're anxious to bring the trip to an end sooner than later, huh? This is hardly a leisurely drive as Hannah had called it. I feel like I'm on an amusement park ride."

Jack decelerated somewhat and quickly glanced at her. "How are you doing?"

"I'm queasy," Jane replied. "Apparently I'm prone to motion sickness."

Jack continued talking. "You know, I'm going to miss you. I...I kind of became attached to you. I haven't felt that way before, ever. I just wanted you to know that." Jack reached over to take her hand in his and gave it an affectionate squeeze.

Tears formed in Jane's eyes and trickled down her cheeks. She thought about how Jack was there for her when she was in crisis. Like a parent to a child, he had given her new life and a name. As she looked at him she was struck by his good looks. She remembered how pleasantly surprised she was at his transformation when he appeared out of nowhere near the Snoes' cottage.

"Well, you know, you saved my life, Jack, and you even gave me a name, so I feel a strong bond between us. I'll never forget that, and I'll certainly make it known to everyone. You'll always remain very special to me, and one day I promise to come back to visit. You'll see."

Jane leaned over to ruffle Jack's hair playfully, and she noticed traces of tears on his face just before he wiped them away.

In the distance, Jane spotted jagged mountaintops screened by a gauzy haze. Clouds were gently floating across the sky until suddenly the vehicle became immersed in them. The vapors were so dense that Jane fantasized stepping outside and having the chance of a lifetime to actually walk on clouds. She was feeling better already but the euphoria was short-lived. Jane's peaceful sojourn was suddenly disrupted by a period of hail and extreme wind gusts. She began to shiver.

"Jack!" she called out. "Please turn the heat on." She thought she detected a response, but it was unfamiliar and very distorted. She couldn't quite make sense of it. Her vision was blurry so she closed her eyes for relief. She thought about Goldie and Pearl and hoped they were OK.

When Jane opened her eyes and blinked she was amazed to see how dramatically the landscape was changing from the rock covered, barren terrain they had been driving through since leaving Levi's Town. Pine trees had emerged, and the narrow road twisted and turned as it proceeded down very steep grades. She was delighted to see a herd of sheep with large curved horns climbing along one of the many mountain ridges that surrounded them. Ahead she glimpsed a refreshing world of lakes and forests ablaze in the colors of yellow and red. It was a promising sight indeed, and Jane was overwhelmed with anticipation of good things to come at last.

"Jack, oh my God! Jeez! Watch out!" Jane looked over her right shoulder and cringed. About a foot away and beyond the outside edge of the road, was a sheer vertical drop. She looked at Jack who was gripping the steering wheel very tightly. His grimaced face was frozen in terror, like two eyes staring out behind a stone mask.

Jack abruptly shifted to low gear as they approached a large sign posted up ahead saying, "Warning. Do Not Ride Your Brakes. Put Your Car in Lowest Gear." Jane's heart was in her mouth as he slowly maneuvered the truck through harrowing switchback turns, hugging the inside of the road as much as possible. She felt like a vulnerable bubble floating in the air at the mercy of the wind. Again the warning signs appeared, one after another: "Do Not Ride Your Brakes" "Hot Brakes Fail" "Use Lowest Gear."

"Hot Brakes Fail" echoed in Jane's mind as the horror of a pungent burning smell pervaded the space around them. She started choking. Moments later, the truck began slipping and careening wildly down the steep incline with the girls' piercing screams trailing behind in the air. It lost some speed as it slammed broadside into an inside rock wall before whipping around towards the outer edge. Her door flung open and she felt a powerful force thrust her through the opening just as the vehicle plunged into the tree-covered abyss beyond. At that precise moment, seeing the world about to engulf her, Jane assumed the innocence of a child who believes that wishing makes something so. This is it, she realized. She was going home at last.

EPILOGUE

"What was that? You said something. Can you hear me, dear? Say it again. I'm Gilda, your nurse. You're in the hospital intensive care unit."

"Ah. Mmmm…"

"I'm still here. I'm going to page the doctor."

Within minutes the woman in the bed heard the public address system: "Dr. Deleo… Dr. Petra Deleo…"

Gilda tapped her patient's face gently with her fingers and detected a slight grimace. She lifted the lids to check the pupils with the penlight. "Your eyes look good, and you have a bit of color in your cheeks, dear." Gilda recalled how ashen the patient's face was when she was first brought in. How she had clung to a thread of life.

Gilda grabbed the patient's chart hanging at the foot of the bed and pulled up one of the little side chairs, almost sitting on a pair of men's eyeglasses. She checked the dressings on her stitches and began to gently stroke the limp hand through the raised bed rail, carefully avoiding the IV tubes snaked around it. The fingers twitched. She glanced at the reassuring red and green flashing lights of the monitors and life support equipment and quickly logged the time and the patient's vital signs on a progress sheet. The machine next to her beeped repetitively.

The phone buzzed. Gilda answered.

"Hi. Dr. Deleo here. I was paged. Who's this?"

"Yes, Dr. Deleo. It's Gilda in ICU 3a. My comatose patient—the one with the intracranial hemorrhage and cerebral edema—is waking up. She's mumbling something."

"Call the attending neurologist," Dr. Deleo said. "I'll be right there."

"Of course doctor, right away."

Gilda studied the injured woman lying in the bed. With cases like this it was wait and see. Recoveries were rare, but not unheard of.

"Hey Gilda, how is she?"

Gilda looked towards the adjacent nurses' station where Dr. Deleo was already on the computer. "I'm reviewing all the labs and CT reports. They just came through."

"That was quick," Gilda replied. "The patient's squealed, muttered, and moaned several times in the last hour. Her eyelids have been fluttering, she's flinching, and she squeezed my hand. I put it all in the chart."

"Excellent," Deleo said. "Very promising. Where's the family?"

"They're getting something to eat," Gilda said. "They're so engaged in her recovery. Her husband is into holistic remedies like sound therapy and aromatherapy, and I have to say I'm amazed at how persistent her two young daughters have been in talking and reading to her from some storybooks. In spite of the noise around here from all the equipment, they insist she's aware of their every word."

Deleo came to the far side of the bed. "Maybe there's something to all that. I'm constantly intrigued by the mysteries of the brain."

Deleo held the patient's pulse and counted. She patted her arm and observed her face intently. Both eyes moved slowly under closed lids, as if in a crude kind of REM sleep. "Hi sweetie. I'm Dr. Petra Deleo, the ICU chief resident. Do you understand what I'm saying?"

The patient murmured, "Mmmm."

"Can you squeeze my hand?" She felt a slight twinge. "Excellent." She smiled. "Can you open your eyes for me?" The lids flicked slightly.

"Welcome back," the doctor said.

Nancy Brennan is an editor and college admissions coach for under-graduate and post-graduate applicants. During her professional business career she held various positions as a fiduciary accountant, financial analyst and human resources vice president for a large New York City financial institution. Her area of specialization in employment risk management includes expertise in resolving difficult workplace situations and conducting internal discrimination and sexual harassment investigations. She holds a B.A. in English, an M.B.A. in Finance and an M.A. in Psychology. She is an avid gardener and life-long resident of Long Island where she raised two sons, as well as a dog and several cats.

www.ingramcontent.com/pod-product-compliance
Lightning Source LLC
Chambersburg PA
CBHW072235190626
46809CB00018B/2074